I0699575

SEASON OF FIRE

THE NIGHTINGALE WITCHES
BOOK ONE

CIDNEY MAYES

CROW QUILL PUBLISHING

ISBN 979-8-9916361-3-1

First Edition.

To my sisters.
May we always believe in magic.

Please take care while reading.

This book features descriptions of suicidal ideation. If you or anyone you know is in need of mental health support, help is available by calling or texting 988 in the United States. You can also reach out to NAMI by calling 1-800-950-6264 or texting NAMI to 741-741.

You are not alone.

CHAPTER 1

Rose Worthington stared at the shattered fragments of porcelain scattered across the breakfast table. The letter she'd finished reading shook between her fingers. Her pulse pounded in her ears, and her lips felt strangely numb. Distantly, she noted how the pieces of her teacup looked like bones, bleached and jagged. They looked out of place among the plates of food and tea service.

Her chest fell in quick, ragged breaths, and her face felt hot. The scent of burnt wood and smoke mixed with the aroma of spilled tea. A stain crept across the already dingy linen, ruining it further. Rather than replace the tablecloth with another, she and her mother continued to dine on the same timeworn linen, chipped plates, and tarnished silverware. Their monthly allowance would never allow them to purchase new china and silver. So, the good linen was sequestered to the linen closet, reserved for entertaining.

Not that they'd hosted any parties or gatherings in years.

Rose's mind continued to churn as she beheld the mess she'd made. It was the second time this month that something had shattered. She twisted her mouth into a grimace as her face gradually cooled. Her mother would scold her for her clumsiness. But Rose wasn't sure that clumsiness was to blame for this most recent offense.

She'd snatched the letter from the tarnished silver tray with little thought. It irked her mother endlessly that Rose opened the household correspondence without her permission, but that never stopped Rose before. Brushing crumbs from her fingers and swallowing a mouthful of tea, Rose had cracked the letter's seal. Her eyes scanned the page, snagging on words that had no right to be there. She flipped the letter over, noting the postmark. It was, indeed, from Boston. An ocean away. Anger had washed over her, blackening out all thought and twisting her stomach into a writhing knot. She'd heard the cracking of china, and felt an enormous pressure bubble from her chest, down her arm, to her fingers. When she'd blinked away the worst of her rage, the teacup was no longer nestled in its blue patterned saucer. It lay in pieces around her place, and tea bled into the tablecloth.

There was no room in her head to contemplate the ruined china. Instead, Rose read the letter once more, bracing one hand firmly atop the table.

Lady Worthington,

It is my pleasure to inform you that I will be traveling to Worthington House within the next month. The most recent report from my solicitor has indicated that my presence is needed if we are to increase the profit margin on the estate. I shall keep you informed of my expected arrival date.

Yours,

Cornelius Worthington

Rose fought the urge to crumple the letter and throw it into the fireplace's modest blaze. How dare he? Cornelius Worthington was named heir of Worthington House after George's passing seven years ago. Until now, he had been content to continue living in the States, overseeing the estate from afar. Why was he suddenly interested in his inheritance?

What smarted almost as much as his impending arrival was his comment about the estate's profits. Rose had overseen the family's accounts and her home's affairs since she was sixteen years old, throwing herself into managing Worthington House after her brother's death. Her mother certainly wasn't up to the task, and Rose would be damned before she let a distant third cousin of the family be in charge.

Rose felt her cheeks grow warm again as indignation swept through her. The estate was doing fine. It wasn't her fault that she and her mother were only allowed a few pounds a month to see to their own affairs. The law was ironclad about that. But the farms produced well, the inhabitants of the village were happy, their businesses successful. They did not need a clueless American barging into Ashford and mucking things up.

Footsteps down the hall jerked Rose from her stewing. She placed the letter back onto the tray and swept the broken pieces of her cup into a pile. She placed her napkin over the tea stain and tried to blot it.

Her mother stopped next to her chair, taking in the mess Rose had made of the breakfast table. Her eyes narrowed as she spotted the open letter. "Rosalind Frances Worthington."

Rose forced herself to look up at her mother. She did her best to school her face into once of innocence. "Yes, Mama?"

Her mother's eyes, the same bleached-gray as Rose's, were steely. "What have I told you about opening letters that are not addressed to you?"

"I thought it was of no consequence." Rose's attempts at nonchalance were smothered by her quickly rising panic. It had been hiding beneath her anger. But now that her rage had come and gone, only an ocean of churning anxiety remained. "Mama, you must write him back and tell him we do not need his help with the estate."

"What nonsense is this?" Her mother grabbed the letter and read. When she finished, she lowered herself gingerly into the chair across from Rose. Then she read the letter once more.

Rose waited for her mother to say something with her hands gripped tightly in her lap.

Finally, her mother folded the note carefully. "I see," she murmured.

"So, you'll write him? Tell him to stay in America?"

Her mother began to assemble her breakfast with perfunctory efficiency, placing fruit and a piece of toast on a chipped plate. "Certainly not."

"But, Mama —"

"He will be our welcome guest. Besides, this is further reason to go to London this spring."

Rouse ground her teeth. This again. They argued about the London season at least once a year. Ever since Rose was seventeen and past the age that most girls made their debuts.

"I have allowed you to refuse a social season against my better judgement until now, but it is time you were married."

"There's *no* reason for me to marry."

Her mother shook her head. "You cannot live like this forever, pretending to be master of this house. I've heard that you've been asking about the crops in the village again. It's not proper for you to be doing so. You'd be so much happier with a husband, and child—"

"That's ridiculous," Rose snapped. "You know I check on the tenants, and the farmers, and the livestock most days. Who else is going to?"

Her mother let out an exasperated huff. "It is no business of yours. Your cousin already receives reports from Mr. Barton."

Rose rolled her eyes. "Oh yes. That odious man knows *exactly* the state of our farms and holdings."

"Don't be impolite. That behavior will be completely unacceptable when we go to London this spring."

"We're *not* going to London this spring."

"London certainly isn't going to come to you."

Rose felt a strange pressure building in her chest again. It pulsed in time with her pounding heart. "I will not be married."

"Your father would have wanted you to marry, have a family of your own. George would have wanted you to have a husband, too."

Rose flinched as if her mother had smacked her. The anger in her chest went cold, as if she'd jumped into an icy river.

Her mother continued, unmoved by Rose's sudden change in countenance. "You need to prepare yourself. Your cousin will take up residence here permanently before the year is out. I'm sure of it." She held up the letter, as if it were the only proof she needed. "Which means you have no alternative. We must go to London and find someone suitable for you to marry. Unless you would prefer to remain here, as you have said many times, but that would require you to secure an offer of marriage from your cousin instead."

Rose inhaled sharply. "You want me to marry Cornelius?" He was a complete stranger. Apparently, they had met when she was five years old, but Rose didn't remember him at all. The Worthington family never spoke of him. It wasn't until he was named as the last remaining heir to the estate that Rose was reminded of his existence.

"It's your only option if you want to continue to live in this house," said her mother.

Until now, the threat of marriage had been empty. Rose had evaded all serious plans for matrimony and a social season so far. Her mind fumbled for a plan, anything to get out of her mother's latest schemes. She fought to swallow her rising panic.

All she had, all she wanted, was Worthington Estate. The beginnings of a plan collected in her mind, but she needed time to think without her mother staring daggers at her.

"I shall consider it," Rose said faintly.

Her mother, clearly about to provide a litany of reasons Rose should vie for Cornelius's hand, snapped her mouth shut. "Very well. It's the best I can hope for, I suppose."

Rose shot her mother a withering look.

"I will still make the arrangements for us to travel to London in April. As a precaution," she emphasized as Rose continued to glare at her. "With any luck, we will simply cancel the trip," her mother placated.

Something wasn't quite right. Rose's eyes narrowed. She knew the state of their personal accounts. "With what money? We don't even have enough to buy new linens." She gestured to the stained tablecloth.

"Funds were set aside for this very purpose. Your father took care of everything," her mother said smoothly.

"I've seen no record of them."

Her mother spread marmalade a touch to vigorously over her toast. "The money was encumbered when you were born, Rose. I know you think you know everything that goes on in this house, but I have been managing it far longer than you."

Rose shot to her feet, unable to stand the conversation, or the thought of parading around a ballroom for suitors a moment longer. The fire flared unexpectedly in the grate, surging brightly against the chill in the room, before settling. Rose ignored the flare, despite the nagging disquiet that bloomed beneath her anger. "I'm going out." She stood next to her chair, waiting for dismissal.

Her mother stared at her with her mouth set in a hard, thin line. "The sooner you accept this, the better it will be for you."

Rose stood ramrod straight and dug her fingers into the back of the frayed chair. She didn't trust herself to speak civilly to her mother.

Tense silence hung between them.

"Be back for supper," her mother finally said. "You will read psalms after we dine for the next week, as a penance for your disobedience."

Rose nodded curtly, swiped another muffin from the basket on the table, and strode out of the breakfast room, leaving her mother staring at her plate, alone.

* * *

ROSE'S FOOTSTEPS echoed forlornly in the cold, dark hallway as she made her way to the study that once belonged to her father and brother. A bite of winter chill made the tip of her nose grow cold as she marched, anger still burning in her chest. When she was a child, the house had always glowed with warmth and light. She and her brother were often scolded for running down the halls, slamming doors, and behaving in an altogether unsuitable manner for children of their station. But their father had never minded. When he needed a break from his letters and accounts, he often joined his children in their romps outside. The three of them returned to the house covered in mud or snow too many times to count, trailing muck across the fine rugs and wooden floors.

Now the house was perpetually cold, as the Worthington women had to stretch their allowance to purchase fuel, food, clothing, and other necessities. The house held a gloom that would not leave. It was a gloom that Rose had grown accustomed to, one she was now quite fond of. It mirrored the heaviness that she carried with her always, like a mist that would not burn completely away, no matter how bright the sun shone.

Still fuming, Rose let herself into the study.

A large window let a modest amount of light into the room. Bookshelves lined the walls. Novels, plays, histories, and treaties occupied every available space. Her father's desk, a solid construction of deep mahogany, sat on a deep green rug in the far corner of the room. The fire place was empty, but clean. A few chairs sat before the mantle, a small table set between them.

Instantly, Rose felt her anger ebb away. This room had always calmed her.

Rose brushed her fingers over the spines of the books on the walls. She'd read every book in this room at least once, some of them two or three times over. Gothic tales were her favorite, but they were in short supply. She pulled her fingers away from the shelves, expecting to find them covered in dust. Rose frowned as she rubbed the tips of her fingers together. Not a speck on them. The cleanliness made the disused room feel more like a mausoleum than a shroud of dust would have. The ache of grief grew heavy in her chest, but only for a moment. She quickly shut out the sadness, locking it back into the small part of her she refused to open after her brother had died.

A book bound in deep green caught her attention as she dropped her hand. Or, rather, she felt an inexplicable pull towards it. A tingling in her fingers and a squeeze of her heart made her squint at the faded embossed lettering on the spine. Rose plucked the book from its resting place and ran her hand over the rough linen cover. *The Raven's Song and Other Stories.* She vaguely remembered reading it as a child. She cracked open the cover and saw an illustration of two ravens. It was a book of fairytales. She ran a finger over the beak of one bird, trying to recall the stories inside.

Down the hall, a door slammed shut. The bang echoed loudly in the otherwise silent house. Rose placed the book back on the shelf and returned to her task. She sat at the desk and withdrew a tiny key from her pocket. Unlocking the top drawer, she withdrew the Worthington ledger. She unwrapped the book's cord, her fingers sliding over the worn, supple leather. She opened the ledger and looked for any notes about a dowry or funds set aside for her to find a husband.

The small clock above the mantle chimed eight o'clock. Rose

read for a quarter of an hour longer, but could find nothing. She sighed and flipped to the most recent pages. Rose had carefully adjusted the ledger last week, overriding Mr. Barton's figures again. The solicitor visited a few times a year, descending from London to evaluate the estate. He had no real understanding of its profits and expenses, so Rose fixed the accounts herself, despite her mother's insistence that it was not a proper activity for a lady of her age and station. Never mind that the Tilneys and the Fosters had their eldest daughters managing their family accounts.

Satisfied that things were still in order, Rose placed the ledger back into the desk and locked it. She rubbed her hands together, dispelling the chill that had settled in her bones as she glanced out of the window at the frost covered gardens. The sun was breaking timidly through clouds that lay as heavy as wool over the horizon, finally showing itself after over a week of absence. Two ravens cawed to one another from somewhere in the hedgerows, breaking the stillness of the morning. She studied the sky a little longer, watching the weak sunlight grow stronger. It looked like she could take Fern out for a ride today, after all.

There was one person who would make her feel better after the morning's vexing news. Rose felt the corners of her mouth lift at the thought of visiting Philip. She left the study to change into her riding clothes, closing the door behind her, pushing the gloom away for now.

CHAPTER 2

The cold air bit her face as she rode past the lone, small tree marking the end of the immediate grounds of Worthington House. She relished the feeling of crisp air in her lungs as her breath made clouds before her, and her anger ebbed away like the ice melting from the tall, frozen stalks in the fields. Fern had an extra bounce in her step, happy to be let out of the stables.

Her heart beat a fraction more quickly as she rode to the small glen where she knew her best friend would be working. As she entered the clearing, she spied him hunched over a hulking mass of wood. He wore only a loose-fitting shirt, forgoing a jacket despite the cold. His sleeves were rolled, exposing his forearms.

Philip straightened at the sound of her approach, his frown of concentration breaking into a wide smile when he saw her. He waved, the hammer still clutched in his hand. He shoved his thick brown hair back from his brow, wiping away sweat.

Rose tied Fern to a tree and picked her way through the last stubborn patches of ice and snow towards the strange machine Philip had built. "What new contraption is this?"

"This," said Phillip, "is a new type of blade for sowing the fields."

Rose squinted at the ramshackle pile of lumber. She knew what a plough looked like, and this certainly was not one. "It's made of wood."

"Well, this is only the frame. The blades will go here and here," he gestured to some oddly angled portion that stuck up into the air and another pointed at the ground. "If you think this is bad, you should have seen last week's attempt."

"I'm sure it was a marvel of modern invention." Rose teased. "Have you been able to test it?"

"Have to wait for the ground to thaw a bit more. Should only be another week. How was your morning?"

Rose glowered, her sour mood creeping back. "Not pleasant."

"What was it this time? Your needlework requiring some more improvement? You know, your stitches will never get better on their own. You have to actually sit down for more than two minutes to practice." Philip went back to tinkering with his machine, waiting for Rose to take the bait.

Rose thought about playing off the spat she had with her mother as nothing important. It would be easier to bemoan her tragic needlework and brush off how upset she was, but she couldn't bring herself to do it. Her heart was too heavy.

"She wants us to go to London in April," she said dejectedly.

"That doesn't sound too terrible," Philip dismissed as focused on his work. "You'll miss the spring sowing, but the summer harvest is more important, anyway."

"She wants me to go to London to find a husband. To get *married*."

Philip's hands froze. His brows knit together. "I thought you told her you would prefer to stay *unmarried*."

"Apparently, my opinion doesn't matter any longer. And the worst thing is she is using horrible tactics to try to convince me it would be a good idea. 'George would want you to.' How could she say that?" Her throat tightened.

Philip straightened. "She didn't."

"She certainly did." Rose folded her arms, willing the tightness in her throat to dissipate. It was easier to be flippantly irritated than to admit how much the words truly bothered her.

"I'm sorry." His mouth twisted downwards.

The ache in her chest eased. She knew he would listen. Not offer a solution, or tell her not to worry about it, but simply hear her.

Rose blurted the question before she even knew she was going to ask it. "Do *you* think it's what he would have wanted?"

"I think," Philip said, weighing his words, "he would have wanted you to be happy."

Rose uncrossed her arms and placed her hand on the rough wood of the machine. The sun felt good on her face. She breathed deeply, inhaling the crisp winter air. "I am happy. I would *not* be happy married to some stranger just so I can have his money."

"You certainly wouldn't." His frown deepened. "But I don't think he'd have wanted you to be alone, either."

Alone.

Rose's heart squeezed painfully. "Perhaps." She took a breath, trying to dispel a wave of sudden, suffocating anxiety. Her pulse quickened despite her efforts. "There's more. Cousin Cornelius is coming to the house. Mama thinks he means to stay permanently."

Philip's frown deepened. "Why?"

"His letter said that he wants to increase the profit margins on the estate."

"We're doing all right."

"That's what I said."

Philip rested his hand on the wood next to hers, close

enough for their fingers to touch. "Maybe a gift will lift your spirits? I have something for you."

Rose smiled. Her anxious thoughts faded to a quiet murmur in the back of her mind. "You do?" He'd never given her a present before. Her face fell as guilt squirmed in her stomach. "I can't accept a gift and not give you one in return."

"Well, you'll just owe me one, then." He poked her in the side.

She batted his hand away and grinned.

Before Rose could protest further, Philip reached into his pocket and produced a small cloth bundle. "For you, Miss Worthington," he said with a lavish bow.

Rose laughed at his pantomiming. She untied the package, but Philip stopped her.

"Don't open it now. Wait until you get home."

"Why?" Rose asked, fingers hovering over the knot in the cloth.

"Just because." Philip shoved both hands into his pockets. "I've got to go help my father."

"Right," she said slowly. "I best be off, too. I'll see you soon?"

"Sure." Philip grinned impishly. "You owe me a gift, after all."

Rose rolled her eyes. "How will I ever forget?"

Philip helped her onto Fern, then disappeared into the trees, whistling a cheerful tune.

As soon as he was out of sight, Rose opened the small bundle. Inside was a tiny wooden rose strung on a thin cord of leather. She knew he had carved it himself. She smiled.

She fastened the charm around her neck, tucking it into her dress. Then, she galloped homeward, heart as light as a feather blowing in a warm, spring wind.

THE NEXT TWO weeks flew by in a dizzying effort to ready the house for Cornelius's arrival. Rose's mother had taken to the task with an enthusiasm she hadn't displayed in years. She dragged Rose along for meetings with the household staff to discuss the sprucing up of various disused rooms, going so far as to hire an additional maid from the village. They could not afford to refurnish any of the rooms, but they made do with what they had, bringing out the good linens and china from their cabinets.

At first, Rose was annoyed with having to attend so many frivolous appointments with the staff at her mother's side. She huffed every time her mother requested her presence. The meetings were keeping her from her regular tasks in the village and across the estate. After Rose complained that she hadn't been able to check on the sheep in eight days, her mother had snapped that just because Rose thought she could manage the grounds of the estate did not mean she knew how to run a home.

After that, Rose paid closer attention to her mother's instruction. With her cousin's impending arrival, she had realized that being married was not the only threat. Cornelius could claim the house as his. In the eyes of the law, it belonged to him outright. He could find lodgings for Rose and her mother elsewhere, banishing them to a cottage in the village, or a meager home in London. The thought had brought about an attack of anxiety, and Rose had broken a saucer. She'd quietly disposed of the broken china, grateful that it hadn't been one of the unblemished pieces retrieved from storage.

Worthington Estate, its fields and rivers, were hers. They were her home, and she would do whatever was necessary to remain on the land where she felt most free. Her plan for remaining began for form in earnest. So she stopped complaining about helping her mother prepare for her cousin's arrival. If she was going to convince Cornelius to let them stay at the house, she wanted to hold as many cards as possible.

Messages were sent out the second week of March to old friends and acquaintances in the village, inviting them to a party to celebrate Cornelius's arrival. Rose knew the party was only partly for that purpose. Her mother would get to parade her in front of Cornelius as a potential wife at the gathering, too.

The day arrived much faster than Rose liked. She and her mother dressed in their best daywear and sat in the parlor to wait. They made futile attempts to busy their hands and minds, but neither of them was very successful. Rose could feel her mother's worry hovering around her like a thick grey cloud, which made her only more anxious. She hated how easily other's moods influenced her own. Shortly before two o'clock, a carriage crested over a distant hill, signaling Cornelius's arrival.

The house staff arranged themselves according to rank in the foyer. Rose and her mother stood in the middle of the hall, backs straight and heads held high. Betsy, their maid, had styled Rose's hair in a simple up-swept bun instead of her usual hasty braid. The back of her neck was uncomfortably exposed. Gooseflesh sprang over her arms as the front door opened, letting in a gust of early-spring air.

The man who entered was tall and had onyx black hair that fell into his eyes. He was slender, his V-shaped face thin. He looked gaunt, almost underfed, but it was hard to tell exactly how lean he was under his traveling cloak. It was a long journey from here to America, after all.

Rose's throat tightened as Cornelius shed his coat, handing it to their butler, Graham. She felt awkward in her own skin and wanted to yank her hair down. She'd thought the hairstyle would help her feel more confident, not self-conscious. Her breath hitched as Cornelius approached them.

He bowed to her mother. "Lady Worthington."

His accent was strange. Mostly British, but the vowels were flattened slightly. From this distance she could make out the high set of his cheekbones. His eyes turned upwards at the corners.

"Dear Cornelius," said her mother. "It is an honor. We hope your journey was not too taxing. May I present my daughter, Rose?"

Rose took a breath. If she was going to play her part, she had to start now. She shoved away the instinct to run to her bedroom. "Welcome, cousin," Rose said, faking warmth as she bobbed a small curtsey.

"You are quite grown up now, Miss Worthington. If I recall correctly, the last time we met you were not yet out of leading strings."

Her apprehension returned in full force as his gaze swept up and down her body. She was not used to being looked at so appraisingly.

"It is a pleasure to meet you more formally," he said.

Her mother swept in, saving her from trying to force a reply past the choking feeling in her throat. "You must be quite exhausted. Graham can show you to your room. Tea will be served at four o'clock, but I shall send some refreshment upstairs now, if you'd like?"

"There's nothing quite like English tea, is there? I didn't realize I had missed it so much. A small tray would be fine, Lady Worthington. Thank you." He inclined his head and followed Graham to his chambers.

Rose and her mother watched him ascend the stairs. As soon as he was out of earshot, her mother launched into her assessment of his character. "He appears quite amiable. And handsome, too. Though he could do with a good meal. He seems a perfect gentleman. Don't you think?"

It was hard to say. Usually, Rose found she could easily read the moods of those around her. However, there was something closed-off about Cornelius, something she could not quite describe. Her stomach clenched.

"It appears so," she said, hoping that would appease her mother for now.

"Well, let's not dawdle. There's still much to do before the party tomorrow. Come, Rose."

With a last look up the stairs, Rose followed behind her mother, maintaining her role of obedient daughter.

CHAPTER 3

ose sat stiffly between Cornelius and her mother at the end of their long dining table. Soft candlelight cast a golden glow on the assembled guests as they began to relax with the consumption of fine wine. Soft chatter floated through the room, echoing loudly in Rose's head. She had grown so used to silence.

Greeting the guests as they arrived had been excruciatingly embarrassing. Their once-friends had become strangers since her brother's death. As the stream of people entered her home, Rose's stomach had pitched violently with nausea. But she had swallowed her discomfort and stood beside her mother and Cornelius in a hideous red dress, determined to play her part.

Thankfully, Cornelius commanded all the attention. Everyone wanted to talk to him. Even Rose had to admit that he was quite charming. She had assumed he would be more aloof, given the tone of his correspondence, but he greeted their dinner guests as if he were welcoming old friends.

Rose was still waiting for the perfect moment to make her appeal to her cousin. She'd rehearsed what she would say for hours, laying out all the reasons she and her mother should be allowed to continue to live at Worthington House. She hoped the dinner would give her an opportunity to make her case.

Rose sipped from her water glass as she watched her cousin converse with Lord Percival Reeves, a stodgy old man who owned a massive estate to the southeast. Lord Reeves was a viscount known for being stubborn and ill-tempered, rarely speaking at the gatherings he attended. Through some mysterious sorcery, Cornelius had charmed him, and Lord Reeves was going on animatedly about some new business in the House of Lords.

She listened keenly for any talk of the estate as she swirled her spoon idly through her soup, too distracted to eat. She glanced down the table at the other guests. Small families like the Smyths sat farther down. More well-to-do families were closer to the head of the table. Even the parishioner was present and was busy lecturing the Smyth girls. They grimaced at one another when they thought he wasn't looking. Towards the far end of the dining table, Philip sat with his parents, Mr. and Mrs. Harlow. Caroline Barnes, the pretty daughter of a merchant in the village, was on Philip's right, the rest of the Barnes family beside her.

A pulsed squeezed through her chest as Philip laughed at something Caroline said.

Philip caught Rose's eye and winked at her.

Rose's cheeks flushed. She took another sip of water, forcing her gaze away.

As the next course of mutton and potatoes was set on the table, she tried to bring her attention back towards Cornelius and Lord Reeves, but she could not tear her eyes away from the sight of Caroline leaning towards Philip. Her high-pitched laughter was incredibly irritating. She was a simpering flirt. Rose's hand tightened around the stem of her glass. She ignored the savory smell of roast mutton that wafted from her plate. She fixed her focus solely on Philip and Caroline.

Caroline whispered something in Philip's ear. His eyes were downcast, looking at Caroline's generous cleavage.

Rose's fingers dug into her glass, her grip tightened until the thought her fingers might break.

CRACK.

Rose yelped and clutched her hand as the sound of breaking glass interrupted all conversation. But her hand remained unscathed, her glass whole. Instead, the goblet Caroline had been holding was in pieces all around her. Wine had spilled onto the white tablecloth, and a trickle of blood oozed from a gash on her wrist.

"I beg your pardon, I've no idea what happened," Caroline said, clutching her injury as Graham bustled over to clean up the mess. Philip left his seat and wrapped his dinner napkin around Caroline's wound. Mrs. Barnes escorted her daughter to the ladies' retiring area to attend to her.

As the commotion settled, Rose looked down at her own hand. Nothing appeared out of the ordinary. She didn't know why such pain had coursed through her fingers and wrist, as if she had been cut with glass, not Caroline.

She felt someone staring at her. Rose looked up, and caught Cornelius staring at her with his intense, dark eyes.

"I—I was quite startled by the noise," Rose stammered, dropping her hand into her lap. "Weren't you, Mama?"

"Yes, I hope the poor thing is unharmed," said her mother. "I'm terribly sorry for the fright, my lords."

"Quite all right," Lord Reeves sniffed.

The rest of the party took up their conversations, and a soft hum filled the dining hall once more.

"No harm done," Cornelius added. Then he shifted his attention to Rose. "You must forgive me. I have neglected you all evening. You must tell me how you spend your time here at Worthington House. I would think that London would better entertain a woman of your age."

Rose spotted the glimmer of opportunity before her. "Not at all. There is much to occupy my time here."

She felt her mother stiffen beside her, but she forged ahead. "Especially around sowing and harvesting times. I am quite busy with overseeing the affairs of our holdings. The tenants are, of course, quite capable of attending to their work without my supervision, but it is good to know what goes on at one's estate, is it not?"

Lord Reeves punctuated her rehearsed speech with a snort. "No daughter of mine would be permitted such liberties! The very thought."

Cornelius said nothing, but a smirk played upon his lips.

Rose's heart sank. A roaring filled her ears as Cornelius once again gave his attention to the odious old man, who was on a tirade about what became of females without proper fathers or chaperones.

The look on Cornelius's face had told her exactly what he thought of her running the estate. She blinked hard, steadying her breath as sound gradually regained its clarity. Scraping chair legs drew her attention down the table. Philip held Caroline's chair out for her as she and Mrs. Barnes returned. Caroline's arm lingered on Philip's as she took her seat.

Rose pushed her food around her plate and kept silent for the rest of the meal.

While the guests mingled about after dinner, Rose remained pinned to her mother's side, forced to make polite conversation. Across the room, Cornelius kept company with the gentlemen, Lord Reeves among them. Caroline and Philip stood on the fringes of the group, their heads closer together than what was entirely proper.

Rose's heart beat loudly in her ears. She couldn't make out the conversation taking place at her elbow. She rubbed the place on her wrist where she had felt the sudden jolt of pain during dinner when Caroline's glass had broken. It was a strange coincidence. Nothing more.

She couldn't shake the image of Cornelius's pitying smirk either. Self-pity, rage, and helplessness all twisted inside her. They swirled viscously and threatened to choke her, to eat her alive from the inside out.

Rose watched Caroline tip her head back and let out a tinkling, loathsome laugh. She couldn't stand it anymore. She needed to get out of this stuffy, over-packed dining room. There were too many people here, in her space, in her house. She mumbled some excuse to her mother about needing to freshen up and picked her way as quietly as she could through the groups of chattering guests.

She was halfway down the darkened hall when she heard the soft sound of footsteps. Rose slowed her pace, not daring to see who it was. She hoped it was Philip, but knew, somehow, that it was not. It didn't quite *feel* like Philip. Reluctantly, she turned around.

Her eyebrows shot up as Cornelius took long, powerful strides towards her, closing the distance between them quickly.

"Cousin," Rose blurted as she bobbed a dutiful curtsey. "I needed some air."

"Then we are here for the same purpose," Cornelius said. "I am not as accustomed to entertaining as I thought. It's quite taxing, don't you think?"

She knew her mother wanted to give Cornelius the impression that they entertained regularly, so she settled on a noncommittal smile, unwilling to betray just how much she hated it.

"Let's find somewhere more comfortable. Graham said he had prepared the study for me, but I am still learning my way about the house. Would you escort me?" Cornelius offered his arm.

Rose had to keep her mouth from twisting in revulsion. The study was her father's. It was *hers,* goddammit. Not Cornelius's. But here she was, being given a second chance to convince Cornelius to let her and her mother stay. How could she refuse?

She took his arm. "It's a bit further down the hall, on the right."

"Perfect."

They walked silently towards the study. The noise from the party faded behind them.

Rose didn't know what to expect when they opened the solid oak doors to the study, but she hadn't thought that all traces of her father's and brother's belongings and trinkets would disappear. The room felt cold and soulless despite the fire blazing in the grate. It was worse than the untouched shrine it had become in the last eight years.

Cornelius walked Rose to a soft reading chair near the fireplace, then leaned against the mantle, crossing his arms as she sat. His narrow eyes gleamed in the firelight as shadows played across his thin, striking face.

Rose gripped the arm of the chair, unsure of how to begin a conversation with him. They were still strangers to one another. The way he looked at her made her uneasy, but she refused to be intimidated and held his gaze steadily.

"Well, Miss Worthington," he finally said, breaking the silence. "You are not at all what I expected."

She was still not quite used to his accent, the way it slipped between round and flat vowels, caught between his homeland and America.

"What were you expecting?" Rose asked carefully.

"Someone…" he searched for the right words, "more timid, I think. Certainly no one as interested in the land as you."

Rose opened her clenched hands. "This is my home. Why

should I not take an interest in it? Care for it?" She finally broke his gaze. "No one else could."

"It must have been difficult, losing both your father and brother. I still miss my brothers. It was lonely in the States."

Rose was bursting to know why he had left for America, of all places. It was such an odd thing to do. "Why did you leave for America, then?"

"My father and I did not get along. There was nothing for me to do. I was a third son, after all. I had no significant contributions to be made. So, I left."

Rose nodded. He hadn't revealed what his business was across the sea, but she had done enough prying for the moment.

"I have a sense that you wanted to ask me something else," he said as he moved towards the freshly stocked liquor cabinet on the opposite side of the room. Cornelius poured himself a drink from a crystal decanter and waited for her reply.

Rose's mouth grew dry. He had smirked at her at dinner. Was he so two-faced to pretend to agree with someone at the dining table, then adopt another opinion as soon as he was out of their company?

"I was under the impression you did not think it proper for a lady to be so involved with the affairs of her estate."

"Forgive me. You simply surprised me at dinner. Again, not what I expected." He lifted his glass to toast her, then took a hard swallow of the amber liquid.

Something smacked of mockery in the gesture, but she wasn't sure if he was making fun of her or not. If this was her chance, then so be it. Rose smoothed her skirts disinterestedly. "I gather you are a man of business."

"That is true."

"Then I have a business proposition for you, sir."

Cornelius set down the glass and took a seat behind the large mahogany desk. He moved aside a leather-bound journal with an odd symbol pressed into the front. "I'm listening."

Rose stood and faced her cousin, glancing briefly at the ledger. An upside-down triangle against three interlocking ovals with an eye set in the center was carved into the cover. Though she longed to ask about it, she remained focused on her task. Her heart leapt into her throat, threatening to choke her.

"You are concerned about the profits of the estate. Mr. Barton has advised you incorrectly, I think, that the estate needs improvement. Forgive me, but it is hard to trust the word of a man who only surveys the land twice a year. There are far more advantages to using someone more familiar with daily operations in carrying out whatever improvements you desire. I can help you, as your envoy for the estate. I assume you will want to return to your business in America. You can trust the management of Worthington Estate to me."

The speech she had been rehearsing for the past month finally came out right. Her palms were damp, and her heart remained stuck in her throat.

Cornelius blinked, stunned, before he barked with sharp laughter. "Oh, dear Rose." Cornelius shook his head. "I was expecting a proposal of quite a different nature."

Blood drained from her face, but she would not back down. She held silent.

"Your mother had suggested that you were in need of a husband."

Rose could not breathe. The stays of her ridiculous gown were tight against her chest, crushing her.

"I had assumed you were going to ask me to marry you."

"You seem to do a poor job of making assumptions," Rose snapped, air rushing back into her lungs.

"Indeed." Cornelius rose from behind the desk and stood very close to her. A coppery scent wafted from him.

"The fact remains that you must marry, Miss Worthington, and soon. It is my duty to see you cared for," Cornelius said.

Rose took a step back. "That's hardly necessary," she said icily.

He cocked an eyebrow. "Your mother desperately wants to see you settled. I know I should have come sooner, but there were other obligations that kept me away. This is a difficult transition for us both, and —"

"Stop." Rose cut him off. Anger rolled off her in waves. Her skin crawled with it, and she felt the warmth of the fire behind her, adding heat to her boiling temper. It made no sense. Cornelius had forsaken his own lands and titles before moving to the United States. Why would he suddenly have an interest in settling at Worthington House, and why was he so keen to be rid of her? "I don't know who you think you are to come into my home, into my life, and try to marry me off so you can play lord, but I will *never* marry."

Cornelius's brow furrowed as his gaze flicked to the grate behind her. The fire danced in his dark eyes, too bright. His lips pursed, a question blooming on his lip.

A soft tendril of hair had escaped Rose's carefully pinned bun. Cornelius reached out and twirled it between two fingers. Rose held still. Every inch of her wanted to smack his hand away and bolt out the door, but she knew that would accomplish nothing. His fingers brushed her bare neck, and a jolt raced through her skin. A wave of foreboding stole her breath.

Something was happening to Cornelius. His eyes went dark, his shoulders curled inward, and a dark, menacing shadow seemed to radiate from him. The coppery, acrid smell grew stronger.

"I believe I could make you happy," Cornelius said, his voice now clipped.

Rose took a step back. "You forget yourself, sir," she said. Any ounce of affability he possessed had gone.

Cornelius cocked an eyebrow, letting her lock of hair fall. "You would continue to be the mistress of this house. Isn't that what you want? Though your responsibilities would be confined to the house itself, of course, as is befitting a lady of your standing."

Rose's blood chilled. Cornelius wanted to put her in a marital cage. She would be nothing but a pretty wife to do his bidding and manage his home while he ran the estate. It made no sense. He had forsaken his family's lands and titles before moving to the United States. Why would he suddenly want to settle at Worthington House with *her* as a wife?

Fear of a life in which she was a prisoner within the walls of her own home replaced her burning anger.

"*No,*" she spat, the word springing from her lips before she could stop it. She took another step back, but Cornelius grabbed the back of her neck and forced her to look up at him. Another tingle raced down Rose's spine.

"You would throw your life away so easily? You would refuse me, and then what, Miss Worthington? Where would you go?"

Cornelius's eyes glittered with anger. Rose looked past him, eyeing the door. Surely someone would wonder what had kept them both so long and come looking for her.

Cornelius gripped her even tighter, forcing her to look into his burning eyes. "There are far worse things than being married to *me.* Things a spoiled brat like you can't even dream of."

She would not beg, would not plead to be let go. Rose sensed that would amuse him, and she would not give him the satisfaction. She clenched her jaw and said nothing.

Suddenly, Cornelius released her as the study door swung open and Graham entered, carrying a few fresh logs for the fire.

He looked surprised to see them there. "Forgive me, my lord, Miss Worthington. I thought you were in the parlor." He moved to leave, but Cornelius stopped him.

"No, please, carry on. Miss Worthington and I were just

returning to our guests. I had forgotten where the study was, and she was kind enough to escort me."

"Very good, sir."

Cornelius gestured to Rose, suggesting that she should leave the room first.

Rose held her head high as she marched down the hall, still fuming. She did not wait for Cornelius, whose footsteps echoed close behind her.

CHAPTER 4

The Worthington family bid farewell to their guests. Rose was numb as the Harlow family bowed and curtsied their thanks. Philip performed well in front of her mother, careful to conceal the depth of his friendship with her. He offered a quick bow to them both, but his eyes, did they linger a little longer on hers? Or did she only wish that he would look at her longer than he looked at Caroline?

Cornelius caught Lord Reeves as he was leaving and set up an appointment to discuss a matter of business in a few days. The stench of the old man's stale, warm breath made Rose want to wrinkle her nose as he bent to kiss her hand farewell.

Finally, the guests were gone, and the halls of Worthington House were quiet once more. Rose bade her mother a quick goodnight, but did not speak to Cornelius. She climbed the steps to the second floor quickly and shut her bedroom door firmly behind her, waving Betsy off to go help her mother undress instead.

After clumsily tearing herself free from the horrible red dress and ripping her hair out so that it tumbled around her shoulders, Rose sat in front of her mirror. She wasn't ready to sleep. Her encounter with Cornelius had left her shaken. Her fragile hopes lay shattered, their jagged edges pricking her heart. She was so sure her plan would work. It was only logical to rely on her to help him with the estate. But he had laughed at her and shown that he was nothing more than a monster.

Rose hugged herself, warding off the chill in the air and within her heart. Her plan had failed. She had not convinced Cornelius that she could be of use to him. He had thought her a fool and now she was hopelessly out of options.

She felt the yawning of a great pit opening inside of her. She had been here before, stuck at the bottom of this dark well with no way out. Even Philip's kindness had not truly pierced the gloom of those months of despair after her brother's funeral. The familiar, cold embrace waited for her to step into its open arms. She could feel herself falling into the dark chasm and closed her eyes against the crushing weight of her despair. Rose was just about to let herself tip completely over the edge into darkness when something hit her bedroom window with a *plink*.

The lone candle at her bedside flared brightly, increasing three times its size, as she whipped her head to stare at her windowpane. Unease coursed through her veins as the candle's flame returned to normal. A minute passed. Perhaps she had imagined it.

Another *plink*, louder this time, made her tiptoed to the window. Someone was down there. She slowly opened the window a tiny crack.

"Rose," Philip called softly, his voice barely above a whisper. "It's me."

"Philip?" Her heart stopped beating.

"I need to speak to you."

Her shock and curiosity stalled her plummet into the dark well of despair. "I'll be down in a moment."

She grabbed a soft, silk dressing gown and threw it hastily

around herself, then donned her cloak. She padded down the hallway towards the stairs, softening her footsteps as she went. If she were caught, she would merely say she couldn't sleep and was heading to the kitchen for a cup of tea. With her cloak on.

Her mind raced with questions. She opened the side door as quietly as she could.

The sky was clear, and the moon was half-full, casting enough light to see by. The gravel on the garden path crunched beneath her hurried steps. She didn't feel the early spring chill as she moved around the side of the house, deeper into the gardens.

Rose slowed her pace as she approached Philip. Even in the shadows of the moonlight, she knew it was him. His tall, broad-shouldered figure paced fervently. He stopped as she drew near.

"Philip? What are—?" Rose didn't have time to finish before his lips were on hers.

It happened so suddenly. One moment they were several paces away, the next she was being kissed. The heat of his body was tremendous. She could feel it even through her cloak. His hands were in her unbound hair, pressing her to him. He felt so solid, so strong. Her lips burned with his kiss, but she stood still, refusing to give into the strange heat coursing through her.

Philip broke the kiss and stared into Rose's face, searching.

Rose tried to speak but found she could not. How could he be here, kissing her, when he had been so preoccupied with Caroline Barnes that evening?

"Rose," he said hoarsely.

Rose leaned back, causing a waft of cold air to travel between them. "Was Caroline otherwise engaged this evening?" she said.

"Oh, Rose," Philip said. "It's not like that. Really, it's not."

"Isn't it?" She wrenched herself fully out of his grasp. "I saw you tonight with her, Philip. You were acting like a bloody fool."

"Rose —"

"You were so busy flirting that you weren't there when I needed you." Her throat tightened.

Philip paused. "What are you talking about?"

"Nothing. Cornelius." Her throat closed, and she could no longer speak as fear and shame washed over her.

"Did he—did he hurt you?" Philip asked, his voice a deadly quiet. He did not want to know, couldn't bring himself to ask if Cornelius had forced himself on her.

"N-no," Rose stammered. "No, he didn't hurt me. I tried to convince him to keep me on here, to help manage the estate. He refused. He said that I have to marry. Soon." Rose covered her face in her hands.

Saying it aloud, that Cornelius had insisted that she marry made it real — and all the more terrifying. Rose whipped her head up when she felt Philip move her aside. He was walking away from her, his hands clenched into fists.

"No, Philip." She ran and caught his arm. "You can't."

He stopped, took a long breath, and ran a hand through his hair in exasperation. "I'm sorry, Rose. I'm sorry for tonight. I shouldn't have acted that way with Caroline. I don't want her. I want you, and the thought of someone else marrying you, I can't stand it."

I want you.

Rose's heart stuttered.

Philip's shoulders sagged. "I love you," he said, not daring to look at her face.

I want you. I love you.

A month ago, she would have laughed at the idea of Philip being in love with her. They were friends. When George had died, Philip had been there for her, as best he could. He had his own life, his own work, while she had nothing to do but sit in an empty house of memories.

But she could not deny that something had changed between them over the years. How could she be sure that it was love?

"You don't love Caroline?" she asked, dumbfounded.

"No, I don't love Caroline. I wanted to make you jealous. Did it work?" His mouth twitched ruefully as he finally met her gaze. He peered up at her through his thick eyelashes, and Rose felt her heart squeeze.

"Philip." All other words failed her.

Philip grabbed her hand and kissed it gently. "I just wanted you to know." He held her hand in both of his. "And to say I'm sorry. Are you all right?"

Rose blinked hard as Philip searched her face. "Yes," she lied. "I'll figure something out with Cornelius."

"You don't have to marry him, or anyone else," he said, shaking his head. "In fact, I would really, *really* prefer if you didn't."

Rose laughed. She couldn't help it. She could always count on Philip to make her smile, even when all she wanted to do was cry. "I'm definitely not marrying him. He said that cousin-marrying is quite out of fashion, thank goodness. I never want to get married."

"I know," he said. He thrust a fist in his pocket, fiddling with something there. "I can still knock him senseless if you'd like," he offered.

As much as Rose would love to see Cornelius unconscious, she knew it would not help her. "I will call upon your services when I need them. Unfortunately, I don't think that will be soon. I will figure something out."

"If anyone can, it's you. Come see me tomorrow."

Rose hesitated. "I'll try."

Philip nodded his approval. "Goodnight, Rose." He turned on his heel and dashed through the garden, turning to wave goodbye over his shoulder.

Rose watched him go until the night cloaked him in darkness and she could no longer see him through the shadows.

CHAPTER 5

Thoughts of Philip dragged Rose from her bed early the next morning. The things he'd said played repeatedly in her head as she fell asleep and were the first thing she thought of when she woke.

I want you. I love you.

His declarations had shaken something within her. She pressed her fingers to her tingling lips, remembering the feeling of his kiss. She had liked it, wanted more of it, but her jealousy of Caroline had stopped her from giving in fully to the desire she felt. Now she felt light and giddy.

Rose winced at the stiffness in her neck as she dressed in her riding habit. Twisting in the mirror she spotted thin bruises, just the width of a man's fingers, branded on her flesh. She left her hair half-down, as usual, to hide the garish purple marks. There was no way in hell she was marrying the man who put them there. She vowed to avoid Cornelius as much as possible until she came up with a plan.

Rose raced through breakfast and was out the door before her mother and Cornelius had emerged from their rooms. It took her almost half the time as usual to get to the clearing. Her hair whipped behind her in a tangle as she galloped into the woods. Wind-blown and breathless, she tied Fern quietly to her usual tree, but did not approach Philip, who hammered at his invention.

Her breath caught unexpectedly in her chest. She pressed a hand into the rough bark of the tree as, steadying herself as she observed him. The day was warm. The soft *drip, drip* of ice melting from tree branches carried through the woods. Philip wore a thin linen shirt that strained against his muscular back, perspiration making the cloth cling to his frame. With a grunt that sent a strange hum through her, he hammered a large piece of wood into place and stepped back to inspect his work. He wiped his brow with the back of a taught forearm, then spotted Rose staring at him across the clearing.

"Admiring the view?" he called, teasing.

She laughed. As she walked towards him, the pleasant hum grew stronger. "Sorry it took me so long to get here."

Rose waited for him to sarcastically note the earliness of the hour, but he did not.

He looked at her with an intensity that made her blush. She looked down at his latest contraption, suddenly shy. "That's fine work you've done."

She was painfully aware of how close they were. She could feel the heat of his body travel the small space between them. The desire to kiss him again whipped through her.

"It's nearly finished," said Philip, his voice oddly strained. "See just in there? There are some wooden cogs that I need made of metal. Nick is going to forge some for me when he gets a spare moment."

Rose crouched to peer into the machine at the place where Philip was pointing. "What—"

"Rose." Philip cut through her question. "Never mind that now."

Philip pulled Rose close, pressing her against him. She could feel Philip's pounding heart through their clothes. Or, perhaps, it was her own.

He kissed her softly on her forehead, then on each of her closed eyelids. He kissed the bridge of her nose, her cheek, everywhere but her mouth. It was maddening. She couldn't take it any longer. Rose lifted onto the tips of her toes and turned her head, pressing her mouth to his.

Philip inhaled sharply. His hands, which had been softly resting on her back, cupped her jaw. He ran his fingers through her hair and gripped her waist, all while deepening the kiss.

Rose had never thought a kiss would feel like this. It felt like she was melting from the inside out. Her knees went wobbly as she kissed him back. She fell back into the wooden machine, letting it and Philip support her weight.

It felt so good, losing herself in Philip's touch. All worry was driven from her mind by the heat of him as the feeling of fire burning through her. The smell of smoke and fire tingled her nostrils as warmth continued to course through her, igniting in her belly and spreading through the tips of her fingers and toes.

Philip abruptly wrenched his lips from hers, though his hands still gripped her waist and the back of her neck. "If I don't stop now," he said hoarsely. "I won't be able to at all."

"So?"

Philip laughed ruefully. "I'm not sure you know what that means."

Of course she knew what he meant.. Or, at least, she thought she did. She had heard Philip and George joking about dallying with women whenever her brother had come home for visits from Eaton. And some books on the upper shelves of the study had been quite instructive.

"I think I can handle it," said Rose.

Philip brushed his fingers softly over the curve of her cheek. "Of that I have no doubt." His green eyes, usually bright green, were the color of moss on the forest floor. His lids were heavy with desire.

Rose didn't realize how much she craved being looked at like that.

Then, the most foolish idea sparked. Here was a way out, standing right in front of her. A lightness, pure and buoyant, filled her chest as the possibility unfurled like a spring fern. "Let's run away."

It was the perfect solution. She would be happy with Philip. After last night's failed attempt to sway her cousin, she knew her time at Worthington House was limited. Soon she'd be packed off to London, or sent to live elsewhere by Cornelius. Or, God forbid, forced to marry. Then she'd be required to reside with her new husband. Rather than wait for one of these horrible scenarios, it would be best to circumvent them altogether.

"Run away," Philip repeated, as if just settling on the idea himself. "Where would we go?"

"Does it matter?" Rose didn't dare breathe.

"I have money," he mused. "Not a lot, but some. I will take care of you, I promise."

Though it was her idea, Rose hesitated. She could not put the logical part of her mind to rest, it fixated on small details. "What about my mother? Your family?" For all their disagreements, she didn't want to hurt her mother. She knew running away would wound her deeply. And Philip's mother and father had always been kind to her. Would they blame her for taking their son away from them?

"We can write after we've settled somewhere and let them know we're all right."

What waited for Rose at home was monstrous: a life where she would be married off and forced to spend her days in idleness or raising a brood of children she did not want. But it was not only that loathsome thought that drove her decision. She was tired of clinging to the past. Cornelius's arrival had shed light on just how futile it was for her to take her brother's place. She had been safe the past few years, carrying on as best she could to fill the hole that he had left. But it was a false sense of security, and it had splintered like shards of glass as soon as Cornelius had barged into her life.

Her ridiculous bid to convince Cornelius to let her be an equal partner had shown her how powerless she truly was. The realization that there was no place for her any longer at Worthington House threatened to push her into an infinite well of anguish, so black it would extinguish her light forever. If she stayed, if she allowed her family to dictate her life, then there was no hope for her at all.

She would not subject herself to a life that left her empty and hollow, the kind of existence that slowly killed her. She could avoid that dark despair, a meaningless existence, if she ran away with Philip. With someone she knew she could grow to love.

"When should we leave?" she asked.

Philip kissed her, smiling widely against her lips. "Tonight."

There was no going back now. She gripped his hands, assuring herself that this was the right decision. "Tonight."

Rose paused at the foot of the main stairs of Worthington House, her hand resting on the smooth and solid banister. Her cheeks and the tip of her stung with lingering cold from her ride back from the clearing. A wave of uncertainty made her chest constrict. Could she really go through with this? Abandon the only home she had ever known to run away with Philip? She studied the main entryway's polished floors, the delicately carved ceiling, the soft, green papered walls. Her heart ached to think that this would be one of the last times she ascended these stairs or walked through this room.

She had to pack. Rose willed herself to move, to climb the stairs so she could prepare for her farewells, but before she could move, the parlor door down the hall opened. Her breath caught as Cornelius and her mother exited the room. The sight of him made her clench her jaw.

It was so unfair.

Cornelius would never appreciate her home as she did. He viewed the land as a source of income, nothing more. The thought that her beloved, sacred places would now fall prey to his pillaging made her stomach roil.

Rose contemplated running up the stairs to her room, but she knew she would not make it in time. She lifted her chin and strode towards her family.

Cornelius's icy gaze swept over her as she approached, lingering over her neck. Did he know he had left his mark upon her? Rose suspected that she was not the first woman he had handled that way. It only added to the fire of hate that smoldered in her stomach.

"Your mother and I were just discussing the plans for this evening. We're hosting a little dinner party tonight," said Cornelius.

"Lord Reeves will be joining us," said her mother, a tiny note of disapproval in her voice.

"His conversation may not be the most stimulating, but, he has no sons or any family for that matter. It is a small act of charity that we can extend by inviting him to dine with us."

Rose nearly gagged as her mother's eyes softened. She couldn't believe her mother would fall for his act.

"You are such a dear." Her mother smiled. "I know he will be delighted to attend."

That evening, Betsy helped Rose slip into a light lavender evening gown that suited her dark hair and grey eyes. Rose had picked it specifically because it was one of her more flattering dresses. Cornelius wanted her. Maybe not in the same way that Philip wanted her, but he must, to some degree, if he wanted to marry her. If she could distract him, play into his fantasies a bit, she hoped he would be blind to the plans that she had laid.

Rose's hair was pinned into its final coils. Betsy's eyebrows had shot up in surprise when she'd seen the marks on Rose's neck, but had said nothing. Rose didn't try to hide it, but she didn't offer any explanation, either. Betsy styled her hair into a low bun with intricate curls and braids, with one loose lock of hair that curled around the back of her neck. It added a layer of concealment. No one could see the marks.

"You look lovely, miss," Betsy said as Rose slipped on her white evening gloves. They still smelled musty from being in storage for so long.

"Thank you. You did wonders with the hair." She could at least admire her maid's skill, even if she hated being dressed like a doll. Betsy murmured her thanks and held open the door for Rose.

Cornelius waited for her at the top of the stairs, lurking like a vulture contemplating the carrion he would soon feast upon.

Gooseflesh erupted down Rose's arms.

"I thought I would escort you in," he said in a honeyed voice.

Rose couldn't bring herself to say anything, so she nodded and reluctantly grabbed Cornelius's outstretched arm. Betsy emerged from Rose's chambers, the door closing with a *snick*, and Rose was grateful for her presence. Now Cornelius had to walk her into the dining room, no side trips or new bruising. For now.

Betsy locked eyes with Rose as she murmured her apologies and hurried down the main stairs. Not the servant's stairs at the other end of the hall, as was proper.

A jolt went through Rose. Betsy must know that it was Cornelius who had bruised her.

Rose's eyes pricked with unshed tears as Cornelius marched

them down the stairs and into the drawing room, where her mother and Lord Reeves waited for them.

Rose and her mother ate the first two courses, soup and mutton, in almost complete silence as Lord Reeves and Cornelius steered the conversation from remarks on the weather to land, property, and profits. It was hardly suitable talk for a dinner party with women present.

It was clear Lord Reeves thought that Rose and her mother were below his acknowledgement.

The conversation wandered to Lord Reeve's own estate and lack of sons to inherit. Rose's ears perked up as Cornelius said, "It is such a shame. No family at all? No surviving nephews, cousins?"

Lord Reeves shook his head, smacking his gums. "No, no. All long gone with the war and sickness. Terrible, just terrible."

"Have you thought of taking another wife?" Cornelius asked. He lifted a glass of wine to his lips.

"My dear boy, who would want to marry an old man? Besides, there is no chit of adequate rank in these parts whom I have been able to persuade."

Rose thought he must be truly old if he was willing to admit his inability to persuade someone to marry him. He looked about eighty.

"Surely, in such a situation as yours, rank may be over-looked?" Cornelius signaled for their wine glasses to be refilled and for the cheese course to be cleared. "It's our duty to produce heirs to inherit our titles and lands. I'm not an overly devout man, my lord, but God has ordained that it is our divine charge to do so. Perhaps a woman in the village might suit you?"

Lord Reeves gulped more wine. Some of it sloshed down his front. "Perhaps you're right."

Rose twisted her napkin in her lap as rage smoldered in her chest.

"If it is not too forward of me, perhaps you'd allow me to

help find a potential wife for you? I'm sure I could find someone to your liking, who would have no objections to being provided a stately home and given the chance to raise a family."

Rose stopped twisting the napkin. Her mouth popped open. She knew exactly what Cornelius was trying to do. She felt the blood drained from her face.

Cornelius grinned wolfishly at her. *It's me or him,* the look said.

If Rose had any remaining doubts about her plan to run away, they vanished in an instant. Cornelius's plan to marry her off made Rose want to scream and bolt through the front door now. She would not be trapped by this repulsive man.

Rose didn't dare speak, lest she raise attention to the fact that *she* was a woman of marriageable age, who by all rights should not be in a position to refuse a comfortable home and the chance to raise a family. She took a sip of wine instead, daring a sidelong glance at her mother. She sat with pursed lips, and had barely touched her dinner all night. The course of fish in cream sauce was cold on her plate.

After dessert was served and cleared, Cornelius invited Lord Reeves to his study for a glass of port. Rose and her mother retired to the parlor. She whirled on her mother as soon as they crossed the threshold. "I won't marry him," she said through clenched teeth.

Her mother raised her hands. "I do not wish for you to marry Lord Reeves, either. I don't think you would suit each other."

"*Suit* each other? Mama, he is horrible! The way he treated the both of us at dinner! Like we were cattle that needed feeding and not worth a second thought."

"Lower your voice, Rose. Our guest is still in our home."

"It's not really our home, though, is it?" Rose asked. She twisted her hands together.

"No. It's not. And it is high time you accept that. Do you see now why I pushed for months for you to think about marriage? I wanted you to have a *choice* in the matter, not wait for someone to come along and force your hand."

Rose swallowed, trying to clear the lump in her throat. She scrambled for something, anything, to get her out of this arrangement, temporarily forgetting her plans to run away. Panic was making her thoughts wild and slippery. "Let's go early to London. I can have a greater chance at finding someone more suitable, rather than waiting for Cornelius to fix something without our consent."

Her mother shook her head. "The house will not be ready for another week. You will look too desperate if we arrive too soon."

She dropped her hands in defeat. "Then what should we do?"

"I will speak to Cornelius. Perhaps he will be more interested in making a proposal if he knows we are determined to go to London."

Rose bit back the instinct to tell her how horrible Cornelius truly was. If she hadn't realized it by now, she never would, and Rose wasn't entirely sure she would believe her. She sat down on a chair by the fire and waited for the men to return.

Lord Reeves emerged a half hour later, face flushed red with wine, followed closely by Cornelius who was grinning broadly. Whatever transpired between them in the study had pleased both of them.

"Lord Reeves is ready to retire. Come say your farewells, ladies," he ordered.

Rose bristled but was happy to oblige. Anything to get Lord Reeves out of the house.

"I am sure I'll be seeing more of you, pet." Lord Reeves hiccuped as he sloppily kissed Rose's hand goodbye.

She wasn't sure if she wanted to vomit her dinner or smack him across the face. She did neither. Instead, she plastered a small smile on her face, and held her tongue.

Cornelius looked at her approvingly over the top of the stooped man's frame, then led him to the door.

After Lord Reeves's carriage whisked down the drive, Cornelius's re-entered the parlor. "It seems we may have a potential suitor for Miss Worthington."

Rose opened her mouth to protest, but her mother spoke first. "We're overjoyed that you are already taking such great pains to look after us, my lord. We truly cannot express the depth of our gratitude. Of course, we are still quite looking forward to Rose's debut in London this season. It will be such an excellent opportunity for her to meet new friends and potential suitors. Don't you think?"

Cornelius kept his grin plastered on his face, but his eyes darkened. "I did not realize you were still set on a debut."

"Certainly. Rose and I were just discussing how much she was looking forward to it."

Rose kept her eyes trained at a spot over the wall behind Cornelius's left ear. The glint in his eyes knotted her stomach. A cold sweat dripped uncomfortably down her back. She hated that he made her feel as timid as a rabbit.

"Is that so?" Cornelius turned his fox-like face to her, pinning her to the spot with the intensity of his stare.

Rose cleared her throat and found her voice. "Yes, I am," she lied.

"Perhaps we should take the season together, then. I've never had the pleasure. Besides, one of my duties as lord of the estate is to find a suitable wife. I am sure I'll find someone in London."

Her mother did not falter. "An excellent idea, my lord. Your company would be most welcome. I believe you will find several young ladies of suitable nature."

"It's settled then. I will arrange for accommodation tomorrow. Though, if I should take my own house for the season, you will be left quite without any household staff to accompany you."

Her mother paled. It was a major detail that she had overlooked. The staff did belong first and foremost to Cornelius, not to her.

"How silly of me. You are right. We will simply need to hire another staff."

"If I may be so bold, there is a simple solution. We will stay in the same house in London, sharing the staff as we do here. As you have already reserved a house, I wonder if you would have any objection to our family staying together for the season. Of course, the estate would cover all expenses, and I may be of some service in helping find a husband for our dear Rose."

From what little Rose did know of the social season, she knew they would be invited to all the best parties if the unmarried Lord Worthington were a member of their party. Her mother knew the offer was good, too. A widow and her daughter would receive some invitations out of pity, but more social circles would be open to them with Cornelius's presence. And if the expenses for the house did not come out of their small allotment, they could use their money for the clothes, shoes, and other finery that would help Rose attract a potential suitor.

"That is most generous, Cornelius. Thank you."

Bile surged in Rose's throat at the sincerity of her mother's gratitude.

"It's settled then."

"Splendid. I do believe it is time for us to retire. Rose?"

She took the hint. "Goodnight, Mama. Goodnight, cousin." Rose held her head high as she walked straight past Cornelius and ascended the stairs. She heard her mother bid goodnight, and ascend the stairs behind her.

Her mother stopped her in the hall. "Going to London is the right choice, Rose. I'm proud of you."

Rose stared at her. It was the kindest thing she had said in months. "Thank you, Mama," she whispered.

Her mother gave her a faint smile, and closed her bedroom door behind her.

Rose pressed a fist into her stomach, breathing heavily through her nose. The floor swam before her eyes. She reminded herself that she wasn't really going to London. She'd only agreed to the plan because her mother did not know that by tomorrow morning, she'd be long gone. A sense of calm washed over her at the prospect.

She went to her wardrobe and withdrew the satchel buried at the bottom beneath old shoes and dresses. She stuffed clothing haphazardly into the worn leather bag.

Running was the only path forward now.

When the house grew quiet and the clock struck eleven, Rose slung her satchel over her shoulder and crept out the front door, her heart pounding.

The moon was mercifully bright as Rose slipped out into the night. Her footsteps crunched lightly on the gravel as she made her way towards the back corner of grounds. Rose's fingers brushed the latch on the garden gate. Four ravens exploded out of the bushes to her right, cawing loudly. She stifled a scream and clamped a hand to her mouth. Heart pounding even faster than before, she glanced back towards the house. It lay in quiet stillness, undisturbed.

The sight of the house gave her pause. A dull ache settled in her chest. This was goodbye. The lush meadows, trickling streams, and vast open fields would no longer be hers. She would never supervise the sowing or harvesting of another wheat field. She would never again ride along the wide, muddy lanes to the village, and never spend another lazy summer afternoon in the woods. Every spot that she had treasured with her brother, while he was still alive, would be lost to her. It was how she kept memories of George close. Rose knew that with her leaving, those memories would continue to fade until she could only recall the ghost of them.

"Goodbye," she whispered. The stillness of the night swallowed her words.

Rose broke into a light run before she lost her nerve, determined to put distance between herself and the house. She let herself out the side gate and continued to run down the muddy lane, flanked by frozen wheat on either side. She paused long enough to touch the lonely tree that marked the border between the grounds of Worthington House before continuing on.

She didn't see the single candle that flickered to life in the study overlooking the gardens as she let the woods enfold her in their darkness.

Philip waited for her on the side of the road with his hands shoved in his pockets, pacing to keep warm. He bowed extravagantly before her when she approached, balancing a rucksack over one shoulder. "My lady. You look ravishing this evening."

Rose swatted his arm. "Don't be rude," she chided.

He grabbed her hand and held it. "I meant it. You're beautiful."

The cold trickle of fear she had felt since agreeing to run away vanished. She had done it. No matter how much it pained her to leave behind everything, how guilty she felt for abandoning her mother, she knew she would be happy. She shoved her remaining guilt away.

Rose let her satchel slip off her shoulders to the ground. "Kiss me again, Philip," she demanded. She needed to be sure, to know without a doubt that he loved her, or she would wonder for the rest of her life if she had made the right decision.

Philip held Rose's face in his hands and tilted her head so he could reach her jaw. He trailed kisses lightly, sweetly, and with unbearable slowness along the sensitive spot between her ear and neck. Rose let out a gasp of delight. He made his way to her mouth and kissed her deeply.

Slowly, agonizingly, Rose withdrew from the kiss. She thought it would convince her, but she had to hear it.

Philip's brows knit together as she broke from him.

"When did you know you loved me?" she whispered.

"I'm not sure," he said. He leaned back so he could see her face, bathed in silver moonlight. "I didn't wake up one day and say, 'Oh, I love her now.' It happened slowly. When your brother died, you were so lonely and sad. I liked when we spent time together, because I knew I could keep you company. When you started laughing and smiling again, it made me happy. Then I missed you more and more on the days you weren't here with me. I found myself looking for you in the village or in the fields. Waiting for you to come visit was maddening. Every day I didn't see you, it took all of my will to not march right up to your front door and demand to speak to you."

Philip smoothed Rose's hair away from her face with a gentle caress.

Rose's mouth parted. She realized with sudden clarity that she, too, must have been in love with Philip for some time. She had expected to wake up one day and know she had fallen in love, like in the romance novels she liked to read, but it hadn't happened that way. There had been no sudden epiphany. But this feeling that grew from the seedling of kindness and friendship, to bloom into whatever tender, beautiful thing was now between them? Rose knew that *this* must be love.

She put a hand on Philip's chest, above his pounding heart. Her pale grey eyes reflected the moon and stars in the sky above them. "I love you, too."

Philip held the back of her head and brought his lips to hers, pouring everything he felt into a searing kiss.

Her blood roared in her ears. She heard Philip saying her name, but it barely registered over the pounding of her pulse. He kissed her deeply, his tongue explored her mouth. Her insides were burning, turning to flames of want and need.

A distant clattering broke through the haze of her desire. She placed her hands over Philip's, stilling them. "Wait," she said breathlessly. She strained her ears. The sound of carriage wheels on the road made her blood run cold. They were coming down the lane from Worthington House.

"We have to go. Now." Panic jolted through her, squeezing the air from her lungs.

"Damn it." Philip grabbed their bags. "Run." He clutched her hand, and they sprinted down the road towards the woods.

The carriage sped up.

They ran as fast as they could, the moon casting enough light to see by. Rose's side burned as she gasped for air. Her legs pumped wildly as she struggled to keep up with Philip. They flew towards the safety of their clearing, towards the dark shadows of the trees that would conceal them.

Suddenly, her hand wrenched from Philip's as her ankle turned on a loose stone. She fell hard, letting out a cry of pain as Philip shouted her name.

"Go!" She struggled to get to her feet.

"Come on, Rose. Get up. I'm not leaving you."

She tried to stand, but her ankle buckled beneath her weight. She hissed through her teeth.

The carriage came to a halt a few paces away. Rose's blood turned to ice as Cornelius jumped down from the seat of the coach.

If the moon had not been so bright, Rose wouldn't have recognized the man who stood before her. His eyes were dark and glittering, mouth set in a thin line. Anger radiated from him in waves. He was not the polite gentleman who had charmed her mother and their guests. Fury carved deep lines on either side of his mouth.

Rose's body tensed in fear.

"Stop," Cornelius commanded, his voice cold. He extended his arm, and a soft *click* reverberated through the night. Moonlight glinted off the metal in his hand, and Rose realized with horror that he held a pistol.

"Rose, you will return home at once."

"She doesn't have to go anywhere." Philip tightened his grip around her waist, supporting her weight.

Cornelius aimed the gun at Philip's chest. "I won't say it again," he said to Rose.

Her mind fought to comprehend what was happening. The man who stood across from them was not the same person who had been living in her house the past few days.

Tears streamed silently down Rose's face. She could hardly breathe. The moonlight shone off her cousin's pale face. His eyes were so dark, it looked as if his pupils had blown out, making them wholly black. But that couldn't be. She squinted at him through her tears, even as her heart pounded. Something about him was not right. His lips curled in a derisive sneer and anger rolled off him in waves.

Philip dug his fingers around her waist, pulling her even closer to his side. Rose could not tear her eyes away from the pistol pointed at them. If anything happened to Philip, she would never forgive herself. She cared for him too much to risk his injury.

She gathered all her hopes and tucked them into a box deep within herself. She shoved away her desire for freedom, the powerful pull of desire to be with Philip. Then she took a limping step towards the coach, disentangling herself from Philip's arms. Her heart shattered.

"Rose, please," Philip begged.

She took another step, unable to speak. She couldn't let the monster before her hurt Philip.

Cornelius lunged for her as soon as she was within reach and grabbed her arm.

At the contact, bile rose in her throat. Everything about him repulsed her. Something hot and acrid burned in her stomach and pulsed down her fingertips. As his fingers dug into her flesh, an utter sense of wrongness surged through her. A deep, primal instinct took over. What had she been thinking, going to him willingly? She needed to get away. *Now.*

"Let me go! Let me *go!*" She fought to twist her arm free. She reached up her free hand to claw his face. As her fingers brushed his skin, she felt the chill of metal burn against her neck.

She stopped fighting, but could not stop the flow of tears. Her gaze met Philip's and her heart threatened to shatter completely at the look of utter terror on his face.

Cornelius dug the pistol harder against the side of her throat.

"You won't shoot me," Rose said with sudden ferocity.

"No?"

"Do it, then," Rose hissed. She closed her eyes. At that moment, death called to her very sweetly. Death was dark and silent, as comforting as a heavy quilt. She could feel the tendrils of it swirling and reaching out to her, caressing, and enveloping her in an inky cocoon. A soft smell, like decaying leaves on a warm autumn day, flooded her senses. It was a familiar feeling, one she had lived alongside for many years. Though there would be entire weeks or months that might go by without her thinking of it, she knew it was always there, watching her, waiting for her to step into its soft embrace.

"Rose."

Her eyes snapped open. The darkness vanished. Philip stood with his hands at his sides, utterly broken. Rose's resolve faltered.

"Interesting," Cornelius said through gritted teeth. "I would be well within my rights to shoot this man for kidnapping you," he spat, venom coating every word. The pistol gleamed brightly as he brought it away from Rose's neck and aimed towards Philip.

"*No,*" Rose snarled and bucked against Cornelius's grip. He brought his arm around her throat and shoulders, pressing her close to him.

"Careful. My finger might just slip over the trigger. You don't want me to kill your lover, do you?"

She froze, eyes still locked with Philip's. She poured as much love into her gaze as she could.

If she died, she would be freed from the horrible circumstances she now found herself in. But if Philip died, she would be haunted by it forever, knowing that she could have saved him. Her mind was made up. "Don't. I'll come home. Swear you won't hurt him. Please." She hated herself for uttering that single plea, but she knew it would catch his attention.

Cornelius pressed his lips to her ear. "What was that?"

She swallowed the bile that rose in her throat once more. "*Please.*"

Cornelius laughed darkly. He kept the pistol trained on Philip as he steered her towards the coach.

Rose hauled herself into the carriage, hating every step she took away from Philip. Cornelius climbed in after her. Hot tears fell down her cheeks. She ground her teeth together as terrible, blinding hate burned in her chest.

"One last thing, dear," he said. He withdrew a rag from his pocket, and pounced towards her. Before she could blink, he covered her nose and mouth with the cloth.

Rose thrashed and kicked until she ran out of air. Her lungs burned from lack of breath. She gasped, desperate for air. An acrid stench made her mind go fuzzy. Her ears and mouth felt like they were stuffed with cotton. The world dimmed.

Faintly, as if he were miles away, she heard Philip shout her name. She tried to call back to him, but found she had no control over her own body. Her eyes grew impossibly heavy. She felt her body slump against the seat as every muscle went limp. She heard Cornelius leave the carriage. There was shouting, cursing, pleading. Then, a horrible *BANG* reverberated through the night.

With her last ounce of strength, Rose screamed as anguish crashed through her. The windows of the carriage cracked, then shattered as if hit with an invisible force. Cold air kissed her face as shards of glass tumbled all around her like fallen stars.

Rose willed herself to move, to go to Philip. She needed to make sure he was all right. But she was powerless to fight the exhaustion that drew her under, suffocating her. Another heartbeat, and her world went dark.

CHAPTER 7

*R*ose slowly blinked her eyes open. The tiny movement sent waves of nausea through her head into her stomach. She closed them again, swallowing the saliva that pooled in her mouth. Where was she? Rose floated in a sea of buoyant nothingness, content to let the waves rock her gently up and down. She decided she could be content to stay in the dark forever. No hurt, no pain, no fear. Just blissful, quiet darkness. She thought she smelled the scent of decaying leaves, sweetened by warm autumn sunlight as the dark cocooned her in silent nothingness.

A distant boom of thunder and the crack of lightning called her back to her body, and Rose open her eyes once more. A room she did not recognize came into focus. She took in as much of the room as she could without moving her head too much. Blush colored curtains hung around the bed. Dusty pink and white wallpaper covered the room, and a golden chandelier hung from the ceiling. Rain pounded on the widows to her left. A bolt of lightning illuminated the sky, and a clap of thunder boomed, rattling in her chest.

The sound jolted her memory. Her whole body grew icy

cold. She couldn't even cry out, the fear gripped her so tightly. The sound of a pistol reverberated in her skull. A silent scream of horror built in her chest. Through her terror, she realized someone was with her in the room.

Rose turned her head as quickly as she could to face the figure at the side of her bed. A fresh bout of nausea rocked through her.

Her mother leaned across the bed and grasped her hand. "Oh, thank God." Relief broke the tension on her face. "I was worried sick."

"What happened?" Rose's voice was hoarse. Her throat felt scraped raw, but she ignored the pain. "Where is Philip? And Cornelius?"

"Shhh," her mother soothed. "You're safe now." She smoothed her hair away from Rose's clammy brow. A frown carved deep lines on either side of her mouth.

"Mama, *what happened?*" Rose fought against the heavy fatigue that made her tongue thick and mind foggy. She struggled to sit up. She had to go to Philip immediately. The possibility that Cornelius had shot him — No. She couldn't think about it.

Her mother perched on the bed, and gently pressed her back into the pillows. "Cornelius rescued you from being kidnapped. He had to fight the boy off."

Rose fought again to sit up, to get out of this strange bed. She had to know that Philip was all right. But her body would not obey her. The room swam before her eyes.

She felt a glass of water press to her lips, forcing her to drink. Rose swallowed, grimacing at the bitter taste. Her mother placed a tiny dropper back into a brown bottle, and horror constricted her chest. Laudanum.

"No, please. I don't want it," she protested. She knew the dangers of the drug. It drove some people mad. She felt herself falling back into her pillows, unable to keep her eyes open.

Rose sobbed as her mother closed the door. It wasn't long before the dark, sickly sweet drops took effect and she fell down into darkness once more, the sound of rain lashing the windows lulling her to an uneasy, dreamless sleep.

Several hours later, Rose sat up in bed, staring at the sky as it slowly turned from pale blue to dark grey. She felt hollow and wished the storm had lingered. Her thoughts were slow, as if blanketed in lamb's wool. Her limbs were weighed down with rocks, her mouth was too dry. This body was not hers, yet she was trapped within it. She watched a lone raven fly by her window, cawing mournfully in the twilight.

She couldn't allow herself to think about what had happened, so she focused on the drifting clouds. Because if she thought about it, she would tumble so far into the well of her despair that she could never claw her way back out again. So, she sat with her mind blank, and watched the sky as it became stained with inky night.

Rose wanted to be furious. She wanted to feel so angry that she tore her bedroom apart, stormed out of the house, and raced to Philip's side. But she couldn't. She felt nothing but melancholy through the fog of the laudanum.

"Good evening, Rose."

She stared blankly at her cousin. He looked even more pale than usual. The circles under his eyes were dark.

"You know, my sweet Rose, a simple thank you would suffice."

"Where are we?" she heard herself ask, after she unstuck her tongue from the roof of her mouth.

"London," he said simply.

A trickle of fear made her hands go numb. She must have been dosed with a significant amount of laudanum to have traveled all this way without realizing she had left home. Pieces of memory floated through her mind. The sight of the family carriage being repaired as she looked out her bedroom window

—inexplicably, all the panes of glass had shattered. The feeling of the carriage rocking her to sleep. The hushed voices of her mother and Cornelius. And the memory of gunfire echoing through her head and chest.

She had to ask. She knew the truth might break her forever, but she had to know. "Did you kill him?"

"Yes."

A great wave of despair drowned out all else. She had been keeping the tide at bay all day by refusing to think about it. Now terror and grief came to her in a sudden rush. Her body shook. Rose curled forward and clenched the sheets, unable to remain upright under the weight of her loss. She stayed like that for a long moment before she felt a hand on her shoulder. She jerked her head up and scrambled away from the unwanted touch.

Cornelius's eyes were mournful, his expression wan. His voice was soft. He sounded like the man who had first walked into Worthington Estate, not the one who had taken her at gunpoint. "I'm sorry," he said.

Rose blinked, and Cornelius's eyes regained their glittering cunning. It was like a switch flipped inside of him. It scared her. Rose continued to shake, and she shrank further into the bed, trying to put as much distance between them as she could manage.

"There is nothing to fear. He won't harm you again."

Rose's throat grew tight. "I'll tell my mother the truth."

"Your ordeal has left you confused, Rose. He must have told you very pretty things to get you to agree to run away, but he had no intention of taking you anywhere. He only wanted to defile you. Fortunately, I arrived in time to spare your virtue and defend your honor. Your mother is extremely disappointed in you. I have convinced her you have learned your lesson and suffered enough. You will be spared her lecture, I'm sure."

Rose shook her head. The room swayed. This wasn't right. She and Philip were supposed to be far away from here. Philip was supposed to save her from an arranged marriage, from giving up her entire life. She squeezed her eyes shut. The well opened before her and she felt herself falling into it. Down into nothing, into blackness, into a void so crushing it left her breathless. She could not bear this. Not again.

Cornelius sensed the shift in her. "You will marry whomever I choose and leave Worthington House to me so that I may undertake the rest of my duties."

The last remaining piece of Rose that had not yet fallen into the well was her rage. It kept her tethered to the world around her and made one last effort to keep her out of the despairing dark.

Rose blinked at the sudden stinging in her palm. A red mark the size of her palm bloomed across Cornelius's cheek.

He looked down upon her, menace seeping from every pore.

"No." She clenched her jaw tight.

His face paled with fury. Rose braced herself for violence.

But he turned on his heel and left the room without a word. She heard him stomp down the hall until his footsteps faded, leaving a suffocating quiet.

A few minutes later, her mother came into the room with a cup of hot tea. Though she was in no mood for it, she drank it anyway under her mother's reproachful gaze.

The drops of laudanum hidden in the drink coursed through her quickly, lulling her to sleep once more.

* * *

A FORTNIGHT LATER, Rose stood with other wallflowers and their mamas in a corner of the ballroom at the biggest opening event of the season. Her mother had declared it a personal victory that they had been invited. In truth, Rose suspected Cornelius's recent visits to the popular gentlemen's club had secured the invitation, rather than their own mingling with the other eligible ladies and their chaperones at the various gatherings they had attended.

Rose hadn't left her bed for days after Cornelius's visit, crying until she felt utterly empty as the heavy stickiness of laudanum slowly left her body. It was only after her mother asked if the doctor needed to be called again that she forced herself out of bed. After that, it grew easier to go through the motions of the day, though part of her still felt like it was sleeping.

The past two weeks had been a blur of chiffon, dancing, music, garden parties, promenades, and simpering conversation. Rose had refused to step into her role as husband-hunter. She made no effort to dance or showcase herself as an object of desire to the bachelors of London, much to her mother's chagrin. Despite much prodding and encouragement from her mother over afternoon teas, Rose hadn't been able to muster the energy to feign any enthusiasm. She could barely find the energy to rise from her bed each morning.

It was easier to focus on the little things she missed, rather than linger on the despair of her grief, like riding through fields and the feeling of the wind blowing through her hair. She was now forced to wear it pinned and braided and curled into complicated knots during the day. Tonight, Betsy had woven her curled hair into a delicate knot and decorated it with tiny pearls. She wore a simple necklace and bracelet, tiny pearl earrings, and a soft gown of pale blue.

Rose knew she looked positively plain next to Effie Crawford, the daughter of their hosts this evening. Effie was the season's incomparable. The diamond collar she wore looked like it weighed a stone. Rose wondered how she could stand up straight. It would have had her bending over like a woman sent to the guillotine. Men flitted around her like moths to a flame, blinded by her warm brown skin, white-blonde hair, and cerulean eyes. They were so distracted by her beauty that they failed to see the spiteful, spoiled girl she was beneath her glamor.

Effie employed her talents ruthlessly, abusing other girls with thinly veiled insults while charming eligible suitors with her sickly sweet temperament. So far, Rose had emerged unscathed from her interactions with her.

Rose scanned the room with her back pressed to the wall. She had danced twice that evening, once with Lord Edward Moore, a middle-aged widower whose hands wandered too much while dancing, and with Alexander Crawford, Effie's older brother. Alexander was kinder than his sister. He took extra care to dance with each wallflower at least once at every party he attended. Rose had seen Effie roll her eyes at her brother as he escorted the hapless girls to the dance floor, but he was unperturbed by his sister's derision.

Rose watched as the dance ended. Couples strolled onto the large balcony that overlooked an impressive garden. Wide French doors flung open to let in the crisp evening air. The oppressive heat of the ballroom eased as a breeze swept through the ornate room. Some ladies and their mamas took a turn about the room, but Rose made no move to join them.

Spring had overthrown winter all at once. Green spaces had fully bloomed, and the sweet scents of flowers floated through Mayfair, signaling the official start of the London season. She let the cool air kiss her face and longed for home.

Her mother interrupted her thoughts. "Lord Crawford seems quite amiable. Maybe he will dance with you again tonight."

Rose continued to scan the few parties who remained in the ballroom, shoving thoughts of home away. "We'll see," she said. She wondered what time it was. It wasn't socially acceptable to leave before midnight, but it felt like they had been here for hours. She was so very tired.

Her throat grew tight as she and her mother stood on the

fringes of groups of people who were clearly comfortable with one another. They laughed and smiled, enjoying the night and the company of friends. No one spoke to them. She wished she had something to do instead of standing here like a fool.

"I need some air," she said, and made for the balcony, leaving her mother behind. She kept her eyes lowered as she walked.

She hated feeling like an outsider. Rose didn't mind solitude. She ached for it during nights like these when the sounds and lights and heat grew overwhelming. But she also could not stand feeling like she was being purposefully ignored, cast aside. The war between wanting to be alone and wanting someone to talk to tugged at her heart.

You are different. We see that you are different. We do not accept you.

That was the obvious message Rose had received her first weeks in society. She didn't know why she cared what others thought. She didn't even like most of the people who attended these parties, but it was hard to be ostracized night after night.

She stepped into the night, stopping when she reached the end of the long balcony, out of earshot from the few couples who were engaged in various stages of flirtation along the perimeter.

Rose leaned against the railing. Sounds from the party floated towards her, carried on a soft breeze. She wondered, in a detached manner, what would happen if she jumped from the balcony. How long would it take to discover the broken girl lying in the gardens?

Rose felt the hairs on the back of her neck prickle as someone came to stand at her elbow.

"Good evening," Cornelius said.

She did not return his greeting.

Cornelius made a pensive noise and looked out into the night. His dark circles had disappeared in the last two weeks, and his cheeks had filled out. The limp strands of dark hair now shone, and he walked with his shoulders back instead of hunched. He was looking less like a bedraggled vulture and more like a stately crow. Rose observed him silently as her stomach clenched.

"Why do you do that?" he asked. He kept his gaze fixed on the sprawling gardens below.

"Do what?"

"Watch me like I'm a viper, about to lash out and bite you. Like you're frightened of me."

Rose's brow furrowed. "Maybe because you brought me here against my will, or that you drugged me with laudanum. Or that you *shot* Philip." Her eyes stung with tears and her breath hitched. It was the first time she had spoken, or even allowed herself to think of Philip's name in days.

The color drained from Cornelius's face. He griped the banister so tightly his knuckles turned white.

"You *killed* him. You've ruined every chance at my happiness ever since you stepped foot into my house. And now you ask why the sight of you makes me turn away from you in disgust? What sick game is this to you?" Somewhere in the empty void within herself, a burning ember of rage smoldered to life, burning past the suffocating ache of sadness.

A muscle worked in Cornelius's jaw. He continued to stare at the moonlit gardens, refusing to meet Rose's blistering glare.

She'd had enough of this. Fire burned her chest, radiating through her limbs. "You're a coward. I hate you." Rose left the balcony, fuming.

Rose kept her eyes on the ground as she walked back to the ballroom. With every heartbeat, Philip's name reverberated in her body.

It was all her fault. It had been foolish to try to run away. Cornelius was dangerous and violent. She should have tried harder to handle him, maybe even agreed to marry him. If she had, Philip would still be alive.

Rose stopped midway down a wide, dimly lit hallway, her grief arresting all movement. She had to think of something else before she collapsed onto the ground and never moved again.

The candles in the sconce nearest Rose guttered and went out. She put a hand on the wall to steady herself, fighting the urge to slide down in a heap.

It was her fault, yes, but the blame also lay with Cornelius. The man who pulled the trigger, who used fear and violence to achieve his ends.

Her sadness twisted, transforming into fist-clenching anger the more she thought about him, about what he had taken from her. Her blood pounded in her ears, muffling the sounds of the party down the hall. She clung to the burning ember of rage deep within her, holding onto it so she could stay upright, so she could feel some reprieve from the horrible sadness that threatened to drown her.

He is a coward. He is cruel and despicable.

Rose felt the ember of her anger ignite into a burning flame *of hate.* He had taken everything from her. He had reduced her to an empty shell, and plunged her back into the well of despair that had taken years to climb out of since her brother died. She had climbed out once before. She would do it again.

She didn't see the candles relight themselves as she removed her hand from the wall, or the figure, cloaked in shadows, who watched her from afar.

Rose pushed herself off the wall and marched to the ballroom with the heat of her resentment still burning within her.

She sidestepped along the perimeter of the room and spied her mother chatting with Lord Reeves. Her mother was doing her best to entertain him, but she scanned the room, clearly looking for her. Rose sighed and made her way to them.

Her mother looked relieved when Rose emerged from the crowd. "Ah, here she is."

Rose curtsied and murmured a greeting.

"What's that? Speak up, girl."

"Good evening, Lord Reeves," Rose repeated over the boisterous music.

Ever since he'd dined with them back in Ashford, Lord Reeves had appeared at whatever gathering Cornelius attended and paid special attention to Rose and her mother. She hadn't been able to shake him, but because she had no intention of trying to get anyone to dance with her, she had no excuse to avoid his company. She thanked the powers that he relied too heavily on his cane to even consider asking her to dance.

"Yes, very good." He nodded and tapped his cane on the ground.

They stood in awkward silence as the reel continued.

"Be a good girl and get me something to drink," Lord Reeves commanded.

Rose walked slowly, prolonging the time away from him. The music ended as she reached the refreshment table.

Rose reached for a glass as the smell of jasmine flooded her senses. Then a soft, melodious voice spoke near her ear. "Hello, my dear."

$\mathcal{A}$ petite, older woman with obsidian black hair and small, dark eyes smiled up at her. Rose hadn't yet been introduced to her, but she curtsied politely. "Good evening."

The graceful, round-faced woman inclined her head in return. "I don't believe I have had the pleasure of making your acquaintance. This must be your first season?"

"It is." Rose shifted from foot to foot, still clutching a glass of lemonade in one hand.

"I am Lady Nightingale."

Though the top of her head came to Rose's chin, Lady Nightingale seemed to tower above all those around her. Her silk, emerald-green dress shone in the candlelight, refracting a depth of color that seemed impossible. The smell of jasmine wafted from her with every slight movement. She was striking.

"Rose Worthington." Rose covertly looked past the petite woman's shoulders for her husband. Then again, if she had attended the ball with her spouse, he would have been the one to make the introductions. She must be a widow, well past her mourning period, since she wore such resplendent colors.

A spark of recognition brightened Lady Nightingale's

features at her name, though Rose knew they had never met before.

"It is a pleasure to meet you, Miss Worthington. Is your family with you tonight?"

Rose gestured to where her mother stood with the odious Lord Reeves. "My mother, Catherine Worthington. My cousin was here a moment ago." Rose did not try to ascertain where Cornelius had gone. She hoped he would stay out on the balcony for the rest of the evening.

Lady Nightingale clasped her gloved hands demurely in front of her. "Might you introduce me? I do enjoy making new friends."

Rose swallowed the lump of anxiety that swelled in her throat. "Of course."

There was no simpering or falseness in the woman's tone. Lady Nightingale appeared rather genuine. As they crossed the room, Rose couldn't help but wonder why such an obviously important person had singled her out.

She cleared her throat when she reached her mother's side, interrupting whatever dull topic Lord Reeves was going on about.

"Mama, this is Lady Nightingale. Lady Nightingale, my mother, Lady Catherine Worthington, and Lord Reeves."

"Good evening," Lady Nightingale said warmly. "Have you been in London long?"

"We arrived at the beginning of the season." Her mother's eyes danced from Rose to the striking woman beside her, brow pinched with curiosity.

"Eh? What's that?" Lord Reeves interrupted.

Lady Nightingale surveyed him coolly. "Lord Reeves, I believe Miss Crawford was saying she was quite exhausted by all the dancing she has done this evening. Perhaps you might oblige her by filling a spot on her dancing card so she may have a rest? It would be a great relief to her, I am sure."

Rose felt the corners of her mouth turn up. What a clever woman. She fought to keep her face as neutral as possible, but had to resort to coughing into her gloved hand to conceal her delight.

Lord Reeves licked his dry lips. "Of course, of course," he said. "I am happy to assist Miss Crawford." He cast a lecherous eye towards Effie, who was surrounded by no less than three suitors. All very handsome, and all had previously danced with Miss Crawford that evening. Effie couldn't dance with them again without showing her hand at who she favored.

Yes, Lady Nightingale was a smart woman.

As soon as Lord Reeves was out of earshot, she was quick to give her opinion of him. "Odious man. You are out of his league, my dear."

Rose agreed, but it was bold of her to say such things in public, and especially to her mother.

"Lady Worthington, I wonder if I may chaperone your daughter for the rest of the evening, and invite her to a party I am having at my home in two days. I take it upon myself to give special attention to one newcomer each season, to mentor them and teach them how to excel. It can take some guidance for us to find our natural talents and employ them most effectively. I believe Miss Worthington has great potential."

Lady Worthington put a hand to her throat. "My, that is certainly generous of you," she said. "I am certainly amiable to the idea, at least for the evening, if Rose does not object."

Both women turned their eyes expectantly towards her.

She couldn't believe her mother would give her up so easily to someone she just met. Rose knew that she hadn't taken to the season as her mother would have wanted, but to foist her off onto a stranger? She couldn't deny that it stung. And why should she agree? She had no desire to catch a husband.

Rose watched as Lord Reeves limped through the gaggle of suitors surrounding Effie. The incomparable's nose wrinkled at the sight of him, but Lord Reeves was a viscount. One could not dismiss him without causing serious offense, and the Crawfords were of excellent stock. They knew better than to displease certain members of the gentry.

This strange woman had dismissed Lord Reeves and given Effie a taste of her own medicine in just a few short words. Curiosity burned through the haze of Rose's grief. She squashed her hurt at her mother's quick agreement, and listened instead to the inexplicable pull she felt towards the mysterious Lady Nightingale. Rose felt as if she now stood at a crossroads. "All right."

"Wonderful," Lady Nightingale said. "Miss Worthington, as the hour is late, I believe we only have time for a brief lesson this evening. If you would follow me?"

Rose exchanged a pointed look with her mother as she fell into step behind her new benefactress.

Lady Nightingale led the way out of the ballroom and into the grand hallway. The sounds of the party dimmed into quiet murmurings. Candelabras on either side lined the hall, burning brightly. They passed the ladies's retiring room, where laughter and giggles spilled out from the crack in the door.

Rose said nothing as their footsteps echoed down the hall. Her heart was still unbearably heavy in her chest, but she could breathe more easily as she focused on where Lady Nightingale was leading her.

Halfway down the long corridor, they stopped. The hall was empty, save for themselves.

"I was watching you as you walked down this hallway. You placed your hand here." Lady Nightingale pointed to the spot where Rose had leaned against the wall. "Might you be able to explain that?"

Rose squinted at the intricate wallpaper, then gasped. A black scorch mark in the shape of a handprint burned into the paper. Her handprint. Rose looked at her glove. The satin was smooth and white, no traces of fire or charcoal marred it. She looked again at the wall, then at Lady Nightingale, mouth going slack.

"Can you also explain how I observed the candles go out, then reignite as you held your hand to this wall?"

Rose spluttered, "No. That's impossible."

"My dear," Lady Nightingale cooed. "You do not know what *is* possible."

Rose was speechless. She examined her satin glove again and turned her hand over, looking for some trace of soot or ink. She removed her glove, exposing her hand and arm. Her skin was intact.

"I shall see you in two days. Look for my invitation tomorrow."

Lady Nightingale left Rose in the grand hallway, speechless and confused. When she looked back at the wall, the mark was gone.

CHAPTER 9

*L*ady Nightingale made good on her promise. Her invitation, sealed with emerald colored wax, had arrived the following morning. Rose's mother agreed to let her attend the small salon party unchaperoned, as Lady Nightingale requested in her note, as there were to be no men present at the event.

Rose's heart hammered in her chest, thumping in time with her footsteps as she ascended the wide stone steps that led to Lady Nightingale's front door. She lifted the golden bird-shaped knocker and knocked. She tried to keep her nerves at bay, but her knees wobbled as a maid answered the door and ushered her inside.

The reception room was a vibrant mix of textures and colors. Lush green and purple fabrics, exquisite ceramic vases, and plumes of peacock feathers decorated the space. Rose's pulse calmed slightly as she observed several groups of women idly chatting. There were about twenty guests in attendance, making for a rather intimate gathering. Rose stood awkwardly near the wall. She didn't know any of the women in this room, while they all appeared at ease with one another. No one noticed her. For a moment, Rose considered bolting out the door. This had been a huge mistake. Why had Lady Nightingale even invited her?

Rose pressed her back into the wall, holding her hands behind her. She had never wanted to disappear so badly.

Just when she thought she wouldn't be able to stand the crushing awkwardness a moment longer, Lady Nightingale swept into the room. She radiated elegance in a dark red gown with full skirts. The dress was not fashioned in the current style, but instead of looking outdated, Lady Nightingale looked magnificent. She commanded the attention of the room. The quiet chatter died away in her presence, and the guests bobbed small curtsies in greeting.

Lady Nightingale did not return the gesture.

"Good evening," she said, her voice carrying with warmth. She scanned the small crowd and locked eyes with Rose. "Miss Worthington," she said. "Would you care to sit beside me?"

It wasn't a question. Or, at least, it was not an offer Rose could have refused. She nodded and made herself walk across the room to stand at the woman's side. Lady Nightingale led the way into an adjacent dining room where places were set with fine china. Lit candelabras cast a warm glow across the table.

The guests took their places. Lady Nightingale sat at the head of the polished black table, its surface so smooth that it reflected her face like a mirror. Rose took the vacant seat on Lady Nightingale's left.

Another woman, several years her senior, took the seat across from her. Her deep green eyes flitted over the gathered company. Her flaming red hair was swept into an elegant bun that accentuated her long neck.

"We thank the Mother for this meal," Lady Nightingale said.

"We thank the Mother," responded the guests in unison.

Rose fought to keep her face neutral. Lady Nightingale didn't wear a cross, and Rose had seen no religious symbols decorating the room. Back home, the pastor's dining room had a domineering wooden cross that hung on the wall, and he and his family intoned a prayer of gratitude before every meal. Rose had never heard the phrase Lady Nightingale had used before, in church or anywhere else.

The household staff, composed entirely of women, served the first course, placing bowls of creamy soup before each guest. The guests's soft chatter began once again.

"Miss Worthington, may I introduce you to Lady Clarke?" Lady Nightingale gestured to the red-haired woman.

Rose flashed her a quick, nervous smile. It was hard not to be intimidated. Lady Clarke possessed the same quiet assuredness that Lady Nightingale did.

"Lydia was one of my students several years ago," explained Lady Nightingale.

"For which I am very grateful." Lady Clarke bowed her head in reverence. It was a demure gesture, but it did not diminish the self-confidence that radiated from her.

"Lydia has improved her station in life drastically these past few years."

"I have. Though not through any natural talent. I would have never married Lord Clarke without your instruction."

Rose wrinkled her nose. Was this truly to be the subject of Lady Nightingale's instructions, finding a proper husband? What about the scorch mark on the wall?

Lady Clarke noted the sour look and laughed sweetly. "Oh, there are far more benefits to marriage than simply finding a husband." She touched the necklace she wore, laden with emeralds that matched her eyes. It must have cost a small fortune. So, these women must be fortune-hunters.

"More than money and husbands." Lady Nightingale said, as if she had read Rose's thoughts. "Power, privilege, influence. It can all be yours. If you know how to take it."

Lady Clarke lifted her wineglass, toasting to the notion before she took a sip.

"How?" croaked Rose. There was no sense in pretending she wasn't interested in those things. All she wanted was the power to control her own life, to make her own decisions without the threat of marriage or her mother's expectations hanging over her. "I wouldn't even know where to start."

"My dear, that's why I'm here." Lady Nightingale's eyes shone with kindness.

Rose relaxed as the dinner progressed. Elegant dishes were brought out, and the wine flowed freely. Lady Nightingale introduced Rose to the women seated around them.

Lady Margaret sat to Rose's right. She was an old woman who said little, but whose beady eyes absorbed everything happening around her all at once. With her wricnkled face, gray hair, and bowed back, she had an uncanny similarity to an old vulture.

Beatrice Sedgewick, a girl with mousy brown hair and a pinched face, sat diagonally from Rose on Lady Clarke's left side. She stared openly at Rose, studying her throughout the meal. Her unforgiving stare made Rose shift uncomfortably in her chair.

Rose guessed that it must have been an honor to sit so close to Lady Nightingale. The women in the room were drawn to her like bees to honey. A young girl peered up at the front of the table with dark, wide eyes as she ate her food. In fact, all the assembled guests glanced towards the head of the table during their conversations, and Lady Nightingale would meet their stares, smile, and return to the conversation with those seated around her. With only her eyes, she could convey her message: *I see you, I welcome you.*

After dessert, the party returned to the large parlor, where many small tables were arranged throughout the room. Playing cards lay on each table.

The girl with enormous brown eyes clapped her hands. "It's whist tonight!"

Lady Nightingale gestured for the girl to approach. "Miss Sinclair, why don't you play with Miss Worthington and Lady Clarke this evening?"

The girl's lips quirked mischievously. "I will take you for all you are worth tonight," she said to Lady Clarke.

Lady Clarke laughed. "You probably could, Harriet. But you'll be playing with Miss Worthington, which will spare me the loss of my entire fortune."

Rose had not played card games in a long time. Her mother did not have the patience for them. Even though she knew she would be terribly out of practice, Rose was looking forward to playing the game.

Harriet sat across from Rose. Her face had not quite lost all of its baby fat. Her warm, sepia skin glowed in the soft light of the room. The brown of her eyes was so deep it was almost black. Combined with her doll-like appearance and unbridled joy, she looked all of twelve. "Hello, Miss Worthington. You may call me Harriet," she stated in a matter-of-fact tone. "Have you played whist before?"

"Not in a long time," Rose admitted. "But I am a quick student. I am sure with your help, it won't take me long to remember how to play."

Harriet nodded, assured.

Beatrice, the girl with the pinched face who looked to be about Rose's age, appeared at Lady Clarke's elbow. "You'll be needing a fourth," she observed. "May I join you?"

"Of course, Bea. You shall play with me."

Beatrice looked like a cat who had swallowed a canary as she took a seat across from Lady Clarke.

Lady Clarke shuffled the deck and dealt each player thirteen cards, flipping the last card over to display the trump suit, the clubs. Beatrice placed her first card to begin the trick. The player to place the highest-ranking card each time around won the trick. Beatrice and Lady Clarke allowed Harriet to explain the rules of the game as the rounds progressed.

It was a game of strategy. Each player must play not only their own cards, but pay attention to the cards of their team-mate in order to outwit the other players.

Beatrice and Lady Clarke won almost every trick in the first round. Beatrice's face grew more smug with each passing moment. As they played, Rose observed that both she and Lady Clarke often closed their eyes, tightening their grips on the cards before quickly selecting a card to play.

Harriet stared at Rose. Her eyes grew wider and wider as the game went on. Her little mouth tightened into a firm line of concentration.

When their opponents won the game and the party stood to stretch, Harriet turned exasperatedly to Rose. "Didn't you get any of the cards I sent you?"

"Sorry?" asked Rose, arms stretched behind her back. Card trading or swapping was not part of the game.

"Now, now, Harriet," said Lady Clarke gently. "I don't think Rose knows how to play that way yet."

Beatrice, Harriet, and Lady Clarke burst into laughter, drawing the attention of other players nearby.

Rose's checks burned with embarrassment. She was clearly the brunt of some joke between them, and she didn't have a clue what they were talking about.

Harriet took Rose's hand in her own. "Oh, don't feel bad. It took Beatrice ages to learn how to do it. Now she won't stop trying to beat everyone."

Beatrice scowled.

"I still don't know what you mean," said Rose.

Harriet's small hand gripped her own tightly. "Close your eyes," she demanded.

"What?"

"Just do it," ordered the girl.

Lady Clarke and Beatrice stopped laughing. Other women who had finished their games stopped their chatter to watch them.

"*Close them,*" pestered Harriet.

"Fine," Rose said. She shut her eyes, feeling self-conscious.

Harriet kept her grip firm to steady her. "Now empty your head of any thoughts."

It was impossible. Bits of images, colors, and strands of thoughts were flew through Rose's mind. She couldn't track one before being interrupted by another.

"Picture a still lake. No breeze or anything, just flat water," said Harriet.

Rose felt rather silly, but she nodded and tried it anyway, if only to please the earnest Harriet.

The bits of thought and memory floated away. Rose pictured a flat, still lake in her mind. The lake from the Worthington Estate behind the house. Her father and brother had loved to fish there. Rose let the memory drift away and focused as hard as she could on nothing but the still water.

"Now, what card am I sending you?"

Rose swallowed her discomfort and doubt. She felt so foolish. She refocused. Silence. Still water. Then, a flash of red.

Rose didn't *see* the flash, but simply knew that the color was red. Her pulse thumped and blood rushed in her ears.

"It's red," said Rose, a tinge of excitement in her voice.

"Good!" said Harriet, though her voice sounded far away. "What suit? What number?"

Rose felt her forehead tingle, almost as if the skin was stretching too tightly there. She was losing focus. Another flash of curves rocketed into her mind's eye. "Three? Of hearts?" she asked, opening her eyes. More of Lady Nightingale's guests had turned to stare. Rose's throat tightened at their attention.

Harriet gave her hand another reassuring squeeze. "Close. It was the eight of diamonds." She finally let go of Rose's hand. Rose wished she hadn't.

"You did well for your first time!" Lady Clarke said.

"You mean you did that the whole time we were playing?" Rose asked. It was hard to believe. They had been communicating without speaking. How on earth had they done it?

Beatrice's smug face gleamed. "How else do you think we beat you so terribly?"

Rose didn't know what to think. It felt like she was playing pretend, imagining things and saying them out loud. There was no way she had received any pictures or messages from Harriet. It must have been a coincidence, or they were very good at guessing. All they had to do was pay attention to the cards that were played. It was a game of strategy, after all.

Lady Nightingale approached their group. "Well done, Miss Sinclair."

Harriet beamed at the praise.

"And well done to you, too, Miss Worthington. Not everyone gets something the first time they try it."

Rose's mouth popped open. She couldn't believe that Lady Nightingale would take part in such folly.

Lady Nightingale laughed at her expression. Rose closed her mouth and tucked a loose strand of hair behind her ear.

"What an interesting birthmark."

Rose glanced at her wrist where the crescent-shaped mark, as large as a coin, stood in sharp relief against her skin.

Before she could respond, Lady Nightingale addressed her companions. "I think Miss Worthington has had quite enough of whist tonight, my dears. But I can't send you back to your mother, having only taught you how to play cards."

She extracted a fan from the folds of her gown, splaying it open with a flick of her wrist. "The art of the fan," she said. "Lady Clarke, will you assist me?"

"Of course."
"Then let us begin."

CHAPTER 10

Rose slept late the next morning, exhausted from her evening at Lady Nightingale's. For the first time in weeks, her first thought upon waking was not of Philip. Instead, her mind raced, replaying the strangeness she had witnessed last night. Lady Clarke, Harriet, and pinch-faced Beatrice had claimed they could communicate through their thoughts. Even Lady Nightingale had commended her for trying the strange practice. Rose didn't know what to make of it all. It still felt like she was making things up.

She rubbed the sleep from her eyes. As she swung her legs over the bed, guilt, crushing and bleak, settled on her chest. Philip was gone. She had forgotten, if only for a moment.

After picking at her breakfast, Rose wandered the halls of her new home in search of a quiet corner where she could nurse her aching heart.

The townhouse her mother and Cornelius had secured was near Grosvenor's Square. Cornelius must have paid dearly to secure the ostentatious brownstone building. It had white trim, vast windows, and towering rose bushes of white and pale pink that framed the front steps. Inside, there was a sweeping grand staircase, sparkling chandeliers, and exquisite furnishings.

Rose's bedroom was the worst. Everything was bedecked in a soft pink, from the curtains and walls to the settee in the corner. Accents of gold and white brought some variety in color to the room, but not enough to mask the garish hue.

Rose stared out of a second-story window towards a park and the commanding homes that lined the square. People bustled about the street. Parasols in pastel colors bobbed here and there while the sun glinted off gentlemen's hats. Each couple looked the perfect picture of elegance as they strolled arm in arm. Every pair walked at the same measured pace, stopped to admire the same trees and flowers, proceeding mechanically down the street. The small gardens trimmed to orderly, angular perfection made Rose miss the wild brambles of the woods, the rippling of wheat fields, and the wide, open sky of home.

She turned from the idyllic scene, unable to stomach it.

Rose floated through the house like a ghost. She knew that the cheerful pastels and twinkling golds would have taken any sane person's breath away, but she was not awed by any of it. Room to room she went, noting the finely polished furniture upholstered in floral, shimmering fabrics. Everything gleamed and glistened, throwing her mood into stark contrast. She entered an impressive ballroom with towering ceilings. Her footsteps echoed forlornly in the gloom. The room felt as if it were sleeping, waiting for the chandeliers to be lit with candles and filled with joyous partygoers.

She found a locked door down the long hallway of the main floor. Rose twisted the knob to no avail. She couldn't explain why, but she felt compelled to go inside. It was as if a thread pulled somewhere in her chest, tugging her towards the locked door. She tried the knob again, giving it a fierce twist. The door swung wide. Rose paused on the threshold. It must have only been stuck. She stepped inside and closed the door behind her.

The room was furnished with rich mahogany. Floor to ceiling bookshelves sat against the back wall, and golden candelabras sat atop the desk and small tables. Behind the desk was a well-stocked bar with crystal glasses and decanters of dark amber liquids.

Rose hugged herself as a little shiver went through her. The fire was almost completely out, which meant Cornelius wouldn't be using his study for a few hours yet.

She walked to the table stocked with alcohol. She'd never tried liquor before. It wasn't an appropriate drink for a lady. Rose picked up a rectangular crystal carafe and removed the glass stopper. She poured herself a finger's width of the liquid into a short glass and sniffed it. It made her eyes water. She took a tiny sip.

The liquid burned her mouth, from the tip of her tongue to the back of her throat. It traveled warmly down her throat until it pooled in her stomach. She coughed and wiped her watering eyes, setting the glass down while she waited for her coughing to subside. Warmth filled her insides and made her cheeks tingle.

No wonder men liked the drink so much.

Before she could talk herself out of it, she swallowed the rest of the liquor in one gulp. The burning lessened somewhat, but she still felt the alcohol's fire travel through her, filling her head and limbs with a pleasant buzzing sensation as she coughed again.

She placed the stopper back into the bottle and sat down behind the desk. The room felt a little less chilly now. Idly, she opened the drawers. Rose found nothing of great intrigue in the first few.

The last drawer she tried was locked. Rose felt that strange thread pull her towards it. She tugged on the handle, willing the drawer to open, but it refused to budge. She bent down to inspect it and spied a tiny keyhole underneath the handle. Rose riffled through the drawers again, looking for a miniature key, but found nothing. Defeated, she slumped in the chair.

The sound of approaching footsteps made her straighten. She looked at the bookshelf behind her and grabbed a tome from the shelves. Setting it on the desk, she flipped to a random page and fought to keep her breathing even.

A key twisted in the lock, but she kept her eyes fixed on the book as the door creaked open.

"This room was locked," Cornelius said.

Rose lifted her head from her pretend reading. Cornelius's straight, black hair was windblown. He held a leather satchel in one hand.

She turned back to the book casually, trying to quell the fire of hate that burned in her chest. "It wasn't when I tried to open it."

Rose watched Cornelius out of the corner of her eye as he dumped his bag unceremoniously into a chair. He walked over to the table where Rose had helped herself to some of his alcohol only moments before and removed the glass stopper from one bottle. He picked up a glass and paused, examining it briefly before pouring a generous amount. "I didn't realize you had a taste for brandy, Miss Worthington."

"I don't."

Cornelius moved behind Rose and peered over her shoulder, glass in hand. "Military strategy? How incredibly dull." He took a sip of his drink.

"Oh, I don't know. There may be some useful information in here," she said. The liquor gave her false bravado.

"And are we at war, Miss Worthington?"

Rose looked up. His face was bemused, one eyebrow raised inquisitively. There was no cruelty in his dark brown eyes. His face was smooth.

"You tell me."

Cornelius drained the rest of his glass.

Rose braced herself for an explosion of his temper. She had intruded into his study, after all.

"I have some work to do," Cornelius said finally. "I think it's time for you to go." There was no anger or malice in his voice, only calm.

She placed both hands on the desk and stood. Her head swam. She stumbled as she came around the desk.

Cornelius caught her elbow and steadied her. An overwhelming scent of copper flooded her nose. The warm buzz of the liquor could not dampen the sudden surge of fear that made her heart kick against her ribs.

Without a backward glance, Rose hurried back to the safety of her suite.

CHAPTER 11

That evening, Rose, her mother, and Cornelius stood in the receiving line of Lady Clarke's annual ball. It was the first party that Rose was looking forward to since arriving in London.

For most of her life, she had been preoccupied with endings. Her childhood had ended with the death of her brother. Her dreams of managing her family's estate as an unmarried woman had dissolved when Cornelius dragged her to London. Any hope of finding happiness with Philip had died almost as quickly as it had taken root. For the first time in a long while, Rose was hopeful about a new beginning, even though the pang of losing Philip still throbbed endlessly in her chest.

Rose had chosen a white gown with floral appliques and pearl jewelry for the party, which matched the feathered fan she had been practicing with. Tonight, she would put Lady Nightingale's lesson into practice. Before her instruction, Rose did not know that a fan could be useful for anything other than keeping cool. Apparently, there were many more uses. While her benefactress would not be in attendance tonight, she had suggested that she would know how Rose performed.

The receiving line moved, and the Worthingtons approached their hosts.

Lady Clarke wore a gown of shimmering gold. Her auburn hair looked like flame itself as it shone in the candlelight. She flashed Rose a radiant smile as she approached. Next to her was the extraordinarily handsome Lord Clarke. He had a firm jaw, dark skin, and sapphire eyes. Together, the Clarkes looked the perfect pair of elegance and refinement.

Lady Nightingale had given Rose strict instructions not to appear overly friendly with the women who had attended her salon if she should see them at other social events. Not all the women had been entirely truthful about their whereabouts that evening. Some ladies lied to their husbands or mothers for the chance to get away. The *ton* of London might raise their eyebrows at the idea of women gathering to play whist when they should be at home taking care of their husbands, or doing everything in their power to find themselves one. Rose had assured Lady Nightingale that she could keep her confidence, and thus had to pretend that she had never met Lady Clarke before.

"Welcome. It is a pleasure to meet you. I'm so glad you could join us, Miss Worthington," cooed Lady Clarke affectionately. "And you as well, Lord Worthington. Lady Worthington."

Lord Clarke bowed politely, but let his wife do all the talking.

"You are acquainted with my daughter?" Her mother did not fail to notice that Lady Clarke had addressed Rose first.

Rose's stomach fluttered.

"I have heard nothing but praise from Lady Nightingale. She tells me your daughter is a delight," Lady Clarke said warmly.

Rose felt her cheeks flush. She dipped her chin, acknowledging the compliment.

Her mother beamed. "You're very kind."

Those who were close to them swiveled their heads to see

who Lady Clarke was talking about. More than a few eyebrows raised when they saw it was one of the season's wallflower girls.

"Enjoy the ball," said Lord Clarke in a low, commanding voice.

The Worthingtons left the procession and entered the wide hall that led to the garden where the dancing would take place. Cornelius had taken both Rose and her mother's elbow to escort them further into the house, no doubt to assert his claim over them to the curious observers who had overheard Lady Clarke's praise. A muscle in his jaw twitched as they walked.

Rose gasped as they entered the garden, admiring the glittering spectacle. Every shrub, plant, and trellis was covered in small, twinkling lights and lush greenery. A large archway covered in clematis flowers in every shade of purple imaginable marked the entrance to the ballroom floor. Some blooms were as large as Rose's hand. Pale lavender, deep lilac, and rich amethyst flowers cascaded over the floor of polished wood. Each tiny light was a small candle, immune to the breeze of the warm spring air, staying lit even as they flickered. Other guests exclaimed in delight as they beheld the scene.

Cornelius left them near the perimeter of the floor to seek out some gentlemen from the club. Rose was relieved to watch him go.

Lord and Lady Clarke entered the garden to begin the dancing. Thousands of tiny gemstones in Lady Clarke's gown sparkled in the candlelight. She commanded the attention of every one of her guests. Lord Clarke placed his hand gently on the small of his wife's back as they took their positions.

Soon, other guests filled the floor. Rose spotted Effie Crawford and some dark-haired bachelor jostling for a place near the Clarkes. She fought the urge to snort at Effie's obvious attempt to place herself next to the most important people in the room.

Rose remained at the edges of the dance floor with her mother, content to observe the crowd and bask in the garden's scent. The smell of greenery and living things soothed her. She closed her eyes and inhaled deeply, letting her mind wander back to the woods and fields she so loved and missed.

"Miss Worthington?"

Rose snapped her eyes open. Alexander Crawford, dressed in a dark evening suit, looked at her expectantly. His white-blonde hair gleamed in the golden light.

"I'm sorry?" She wondered how long he'd been standing there.

"Lord Crawford was asking you to dance," said her mother with a hint of chastisement.

"Yes, if you'll have me," smiled Alexander.

"Of course." Rose took Alexander's proffered arm. "Thank you." She was so surprised that he selected her to be his first partner that she nearly neglected her manners.

He led them effortlessly towards the center of the floor. Couples were happy to make room for the darling of society as he flashed appreciative grins at them. As they walked, he asked, "What were you thinking about?"

"Home," said Rose. She took her place across from Lord Crawford.

"I'd like to hear about it," he said.

Before Rose could reply, the music started. A waltz, with simple steps. Rose thanked the stars that it wasn't anything more complicated, lest she make a fool of herself.

She needn't have worried. Alexander Crawford was an accomplished dancer and masked Rose's faltering steps and self-consciousness with exceptional leading.

"Do you enjoy dancing?" asked Lord Crawford casually.

Rose knew it was the politest way of asking, *why do you dance like a cow?*

She couldn't help but laugh. "Yes, but I was too busy horse-back riding to be concerned with dancing lessons. My incorrigible brother was able to persuade our governess to cancel lessons every time we had a spot of sunshine. Dancing was never as appealing as spending a day outdoors."

Alexander's eyebrows rose. "It sounds like you had a wonderful childhood. Personally, I'd much rather be at the park riding my horse than dancing at a ball."

"Maybe we could go riding in the park together someday," she said. She bit her lip, immediately regretting her casual offer. It was a very forward invitation.

Alexander wasn't offended. He smiled as they twirled. "I would like that."

The music ended. Rose's heart beat as fast as a humming-bird's wings. Now was the perfect time to put her new lessons from Lady Nightingale into practice. She didn't know she would get another chance this evening, and she wanted Lady Nightingale to receive a favorable report.

She stepped back from Alexander and curtsied as he bowed, finishing the dance. Rose clasped her fan in one hand and made a show of trying to open it as couples ebbed and flowed around them.

"Drat," she said. "I can't get this silly thing to open."

"Here, allow me," he offered, the perfect gentleman.

The strap of the fan was looped around Rose's wrist. Instead of removing it from her arm, she held her hand between them, allowing him access to the fan. Rose saw Effie Crawford glowering at them from the corner of her eye.

Alexander squinted in concentration.

"There's a little clasp here." Rose leaned towards him. She could smell him. Citrus and birch. She let a moment pass as Alexander brought his face close to examine the fan. Then she opened it with a tiny flick of the wrist, her thumb loosening the catch in one fluid motion. The fan spread wide between them. Their lips were only parted by the soft feathers. Rose peered up at Alexander from behind the plumed screen.

"Thank you," she breathed.

Alexander cleared his throat and blinked once. "You're welcome." He offered his arm, putting distance between them once more. "Shall we?"

Rose fanned herself delicately as he escorted her back to her mother. The eyes of every unmarried man in the vicinity were fixed on them as they walked through the crowd. Rose felt Effie's burning stare trail after them, but she held her head high as they moved through the throng of partygoers.

Lady Clarke caught Rose's eye as she walked towards the edge of the dance floor. She grinned and dipped her chin in a delicate nod.

Pride swelled in Rose's chest. Warmth and a happy, light feeling made her steps buoyant. It was something she had not felt for many weeks.

This was a realm of control she had never explored. Maybe power had many faces. Upturned gazes, the flick of a fan, brazenness, all things she never would have imagined that she could wield to her favor. Rose decided that these subtle powers were worth exploring further.

Alexander thanked her for the dance and left Rose to her mother, who began whispering to her excitedly. "I was watching the entire time. That was simply marvelous. He looked positively stunned by you!"

Rose's stomach clenched violently. Her moment of pride disintegrated. She had succeeded in employing her new skills, but in her desperation to prove herself, she had forsaken her feelings for Philip. Tears pricked her eyes. She should be miserable. She *deserved* to be unhappy. It had only been four weeks since Philip had been killed, and it was all her fault. Rose felt bile rise in her throat. She was utterly disgusted with herself.

Her mother continued to prattle on as Rose fought the urge to cry. She blinked rapidly, ignoring her mother. Instead, she focused on Lady Clarke as she handed her husband her glass of punch and whispered something in his ear before heading straight towards her. Rose did her best to resume her cheery countenance, plastering a tight-lipped smile to her face.

Lady Clarke kept her voice low and leaned towards them. "You did splendidly!" Many eyes were upon them. No doubt, she didn't want the entire party overhearing their conversation.

"She learned that in the course of a single evening," said her mother, puffing with pride.

"Your daughter must be a quick student," said Lady Clarke. "And Lady Nightingale is an excellent teacher."

Rose lifted her chin to meet Lady Clarke's gaze. Her eyes had the same benevolent quality as Lady Nightingale's, but they pierced her very soul. No one had ever looked at her that way before, like she could see her thoughts and emotions as if they were carved into her skin, waiting to be read.

"I still can't believe that Lady Nightingale agreed to take Rose on," said her mother.

"Lady Nightingale has a way of choosing those who are most deserving. Now, I must warn you, Miss Worthington. Be prepared to be quite busy the rest of the evening. You have certainly sparked the curiosity of the rest of our company."

Rose dared a glance towards the hum of people circling the dance floor and gardens. It was almost comical how hard they tried to not stare too obviously at them. Rose would have laughed if she weren't so intimidated and heartsick.

"We have set you up for an eventful evening, between your excellent flirtation with your fan and the prolonged attention from your gracious hostess." She winked.

Rose let out a small snort of laughter. She was glad Lady Clarke didn't take herself too seriously. She was aware of the power and effect she had on people, but she did not act superior for it.

"Enjoy the rest of the ball." Lady Clarke rejoined her husband. Guests desperate for her attention surrounded her, blocking her from Rose's view.

A young man whom Rose had seen dancing with Effie Crawford frequently had been lying in wait for Lady Clarke to leave. He promptly asked Rose for the next dance, and her mother agreed on her behalf. Two other bachelors, both handsome and polite, ask to dance with her after the first left. Her dance card was more than half full in under two minutes.

The next hour passed with astonishing speed. Rose danced with three potential suitors, all who promised to call within the week after their dance was done. It didn't seem to bother them she was a mediocre dancer at best. Her mother practically glowed with happiness. During a break in her dance card, Rose stood at the edge of the party and fanned herself.

Alexander Crawford slid next to her and handed her a glass of lemonade.

"Thank you." She drank deeply, thirsty from her exertions.

"Would you honor me with another dance?" he asked.

Rose's eyebrows shot up as she lowered her glass. It was very bold of Alexander to dance with her more than once. Dancing twice with the same partner showed that there was serious interest in forming an attachment. She wanted to refuse. To correct him and tell him he had it wrong. She wasn't interested in him like that. But she couldn't with her mother standing just a few paces away. Besides, what would Lady Nightingale say? Rose swallowed her discomfort.

"I'm…flattered. Of course, I'd love to," she stammered.

Alexander grinned broadly at her and led her gently into the golden light of the party.

CHAPTER 12

$\mathscr{E}$ffie Crawford was beside herself with rage. Her brother was making an absolute fool of himself dancing with the Worthington wallflower twice in one evening. Cecilia would be devastated. Alexander had given her every sign that he would be officially courting her this season, but now this dalliance with the wild-haired country girl was throwing everything off.

The Crawfords and the Hawthornes were poised on the edge of a fruitful alliance. Her mother had divulged the importance of Alexander's marriage to Cecilia sometime last year after one too many glasses of sherry. Effie had been tactful in gleaning the information from her mother, and had done everything in her power to ensure that her best friend and brother not only agreed to marry to solidify the family alliance, but had the foundations for a love match.

Effie loved her older brother more than anything, and Cecilia had been her best friend since they were small children. As the daughter of a Baron, Cecilia's marriage would be used in a manner most helpful to her family. Since the fortunes of Baron Hawthorn had been in decline for several years, and the

Crawford fortune had grown, Lord Crawford and Baron Hawthorn had long ago agreed to wed their two children. Effie had known this, but it wasn't until her mother divulged how dire Cecilia's fate was that she had devoted her more of her energy to ensuring that Alexander and Cecilia had the greatest possible chance at true happiness.

She understood that Baron Hawthorn could marry his daughter to a viscount or even an earl if he wished, but if her parents believed she and Alexander were actually in love, they would not sway from their plans. Effie also knew that if her brother married the daughter of a baron, her own chances at making an advantageous match would drastically improve. The arrangement suited all of them, and a wedding was to be announced by the end of the season.

But now Alexander was dancing twice in one evening with a nobody. She needed to put a stop to this foolishness. She had to do something drastic, and quickly, before Alexander insulted Cecilia or became distracted by the presumptuous Miss Worthington.

"Reginald, be a dear and fetch me a glass of wine?" she simpered to her most recent dance partner. Her eyes never left her quarry.

* * *

"WHAT WAS it like growing up in Ashford?" Alexander asked as he and Rose sipped on lemonade. They stood near the refreshment table, their second dance having concluded.

"I spent a great deal of time outdoors," Rose said. It wasn't wise to divulge how involved she was in her family's estate and its management. At least, not yet.

"I would like to join you in the park this week, if I may?"

"That would be lovely," said Rose. She was startled to find she meant it. She had been so lonely, and Alexander was proving very easy to talk to. He was kind when others had not been. Besides the women at Lady Nightingale's soirée, he was the only member of the *ton* who had given her any sort of attention. "I feel as if you are the only friend I have made in London so far," she admitted.

"It can be difficult to find friends when all anyone here cares about is the marriage market," said Alexander graciously.

Rose was just about to ask Alexander what he did to pass his time when she felt something cold and wet soak into her dress, right over her derriere. She discreetly pivoted so that her back was facing towards the unlit gardens and brushed a hand over her backside. Her gloved fingers came away stained with red. "What on earth?" She whirled around to take a better look at her gown. A large red stain splashed down the skirt of her white dress.

"Oh dear," said a snobby voice in her ear. "Are you well, Miss Worthington?"

Rose whipped her head around to find Effie Crawford dangling an empty wine glass idly from her fingers.

Effie leaned in close to whisper conspiratorially in her ear, ignoring her brother. "It looks as though you've gotten your menses, Miss Worthington. Perhaps you ought to bring a napkin next time you go dancing," she whispered.

Rose jerked back from Effie. She wanted to slap her. Rose had finally had some footing in the treacherous social circles of London and knew this would shatter all chances of maintaining her precarious position. It was more than a mean-spirited prank. It was targeted and hateful.

Alexander could sniff out his sister's trouble. "Sister," he said, feigning a casual tone. "I did not realize you knew Miss Worthington."

"Oh, I doubt we shall ever speak again." Effie smiled sweetly. She flounced back to the center of the party, where a swarm of suitors instantly bickered for her attention.

Rose kept her hands behind her back. "You'll have to excuse me, Lord Crawford," she said in a tight voice. "I'm unwell and need to retire."

He had not yet seen what Effie had done. His brow furrowed. "Of course. May I escort you to the house?"

Rose looked to where the brightly lit garden path led back to the house. They were at the farthest point from it, on the opposite side of the dancing area. If she went that way, everyone would see the ugly red smear on the back of her dress.

"No, thank you." Frantically, she scanned the surrounding gardens, ignoring Alexander's insistence that he escort her to her family.

She spotted a small path into the garden close to where they stood. Hopefully, it connected to the main path, and she could enter the house unseen. "I'll just go this way." She backed towards the wall of greenery and disappeared into the shadows of the hedge wall. Rose poked her head out around the tall hedge. "Thank you for this evening. I had a lovely time," Rose said to a confounded Alexander. Then she ran into the dark.

Rose knew that being caught alone in the garden would ruin her reputation more soundly than the stain on her dress, but she refused to let Effie win. Her humiliation stuck like tar within her throat and stomach. Effie was a snob, but she had no idea she could be so cruel.

For a few hours, Rose had been so busy that she had forgotten that her cousin was a monster and the man she had loved was dead. But in the stillness of the quiet gardens, it all came rushing in at once. Rose felt her body sag under the weight of her unhappiness. Her steps slowed to a walk as she got her bearings.

She walked along in silence, listening to the sounds of the party to help keep her oriented in the direction she thought she should head in.

Footsteps on the gravel behind her made her hands prickle

as adrenaline spiked through her. Someone must have seen her entering the garden all alone and was coming to take advantage of the secluded location. She prayed it wasn't Cornelius. Rose whirled to see the shadow of a man in the moonlight chasing after her.

Before she could scream, damn the consequences, Rose recognized Alexander Crawford's pale hair.

"Go back," Rose whispered as he drew closer. "If we're both caught in here, we'll be ruined."

"I'm sorry," Alexander said. "But I had to be sure you were alright. You can't just wander around in the dark." He straightened, regaining his breath. "What did my sister do to you?"

Rose pressed the heel of her hand to her forehead. "She spilled wine down the back of my dress." She had been perfectly content to handle the situation on her own. Alexander's presence, as thoughtful as it might be, was more risky than helpful.

Rose was about to tell him off for his foolishness, but stopped herself.

Alexander's face was a stone mask of disappointment. "I apologize for my sister's behavior," he said solemnly.

"Well, you didn't do it." Rose dropped her hand and huffed in frustration. She wanted to ask why his sister was so malicious, but she knew it was his duty to defend his sister, even if she was wicked. George probably would have done the same for her.

"I am grateful for your concern, but what are we going to do? If we're both seen coming out of here together, both of our reputations will be irreparably damaged." She didn't much care about what society thought of her reputation. But she couldn't do that to Alexander.

Alexander paced, brow furrowed in thought. He looked like a schoolboy working through a nasty math problem, but wanted to impress the teacher with the correct answer. The gravel crunched loudly under his feet, making it difficult for

Rose to concentrate. She threw up her hands in frustration just as Alexander exclaimed in triumph.

"I'll create a distraction so no one realizes you have gone, and you can run up to the house. I'll say you have been there the whole time and deal with my sister later."

"And what, pray tell, will this distraction entail?"

"Drunken foolery. It's been a good while since I have made a complete idiot of myself. The lords and ladies of London will forgive me for overindulging for one night. Though I doubt Effie will. Payback for her bullying, I suppose," finished Alexander.

"Oh no. You don't have to—"

Alexander held up a hand. "My reputation can stand it. Now go."

Rose walked quickly towards the main garden path as Alexander ran back in the direction he had come from. By the time she remembered to thank him, he was already out of sight.

Rose hesitated around the corner of the brightly lit main path. She needed some cue that Alexander's distraction had begun, but heard nothing. The music was still playing, guests were still happily chattering. Rose held her arms around herself and waited. The music finally stopped, signaling the end of the latest dance.

Suddenly, she heard Alexander's voice boom across the party, "My dear sister!" He sounded quite drunk. "Just how many of my friends were you planning on wringing marriage proposals from tonight, eh?"

The party grew quiet. The crowd beheld the spectacle with bated breath, bloodthirsty for a scandal.

"Probably all of us if she could manage it!" said a voice Rose didn't recognize. A hushed burble of laughter rippled through the party, mostly from the gentlemen.

To her surprise, it was Effie who responded with a brightness in her voice. "Alexander, don't be jealous. It's not my fault that your friends prefer my company to yours, even if you are much prettier than I am!"

Loud laughter erupted from the guests.

Rose sprinted up the path. She made it to the house without being spotted. Chest heaving, she halted by the wide French doors. Lady Clarke stood in the middle of the large drawing room with her hands clasped before her. She looked like she had been expecting her.

"There you are! Where have you been? I was worried when I couldn't find you for some time."

"I was just on my way to the retiring room," said Rose lamely, holding her hands behind her back and trying to ignore the stitch in her side. Maybe she could conceal the spot on her dress long enough for her to sit down and wait for her mother to find her. Then they could leave and Rose could forget this terrible evening had ever happened.

Lady Clarke placed her hands on her hips. "Really? Then why did you come in through the back garden?"

Rose sighed. Perhaps Lady Clark had a spare dress she could wear for her ride home. She might as well tell her what had happened. After giving her explanation, Rose twisted her gloved hands. Would Lady Clarke chastise her for being alone in her garden with a man? She didn't want Alexander Crawford to get into trouble.

"Though that was rather foolish," said Lady Clarke, holding a hand to her cheek. "I can't say that I blame you. That girl is despicable. Turn around."

Rose obeyed.

Lady Clarke tittered. "Not all bad. We can fix this."

"How?" asked Rose. The wind had spread, staining a wide swath of her dress.

Lady Clarke removed her glove and held her hand over the fabric. She moved her hand slowly down the stain. Rose peered awkwardly over her shoulder to watch. She gasped at what she saw. The stain lifted from the dress as Lady Clarke's hand moved over it, as if she were sucking the liquid from the fabric. Droplets of wine flew up toward the woman's outstretched palm.

As Lady Clarke reached the edge of the stain, she clenched her hand into a fist. Rose wrenched the fabric of her dress around towards her front so she could get a better look. It was pure white. She was about to ask Lady Clarke how she had managed it, but stopped when she saw beads of sweat on her brow. Whatever she had done had been taxing.

Hand still clenched, Lady Clarke moved towards the mantle where a fire crackled in the hearth, despite the warm summer night. "An offer for the Mother," she whispered. Lady Clarke opened her hand and a stream of red wine poured from it, hissing as it struck the flames. The fire burned a deep ruby red before returning to shades of yellow and orange.

Rose gaped at her as Lady Clarke's mouth twitched upwards. "There is much more for you to learn, Miss Worthington."

CHAPTER 13

Another invitation to Lady Nightingale's waited for Rose at breakfast.

Rose was impatient to learn how Lady Clarke had siphoned wine from her dress with nothing but her hands. But despite her pestering, Lady Clarke said she would have to wait for Lady Nightingale to tell her what she wanted to know.

"She must want to review the evening with her star pupil," said her mother, eyeing the invitation as she spread jam on toast. "You were wonderful last night, dear. Though I wish you hadn't disappeared, it was most odd. We wouldn't want to invite any unwanted speculation."

"I'm sorry. Next time I'll inform you straightaway." Rose stirred her tea and left the matter at that. Lady Clarke had helped cover for her absence last night. She'd had Rose lie down in the ladies' retiring room, claiming a headache.

"It's no matter," said her mother. "I am glad you're feeling better this morning. Lord Crawford seemed most taken with you last night. You should be prepared to receive him this morning."

Rose shrugged. "I hardly think two dances warrants a proposal, Mama. He was doing me a kindness. Like any friend."

Her mother's hand stilled over her toast, the knife still grasped between her fingers. "You're not here to make friends, Rose. You're here to find a husband."

Rose sipped her tea in silence, ignoring the comment. She did not feel like arguing this morning. She had other things to think about.

She did not understand how Lady Clarke had removed the stain from her dress with nothing but her bare hands. She wandered aimlessly down the halls of the townhouse as early afternoon sun pooled inside, replaying the scene repeatedly. Alexander did not call, despite her mother's insistence that he would. Rose tried to piece together a logical explanation, but the vision of droplets of red wine hanging suspended in the air, caught between her dress and Lady Clarke's hand, could not be reasoned away. When she got a headache from thinking about it too much, her thoughts drifted to darker, softer places.

Melancholy wrapped around her like a heavy blanket as she walked the halls until she found herself at Cornelius's study. Rose felt that strange tugging sensation within her chest again, pulling her towards the door, begging her to open it.

She twisted the doorknob half-heartedly and found it locked. The tugging sensation in her chest grew stronger, demanding she try again. She grasped the doorknob and felt it grow warm in her hand as her palm tingled. She felt the clicking of the lock somewhere in her bones and the door swung wide. Rose brought her nose close to the handle, examining the lock. After careful study, she concluded the door was ordinary and closed it behind her.

Rose felt another incessant tug towards the desk in the back of the room. She followed the thread that pulled her to the bottom drawer with the tiny keyhole. Rose yanked on the handle, but found it, too, was locked. She held her hand there, as she had done with the doorknob, and waited for her palm to grow warm. Instead, an icy chill leeched into her skin, burning with intensity. She jolted back, releasing her grip. Whatever was in there did not want to be found.

"What are you hiding?" Rose ran her hands over the tops of the books on the shelves, the mantle, under the reading chair. She looked in all the bottles of brandy and in all the crystal glasses, but she could not find a key. She removed a hair pin from her styled curls and jammed it into the lock, but only succeeded in bending the metal. Rose threw the ruined pin into the fireplace with a huff.

Defeated, she drank a mouthful of brandy straight from the decanter. The familiar warmth of alcohol trickled through her, relaxing her limbs. Her throat burned as the brandy went down, but she no longer coughed and spluttered when she drank it.

She settled into an armchair by the fire, idly paging through books from the shelves and trying not to think about how guilty she felt for enjoying Alexander's company last night, or how much she missed Philip. But the alcohol burning through her veins did not aid her attempts to keep her thoughts from him. She let the books drop to the floor as waves of memory and emotion slammed against her. Her body bent until her forehead touched her knees. The room swayed, catching her in an invisible current.

Rose remembered the feeling of Philip's warm embrace, and how the heat of him seared right through her. She remembered the taste of him as she kissed him, the sound of his laugh, his smile. She remembered that he was dead and felt herself shatter into a thousand pieces. How could she dance and laugh when Philip was dead? She had wasted so much time. She wished she had realized sooner that she loved him. But it was too late, and she would carry this ache in her chest for the rest of her life.

Her body wracked with sobs for the rest of the afternoon.

* * *

ROSE ROUSED herself just in time to make it to Lady Nightingale's party. She had nearly sent her regrets, exhausted by her crying and grief, but her curiosity won out in the end. Maybe tonight she would finally get some answers to the mysterious things she had witnessed since arriving in London.

Harriet beamed at Rose when she entered the drawing room and took a seat next to her at supper. Rose was burning to ask Lady Nightingale all her questions, but she was occupied with other guests. Harriet proved a welcome distraction, and Rose felt her melancholy lift a little as they conversed over their meal. Harriet wanted to hear all about Lady Clarke's ball. Her dark eyes grew wide with delight as Rose described the garden, lights, and dancing.

"I'm so jealous," Harriet pouted. "My mama says I'm not to attend any balls until I have made my debut, even though I come here all the time. You must continue to tell me positively *everything* about the season's balls. No one else will."

"Of course I shall." Rose fought the urge to ruffle the girl's wavy tresses affectionately.

After supper, the ladies played whist again. Harriet partnered with Rose against two others, and they were beaten soundly. Harriet did her best to think the cards to her, but Rose couldn't concentrate enough to pick up anything. She felt as if she were guessing at random and played the game as best she could. Harriet had comforted her after a few losses and offered to try with Rose in a more private setting, away from the other players at their small tables, but Rose declined. She was flattered that Harriet had taken such an interest in her. She enjoyed her company, but she was too unsettled. Disappointment made her heart sink as she realized that speaking to Lady Nightingale might not happen. The hour grew late, but her hostess did not show her the attention she had given her first evening.

As the party drew to a close and the guests departed, Lady Clarke caught Rose's elbow. "Meet me in the parlor," she whispered. "After everyone else has gone."

Goosebumps raced over her skin. Rose said goodbye to Harriet and excused herself to use the washroom, lingering for much longer than was necessary. When she emerged, the house was quiet.

Lady Nightingale and Lady Clarke waited for her in the parlor. The drapes were closed, and the candles cast long, flickering shadows throughout the room.

"Welcome, my dear." Lady Nightingale's eyes creased at the corners as she held out a hand to Rose.

Rose took it and was led to a seat by the fireplace. The women settled into their seats.

"So, what do you think of the season so far?"

Rose fidgeted with her dress. She was bursting with questions, but didn't want to be rude. "It's quite diverting."

Lady Nightingale raised an eyebrow, and Lady Clarke's face twisted into a wry smile.

"Actually, it's quite taxing," Rose admitted. She clasped her hands together in her lap. "And I'm not interested in finding a husband, much to my mother's dismay."

"I thought as much." Lady Nightingale leaned over and grasped Rose's clenched hands, giving a reassuring squeeze. "It's difficult to be a woman in this world. Luckily, we have found ways to make it more bearable."

"You mean with magic?" Rose asked bluntly. "That *is* what it is, right?" There was no logical explanation for the things she had seen, or felt, these past few weeks. What else could it be? She had not allowed herself to even think the word, but now was her chance to see if it could be true.

"Before we continue, you must promise never to reveal what

we are about to share with anyone. If you cannot make that promise, we will ask you to leave and never return. There are those who would do great harm to the women here. For gathering without their family's or husband's consent. For using their talents in a way that some deem dangerous. You must swear to secrecy. There are lives that depend on it."

Rose swallowed. She'd seen so much already. She couldn't turn back now. Even though the consequences for indiscretion were dire, it took no thought to form her answer. "I promise."

Lady Clarke grinned at her, and Lady Nightingale nodded approvingly.

"Some may call it that magic," Lady Nightingale continued. "Regardless of what the power is called, it is important to know that we use it for a higher purpose, for more than simply finding a good husband on the marriage mart."

Rose wanted to sob with relief. This was it, her way out of having to marry. She wouldn't have to accept society's demands that she wed and bear children so a family line could continue. She would be worth more than a marriage contract. "Teach me. Please," she whispered. Her hands trembled.

"You have natural abilities and great potential. You understand, we had to assess your character and determine whether you could handle such things," said Lady Nightingale.

"The burden you bear is heavy. Your heart is clouded with grief," said Lady Clarke. "We weren't sure if this was something that would interest you."

"I'm *extremely* interested," said Rose.

"We are the Nightingales," said Lady Clarke solemnly. "Everything we know and are, Lady Nightingale has taught and provided for us. She is our teacher and leader, and we obey her instruction in exchange for certain protections."

"You make it sound so dramatic." Lady Nightingale waved a hand, dismissing Lady Clarke's ceremonious statement.

"And she is very modest," countered Lady Clarke.

"The Nightingales are unique, but there have been others like us before. Not all of them as successful. Once, there was a group of women who overreached with their abilities and were ruined. Not all those girls deserved to die, of course, but their leader led them astray. They diverted so far from their path that they could not be saved. When they were discovered, their neighbors executed them for practicing witchcraft.

"We are not so reckless as to allow that kind of discovery here. We reach within the realms of what we can control, and influence those that we cannot control directly."

Control. Influence. Rose's scalp prickled. "What do you mean? They executed women for doing what, exactly?"

"For daring to be different. For refusing the path that was expected of them and trying to forge their own."

"But how do you select who you will teach? Why me?" asked Rose. She looked to Lady Nightingale, for it was she who had first invited Rose to her home and promised to offer her more from life than she ever thought possible.

"Magic is not accessible to everyone. Only those who are born with the proclivity for it can be taught. You have a great natural talent for it. We aren't sure why it takes root in some and not others. We know that magic manifests in a surprising number of girls, but it is often squashed or dismissed. When not nurtured, it withers and dies. For a rare few the power can grow stronger over time, instead of weakening. You can use what we teach you to forge your own path. We want to help those who want something better out of life."

It sounded too good to be true, but Rose held her tongue as her benefactress continued to explain.

"Miss Beatrice Sedgewick, for example, has a brother who was gambling away their entire fortune. She entered her first social season two years ago with hardly any credibility or fortune. We taught her the skills she would need to persuade her brother to find something else to occupy his time, and she has since enjoyed the many comforts London has to offer to those with the proper affluence. She can choose whom she wishes to marry, rather than settling for the first man with coin in his pockets who would take her."

"So, this control and influence is…?"

"About making the most of our situations, and making choices for ourselves," finished Lady Clarke.

Rose frowned. "But you still married."

Lady Clarke laughed. "Well, not everyone is as opposed to the idea as you are, Miss Worthington. I quite like my husband. Which, I admit, was an unforeseen prize in my scheme to secure a comfortable home and position of power within society. But I fell in love. I'm happy."

"Your own destiny will become clear to you, Miss Worthington. It only takes time," said Lady Nightingale.

Rose looked at the two women. She felt like she was dreaming. "And the way you removed the wine from my dress. Is that another unforeseen advantage as well?"

"There are things, large and small, that we can do to help improve the circumstances around us."

Rose felt as if she were floating, as if she were not quite settled in her own body. Magic was *real.* It was an enormous amount to take in. She gripped the edges of her seat, searching for anchorage in this sea of uncertainty. A entire world had opened before her. All she had to do was step into it.

"But why has my magic grown stronger? Why do I even have it at all?"

"We're not entirely certain," Lady Nightingale said.

"The scorch mark on the wall. You said I made it. But I don't know how."

"What do you remember about your emotional state that evening?" asked Lady Nightingale. Her onyx hair gleamed in the firelight.

Rose thought back to the night of the Crawford's ball. She

bit her lip as waves of grief surged within her. Beneath the waves of despair lay the simmering anger at Cornelius. He had mocked her again, claiming ignorance of the murder he had committed.

The fire in the grate flared white-hot as Rose felt completely engulfed by her own emotions. Rose flinched at the sudden rush of heat. The flames returned to their ordinary color and size.

"There," said Lady Nightingale. "What was that? What did you *feel*?"

"Sadness, anger," said Rose. Her voice was strained. She felt lightheaded.

"And has your sadness and anger caused anything else strange to happen? Fire talks to you especially, but it doesn't always come through one way," prompted Lady Nightingale.

Rose fought the heaviness that had descended on her. She had opened herself up to her emotions and had trouble subduing them now that they were crashing over her. After a few breaths, she was able to think more clearly.

The glass . . .

When Philip was flirting with Caroline, she'd felt betrayed. She remembered how her own hand had pricked with pain when the glass Caroline was holding exploded. And the windows of the carriage had shattered the night that Philip had been killed. "I may have caused a wine glass to shatter. And a few carriage windows. But surely those were coincidences?"

"If there is one thing I have learned these past few years, it's that there are no coincidences," said Lady Clarke. "We all have a connection to the Mother, what we call the source of our power. She grants us our abilities and allows us to use what you called magic."

Lady Nightingale perched forward in her chair. "Are you ready to embrace your power and change your life?"

Rose took a long, steadying breath. Some part of her she did not fully understand pushed her to say accept. She thrust her shoulders back and lifted her chin. "Yes," she said, in as firm a voice as she could muster.

With a smile, Lady Nightingale stood and gestured for Rose to follow.

Rose pushed herself to her feet and fell into step behind her benefactress. There was no turning back now.

CHAPTER 14

$\mathcal{R}$ose followed Lady Nightingale's tiny frame as she led the way to back of the house. Lady Clarke walked beside her. The passed long, dark hallways that stretched for an uncanny length, rooms filled with art and books, a ballroom, and many doors that were shut. Eventually, they stopped in from of a painted green door that opened onto a small landing. The smell of herbs, beeswax, and smoke grew strong as Rose descended the stairs into a cellar. Another thick wooden door waited for them at the bottom, and they passed through it into a small antechamber, its wall made of earthen stone. Lady Nightingale snapped her fingers, and a small orb of emerald light appeared, brightening the darkness.

The party stood in a low-ceilinged chamber. Hundreds of jars of varying sizes and shapes lined the walls, perched on wooden shelves. Some were filled with various types of stones, others with dried plants. Herbs hung from a rack on the ceiling, drying. Copper instruments worn smooth with age sat upon a large worktable.

Lady Nightingale bent over the small hearth on the far wall of the room. A fire ignited a moment later, as if it had been burning for hours. "There," she said. "You will lie here, Miss Worthington." She pointed towards a chaise lounge set off in the corner. She turned to the shelves and grabbed jars, seemingly at random, from the shelves.

Rose studied the chaise. It was an odd piece of furniture to have in one's cellar. The polished elegance of the chaise clashed with the rustic earthiness of stone, herbs, and wood. Her mouth twisted. Skepticism kept her from obeying immediately.

"Don't worry," Lady Clarke said. "All you have to do is lie down and we'll do the rest."

"The rest of what?" asked Rose.

"It's helpful for Lady Nightingale to know what power you posses. The fact that your magic has bloomed so late leaves many questions. In order for you to harness your power, we have to understand it. There are a few tests we can run to help us."

Rose couldn't deny her curiosity, nor did she want to disappoint Lady Nightingale or Lady Clarke. She swiveled onto the chaise lounge and rested her head on the pillowed arm of the seat. She stared up at the ceiling as the two women busied themselves at the worktable. The clinking of small glass bottles and the snapping of the fire rang in her ears. She blinked slowly. The smells of herbs and the warmth of the cellar were making her sleepy.

"Close your eyes now, Miss Worthington," instructed Lady Nightingale.

Rose obeyed.

A sweet, resinous scent filled her nose. Lady Nightingale spoke in soft, hushed tones. Her words blurred together, and Rose quickly lost track of them. The heady smell of the burning herbs soothed her, and Rose she felt as if she could take a deep breath for the first time in days. She let the cloying scent and feelings of weightlessness wash over her. She saw flashes of color and objects.

Two black birds. The ocean and white cliffs. Leaves of orange, gold, and red. A bird flying out of a cage.

Rose floated out of strange images and dreams. Some things she felt, and some things she simply *knew*. It was hard to explain.

Voices from far away drifted to her.

Shadow-touched.

We must be careful.

Not tell her yet.

She tried to make sense of what they were saying, but it was like trying to grasp dandelion seeds on a windy day.

Then the scent diminished, and clarity returned.

"You can open your eyes now, dear," said Lady Nightingale.

Rose blinked her eyes open slowly, fighting against the heaviness, and sat up. The ghost of an herbal scent still wafted through the air, accompanied by a new smell. The sweet smell of autumn leaves on a warm day swirled around her. Rose rubbed her eyes. Her body grew more alert. Less heavy.

Both women sat on wooden stools next to the chaise lounge.

"Well?" Rose's eyes flitted from Lady Nightingale to Lady Clarke, looking for some sign of approval or displeasure.

In the room's corner, a man, no older than thirty, stood in half-shadows. He was about as tall as Rose, and had an unshaven face and wore a dark, simple suit. He dipped his chin solemnly, acknowledging her stare. The sickly sweet smell of an old forest floor wafted towards her. How long had he been standing there?

Confused, Rose returned the nod. She didn't want to be rude and ask who the man was, but it was odd that neither Lady Clarke nor Lady Nightingale had made an introduction. She slid her gaze to the women seated next to her.

Lady Clarke's eyes were wide. Even Lady Nightingale looked a little shocked.

"She reacts rather strongly to the stimulants," remarked Lady Clarke.

Lady Nightingale cocked her head. "Who is here with us, child?"

Rose looked to the corner to ask the man his name, propriety be damned, but it was empty. Only shadows remained. "How odd. I swore I saw someone." Unease made her stomach swoop.

"Spirits are usually drawn to magic. With more practice, you may see more of them," said Lady Nightingale.

"Spirits? You mean that was a ghost?" Rose stared at the still-vacant corner. Her scalp prickled.

"Ghost, spirit, apparition, they're all the same," said Lady Clarke. "Though we prefer the term spirit."

Rose rubbed her brow, trying to dispel the itch that lingered. It was a lot to take in. Her mind felt full of fog. "So, that's my ability? I can see spirits?"

Lady Clarke tucked a tendril of her fiery red hair behind her ear. "You have an affinity for fire, and you are very aware of the emotions of others around you. The herbs we burned temporarily strengthen your link to the Mother's power. One effect of those herbs is increased spiritual awareness, which explains why you could see a spirit."

Rose felt the color drain from her face as a thought entered her mind. It was a dangerous, hopeful question. One she could barely bring herself to ask. But she had to know. If it was at all possible, she had to try. "Can you talk with particular spirits?"

"It can be done. Though the spirit themselves has to be willing."

A tiny bubble of hope bloomed in her chest. She would give anything to speak to Philip and her brother. She had so many questions for them both. But if she could just talk to Philip again, beg for his forgiveness, maybe she would feel better. Maybe the ache of loss and despair would ease.

"Teach me. Please." Her plea was only a whisper.

"In time we shall. For now, we have an important party to prepare for."

The bubble popped, leaving her aching and hollow again. How could she think of parties at a time like this? But she didn't want Lady Nightingale to think her ungrateful. She twisted her hands together in her lap. "Whose?"

"Mine," said Lady Nightingale.

"Oh." Rose tried to conceal her disappointment, but her shoulders sagged. A familiar heaviness settled on her bones.

"Perhaps we could assist Miss Worthington with an interview before we begin?" Lady Clarke said.

Unspoken words traveled between the two women. Lady Clarke's eyebrows raised beseechingly.

Lady Nightingale nodded. "Very well. With whom do you need to speak to?"

Rose fought to maintain her composure as oceans of sadness threatened to swallow her. She cleared her throat, trying to dispel the lump that choked her. "His name is Philip Harlow."

"Do you want to tell us about it?" Lady Clarke placed a hand on Rose's shoulder.

Rose shook her head. "I don't want to trouble you with my problems."

"Burdens are meant to be shared. We don't mind."

"It may be beneficial to your lessons to unburden yourself. It's easier to find one's path with a lighter heart," Lady Nightingale said.

Rose clenched her hands in her lap. She had no choice but to trust Lady Nightingale and Lady Clarke. She took a shuddering breath and told them about her cousin; her failed escape attempt, and being forced to come to London.

By the time she was done, she couldn't conceal the shake of her hands. "It's my fault that he died. If I had simply done my duty, then Philip might still be alive."

"It's not your fault, Miss Worthington," said Lady Nightingale.

Lady Clarke crossed her arms. Her cheeks were pink. "I'd like to murder your cousin in his sleep if I felt it would help. And your mother as well, for allowing this to happen to you."

Rose hadn't considered that her mother might also be partially to blame. Her eyes pricked with unshed tears.

"We will try to contact Mr. Harlow. Hold my hand and close your eyes," said Lady Nightingale.

Rose's throat was too tight to utter a word of gratitude. The three of them sat linked, eyes closed. Rose felt her hands grow warm. Her brow tingled again as Lady Nightingale attempted to summon Philip's spirit.

They were quiet for a long while. Rose didn't dare interrupt, but she couldn't help but worry as the minutes ticked slowly by. She concentrated on Philip with all her might. Every cell in her body yearned for him. Surely he would come. He loved her. He *had* to speak to her.

After another minute of stillness, Lady Nightingale dropped her hand, breaking the circle.

"What happened? Why didn't he come?"

"I'm not sure he's passed on," said her benefactress.

Rose's world ground to a halt. She couldn't breathe. "What do you mean?"

"His spirit may linger near the place where he died. He might not be ready to transition completely to the spirit realm. Or there is a possibility that he is still alive."

Rose's hand flew to her mouth. "Alive?"

"Only a possibility," repeated Lady Nightingale. "We may try again in a few weeks, if you'd like."

"Yes. Yes, of course. Thank you for your help," said Rose. A single tear ran down her cheek. She didn't bother to brush it away. Philip loved her. He *loved* her, and if his spirit had not come when she had called, then maybe he was alive. She could not stop the hope from blooming in her chest.

"Now, then. We must prepare you for the party," said Lady Nightingale.

Rose snapped her attention back to her. "What sort of preparations?" She didn't think she would be able to focus on anything other than the singular thought that Philip could be *alive*.

"I'd like your help with the entertainment for the evening. Think of it as an exam of sorts for your lessons in magic. And we must further instruct you on how to charm men on the dance floor. Lady Clarke informed me that your previous lesson yielded great results."

Though her chest warmed at the praise, her nose wrinkled at the thought of trying to catch a suitor. "I'm not sure that's necessary. I have no intention of marrying any of them. Though I have no objections to helping with your party."

Lady Clarke waved her hand through the air. "You don't have to marry them. You can turn down every one of them if you so choose. But your cousin can't say anything about your lack of trying if you have a line of callers at your door every morning."

"And if your visits continue to improve your social skills, then your mother can have no objections to you continuing to come and study witchcraft," Lady Nightingale said.

"Witchcraft?"

"The Nightingales are witches," Lady Clarke said. "Wouldn't you like to be one, too?"

Rose didn't hesitate. "Yes. I would."

CHAPTER 15

The sun shone brightly as Rose and Alexander Crawford rode through Hyde Park, though the warm light did nothing to ease Rose's exhaustion. She had returned home from her evening at Lady Nightingale's after midnight, but had been too exhilarated to sleep. She'd dozed off before dawn and had been looking forward to a morning of languishing, but Alexander Crawford had at last made good on his promise to visit and called shortly after breakfast.

As they rode side by side, Rose's thoughts drifted. Last night's attempt to contact Philip's spirit had rattled her. The crushing grief she fought to swim through every waking moment had ebbed. Now, she had a reason to stay afloat. Philip could be *alive*. She could not help daydreaming and indulging in wild fantasies of their reunion, of how good it would feel to kiss him again.

"Miss Worthington?"

Rose tightened her grip on the reins of her horse. "I'm sorry." Her cheeks grew warm. She cleared her throat and mentally chastised herself for being rude. "I was thinking of home."

"It looked like a pleasant reverie." Alexander's bronze skin glowed in the sunshine. His pale blonde hair was nearly white. He flashed a patient smile.

Rose adjusted her hat, flustered that he'd caught her being inattentive. But she didn't dare tell him what she'd really been thinking about. "What were you saying?"

"I was wondering if you would be attending Lady Nightingale's masquerade ball later this month."

"I shall. I've never been to a masquerade before. What's it like?"

"The same as every other ball, though everyone wears a mask and pretends that they don't know who is lurking beneath them. There's typically a grand reveal during the evening, but I don't think anyone has ever been surprised by who is behind the masks. Lady Nightingale usually plans some sort of spectacle for her guests at the beginning of the party. Last year, a gaggle of pigeons turned into peacocks and strutted about the garden."

"How enchanting," Rose said as the horses brought them further down the park path towards a grove of shady trees.

Lady Nightingale had not told her how she would help with the soirée, but now she had a good idea that it would involve an exhibition of this nature. Before her thoughts could fly too far away, wondering what manner of magic was used to complete such a transformation, Alexander brought her back.

"Tell me about your family."

Rose tilted her chin up to the sun, catching the warm rays on her face and closing her eyes. She inhaled the lush spring air, wondering exactly how much to divulge to Alexander Crawford about the state of her family. If he wanted to befriend her, he should know at least most of the truth.

"My father died when I was eight. He was a kind man who loved my brother and I very much. My mother still grieves his passing tremendously."

A long moment of silence passed. Rose squirmed, adjusting

her position in the side-saddle. She studied the fine hair of the horse's mane, unwilling to see just how uncomfortable she's made her companion.

"I'm sorry. It must have been terribly difficult for you all. I can't imagine growing up without my father," said Alexander. "I wasn't aware you had a brother. Is he on tour?"

Rose continued to stare at her horse's mane, unable to meet Alexander's gaze. It had been years since George's passing, but his absence felt like a knife wound. "He is also dead. Seven years ago. There was an accident."

Alexander pulled his horse up to a stop. They had reached a quiet corner of the park, out of earshot of the promenading couples.

Rose reigned in her own mount. Had she frightened him away with her grief? A shard of disappointment lodged in her chest.

Wordlessly, Alexander dismounted and handed the reins to the footman who was accompanying them. He approached Rose's side and extended a hand. "This is not a conversation I wish to have on horseback. Walk with me?"

"It's all right," said Rose, taken aback by his serious nature. She felt her cheeks grow warm. She mentally chastised herself for not keeping her emotions in check. It had been so long ago, after all. She'd ruined the mood of their outing.

Alexander continued to stand, hand outstretched.

Realizing that he would stand there for the rest of the afternoon if she did not relent, Rose placed her hand in his and slid from her horse.

He took the reins of her mare and handed them to the footman. Rose glanced at Betsy, who had come along as a chaperone. Her maid raised her eyebrows, but gave an imperceptible dip of her chin. She would wait on the path for them to return.

Rose settled her hand in the crook of Alexander's elbow as they walked onto the grass and into the cooling shadows of a cluster of willow trees. The lawn was springy underfoot. Birds sang in the branches, their song echoing across a small, still pond. Rose untwined her hand from Alexander's arm, unpinned her hat, and shed her riding gloves.

"I can't begin to express the sincerity of my condolences for your losses, Miss Worthington."

"Thank you." She hoped he would not ask for the details of her brother's passing. She rubbed the little crescent-shaped birthmark on her left wrist idly, then forced her hands to her sides.

"Forgive me for asking, but is that why you know so much about running your family's estate?"

Rose finally met his bright cerulean eyes, grateful he had not asked for details she couldn't bear to give. "No one else was around to do it. All I knew was that everything had passed to a distant relative who lived in the United States. His solicitor made his rounds twice a year, but there was no one to see to the day-to-day necessities. It kept me busy and gave me something to do instead of sitting around all day in mourning."

"And when was the last time someone asked you how you were doing with it all?" asked Alexander.

"I believe the estate is running fairly well. Though Cornelius —Lord Worthington, I mean, says he wants to make improvements. I don't know what he means by that."

Alexander shook his head. "Not the estate. How are *you?*"

Rose blinked. No one had asked her how she was in a long time. Especially regarding the loss of her family. It had been seven years ago since the last funeral at Worthington House.

Not even Philip has asked her. He hadn't needed to. He had left her to process her grief in the way she needed. She didn't feel the need to talk about it with him, and he had never shared his feelings about it openly with her. They had mourned in comfortable, quiet companionship.

Alexander was the first person to ask in years, and she was

unsure of how to respond. Rose tugged on the long-leafed branch of the willow tree that shielded them, admiring the silver leaves.

"I think it's not something you ever completely heal from," she said finally. "Though some days, the sting of the loss is less painful than others. I do still miss him terribly."

Alexander nodded, eyes full of empathy.

Rose felt her affinity for him grow. He truly was as kind as everyone said. "And what of your family?" she asked, breaking his stare. "Tell me about them." She didn't want to dwell on such sad topics any longer.

"Well," he crossed his arms and leaned against the tree trunk. "You've met my sister. My parents are loving and give their children everything they could even want. Except their attention."

"Is that why your sister is the way she is?" Rose wanted to ask if that was the source of his sister's cruelty, but she didn't want to hurt Alexander's feelings.

He understood her meaning, though. "Effie desires the attention of our parents. But she's not all bad, only very protective. I apologize for her behavior the other night. I know it would mean more coming from her, but I'm very sorry for what she did. It won't happen again."

Rose tightened her lips into a wan smile.

"Perhaps you will get to know her better if we are to continue to spend time together."

"Unfortunately, I think your sister made her feelings for me quite clear."

"That doesn't change how I feel about you."

Rose swallowed hard. Her mouth was suddenly dry as her heart beat a fraction harder in her chest. Had he mistaken her friendliness for something more? "Lord Crawford, I must tell you—" began Rose, her hand reaching up instinctually to cover her heart, as if to guard it. She felt the tiny wooden charm under her dress, pressing into her skin. Her gift from Philip.

"Don't worry," said Alexander with a caddish grin. "I didn't mean like *that*."

Rose dropped her hand from her chest. "Oh." She felt foolish for presuming that Alexander Crawford was about to make some unwarranted declaration of affection. She felt her face grow warm again. "What was your meaning, then?"

"Just that you're one of the few sane women I've talked to in months."

Rose bit back a snort. "Goodness. Does the young lord grow weary of eligible ladies throwing themselves at his feet?"

Alexander's brows rose in feigned shock. "Miss Worthington. You wound me."

"From what I gather, it's high time someone does," Rose quipped, fighting to keep laughter from her voice. She hadn't enjoyed anyone's company this much in quite a while. The last person she had laughed with this much had been Philip.

Philip.

Her smile weakened, but she did not let it fall completely.

"Are you happy here in London, Miss Worthington?" asked Alexander, sensing the shift in her emotions.

"I am finding I grow happier by the day." It was the closest thing to the truth.

"Shall we return to the horses? I believe tea is in order."

Rose donned her hat and took his outstretched arm. Their feet left the lush grass and crunched on the sandy gravel path.

Alexander led the way to her horse. "I'm quite glad to call you my friend, Miss Worthington."

"So am I," Rose said. She was glad that he had spoken plainly of his feelings. She only hoped it didn't blossom into anything more.

CHAPTER 16

*R*ose's foot bounced with impatience as her last gentleman caller finally left the townhouse. It was hard to focus on entertaining when she knew her first lessons in magic were only hours away. She had been forced to suffer through a morning of entertaining not one, but three gentlemen callers. Word had gotten out about Alexander Crawford's visit to the Worthington home. The morning's gossip column, which used only the initials of its subjects, could not have been more clear.

London's finest and most eligible bachelor, Lord C, was seen riding with the peculiar and withdrawn newcomer Miss W. Though this wallflower is yet to bloom, it appears that Lord C glimpses a beauty that we have yet to see.

The widowed Lord Moore, the young Mr. Finnegan, and his friend Mr. Reid had drawled on about themselves for the better part of two hours while Rose was forced to sit, smile, and nod. Her mother supervised, pretending to work on her embroidery while listening to every word, and constantly offering more tea and refreshments.

The only thing that kept Rose from slamming out of the

room was the promise of her meeting with Lady Nightingale and Lady Clarke that afternoon. Her first lesson would be conducted at the Clarke townhouse. Too many visits to the same household in one week looked peculiar, and the *ton* was always sniffing for any hint of impropriety. Lord Clarke was away on business for a few days, so the ladies would have the house to themselves. Rose's mother had beamed with pride at the invitation, and agreed to let her go without a second thought.

As soon as she was free of her unwanted company, Rose retreated to her rooms and flopped down on her bed. She sank into the feathery softness, slung an arm over her eyes, and tried to clear her mind of guilt. Lady Nightingale and Lady Clarke said the charade of entertaining suitors was necessary. So, even though she was sure she'd chipped a molar with how hard she'd ground her teeth, Rose accepted that this was a necessary evil.

She wanted the control she'd been promised. She could suffer through a few unpleasant hours if it meant she'd never have to marry.

* * *

Lady Nightingale and Lady Clarke sat comfortably in the parlor, nibbling from little plates of food and sipping from gold-rimmed teacups. A spread of cucumber sandwiches, cream scones, and lavender lemonade filled a table in the extravagantly adorned room. The lace tablecloth was starched to snow-white cleanliness. Every surface gleamed with polish. Gilded mirrors, giant oil paintings of landscapes, and a chandelier of glittering crystal radiated elegance and wealth.

Rose's heart sank a little as she eyed the perfectly normal tea service. She'd been taught how to play a card game, dance, and use a fan to flirt — all skills which would aid her in gaining the attention of suitors at parties. She was eager to learn more about the magic Lady Nightingale and Lady Clarke claimed she had. But perhaps this was another sort of test. Though she was weary of idle chatter, Rose joined the women, and acted as if she had come for nothing more than a social afternoon.

Despite her anxiousness to begin her lessons, Rose found herself enjoying their company. Lady Clarke was especially amused by her recounting of Lord Finnegan's awful poetry recitation in the Worthington drawing room that morning.

After the tea service was cleared away, the parlor door firmly shut, and the curtains drawn, Lady Clarke announced the subject of today's lesson. "Fire magic."

Rose leaned forward in her chair. Her heart pounded so loud she was sure Lady Nightingale and Lady Clarke could hear it.

"Don't be too eager, Miss Worthington," cautioned Lady Nightingale. "We rarely start with this subject. But as you have shown a strong affinity for it, I want to see what you can do. Fire is one of the most fickle elements to control. It requires great self-discipline and respect for the power it holds. Don't be vexed if we make little progress at first."

Rose swallowed, trying to calm her racing heart in vain as Lady Clarke put a small white taper nestled into a short candlestick on the table.

"Everything is connected. The threads of the universe that weave and bind us all together create one giant tapestry. Each blade of grass, each grain of sand, each star in the sky is but one of millions of threads that weave together to create life. Those threads can be manipulated." Lady Nightingale snapped her fingers and the candle wick ignited.

Rose inhaled sharply. Something stirred within her ribcage beneath her galloping heart. A warm pulse as soft as a kitten's purr.

"By visualizing the threads of the things you wish to control, you can tap into their energy and influence them." Lady Nightingale snapped her fingers again, and the candle went out.

"Where one thread pulls, another must give. Everything must be kept in balance, the picture must remain intact. I cannot light a candle without finding some give in the threads, or offering the energy required to complete the task."

Rose gripped the edges of her chair and stared at the candle. It was dizzying to think about. Rather than fight her way through with logic, Rose did her best to accept her teacher's explanation. She forced her hands to release their iron-grip on her chair and tried to create a mental picture of threads and tapestries. "If the threads of energy need to be slackened in order to be manipulated, what threads are you pulling to light the candle?"

"Sparks from the kitchen's hearth. I am transferring their light and energy to this candle."

"But a spark would go out on its own. Wouldn't changing the spark's destination alter the tapestry?"

Lady Nightingale nodded. "You're a bright girl. Fortunately, the threads are pliable. There is more give to them than simple embroidery thread. With minor alterations, such as a single spark, the tapestry can stretch to accommodate the change. Larger changes require more energy, and therefore more consideration where the energy is coming from."

"I've never tried anything that large myself," chimed in Lady Clarke. "Altering the tapestry significantly requires a great deal of magic, fortitude, and stamina."

Rose rubbed her chin. "When you removed the wine from my dress the other night, what threads were you pulling?" Siphoning a stain from a gown seemed like a much larger task than lighting a candle.

"I dispersed the water back into the air, heating it to steam with the threads already present from the fire in the room. It was a simple change of state. I moved the liquid from one place to another, changing its form, using energy already being supplied by another source in the room."

Rose recalled the words Lady Clarke had said as she let the wine fall from her hand into the flames. "You said it was an offering."

"The Mother is the Great Weaver of the tapestry," said Lady Nightingale. "She is the source of life itself. Whenever we make alterations to the tapestry, large or small, we ask the Mother for her blessing or make her an offering. Even a positive thought of gratitude can be sufficient."

It was utter blasphemy. If the wrong people heard the way Lady Nightingale was talking, she would be persecuted as a heretic. Rose was becoming more skeptical with each passing moment. If she hadn't seen these small feats with her own eyes, she would never have believed them.

Lady Clarke seemed to sense her enthusiasm cooling. She gripped her arm and squeezed reassuringly. "Let's have you try now, hm? When you experience it for yourself, it will all make sense."

Rose bit her lower lip. "All right. I suppose it won't hurt to try."

"We will help you see the threads, then let you practice on your own. Close your eyes and take my hand. That's it. Now, place your other hand on the candle."

Rose did as Lady Nightingale instructed.

"Empty your mind of all other thoughts. Think only of the threads that connect us. Visualize them in your mind's eye."

Rose imagined tiny, invisible threads connecting everything together. They were gold and shimmered. She tried not to feel foolish. Was she really seeing these threads, or playing pretend again? Where did her desire to see them stop and the reality of them begin?

"I'm going to bring a spark from the fireplace to you. Feel the spark's thread in our connected hands. It is warm and bright," said Lady Nightingale. The woman's voice was soft and warm.

Rose kept her eyes shut and tried to feel something. She slowed her breathing, letting that faint tug between her ribs pulse stronger.

Yet she felt nothing. She didn't know what she was supposed to be feeling. Several long moments passed.

"You're doing well. Keep trying," encouraged Lady Clarke.

Rose's brow furrowed into deep lines as she concentrated. Impatience curled up the back of her throat, cloying like smoke. She tried to stamp it down, but it was hard to control. A surge of frustration broke through her calm thoughts. The whole thing was utterly ridiculous.

As soon as the thought crossed her mind, a sharp pain pinched her hand. She bit back a yelp as she opened her eyes and let go of Lady Nightingale's hand.

An angry red mark blistered on her palm, just the size of a stray spark. "Did it hurt you, too?"

Lady Nightingale showed Rose her unblemished hand. "Fortunately, I have long since learned to ward against stray embers when working on fire magic with a novice."

Rose frowned. If she was supposed to have an affinity for fire, then why was it so hard?

"Let's try this instead," said Lady Clarke. She struck a match and lit the candle. "I have more of an inclination for water. It would take far too much time for me to light this candle with magic. There is wisdom in knowing when to use a gift and when to take a more mundane approach."

She blew out the match and set it on her saucer. "Concentrate on this candle's flame. Observe it. Note the colors and shapes. Focus until you see nothing but the flame. Then, try to feel out with your ability for the fire's thread."

Rose stared hard at the candle. The room was dim with the curtain drawn, making it easier to focus on the frail light. The shape of the flame shifted as it burned, changing color from yellow to pale orange and back. Her eyes slid in and out of focus. The wavering fire filled her vision.

Something in her mind took hold of a tiny, delicate thread. There was no other word for it. It felt impossibly thin and fragile. Rose had the sensation of holding the tenuous link between her forefinger and thumb, even though her hands lay in her lap. She gave the thread a tiny tug, but the thread snapped. In the same moment, the candle's flame grew small, then sprang back to its original height.

Rose huffed in exasperation as her eyes snapped back into focus and the rest of the room regained clarity.

"I think I felt something that time," she said skeptically.

"It's a wonderful start." Lady Clarke relit the candle.

Lady Nightingale inclined her head towards the flame. "Try again."

Rose's subsequent attempts at grasping the candle's thread of power were not as successful. She felt it harder to reach the appropriate level of concentration each time. She grew tired. Her eyes felt scratchy, her limbs heavy.

After seven attempts, Lady Nightingale instructed her to return home, rest, and try again on her own that evening. "Just remember, it is of utmost importance than no one, *no one*, knows of your abilities."

"Of course." No one would believe Rose if she told them, anyway.

"We'll teaching you how to ward against unwanted suitors in no time," said Lady Clarke as she waggled her eyebrows. "It's not too difficult."

Rose clung to that promise as she bade them farewell. Her recent success at balls had made her nervous, as did the visits from gentlemen. She would *not* be married. She would do whatever Lady Nightingale required if that was to be her prize.

As Rose climbed into her carriage, her stomach filled with rocks. Lady Nightingale's masquerade ball was two weeks away. She had made no real progress today. There was too much to learn. If her ability to perform at a party was to be her test, Rose wondered how on earth she was supposed to succeed.

* * *

Rose's mood was not improved by the sight of Cornelius waiting for her when she arrived back at the house.

"Join me for a moment?" He gestured to the receiving room. It wasn't so much a question as a command.

Rose clenched her jaw and obeyed. She was surprised to see him here. When he wasn't locked up in his study, he was at his club or meeting with other gentlemen on manners of business. She hadn't seen him during the day in some time. But here he was.

Cornelius lowered himself onto one of the freshly upholstered chairs, folded his news pamphlet into a crisp rectangle, and gestured to a chair opposite him.

Rose braced herself for whatever was about to transpire and sat with her back ramrod straight. She rested her balled fists on her knees.

Cornelius's shoulders drew forward. His fingers gripped the folded pamphlet tightly, but his face was smooth and composed. Scanning him, Rose couldn't tell if he was in a pleasant mood or a volatile one. It was infuriating that she could not read him.

"What's this about Lord Crawford's son calling on you yesterday?" he asked nonchalantly, setting the pamphlet aside and flexing his fingers.

Though he was calm for the moment, Rose had seen him swing into violence faster than she could blink. She remained on her guard. "What do you mean?" she asked.

"Are you setting your cap for Alexander Crawford?"

"No. Though I'm not sure why that is any of your concern."

Cornelius shifted in his chair. "I don't think you should see him again."

"Why?" Rose crossed her arms. "It's not as if I can turn him out the door if he calls again. People will talk."

"People are *already* talking. I am not sure if you are aware, but he is betrothed to Lord Hawthorne's daughter. The family has wondered if he is going to cry off now that he has been spending time with you."

"And how on earth is this my fault? I am finding it quite impossible to meet anyone's expectations." Rose said hotly. "You and my mother brought me to London to be married off. I have attended these never-ending parties and done what is expected of me, and now you are saying to *not* do the things that will gain me suitors?"

Cornelius rubbed his chin with his thumb. "I'm telling you this for your own benefit. Alexander Crawford will never marry you."

"I have no interest in marrying Lord Crawford. Is it so ridiculous that I should merely enjoy his company?"

Cornelius looked pityingly at her. "You are grossly misinformed about acceptable relations if you believe you may spend time with Lord Crawford's son as a friend. You're both unmarried. The only acceptable time you may spend together is if you were entertaining the idea of matrimony. As you are not, I think it best if you dissuade his attention. He knows these rules, Miss Worthington. The fact that he *is* seeking you out means the idea has at least crossed his mind."

Rose felt heat rise in her cheeks, half embarrassment, half anger. "I see."

"My only intention is to shield you from embarrassment and ensure we stay in society's good graces."

She stood and clenched her fists at her sides. "Is that all?" She could not bear to speak about it a moment longer. Her eyes pricked with tears of frustration.

Cornelius looked up at her through the dark hair that fell into his eyes. They were soft, not brittle with malice.

Rose didn't care. She concentrated on the pricks of pain from the little half-moons she was digging into her own palms. She focused on the sensation instead of the strange look in Cornelius's eyes.

"That's all." He picked up his pamphlet again.

Rose strode out the parlor door, exhausted from her attempts at lighting candles and Cornelius's interrogation. She blinked and found herself in the horrid pink parlor. She didn't even remember climbing the stairs. Rose threw herself into a settee, grabbed a lacy white pillow, and screamed.

Once she started, she could not stop. She felt the force of her anger build and build, rising like a terrible wave. Her throat grew raw. Her scream reverberated through her skull, pulsing and pounding with the force of her rage and hurt.

A delicate crystal vase next to the settee cracked. Shards of glass clinked softly as they fell.

Rose tossed the pillow aside and squeezed her eyes shut. She was so tired of it all. Tired of the grief that crushed her heart, of her inability to meet anyone's expectations, and tired of being so very alone.

A few evenings later, Rose sat at the whist table with Harriet again. She had managed to pick up correctly on three cards that Harriet sent her as they were playing, her brow tingling and tightening each time. Harriet clasped her hands with glee each time she got one correct. It helped lesson the sting of her inability to light any fires on her own, despite her repeated attempts. She was exhausted, and anxious.

"You're improving!" exclaimed Harriet when the game was done and their opponents, Beatrice and the elder Mrs. Finnegan, had departed their table.

"Maybe I'll be as good as you one day," said Rose. It was hard to be completely miserable around Harriet. She was still very much a child and took such pleasure in little things. Rose sincerely hoped she stayed that way all her life.

"Are you tired, Rosie?"

"A bit." Her heart squeezing at the nickname. She must have looked as tired as she felt, as it was still quite early by London standards. Her most recent encounter with Cornelius did nothing to ease her nerves. Rose had stayed awake until nearly three each morning trying to light the candle by her bedside. Each failed attempt only made her feel worse.

"Walk with me. We can get some fresh air."

Rose let Harriet lead her down the hall, away from Lady Nightingale's parlor. The buzz of chatter died away, but her thoughts refused to quiet.

"What are you thinking about?" asked Harriet.

"Busybody," teased Rose.

Harriet's wide, innocent eyes glowed in the light of the sconces. She kept them fixed on Rose, waiting for her to share.

"A lot of things, I suppose." Rose sighed.

"Show me." Harriet extended a hand.

"How?"

Harriet rolled her eyes. "Just think about whatever it is you were thinking about, and I shall know."

Rose doubted that Harriet could actually "see" everything she was possibly thinking and feeling. Cards were one thing, but her mind was in such a tangle, she hardly knew what to make of it herself. But it didn't hurt to let Harriet practice.

She took Harriet's hand and closed her eyes, letting her mind wander. The sources of her anxiety flooded through her. The failed summoning of Philip, the outing with Alexander in the park, Cornelius's locked drawer in his study, all flickered in her mind. Rose wasn't trying to control them, but let the thoughts come and go. She couldn't be sure if Harriet was the one flipping through her thoughts, sorting them like items of clothing on wash day into neat little piles, or if she was the one in control. Her mind wandered to the cellar, the night of her test with Lady Nightingale and Lady Clarke, her failed attempts at controlling fire. Rose wondered if Harriet was supposed to know about that. Lady Nightingale has been clear that no one should know of her magic. But surely those who attended her salons were exempt?

Rose and Harriet stood in the hall for what felt like several long minutes before Harriet released her hand. Rose blinked her eyes open.

"Don't worry, I know all about it," Harriet dismissed. She must be referring to the cellar and the strange ritual Rose endured. "Though Lady Nightingale says I am still too young to practice summoning spirits. She says I must wait until next year when I am sixteen."

Rose's eyebrows shot up. Harriet looked twelve, with her big, brown eyes and full cheeks. Not nearly old enough to debut next year.

"I look exceedingly young for my age," said Harriet sagely. "Anyway, your Philip did not come when called? That *is* good news. Lady Nightingale has good success with most spirits. Is he the one with fair hair?"

"No, he has dark hair," Rose said. Something oily twisted in her gut.

"Oh, sorry." Harriet clasped her hands before her as if waiting to recite her lessons for her governess. "They get mixed up sometimes, the names and faces. Especially when there's a lot of feelings involved."

"What do you mean, feelings?"

"Nothing of importance." Harriet shrugged. "I can't tell you what to feel. Though, I will say, you have quite a lot of them. Feelings, I mean."

"Yes, well. Quite a lot has happened since my arrival," said Rose, shifting uncomfortably.

"And before you came to London," added Harriet.

"I suppose you're right." She wondered exactly how much Harriet had gleaned from her brief look into her innermost thoughts. She hadn't really expected Harriet to see anything important. Now she felt exposed.

Harriet tossed her hair. "I usually am."

Rose couldn't help but laugh at the girl's obvious self-satisfaction.

"You know what I think would make you feel better?" asked Harriet, pressing a finger to her cupid's bow lips, a mischievous glint in her eyes.

"Do tell."

"Follow me." Harriet didn't wait for her reply. She turned and dashed further down the hall.

"Wait a moment," laughed Rose, breaking into a jog to catch up with her. She was quick. Her umber hair, tied back with black velvet ribbon, whipped behind her as she raced down the hall.

Rose ran silently behind her, the plush carpet muffling their steps. Harriet stopped abruptly in front of a pair of doors at the end of the corridor. Rose nearly crashed into her.

Harriet waited for her to right herself. "This is an 'ask for forgiveness, not permission' situation. I'm not sure if Lady Nightingale wants you to have access to this room yet, but I will take full responsibility for letting you in."

"What is it?" Rose asked breathlessly, lamenting her lack of physical stamina. Sitting all day in parlor rooms had made her sluggish.

"You'll see," she replied, mouth twisting upwards. She thrust her hands against the double doors. A strange current singed the air as Harriet touched her hands to the smooth wood. A smell like cinnamon drifted through the air as the doors swung open, revealing the largest library Rose had ever seen.

As they stepped inside, candles lit on their own accord, welcoming them. A domed glass ceiling arched over the entire room. Strange brass instruments hung suspended from the ceiling by thick wires, casting light and shadow about the room as they oscillated. Though low clouds darkened the sky, pinpricks of starlight were thrown about the room by the curious machines that spun soundlessly. The far wall, made of white marble, served as a sort of chart where constellations of light glowed.

Towering bookshelves that held volumes bound in cloth and leather stretched from the floor to the ceiling. Standing bookcases were placed in a diamond formation, leaving the space in the center of the room for a long reading table, set with lamps. Against the far end of the room sat several smaller writing desks, strewn with papers and inkwells.

Rose took a tentative step into the room, her steps echoing off gold-flecked tile decorated with deep green vines. Harriet beamed as Rose gaped in awe at the sheer number of books. Her palms tingled with anticipation as she stepped to the nearest shelf and peered at the titles. *Properties of Herbs. Bone Scrying for Beginners. Tarot in Turmoil. Wyrd Lore: Shakespeare's Iambic Incantations.*

"These are all books about magic?" she asked breathlessly.

"Mhm. Lady Nightingale has collected them from all over the world." Her chest puffed with pride. "Some of us get to study them as part of our training."

"This is incredible." Rose tore her eyes from the shelf to admire the rest of the room.

"I knew you would appreciate it. Here, I think you shall like this one."

Harriet handed Rose a brown book the size of her hand, bound in worn leather. *Tales of Citadel.* The book smelled liked autumn, of sun-dappled forest undergrowth and cool air.

"What is it about?"

"They're stories of a place between worlds."

"Are they true?" Rose asked, cracking open the cover and reading the title of the first chapter, "Enter Through a Crossing Darkly."

Harriet shrugged. "Who knows? I have never heard of someone actually going there, but sometimes the point of books isn't that they are true, but is about what is possible within their pages."

Rose glanced at Harriet, who stood proudly with her hands clasped in front of her.

Suddenly, one of the brass instruments chimed. The soft notes reverberated through the domed room. Harriet's dark eyes grew wide. "Oh, drat. We'll come back another day." She took the book back, placed it on a shelf. "Come on, or they'll wonder where we've gone."

Rose had no choice but to follow as Harriet dragged her back towards the party. She dared a glance behind them before the doors swung shut of their own accord. The lights had gone out and the giant bronze machines had stilled, sleeping.

* * *

DESPITE THE DISTRACTION the magnificent library had provided, Harriet's comments about her mixed-up feelings stayed with Rose for the rest of the evening. She continued to think about them as she readied herself for bed.

Rose sat at her dressing table in her nightgown. A lifetime ago, she had been sitting in a similar fashion when a rock had struck her window, and Philip had called her out of the house into the garden. She closed her eyes, remembering that night.

I love you.

Philip could be *alive,* and she was here, dallying at parties and balls that meant nothing. Trying to find some meaning and purpose in a group of women who called themselves *witches,* for goodness's sake.

Rose pushed her thumb into her forehead above the bridge of her nose, head and heart torn. The lure of all that knowledge, of secrets of magic waiting to be discovered in those bound tomes, the promises that Lady Nightingale had given her to teach her how to use magic, had woken something deep within her. She wanted to be a part of it. She wanted to be part of something bigger than herself.

But she could not deny that she also longed for Philip and the comfort he gave her. She loved him, and if there was even the smallest chance he was alive. . .

She had to contact Philip.

Rose pushed herself back from the dressing table and entered the parlor that adjoined her room. She withdrew a piece of paper and ink from the desk in the corner and wrote.

CHAPTER 18

*R*ose stared at the book in front of her, fingers resting lightly on its dry pages. She couldn't make sense of the words. The volume, *Magickal Energy Theory and Practical Applications,* was so dense that she'd read the same paragraph twice and still had no clue what it was trying to say. She braced her forehead with both hands and tried again.

In this manner, the author suggests that the principles of all energetic magicks shall firstly adhere to the notion that magick energies derived from this plane must, first and foremost, be withdrawn from those previously existing energies available to the wielder in their immediate surroundings before undergoing any transformation. The speculation by those illogical wielders, the Moon Daughters, that energy may be derived from the soul itself, is unsupported by evidence and therefore will not be explored in this volume, which is grounded firmly in those principles of energetic matter that are certifiable.

She rubbed her eyes in exasperation and looked up from the small writing desk. The late afternoon sun glinted off the oscillating bronze disks in Lady Nightingale's library.

Rose stiffed a yawn with the back of her hand. She, her mother, and Cornelius had been invited to dine with Lord

Moore last night. It was an intimate gathering, composed mostly of men who knew both Moore and Cornelius from the gentleman's club. Half of them were married and had brought their wives, but did nothing to introduce the ladies to one another, resulting in awkward conversation. It was after midnight before Cornelius had finally announced their departure. Rose was too tired to try to light her candle.

Unable to read the paragraph again, Rose let her gaze wander around the library. Other witches, Harriet among them, were engaged in various degrees of study throughout the room. Two women about Lady Clarke's age drew strange symbols in white chalk in a corner of the marble floor. Nearby, the elder Lady Margaret Templeton had dozed off in a soft chair.

Another witch kept making trips to the cellar, emerging with fistfuls of herbs that she combined in slim glass vials. The woman lit a small flame between her fingers, heating the vials, then watched their contents and the color of the smoke that rose from them. She then discarded the phials onto her desk, shaking her head before traipsing back out the door in search of more plant matter.

Harriet and another girl, only a few years Rose's senior, occupied the writing desks to her left.

While Rose had hoped for more direct instruction from her teachers this afternoon, she was glad to have been invited into the library.

"Normally, we don't let girls so new in here," Lady Clarke had said as she escorted her to the massive double doors. "But Lady Nightingale has made an exception. I think she sees something very special in you."

Before she'd been able to ask what that something might be, Lady Clarke had swung open the doors. Rose did not need to feign her delight. The library was just as impressive in daylight. Lady Clarke told her to pick a book that sounded interesting and left her to her own devices.

Rose stood, stretching her cramped muscles, and wandered to the shelf where Harriet had shoved the book that she'd recommended the other night. She weaved in and out of the free-standing shelves that stood in their diamond formation in the center of the room. Anything had to be better than the drivel she had selected. She squinted at the shelves, determined to make better headway with her next book selection.

She couldn't recall the name of the little book Harriet had shoved into her hands, but figured she would recognize it when she saw it. She didn't get far when she heard the soft patter of feet behind her.

Harriet stood at Rose's elbow, peering at the shelves. "If you're looking for that book again, the library has probably shelved it somewhere else by now," she whispered.

"What do you mean? Who would move the books around?" Rose asked, slightly scandalized.

Harriet continued to scan the shelf in front of her, unfazed. "The library gives us the books we need at that moment. It's complex magic I don't understand. Yet." She made a little noise of satisfaction as her fingers alighted the spine of a slim, dark blue book.

Rose turned her gaze to Rose, hugging the volume to her chest. "And how are your studies this afternoon?"

"Dreadful. I can't make any sense of that book." She crossed her arms.

Harriet nodded sympathetically. "It was like that for me at first, too. But never fear. There are plenty of us here to help."

Steps echoed close behind them. The quiet girl who had been sitting next to Harriet approached.

"Rose, this is Kate," introduced Harriet.

The girl was tall with rich, brown skin and tight curls. She dipped her chin in greeting. "What are you both up to?" she asked in a lowered voice.

"Rosie is having a tough time with her book," Harriet said.

"Which one was it?" asked Kate. "We've found the library gives all beginners the same books."

"*Energy Theory* something or other. It's horrible. I can't understand a word."

Kate's eyes widened. "Are you serious?"

Rose shifted on her feet, feeling self-conscious and terribly unintelligent. "It's probably easy for you, but—"

"Can I see it?" Kate asked, leaning forward slightly. Her eyes were hungry.

"Of course," she replied, surprised at her eagerness. "It's on my desk." Rose led the way back to her workstation, but when they arrived, the book had gone.

"What I wouldn't give to get my hands on that one," Kate said, shaking her head in dismay.

"Where did it go?" Rose moved the stacks of paper around on the small desk, hoping it was simply under her mess.

"The library probably cleaned it up. It will turn up again when you're ready," said Harriet. "It's an advanced book, from what I've heard."

"And has the theory, and counter-theories, for where all magic comes from," Kate added.

Rose's brows knit together. "Lady Nightingale said magic came from the Great Weaver."

Harriet and Kate exchanged a quick glance.

"Of course it does," Kate said. "But where did she get *Her* magic from? And how does it pass on to other girls?"

"Such questions, Miss Miller," said a reedy voice, not bothering to whisper. Lady Templeton had woken from her nap and, sensing mischief, had flocked to them. Her eyes were steely as she regarded them. "As we have discussed on numerous occasions, the only thing you need to concern yourself with is harnessing and improving your abilities using approved methods. The theories are theories. Not the truth."

Kate and Harriet looked at their feet.

"And how do you know that's the truth?" Rose asked, chin jutting forward. She did not like how this woman made Harriet curl inwards on herself.

Harriet made a tiny squeaking sound, but Kate continued to hang her head.

Lady Templeton glared at Rose. "Impertinent child. How dare you question the Council?"

"Please, Lady Templeton. She's new," implored Harriet.

"Quiet. What is your name, girl?"

Rose decided that she did not like this crotchety old woman. But Rose sensed there would be trouble if she did not answer, and she didn't feel like being reprimanded on her first day in the library. Not when there might be a book here to help her with her fire magic. She tried to ignore the fact that everyone else in the room had stopped their activities and turned to watch the exchange. "Rose Worthington," she replied, refusing to break eye contact.

Lady Templeton frowned, deepening the wrinkles on her face. "Hana's current pet," she said disdainfully. She turned her attention back to Harriet.

"Miss Sinclair. You would do well to instruct your new friend on the customs and rank of the Council," she sniffed. "As for you, Miss Miller. I will inform Lady Nightingale of your continued questioning."

"Yes, Lady Templeton," Kate replied, still refusing to lift her gaze from the floor.

Satisfied, the old woman shuffled towards the library's double doors.

Once she'd gone and the other women had returned to their studies, Rose leaned in to whisper to her companions. "She really did not like me."

"She doesn't like anyone," replied Harriet in an even softer voice than before. Her eyes were watery.

"Or people who ask too many questions." Kate crossed her

arms.

"Isn't the whole point of learning to ask questions?"

Harriet's bottom lip quivered. "It is to protect us. There are bad people who would do anything for magic. When the Council deems us ready, we earn the right to learn more, so long as we show them we can keep ourselves, and each other, safe."

"And asking questions about where magic comes from is unsafe?" Rose asked. Unease twisted in her stomach.

"It's more about what the Council says, goes," Kate said. "Not accepting what they tell you, especially when it comes to the Mother or the Great Weaver, is like other people saying they don't believe in God or want proof of an afterlife."

Rose fingered the cord of leather at her neck. The wooden rose charm lay concealed beneath her dress. It gave her little comfort. "What's the Council?"

"Lady Nightingale is in charge, Lady Clarke is second in command, and Lady Templeton is third. There are thirteen witches, including them, that make up the Council. It is their job to monitor everyone's studies, decide which missions should be given to who, and run everything," Harriet said.

Rose pursed her lips in thought, twisting her necklace. There was much more to the Nightingales than she had thought. She had no idea there was a Council of other witches who presided over what went on in Lady Nightingale's house, and who directed what information could be accessed. Her stomach knotted further. By telling Lady Nightingale and Lady Clarke that she wanted to learn more about magic, she had not known she was signing up for all of this as well.

The bronze disks in the ceiling chimed, making her jump.

"Let's have tea," said Harriet, looking at the glass domed ceiling. "I think I'm finished with books for today."

They were halfway across the room when the doors swung

open. Lady Nightingale stood at the threshold with her hands clasped in front of her.

"Miss Worthington," she said, finding her immediately. "If you'll come with me, please."

Rose felt her heart drop into her stomach, certain she was in trouble. She'd never cared about reprimands from her governess, but Lady Nightingale was different. She swallowed and continued onwards, leaving Harriet and Kate.

Lady Nightingale led her down a side corridor to a back door that opened out into the gardens. She grabbed two parasols from a basket and offered one to Rose. "Let us take the air."

Rose took the proffered parasol and stepped out into the garden. Warm spring air kissed her face, and she felt her spirits lighten. If Rose wasn't sure she was about to be reprimanded, she might unpin her bun to let the breeze ruffle her hair. Instead, she forced herself to take slow, steady steps alongside her benefactress.

They walked silently, side by side, for a minute before rounding the hedgerow towards the stables. A wooden archway with climbing ivory flowers stood behind the horse stalls, oddly out of place. Her skin prickled despite the sunshine. Rose wanted a closer look at the peculiar structure, but Lady Nightingale led them back towards the center of the gardens, where stone benches sat surrounded by tall hedges. They continued down the walking path.

"I hear you have caught the sharp end of Lady Templeton's tongue," Lady Nightingale finally said.

"Yes." Rose concentrated on her feet and the dirt crunching beneath her shoes. Guilt lodged in her stomach, despite knowing that she had done nothing wrong.

"Margaret is very traditional," said Lady Nightingale diplomatically, stopping to touch the velvet petals of English roses lining the path. "She does not mean to be so exacting. She has been forced to hide her abilities for many years, and her beliefs are unshakeable. They are what kept her safe. Those beliefs, and the rules of the Council, are what keep everyone who wishes to train their magical abilities protected."

Rose twisted the handle of her parasol. "I didn't mean any offense."

Lady Nightingale released the blossom she cradled, straightening. The petals had opened beneath her hand, creating a flower so large it was a marvel that it could remain upright on its fragile stem. "It is natural to be curious. She informed me that the library gifted you an intriguing book."

Rose fought to steady her pulse and made herself loosen the white-knuckle grip she had on her parasol. She really, *really,* did not want to get into trouble. And she didn't want Harriet or Kate to be reprimanded, either. Even though she hadn't asked outright for the book to begin with. "Yes. It's unfortunate that I couldn't comprehend a single word. It was actually quite dull."

She had a feeling that she would have many more questions for Lady Nightingale if she'd understood the apparently blasphemous theories within its pages. Questions that she was not entirely sure she would be given answers to. Her curiosity about the volume was now piqued. Rose couldn't help but ask, "What is so special about the book?"

"It's human nature to want what we cannot have, or to covet the knowledge of others. Knowledge is its own kind of power. The book appears rarely in the library, that's all. There are a few tomes that make very rare appearances, and when they do, it can cause a stir."

The tightness in her stomach eased. She had been expecting a scolding, but this did not feel like a reprimand. Rose cocked her head. "But can't you access any of the books? Didn't you magic the library?"

Lady Nightingale gave her a wry smile. "I'm merely the library's stewardess, giving it a home. I inherited a good part of the collection and have added to it over the years. It takes a great deal of effort to call specific books from its depths. The library can be very protective of its information."

Rose wondered why the library gave had given her such a controversial book, then. Especially when she didn't understand a word of it.

They resumed their walk. Rose bit her lip, then asked, "Kate won't be punished, will she?"

Lady Nightingale let out a soft, airy laugh. "Of course not. It's natural to be curious."

Rose felt the residual ache in her stomach dissolve.

"Have you had any success with your fire magic after our lesson?" Lady Nightingale asked as they came upon a bed of lavender, the tranquil scent wafting in the spring air.

"No," Rose sighed. "I haven't been able to make so much as a spark."

Lady Nightingale turned her kind, hooded eyes to Rose. "Don't be so hard on yourself, child. It is natural to want to master the magic after your first taste, but Rome was not built in one day and neither did a witch gain full command of her abilities in a single evening."

Her words instantly soothed Rose. How comforting it was to be *seen* by someone. She felt the tension in her shoulders ease. Tall hedges rose on either side of them, shielding them from view. "Perhaps I can try now?"

Lady Nightingale glanced briefly at their surroundings, saw that they were concealed from prying eyes, then nodded.

Rose took a deep breath, inhaling the scent of greenery and life, filling her lungs with the essence of growing things. She felt it in the plants and flowers surrounding them, almost as if she were connected to them by tiny, invisible threads. She fought to contain her elation and maintain her focus, for she knew she was sensing the Great Weaver's threads of magic that bound all things together.

But there was something more than that, something that

flowed and bubbled like the streams on Worthington Estate, just at the edges of her consciousness. It felt familiar, somehow.

Fighting for focus, she brought her hand up and willed a flame to light between her fingers, just as she had seen the other woman summon a small flame in the library that afternoon. Rose felt a pulse rocket through her chest, spreading over her arms. An inner, secret part of herself dipped into a warm pool of sparkling light, and a yellow flame appeared between her thumb and forefinger. She felt the heat from the flame at her fingertips and yelped when it grew too hot. The flame extinguished, and she pressed her fingers to her mouth, soothing the small hurt.

Rose looked at her fingers. They were a little red, but not blistered. She grinned triumphantly at her teacher.

"Very good, Miss Worthington. I knew you would be a dedicated student."

Pride made her chest swell, and she gripped her parasol again, stilling her trembling hands. She was filled with frenetic energy and wanted nothing more than to race through the garden, to feel her blood pumping through her veins and relish in that sense of *aliveness*. She almost didn't want to admit how happy that praise made her feel. Her mother constantly begged her to employ herself in more homely pursuits and frowned at her excessive horseback riding, time spent outdoors, and her meddling in the affairs of their estate. It was always correction, never acknowledgement. With Lady Nightingale, it was different.

"I shall keep practicing," she promised.

"I know you will. We shall meet with Mrs. Kensington in a few days to arrange the finer details of the masquerade. I would like you to be there."

"I would be honored."

They made their way back to Lady Nightingale's house in companionable silence. Rose practically skipped the entire way back. She folded her parasol and perched it on her shoulder, basking in the warm light on her face and the feeling of the lightness in her chest. She resolved she would do everything in her power to continue to make Lady Nightingale proud.

"Now, I daresay you would like to join Miss Sinclair and Miss Miller for tea. Look for my invitation to our party planning within the next few days," Lady Nightingale said, opening the door.

Rose placed her parasol in the rack by the door, then made for the parlor for tea. Kate would be relieved that she wouldn't be punished for her questioning, and she couldn't wait to tell Harriet that she'd finally had some success with her fire magic. She had taken only three steps down the hall before Lady Nightingale called out to her.

"Oh, and Miss Worthington, *do* let me know if that book should turn up again? I would be very interested to see it." Lady Nightingale's face was half hidden in shadow, obscuring her expression.

The joy in her chest morphed into something darker, more wary. But Rose couldn't deny her benefactress's request. "Of course."

CHAPTER 19

The candlewick remained stubbornly unlit. Rose's head pounded from the effort of concentration, but the threads of magic she'd found so easily yesterday afternoon evaded her. Her bedroom was cloaked in cool the cool blue shadows of twilight, but even the dark did not ease her headache. Rose squinted at the wick and tried to channel any amount of heat into the cold taper.

Light.

She had been at it all evening with no success. After supper, she'd claimed that she wasn't feeling well and locked herself in her bedchamber to practice, as she'd promised Lady Nightingale. Her mother and Cornelius were away at yet another stuffy party, leaving her blissfully alone.

Light, she commanded.

Nothing.

She glanced down at the book she had taken home from Lady Nightingale's library, squinting at the diagram. Strange alchemical symbols scattered across the tea-colored pages. The tiny footnotes scrawled in the margins were more confusing than helpful. Rose closed her eyes, took a deep breath, and tried to enter a place of serenity, as the book suggested.

Light!

She cracked one eye open. The taper remained flameless. She let out a grunt of frustration and slammed the book shut. A long, bright orange flame sprang up from the wick of the candle for a mere second before extinguishing. The wax didn't even have a chance to melt.

If the ball was supposed to be an exam, Rose knew without a doubt that if she were tested now, she would fail. Whatever she had done in Lady Nightingale's garden had been an accident. Or she's gotten lucky. She had no proper control over her magic.

She shoved the borrowed book under her pillow and fought to keep waves of despair at bay. She had woken with a heavy blanket of sadness cloaking her thoughts, her mood mirrored by the grey clouds slung low across the city. Despite attempts to rouse herself, she'd been unable to shake her melancholy. Some days were just like that, where she felt too much at once and the weight of the world was too heavy. She slid under the plethora of blankets on her bed and cocooned herself within them.

Philip should have received her letter by now. A seed of doubt had taken root within her. After that disastrous night, what if he decided she wasn't worth the trouble? What if Cornelius had hurt him badly? What if he really *was* dead, and she never saw him again?

Rather than let herself be pulled into a spiral of doubt and despair, Rose reached for the second book she'd taken from Lady Nightingale's library. It was a thin green volume with a dark bird on the cover. *The Raven's Song and Other Stories*, the same one she had at home. She wondered why the library had given her a children's book. She opened the book and read, hoping to distract herself.

A raven alone, misfortune is sown.

Black birds in a pair—a sign's in the air.

Three ravens foretell of good fortune's spell,
But take heed, and beware, of death and despair
What fear ravens bring
on four pairs of wings.

The stories and little poems had always cheered her as a child, but she could not shake a strong sense of foreboding as she read it now. She slid the book under her pillow to join the other, sadness pressing down on her once more.

Her thoughts drifted as she closed her eyes, finally snagging on the day Philip had saved her life.

* * *

SHE HADN'T CRIED for months after her brother's death. She floated through each day with a strange numbness, completing small tasks without even realizing she did them. Her mother wept constantly, but Rose didn't shed a single tear. She wondered if there was something wrong with her, not to cry at the loss of her other half.

One early summer's evening, a few months after they'd lowered an empty casket into the ground, she sat in the glen. She watched Philip as the sun set, casting vibrant pastel colors in the sky. Her pockets were heavy with the river stones she had collected on her way here. She'd wanted to see him one last time. To say goodbye before she walked into the cool rushing waters of the river, weighed down by stones and grief.

She sat on a large rock, still warm from the heat of the sun, and watched him silently, fingers gripping the heavy stones in her dress pockets. Rose observed as he hammered odd bits of wood and metal together. Philip could always see something marvelous in the pieces he held, even if all she saw were scraps of lumber. He never pressed her for conversation, but would talk if she was willing.

He must have sensed something different in her demeanor.

After a quarter hour, he placed his tools back in their oiled leather roll and sat beside her. They watched the sun dip lower and lower until it disappeared into the tops of the trees, and soft twilight stretched across the sky.

Finally, she'd asked if there was something wrong with her, since she couldn't cry over George's death.

Philip turned his eyes to hers, full of his own sorrow. "There's no one way to grieve. It doesn't matter how much you cry. Because no matter what we do, he won't be coming back."

It was something she had known all along, yet to hear it spoken aloud broke a dam within her. The words ran hollowly in her mind.

He won't be coming back.

A single tear fell down her cheek. It rolled down her face and fell onto her lap, marking her dress like a singular raindrop.

"What do we do?" she'd asked, her voice raspy with disuse.

Philip lifted his chin to the night sky as the first pinpricks of starlight shone. "The only thing we can do," he whispered. "We go on. We live."

They sat side by side for a long time until the air became cool and a crescent moon lifted into the night sky. On her way home, Rose dropped the river rocks from her pockets, one by one, leaving markers of her grief behind.

Rose rolled over in her plush bed, dragging herself from the memory. She withdrew the carved wooden rose from beneath her nightgown and gripped it tightly. She didn't know if Philip knew what he had done that day, but she knew he had never stopped fighting for her.

She glanced at the candle, bathed in moonlight. She squeezed the charm and felt a strange tugging sensation on the edges of her consciousness. It felt like stepping into a river's rushing current, swollen with spring rains. Instead of the current pulling at her ankles, it nudged at the very center of her. Rose let herself fall into the gentle lull, and the sparkling sensation of magic crept over her like gooseflesh. She willed that magic to become light, to become fire.

The wick of the candle ignited.

Rose stared at the tender flame as her chest ached with longing. Propping herself on one elbow, she blew out the candle and ensconced herself in her blankets once more.

When she did eventually fall asleep hours later, she dreamed she was back in the starlit clearing with Philip as the stars wrapped themselves closely around them, shielding them from the darkness of the night.

CHAPTER 20

Rose hadn't asked permission to take the book from Lady Nightingale's library. Her palms were damp as she held the book close to her chest and knocked on the door. A maid answered and let her in without question. She was clearly used to the frequent traffic at the Nightingale townhouse. Every time Rose had visited, there had been a plethora of ladies already present.

Now that she thought about it, Rose had never seen any men at the house, or anywhere on the premises before. Rose chalked it up to an oddity of Lady Nightingale's character that she would prefer to employ only women. She was a wealthy widow. Rose had never heard the late Lord Nightingale mentioned. Perhaps London's elite could forgive widowed women their oddities, as long as they kept to themselves or didn't break their rules too badly.

Rose's pulse raced as she stepped inside and made straight for the library. She forced herself to take calm, measured steps. She would return the book, then make for the parlor to bid her teacher good morning and begin her day like usual. Rose was anxious to share her success with her candle lighting last night.

Thankfully, there was no one else in the corridor. She had arrived at the earliest possible time. Her shoulders relaxed as she reached the library doors. Rose breathed a sigh of relief as she gripped the smooth brass handle.

A reedy voice sounded behind her, halting her steps. "Stop right there."

Rose's throat tightened, and she gripped the book tightly to her chest. She forced herself to turn around and face the crotchety Lady Templeton. "Good morning," said Rose, feigning nonchalance. She refused to be cowed by the old woman.

Lady Templeton shuffled menacingly towards her, shoulder hunched forward. "What do you think you are doing?"

Rose bit back a nasty retort about manners. "I'm on my way to the library." She willed her breath to ease, to appear unconcerned with the impromptu interrogation.

Lady Templeton's frown deepened as she spied the book clutched in Rose's sweaty hands. "Books are never to leave the library," she snarled. "Give it to me."

Reluctantly, Rose handed over the book as the old woman muttered about impertinence under her breath.

Lady Templeton squinted at the title. Rose could have sworn she saw a brief flash of disappointment before her wrinkled visage returned to its habitual scowl. "Loss of library privileges for a week for this infraction," she sentenced.

Rose opened her mouth to protest, but Lady Templeton stopped her.

"Defy me and it will be a month."

She knew that the old bat would be happy to dole out more punishment, so she fought to keep her face an impassive mask as anger at the injustice bubbled under her skin. She hated herself for complying so easily, but she could not afford to lose access to the knowledge in the library. Not with the masquerade drawing near. She'd only lit a single candle on her own. Lady Nightingale had not yet shared what her test would be, but she knew it would require more than that. Rose tried not to panic. What would happen if she failed the test? Would she be asked to leave and never return?

Lady Templeton's grating voice broke through her spiraling thoughts. "Lady Nightingale is expecting you in the parlor. We shall tell her about your latest bout of rule breaking together, hmm? You clearly can't be trusted to wander around on your own."

Rose would not give her the satisfaction of taking the bait. She ground her teeth and followed behind the hunched woman to the parlor.

Lady Templeton threw open the door with barely concealed glee. "Your newest pet has broken the rules again," she gloated before Lady Nightingale had a chance to greet them. "She took a book from the library."

Lady Nightingale frowned at her third-in-command from her perch on a bottle green velvet settee. She closed the notebook she had been writing in and set down her ink pen. "Is this true, Miss Worthington?"

Rose felt a strange crackling in the air. A painful lump lodged in her throat. No one explicitly told her she couldn't remove the books from the library. How could they fault her for breaking the rules she didn't even know existed?

Lady Templeton continued to revel in her misfortune. She patted the confiscated book softly as she stared daggers at her.

"It's true," Rose said through her clenched teeth.

Lady Nightingale glanced at the old vulture. Unspoken words passed between them. Rose clenched her fists, waiting for further admonishment.

"Margaret, you may leave us," said Lady Nightingale.

Lady Templeton's shoulders hunched further at the dismissal. "I'll just put this back where it belongs." As she shuffled past Rose, she whispered, low enough so that only she could hear, "I'll be watching you, girl."

Rose waited until the doors closed before launching into her explanation. "Lady Nightingale, I had no idea —"

Her benefactress held a hand up to silence her.

"It is my fault for not telling you. But know now: nothing from this house leaves the grounds." Her warm brown eyes were cooler, her voice tinged with displeasure. "I must admit, I had thought that would be obvious."

Rose's anger evaporated in an instant, replaced by a hollowness in her chest. "I'm sorry." She fixed her eyes on the parlor's intricate rug.

"There is more at risk than you realize, child. What if someone had caught you with it? What then?"

Rose whipped her head up. "I would never say I got it from you, or any of the others."

Lady Nightingale clasped her hands lightly in front of her. "I am glad, but that does not lessen the fact that you did not stop to think of the consequences of what could happen if you were discovered. May I remind you that when we first spoke of the Nightingales, you promised to protect and conceal this sisterhood?"

She was right. She had been incredibly foolish, risking taking the book. Rose's stomach clenched with self-loathing.

"If you want to be one of us, you cannot put us, or yourself, in danger. I will not allow it."

The hollowness in her chest threatened to swallow her. It was hard to speak past the tightening lump in her throat. "Yes, Lady Nightingale."

Her teacher closed the distance between them and placed a reassuring hand on Rose's shoulder. Lady Nightingale's eyes regained some of their familiar warmth.

"I promise to not put you or any of the other girls in danger." Rose hoped her benefactress knew how remorseful she was.

Lady Nightingale nodded. "Actions speak louder than words, I am afraid." She let her hand drop. "I suppose now is the time to tell you. I have not shared this with everyone, but the Council can't deny the signs any longer. Whispers have reached us that people who would wish us harm have arrived in the city."

Rose's palms grew damp. "Who?"

"It's nothing you need to concern yourself with. We are well-protected here. As long as we all follow the rules and keep our powers concealed. But you need to prove that I can trust you. That we can all trust you. Including Margaret."

"I will do whatever you require of me," she said firmly, pulse still racing wildly.

"Then light the fire, Miss Worthington." She looked at the fireplace set against the far wall, its white marble cold and dark.

Rose stared hard at the empty hearth until her vision blurred. She channeled all her twisted emotions into her desire to *burn*. She felt her hands grow warm, and she blinked, causing the room to refocus.

Out of the corner of her eye, Rose saw Lady Nightingale looking at her expectantly. She refocused on the fireplace and tried to remember what she had done last night to light her bedroom candle. She'd thought of Philip, but it was more than that. Rose had poured her heart into the desire to fight for him, to claw her way out of the despair she felt in her every waking moment. It was a sorrow that shifted, sometimes it was light and other times suffocating. Rose reached for the desire to stay, to prove to Lady Nightingale that she could be her student, that she was worthy of being her pupil.

She channeled her focus into that singular desire to prove herself. The stream of magic tugged gently at her consciousness, and she fell into it, letting herself become buoyed by gently sparkling magic. A warm pulse radiated through her chest, surging through her arms like an electric shock. Sparks flew from her fingertips, and the fireplace ignited with a sudden *whoosh*.

Relief crashed over her in waves. Rose wiped away beads of sweat from her brow as she grinned at the now lit fireplace.

"Very good," said Lady Nightingale, satisfied with her work.

Rose's chest heaved as she tried to regain her breath. A seedling of pride took root and blossomed, filling her up with warmth. She had done it. She had willed fire into existence from nothing. Her hands tingled pleasantly, and she flexed her fingers at her sides.

She had *done it.*

Lady Nightingale walked to the hearth and gazed into the flames, dark hair glinting in the light. Rose's eyebrows knit together as she observed, breath finally slowing. Her benefactress's eyes glazed as the light danced eerily within them. A log cracked in the fire, but Lady Nightingale did not flinch. She continued to stare, seeing something that Rose could not, within the dancing fire.

"Alexander Crawford will invite you to the opera tonight," said Lady Nightingale finally, tearing her eyes away from the fire. "This is fortuitous timing." She placed a finger on her chin thoughtfully. "His father has something in his possession that we need. You are to retrieve it and bring it back to me."

Rose bit the inside of her lip, and she reached for the leather cord at her neck. Her hands still tingled with the ghost of her power. Her elation dimmed at the request. "From Lord Crawford?"

"Yes." Lady Nightingale waved a hand over the fire, extinguishing it. The air in the room cooled immediately. "I See that the papers we need are in the Crawford's study, bound in blue ribbon."

Rose stilled her fidgeting fingers. "You want me to steal from one of the most powerful men in London?"

"You want to keep us safe, don't you? To keep everyone here protected?"

"Of course I do." Rose dropped her necklace, ignoring the tightness in her stomach.

"Then you will retrieve those papers for us."

Rose knew she should not question her. But Alexander Crawford was her friend. He had shown her nothing but kindness. Now Lady Nightingale wanted her to steal from him.

She should refuse. A better person than her would decline outright, without a second thought. But she had just conjured fire from thin air, and on command. The impending threat of marriage was being kept at bay by her charade. Cornelius hadn't mentioned or threatened her with an engagement to Lord Reeves in a week, apparently satisfied by the callers she'd entertained after the Clarke's ball. But they had not called again. Who knew how long her luck would hold? Rose had not forgotten that learning how to ward against unwanted proposals was to be her reward for a passing her test at the masquerade.

Lady Nightingale would change her life. She was already helping her to have some control over her future. The Nightingales would help her avoid marriage, navigate the stormy seas of the social season, and advance her skills in magic. If these papers were so important, stealing them for her teacher was the least she could do. Rose was sure she wouldn't ask unless it was important.

But she still felt uneasy. "Why are they so important?" She wrung her hands, hoping she hadn't asked one too many questions.

"Knowledge must be earned, Miss Worthington. Procure those documents, and you shall gain my trust. When my trust is earned, the rewards are great, I assure you. Wouldn't you like to hear what else I Saw in the fire for you?"

Rose eyed the darkened hearth warily. It would be foolish to deny how badly she wanted to know. But, more than that, Rose wanted to prove that she could handle whatever it took to grow her magic and control her own destiny.

She squared her shoulders and locked her doubt away next to the place she kept her grief. "I'll get them for you."

"I know you will."

Rose left the parlor with heavy footsteps and tingling palms. She forced herself to think only about the rush of joy she'd felt as she set the dark hearth aflame. Only when she was halfway down the hall did she realize she hadn't pulled on any threads to light the fire. She knew there must be an explanation. Perhaps she did not always need to visualize the threads of power that connected everything. Maybe she'd accessed them subconsciously. She had completed what had been asked of her. She would do this, too.

CHAPTER 21

There was no point in staying since she was banned from the library. Rose walked towards the foyer, ready to return home. Besides, she needed to prepare for this evening if Lady Nightingale was correct about Alexander Crawford inviting her to the opera. An invitation must already be waiting for her.

Before she made it twenty paces, Harriet and Kate rounded the corner of a side corridor where they had been eavesdropping.

Harriet, her full cheeks flushed with exertion, spoke first. "We heard Lady Margaret punished you. Is it true?" Her doll eyes bulged with curiosity.

"It's true," Rose admitted, crossing her arms. "Though no one ever said that books can't leave the library." She didn't bother to conceal her bitterness.

Kate rolled her eyes. "Girls take books from there all the time. Just not *home*."

"That's terribly unfair!" Harriet cried, eyes growing impossibly more round.

"She was just looking for a reason to punish you, I expect," Kate added.

Rose was fortified by their indignation, but she was still annoyed that she'd been singled out. "Bully for her."

Harriet looked over her shoulder, as if she was afraid the old woman would be summoned by their words. "Come join us in the greenhouse. Kate's project is going well."

Kate squirmed, uncomfortable at the praise. "It's coming along fine."

"It's more than fine. Kate is a singularly talented green witch."

It was only mid-morning. If she was to attend the opera, she had plenty of time to prepare. "I didn't know there was a green-house. I'd love to visit it. And what's a green witch?" Rose asked.

"Magic speaks to us all differently." Kate shoved her hands into the pockets of her pale-yellow dress and rocked back on her heels. "Plants, flowers, vines, they all speak to me."

Rose wondered what plants could have to say.

"Let's go." Harriet tugged her hand, impatient to be off.

Rose let herself be dragged through the lushly carpeted hall and out a pair of French doors. The trio emerged in a part of the garden Rose had never seen before, even though she was certain she had walked the entirety of its paths with Lady Nightingale. A soft, buttery light filtered through the leaves of tall hedges as she walked a step behind Harriet and Kate. The sharp scent of growing things, and something slightly *other* wafted through the air. She wondered if the garden itself held magic.

"Here we are," Harriet announced.

The greenhouse appeared ordinary from the outside. Wood and glass encased a kaleidoscope of green, and bright shocks of color peppered the thick verdancy within. Kate unlocked the door with a small brass key, and the heady scent of perfumed flowers wafted towards them.

Warm, humid air pressed thickly upon Rose as she followed

her companions into the greenhouse. The scent of otherness was even stronger here. Kate walked between several tall, wooden potting benches to a tower of vines.

"Do it, Kate," begged Harriet. She stared expectantly at the strange column of twisted vines.

Kate rolled her eyes and withdrew a hand from her pockets. She extended her palm towards the plants and flexed her fingers.

White buds sprouted along the vines as tendrils of the plant curled with pleasure at the touch of Kate's magic. The buds grew, then opened, blooming in seconds. Each blossom's petals tapered into points. The flowers looked like giant stars with golden centers and released a strange sparkling substance into the air that glittered like flecks of starlight. They smelled heavenly.

Kate dropped her hand. "These are just for show. Lady Nightingale may use them for decoration at the masquerade."

"They're lovely." Rose bent to breathe in more of their heady scent. "They smell so familiar. Like a cold brook on a hot summer's day, and wood shavings."

"They smell different to each person," Harriet explained. "It's tricky magic."

Kate flashed a brief, bashful smile before waving her hand over the vines. The flowers closed, shrank, then disappeared back into the vines, their growth reversed.

Rose looked around at the neighboring worktables. There were more pots of flowers, vegetables, and herbs. Her curiosity was piqued by a table of dark green plants, their veins deep purple.

She reached out to stroke one of the waxy leaves, but Kate barked at her. "Don't!"

Rose jumped back, alarmed.

Kate guided her back to the center of the greenhouse. "Those are poisons. Best not to touch."

A chill crept down Rose's spine as she eyed the dark plants.

"Are you staying for tea this afternoon?" Harriet asked as she waved her hand through the air to stir the floating specks of gold that still lingered.

The weight of Lady Nightingale's orders crashed back down on her.

"I would love to, but I should return home. There's something I have to do for Lady Nightingale." Rose glanced over her shoulder, sure that Lady Templeton would lurch around the corner to admonish them for some new infraction.

"No one comes here this time of day," Kate said, noting her reluctance.

Rose bit her lip. She wasn't sure how much she should share about her errand. Lady Nightingale had demanded secrecy, after all.

Harriet bounced with excitement. "Well, are you going on a secret mission?"

"It's a bit early for her spark to be called, don't you think?" Kate asked.

"My what?" Annoyance wrinkled her nose. It would be far more helpful if there were some sort of newcomer handbook for new witches. It was exhausting, and slightly irritating, that she was learning everything through the other girls, not through Lady Nightingale or Lady Clarke.

"Your spark is the mission or task you have to complete in order to become a full-fledged Nightingale," explained Harriet.

"Have you had your spark called?"

Harriet was certainly gifted, and dedicated enough, to have been invited to become a Nightingale, and Kate's demonstration had been impressive. They must be top-form witches.

Kate shook her head solemnly, and Harriet pouted. "No," they said in unison.

From their genuine disappointment, Rose gathered that this was a sore subject, bemoaned about as other witches had their spark called, and they were left behind. She was eager to assure them she had not been called before they had. "Lady Nightingale didn't mention anything like that. She wants me to retrieve something for her, that's all."

"Oh, I see. Reconnaissance." Kate shoved her hands back into her pockets. "We all do it. It's sort of like a first test. To prove yourself."

"What are you retrieving, Rosie?" asked Harriet. "A book? A secret love letter? Tears of your enemies?"

Rose frowned. "Did someone actually have to collect the tears of their enemies?"

"She's joking," said Kate as Harriet stifled a giggle.

The scowl on Rose's face deepened. "Well, how would I know? No one tells me anything around here." A pulse of frustration ricocheted around her chest.

"I'm sorry. I didn't mean anything by it. And we are telling you things, aren't we, Kate?"

The other girl nodded, tight curls bouncing.

"So, what do you have to collect?"

Rose glanced at the greenery all around them, still unable to shake the feeling that someone could be listening. Her two friends looked at her expectantly. Her chest constricted unexpectedly. The thought that Harriet and Kate were her friends had only now dawned on her. It made her feel better.

"I have to fetch some papers for Lady Nightingale. They belong to Alexander Crawford's father," she admitted.

Kate's shoulders relaxed. "That shouldn't be problem for you. He's half in love with you already, if the talk is to be believed."

Rose rolled her eyes. "He is *not*."

Harriet turned her dark eyes to Kate and whispered, "Rose is madly in love with a boy named Philip."

Rose swatted Harriet playfully. Her neck and cheeks flushed.

"Well, you are," Harriet said indignantly, massaging her arm dramatically.

Kate shifted on her heels, uncomfortable with their playfulness. But her eyes glowed with curiosity.

Rose appreciated that Kate did not press her outright. It was easy to forgive Harriet for her prying, as her bubbling nosiness was innocent. Kate respected Rose's privacy, and for that, she was grateful. It made her feel like she could share her secrets, knowing that Kate would keep her confidence. "He's a friend from back home. Actually, we tried to run away together before I arrived in London."

Kate's mouth opened with silent delight.

"Rosie, tell us everything," Harriet demanded. "Right now."

"It's not an entirely happy tale," admitted Rose, her smile fading.

A small, wounded part of her didn't want to resist that terrible time. But she had told Lady Clarke and Lady Nightingale. She'd felt so much lighter, finally voicing her fears about losing Philip forever. Lady Clarke had said that burdens were meant to be shared. The weight of not knowing if he was alive or dead traveled with her always. He still hadn't replied to her letter. Maybe sharing her story with her friends would help lighten that weight. Even if only for a little while.

Rose bit her lip as she studied the two girls in front of her. "All right," said Rose, exhaling, and began.

By the end, Harriet's eyes were round as saucers, and Kate's mouth hung wide open.

"How terribly romantic," Harriet sighed.

"And terribly *horrible*," Kate said. "We could hex your cousin for you. Give him a nasty rash, make him go bald."

Rose let out an involuntary sound, something between a laugh and a sob. She pressed a hand to her mouth, trying to stifle the tide of emotions. "I think I can handle my cousin," she choked out. "I just hope Philip is all right."

"I'm sure he is." Harriet tossed her hair over one shoulder. "If Lady Nightingale wasn't able to contact his spirit, then there's a good chance he's alive."

She felt lighter with the reassurance, but a nagging tug of doubt remained. "I still don't know about stealing from the Crawfords." Rose reached for her necklace absently. "Apparently, he is inviting me to the opera tonight. It might be my only chance."

Harriet clapped her hands together. "But my parents are going tonight! I can ask to attend with them, and I can help you."

Rose bit her lip. Her fingers traced the smooth leather cord around her neck.

"I wonder what I shall wear, or if my mama will let me put my hair up," babbled Harriet.

"Harriet," Rose interrupted. "I think I should do this by myself."

Harriet's face fell, and Rose felt a twist of regret. Kate gave her a hard look which she ignored.

"Oh. If you're sure, then."

Rose saw her hopes burst like a glass balloon, but she hated to think of what would happen if Harriet was caught. She couldn't afford to botch this. Successfully retrieving those papers was proof that Lady Nightingale could trust her. If she failed . . . well, she didn't want to think about it.

"I'll still need your help with studying magic, since I'm banned from the library for a week."

That brightened Harriet's mood again, and Kate softened.

"I should go. If there's an invitation waiting for me, I'll have to respond straightaway." She bade farewell to her friends.

"Good luck, Rosie! You must tell me all about it tomorrow," waved Harriet.

Kate gave her a somber dip of her chin and turned to tend to her plants.

Rose left the greenhouse, walking through clouds of golden dust that lingered in the air. She hadn't meant to hurt Harriet's feelings. But stealing from the Crawfords was her test. She needed to prove to Lady Nightingale that she was capable. Otherwise, she'd be doomed to navigate the marriage mart on her own. Her stomach flipped at the thought. No, she wouldn't risk it. She would say if she married. Only she would determine her own fate. And it would start with a trip to the opera.

CHAPTER 22

*R*ose's mother thrust a cream-colored letter wrapped in pale blue ribbon, the Crawford house color, into her hands as soon as she walked through the front door.

The letter's wax seal was broken.

"Was it you or Cornelius who read this?" asked Rose coldly as she opened the envelope, scanning the card inside.

"Don't be silly, dear. I'm your mother. I wanted to ensure that your relationship remains…" She cleared her throat delicately, searching for the right word. "Appropriate."

Rose scoffed. "*Mother.*"

"Oh, hush. It was addressed to only you, which is certainly not proper. Perhaps you should remind him when you see him tonight." Her mother frowned, only now registering Rose's accusation towards her cousin. "Why on earth would Cornelius want to read this?"

Cornelius must not have said anything about his reservations about her spending time with Alexander, which was just as well. If Cornelius forbade her to see him again, her mother would uphold his demands, regardless of what Rose herself wanted. Thankfully, he wouldn't know about the invitation until she had already consented.

"Never mind," Rose said.

"Write your reply in the parlor, then sit with me. I feel as if I haven't seen you all week," implored her mother.

It was true. Rose had been preoccupied with her magic lessons and society outings. She wanted nothing more than to go to her bedroom and practice lighting fires in the hearth, but guilt twisted in her stomach. Her mother was exceptionally good at using that guilt to her own advantage. Rose followed her mother to their shared parlor, doing her best to hide her reluctance.

Rose penned her assent and called for Graham to have it sent to the Crawfords immediately.

When her task was complete, and they were alone again, her mother broke the silence. "Do you think he will propose to you?"

"Mama." Rose bristled, swiveling to face her from the writing desk.

Her mother held up her hands. "I'm only asking. You clearly enjoy your time together."

"We do, but we're content to remain acquaintances. He is betrothed to Miss Hawthorne."

"Betrothed is not engaged," her mother sang.

One of Rose's eyebrows shot up in disbelief. Talk of marriage turned her mother into a giddy foal. "We have discussed the matter plainly. Both of our intentions are clear."

Her mother made a noncommittal sound as she sifted through her own stack of invitations.

Rose bit the tip of her pen. A sudden thought entered her mind. "What will you do if I am married?"

"Don't chew on that. What do you mean, 'if'?"

"Fine, *when* I am married," huffed Rose. "What will you do?"

Her mother froze. She did not look at her daughter as

replied. "I expect Cornelius will provide a small home for me on the estate. He has mentioned it. There is some charitable work to be done. I will have things to occupy my time."

A wave of sorrow washed over Rose. After she was married, her mother would be left alone, and isolated, with neither her father nor brother for comfort as she grew old. Should Rose successfully marry, her mother will have fulfilled her life's purpose. Bear children, raise them, marry them off.

Rose would follow that same prescriptive life, only able to visit her mother when her husband gave her permission. An icy dread settled in her heart at the thought. Rose didn't want children. She didn't want to marry. She didn't want to be bound to the whims of her husband, dependent on him for everything. And if he should die first, then she would be left to suffer the same terrible fate as her mother.

Her doubts about stealing from Lord Crawford dwindled. Magic was the only way she was going to seize her own destiny. She needed to become a full-fledged witch. A Nightingale.

With her resolve set, she turned the talk to upcoming parties and shopping, leading her mother away from the subject of marriage. The time passed more quickly than she had expected, and soon it was time to dress for her outing with Alexander Crawford.

* * *

THE OPERA WAS AN AWKWARD AFFAIR.

Against the deep-red velvet and gold filigree opulence of the opera house, Rose felt drab in her simple dove gray evening gown. Her mother had suggested she wear a pale blue one, but Rose had given her a withering glare. She'd surely end up in one of those gossip pamphlets for presuming to wear the Crawford colors while sitting in their box. She'd probably appear in one tomorrow just for attending the opera with Alexander.

Everyone knew it should be Miss Hawthorne who accompanied him, not her.

People ogled as she sat beside him in the Crawford's box, visibly craning their necks to glimpse them. Rose twisted the braided strap of her fan repeatedly as they waited for the show to begin.

She found herself unable to give more than monosyllabic responses to Alexander's attempts at conversation. Mercifully, he did not push her, and they sat in embarrassing silence for a quarter of an hour before members of the royal family arrived. Heads swiveled to gaze upon the prince and his retinue. Rose at last felt that she could breathe normally, though she remained stiff. Their box was only two removed from Her Majesty's.

Finally, the house lights dimmed, and the audience turned their attention to the stage, some more reluctantly than others. Alexander placed his hand on hers in the safety of the dark, stilling her fidgeting fingers. He leaned in and whispered, "Don't be so nervous. They won't bite."

She gave him a wan smile, and turned her attention to the stage, unable to shake Kate's words from her mind as he removed his hand.

He's half in love with you already.

It was complete nonsense. They had clearly established the parameters of their relationship that day in the park. But even so. She felt warmth through her gloved fingers. Her skin hummed pleasantly at the contact, and her chest felt as if it were filled sunlight. Was it wrong to feel this way? Comforted by his touch?

The sweet, low notes of a cello reverberated in the theater, and the audience ceased their hushed murmurings. Rose swept her eyes once more over the crowd seated below. A jolt of panic whipped through her as she spied Cornelius seated in the lower left wing. With Lord Reeves, of all people. She hadn't noticed them when they entered the theater. She prayed they hadn't seen her, either.

Rose fought to slow her panicked, shallow breaths as the music continued to sweep over the audience, the notes reverberating in her chest. She could just make out her cousin in the soft glow of lantern light, and she was thankful for the shadows that cloaked her high in the Crawford box.

She couldn't take her eyes off him. Cornelius looked utterly enraptured by the orchestra. His fingers flexed against his knee, in time with the music. She couldn't make out his face at this distance. Her eyesight wasn't perfect, but she could see his whole body leaned forward, as if he wanted to fall straight into the melody.

Alexander shifted beside her. Rose snapped her gaze to the stage where actors had taken their places. She did not look at Cornelius again.

It wasn't until the first act was well underway that Rose felt her shoulders relax and her breathing return to normal. The music washed over her, and she let herself become lost in the heart-breakingly beautiful songs that filled the theater.

After three hours, the curtain fell, and she realized with a start that she had not yet set her own stage. She had let herself forget, for a time, about everything. Her mind raced as lamps were lit, once again shedding light on the attendees. Rose stood silently next to Alexander as he bade farewell to friends and acquaintances in the grand foyer. Her palms grew slick inside her gloves.

She couldn't think past the terrible truth that she would have to take advantage of his kindness or betray his trust.

Rose was sure Alexander could hear the thundering of her heart as he helped her into his carriage. As they pulled away from the glow of the opera house, she slumped in her seat, relieving the tension in her back and shoulders.

"Did you enjoy the opera?" Alexander asked as the carriage rolled away from the busy steps of the theater.

"I did. It was beautiful. But I must apologize. I'm afraid I was terrible company tonight."

He leaned forward, bracing his elbows on his thighs. His brow creased with concern. "I admit, I was beginning to worry. You didn't seem at all yourself."

"How can you stand it? The way people constantly stare at you?"

Rose could just make out his rueful smile in the dim light. "It used to bother me more. I suppose I've gotten used to it."

"I admire you for it. It makes me seize up like a frightened fawn. I must make it up to you."

"You don't need to apologize, Miss Worthington. Would it suit you if our next outing were a quieter affair?"

Rose fiddled with the fan she clutched in her hands. "I daresay it would. Perhaps we can spend more time together now. At your home?"

Confused, Alexander leaned back. "Now?"

"Why not? My mother won't be expecting me for another few hours. And I... I don't want to go home. Not yet." She stroked the soft feathers of her fan. It wasn't an outright lie. She wanted to avoid Cornelius for as long as possible. If he hadn't seen her himself, it was only a matter of time before he heard that she'd attended the opera with Alexander. Then there would be hell to pay.

"Why is that?"

It was too dim to make out his features, but there was worry in his voice. Her guilt twisted deeper. She snapped her fan shut, steeling herself. "Is it enough to say that I simply enjoy your company? Your friendship?"

"Of course it is." Alexander cleared his throat. "All is well otherwise? You must forgive me if this is too forward, but your cousin seems a severe sort of fellow. I do hope he is a proper gentleman. That he treats you and your mother well."

Rose's chest ached. She wished she could tell him how horribly he treated her with threats and contempt. But what could Alexander do about it? Nothing. It was her problem, and she would fix it.

"My cousin is strict, is all. I think his time in America has made him feel he must overcompensate in his role as lord of our estate. He's most determined to find me a husband, even though I'm not ready."

Alexander made a pensive noise in the back of his throat. The sound hummed pleasantly in Rose's chest.

"As much as I would enjoy taking you home with me, Miss Worthington, I'm afraid the *ton* will talk. I wouldn't want to tarnish your reputation. Perhaps we can take another outing to the park? I have affairs to see to tomorrow, but the day after?"

Bile rose in the back of her throat. She couldn't do this. Her chance was slipping away. She forced herself to answer. "That would be wonderful."

It wasn't a lie. She wanted to spend more time with him. He was kind and understood her in a way no one else did.

The carriage slowed. Rose glanced out of the window and was startled to see they were almost to the Worthington town-house. Her heart sank. What else was she supposed to do? Seduce him? Her stomach swooped with nausea just thinking about it. She did not have the fortitude, or skill, for *that*.

They stopped. Alexander helped her out of the landau, promising to call again soon. His teeth flashed brilliantly as he bade her good night.

She hurried up the front steps, lest prying eyes spot her dismounting the Crawford carriage unaccompanied. When she opened the front door, she found the house dark and quiet. Only when she was safely within the house did she hear the wheels of Alexander's landau pull away from the drive.

Disappointment and despair made her steps heavy as she climbed the stairs to her suite. She sat in an overstuffed pink chair, not bothering to remove her shoes. She had failed.

Hot, angry tears spilled down her cheeks.

Lady Nightingale had given her clear instructions on how to complete her task. Rose was simply weak and unable to do what was necessary. She wiped her face, trying to stem the flow of tears. It was so unfair. Obstacles barred her path at every turn, whether it be the rules of the elite, codes of honor, duty, or her own damned inability to grab the opportunities that lay before her; to use the emotions of those around her to her advantage.

Anxiety made her thoughts spiral. If she failed, Lady Nightingale would expel her as her pupil. There would be no more magic. Her friends would forget about her, and she would be alone. Cornelius would eventually find someone to marry her, and that would be that.

She wished she could just accept that this was how things were.

Rose gritted her teeth in frustration, stray tears still squeezing their way out. It was so easy for some girls to accept the path that had been laid out for them. Girls like Effie Crawford, whose life was charmed and perfect. She'd probably never suffered a day in her life, or cried over the idea of marriage, or worried about money. She was a woman who knew how to wield the power that she had and used every ounce to her advantage. Effie would have no qualms about seducing a man for her ends. She would probably *enjoy* it.

Rose shoved herself out of the chair and paced in front of the fireplace. She glared at the weakening embers, channeled her anger towards the dying fire, and felt no small amount of satisfaction when the flames leapt high, licking the walls of the chimney. They stayed that way, burning hot.

The ease with which she had commanded that fire should have given her pause, but she was too preoccupied to give it much thought. She was making so much progress. She couldn't give it up now. If only Lady Nightingale could see.

Self-loathing coated the back of her throat, tasting like copper. She wouldn't get the opportunity to demonstrate her progress if she didn't deliver those papers. The path that Lady Nightingale had so clearly laid out for her was now gone.

She couldn't stop thinking about Effie Crawford and how she navigated this unjust world, prevailing despite the obstacles. Rose put her thumb on her bottom lip and stared into the raging fire, deep in thought. A plan began to form. It was reckless, but if she could pull it off...

Half an hour later, Rose shed her clothes, draped them over the back of her dressing chair, and fell into bed, exhausted. Her mind was made up.

She would no longer put herself at the mercy of men.

CHAPTER 23

*E*ffie Crawford delicately wiped her mouth, blinking back the tears that inevitably formed when she made herself sick. She rinsed her hands and mouth in the basin of water she kept on her nightstand, then opened her bedroom window, plucking a few leaves from the potted peppermint that grew on the sill. She chewed the leaves and let the sting of the mint fill her mouth, covering the sour taste of sick.

The pulsing crush of emotion that had threatened to smother her had dissipated, subsiding to a gentle throb after she vomited her guts out.

Last night had been wretched.

Lord and Lady Barrington's soirée had been exceedingly dull. They were old and stuffy, and provided no sort of entertainment other than food, drink, and stilted conversation. Her mother and father had dragged her along with them, despite her protests. Her favorite wayward gentlemen had not deigned to grace the Barrington party with their presence, so there had been only the brothers Langley, too young and green for her taste, to flirt with.

Celia Hawthorne was also notably absent. Her best friend

had received a private invitation to listen to a small concert with the queen.

The queen.

Envious couldn't begin to describe how she felt.

Then, on top of it all, the youngest Langley brother had let slip that Alex had taken Rose Worthington to the opera.

It was insulting. Her brother didn't mind if their family name was dragged through the mud, but she certainly did. His actions reflected on her, and if she were to obtain an advantageous match, then he needed to get his act together.

Some calm had settled over her, though her discontent remained. She swallowed the mint leaves and sprayed perfume into the center of her boudoir, decorated tastefully in blue, and walked through the scent, letting it settle into her hair and clothes.

It shouldn't bother her that Celia hadn't been able to attend the Barrington party. Effie chewed her lip absently. She had been looking forward to seeing Celia for the past two days. She found herself more and more wishing to shake herself of the clinging attachments of her suitors for the quiet company of her friend. Her friend who smelled like lemons and sunshine, who made her heart skip an inexplicable beat every time she walked into a ballroom.

Rather than give into the disconcerting longing for Celia's company, she flirted more shamelessly with her suitors than was advisable for a woman of her standing. Maybe the Langley boys could shake her from this strange preoccupation with her impure thoughts of her best friend.

Effie eyed the clock in the corner of her room. Alexander would have finished his breakfast by now. She needed to have a little chat with him. She was nearly to the breakfast room when one of the pimply-faced butlers stopped her. "Pardon, miss. There is a caller in the parlor."

A relaxed smile broke across her face. "Who is it?" It must be one of the Langleys. Haven gotten a taste of her all to themselves last night, they would be wanting more. She touched the back of her hair, making sure her white-blonde curls were in place.

"Miss Worthington is here," replied the butler. Thomas was his name. He extended a simple calling card to her.

Effie reached for the card and scowled. "No doubt she is here to see my brother," she snipped.

"She asked for you," said the butler timidly.

Effie's grip on the card tightened. The card was plain, the penmanship clean and unassuming. "She has some nerve," she muttered.

"Quite so, miss."

She glared icily at the young butler. It was acceptable for her to speak less than fondly of members of the *ton*, but for a butler to presume to do so was not so forgivable.

He coughed, uncomfortable under her withering glare. "If there's nothing else, miss?" Sweat formed on his brow.

Effie let him squirm a bit longer, watching beads of sweat gather at his temples. For what good were the servants if they did not fear you just a little? "You may go," she finally dismissed.

Thomas bowed perfunctorily, then walked stiffly down the hall. Effie got the distinct impression that he was doing his best not to run as fast as he could.

Her fun was over for the time being. She turned her attention back to the calling card and grimaced. She would certainly see Rose Worthington and tell her exactly what she thought of her dallying with her brother. She lifted her chin and marched to the parlor, determined to put the harlot in her place.

Effie thrust open the parlor doors. The dark-haired Worthington wench sat comfortably on a settee. She turned pale grey eyes, glistening with unshed tears, towards her.

"May I help you?" Effie asked in her most scathing tone. It

would be so satisfying to watch those tears fall. She wondered how long it would be before they did.

Rose blinked rapidly before rising. "Miss Crawford, please forgive my intrusion. I find myself in a terrible predicament and believe you are the only person who can assist me."

It was surprising that Rose Worthington had dared to call at all, but to ask her for help? Something was not right. Effie had thought she scared her away when she'd spilt wine down the back of her dress. Apparently, she was wrong. She didn't much care for that.

She scoffed, hoping to hide her curiosity. "And why on earth would I do that?"

"Because it's about your brother," said the wretch, twisting her hands.

The spot above Effie's left eyebrow pulsed. She crumpled the calling card in her fist. "Look, if you're hoping for an ally in your sham of a courtship, you are sorely—"

Rose interrupted her in earnest. "I'm not looking for courtship with your brother. I need your help to convey to him that all I want is his friendship. Nothing more."

Effie's forehead continued to throb in irritation. "Do you not know how this works?" How dare she come into her home and demand she be her messenger? It didn't matter that she had been on her way to reprimand Alex moments before. That was her idea. To have Miss Worthington dictate her dealings with her brother only made her blood boil.

"The only reason you could possibly have for spending time with my brother is because you are interested in marrying him. That is all. It's the *season*. And even if it weren't, our family wouldn't have any dealings with yours, despite your cousin's pathetic reaching for higher rungs in the societal ladder. You were not born into this tier of society, nor have you earned a place here." She exhaled through her nose, trying to steady her rapid, angry breathing.

"Please," said Rose in a small voice. "Say something to your brother, or he will continue to call. I cannot refuse him if he shows up on my doorstep."

"Haven't you ever heard of lying?" Effie asked incredulously. Good God, was she truly this naïve? "You have a headache. You have received other invitations. Your cousin has, rightly, forbade you. You are indisposed. Dare I go on?"

Rose bit her lip, contemplating. "Your brother has already been made aware of my limited social engagements. You made it quite plain that I am not welcome in certain circles. Invitations are few, and I can only have so many headaches a week."

Effie crossed her arms, fist still tightly closed over the crumpled calling card. She squeezed it, wishing she could pulverize it.

"He will continue to call, Miss Crawford, until you and I do something about it."

Damn. Her own desire to ostracize Miss Worthington had worked too well. A word and it could be undone, but still. She hated losing. She hated being wrong. But Miss Worthington was only providing one solution to solving this puzzle. She could do better than that. "Come with me," she ordered, then spun on her heel. She did not wait for her, but continued on to the study where Alex was working.

She knew he was only there because their father was out. Part of her didn't want to disturb him. He only had a limited amount of time to complete the work his father left for him, as they couldn't work together in the same room. Father was too harsh on Alex. Effie knew he tried his best. He just wasn't perfect enough.

But this was an emergency and Alex would understand. Effie knocked thrice before opening the door, not waiting for a response.

Alex sat at the desk, cravat hanging open and shirt unbuttoned. He hadn't even bothered to finish dressing before rushing in here to do what he could. She had no time to feel badly about the intrusion.

"Effie, what have I told you about—" He stopped mid-reprimand as Rose entered the study right behind his sister.

"Miss Worthington." His gaze flicked between the two women, puzzled.

"Yes," Effie spat venomously. "*Miss Worthington* would like a word. I will chaperone, then she will be leaving."

"Are you well?" asked Alex, concern carving deep lines into his face. The question was not directed at Effie, but at *her*.

Effie felt as if a bucket of ice water had been dumped over her head. Cold tingles raced down her spine as Rose replied, "Yes, I am. But there is something that I need to discuss with you."

The look on Alex's face... It wasn't false emotion, but the kind of empathy that society's darling was praised for. He was a sweet boy, a golden child, to be so kind and thoughtful to the wallflowers and lesser sons of society. He was a bleeding heart, too prone to do the honorable thing. But this... this was real.

Her mind raced. She needed to rectify the situation, and quickly, before Alex threw Celia off for good in favor of this *nobody*.

"Actually, Miss Worthington, darling, if you could wait outside for just a moment." She kept her eyes fixed on her brother's face as he nodded silently for Rose to wait outside.

Then his gaze slid to hers, wariness pinching his brow. His mouth was drawn in a thin line, restraining any questioning until Rose was safely out of earshot.

The parlor door closed behind her, and she launched into her admonishment. "You took her to the *opera*?" she asked in a low voice.

Alex at least had the decency to look guilty. "Yes. How did you find out?"

"God, *everyone* is talking about it. You can't do this Alex. You cannot."

He ran his amber brown fingers through his hair, mussing it. He did not look at her.

"Even she knows it," Effie continued. "That's why she's here. If one word of this visit gets out, we are in serious trouble. If Celia knew . . ."

Alex leaned against the desk, bracing himself with his fists. "Shit."

Good. She was getting somewhere.

"Luckily, she had the good sense to call on *me*, not you. I will speak of this to no one. Tell her to do the same. Tell her to leave us alone."

"Effie, I can't."

She didn't let him finish. "Yes, you can. You must. You have no other choice." She threw the crumpled calling card into the grate, where it nestled among the logs. It would burn quickly the next time the fire was lit.

"But what if I want a choice?" He said it so quietly she almost didn't hear him.

It was easier to pretend she hadn't.

She threw open the parlor doors. Rose was awkwardly adjusting her dress, pulling up the low neckline to cover more of her décolletage. "Go in. You can escort yourself out when you've finished," she said coldly.

Rose brushed past her, chin lowered.

Before she closed the doors, Effie said, low enough so only Rose could hear, "May our paths never cross again."

As she swung the doors shut, fingers gripping the smooth brass handles, she glimpsed fiery defiance in Miss Worthington's eyes.

The doors closed before she could say anything else.

She pressed an ear to the door, hoping to catch a fraction of their conversation, despite knowing that in all the years she had done so, she would hear nothing more than muffled sounds. Like every other time she had tried to eavesdrop on the forbidden conversations of the study, she couldn't make out anything coherent.

Effie shoved off from the doors, accepting that she had done all she could, and went in search of the raspberry and lemon tea cakes. She would eat them until she could barely breathe in her stays, anything to quell the churning of feelings within her.

She may or may not make herself sick soon afterwards, depending on what time it was. She needed to visit Celia and soften any damage that rumors of her brother escorting another woman to the opera might do to her sweet-tempered friend.

If anything happened because of this 'friendship' between her brother and Miss Worthington–if the betrothal was revoked, or Celia heartbroken–she would make Rose Worthington pay.

The scroll of papers, bound with pale blue ribbon, sat uncomfortably between Rose's breasts. She had forced it down her stays in the hallway after swiping it off the low table near the door. Effie had nearly caught her shoving it unceremoniously down her front.

Thankfully, the only thing Effie had seen was her readjusting the neckline of her dress, dragging up as high as it would go. Rose knew that if she bent forward at all, the papers would be visible.

It took considerable effort to stand in front of Alexander Crawford with his father's documents pressed against her chest without drawing attention to them, or her nervousness. She shifted from foot to foot, waiting for him to say something as the papers burned against her skin.

Thief. Traitor.

She pushed the thoughts away. She refused to have any regrets.

Fate was intervening on her behalf. Rose had been prepared to make some excuse to wander their house in search of them. Instead, Effie had led her straight to where they waited for her.

Rose had spotted them immediately as she entered the study. They were the only papers bound with ribbon. She'd snagged them with two outstretched fingers, letting her skirts conceal her thievery, as she left the room.

Now she stood in front of Alexander, his piercing blue eyes boring into her. She had to break this awkward silence between them, before her guilt betrayed her. "I'm sorry if I've interrupted you."

Alexander came around the front of the desk. He leaned against it and crossed his arms.

She could not help but notice his partial state of undress. It was hard to ignore the view of his strong chest muscles and the downy tuft of hair revealed by his unbuttoned shirt. He was, objectively, an attractive man. Rose immediately berated herself for even thinking such a thing.

Alexander glanced down and buttoned his shirt with swift, deft fingers. "I admit that I find myself perplexed by your visit," he said as he tied his cravat, the silken material sliding through his fingers. "I had thought you would want to stay well away from my sister."

Rose stopped her fidgeting and swallowed. She'd never had much cause for lying before. Certainly, there had been times as a child when she had stretched the truth, usually to coax sweets from the cook for herself and her brother. And she had never disclosed to her mother that the destination of her horseback rides was usually to see Philip, but that had been an omission of the truth rather than outright deceit. Now was an appropriate time to test how convincing a liar she could be, even if a small part of her hated herself for it.

A good lie was grounded in truth. She would start there.

"My cousin is displeased about our spending time together," she said. "I was hoping your sister could relay the message, but she thought I should tell you directly. He has forbidden me from seeing you." Rose knew Cornelius would make such a decree. It was only a matter of time.

Alexander uncrossed his arms. His dismay was palpable. "If I have done anything to offend you or your family, I am sorry for it."

Rose knew he meant it.

Thief. Traitor. Liar. The words rang relentlessly within her.

"You must know that I enjoy your company. I look forward to the time we spend together, I truly do. But, my cousin…" She bit her lip, pausing for dramatic effect. "He blames me for encouraging you. He thinks it's inappropriate for us to be spending this much time together, especially given your betrothal to Miss Hawthorne."

Alexander rubbed his chin. Rose sensed a current of frustration in the gesture, but knew that it was not directed at her.

"I apologize if my actions have caused you pain."

Rose suspected there was much more he wanted to say about the matter. His jaw set in a hard line, but he said no more.

"You do not pain me, Lord Crawford. But the rest of the world is intent on doing so."

Alexander sighed. "It certainly feels that way some days, does it not?"

Rose gave him a sad smile. "I believe that our private engagements have come to an end. I hope you will still dance with me at Lady Nightingale's masquerade."

Alexander took her hand in his and gave it a chaste kiss. "Of course, Miss Worthington. And every ball after."

The knife of regret twisted in her chest. Her hand buzzed pleasantly at his touch. She shoved both feelings away. "Goodbye, Alexander."

"Goodbye, Rose." He dropped her hand, and Rose wished desperately that he would not.

He held the study door open for her. Rose half expected Effie to be waiting for them in the hall, but there was no one.

"Shall I see you out?" he asked with brittle sorrow.

The knife twisted deeper. "No, thank you. I can manage. Goodbye."

He nodded and closed the door.

The stolen papers burned against her skin.

Thief. Liar. Traitor.

She had succeeded. She should be happy that she had completed the task Lady Nightingale had set for her. But the regret in Alexander's voice was real and weighed more heavily that she had expected on her heart. Rose leaned her back against the study door, breathing in through her nose, trying to dampen the pain within her chest.

She thought she felt a soft thump on the other side of the door. She wondered if Alexander had done the same as she had, thrown his weight against the first available solid surface to keep him upright.

Rose stayed a moment longer, pressing her back to the painted wood, trying to convey her regret through the barrier to him. She allowed herself another breath, then she propelled herself into motion, away from regret and shame, towards Lady Nightingale and the bright, burning future that awaited her.

* * *

SHE WAS five minutes late for the meeting with Lady Nightingale and Mrs. Kensington, the woman who was helping plan the masquerade. Lady Nightingale had said Mrs. Kensington was the secret weapon in all the season's successful fetes. Her eye for detail, taste, and efficiency were impeccable.

It would look bad if she was late for such an important appointment. Rose hoped her tardiness would be forgiven once she handed over the stolen scroll.

Rose dashed through Lady Nightingale's front door and raced to the parlor, stopping halfway to extract the papers from her bodice, now damp with perspiration. Rose waved them in the air as she continued at a walk at a brisk pace, hoping to dry the scroll before handing it over to Lady Nightingale. She knocked firmly on the parlor doors and tried to catch her breath while continuing to wave the papers through the air.

Lady Nightingale herself opened the doors, just wide enough so that she could see Rose. She arched an eyebrow expectantly.

Rose held up the still-bound scroll of papers in front of her.

She was rewarded with a satisfied smile from her teacher, and the doors to the parlor swung open. Lady Nightingale took the scroll from her and whispered, "Well done."

Her cheeks flushed with pleasure. The swell of pride nearly eclipsed the deep cut of her guilt.

"Here she is now," Lady Nightingale said to the woman seated behind the lavish tea service.

Mrs. Kensington tapped a pen in her hand impatiently as Rose took a seat across from her. She clearly did not like being kept waiting.

Rose was slightly cowed by her brisk, business-like manner. Her blonde hair curled prettily at her temples, bobbing as she reviewed a leather-bound ledger clasped firmly in her hands. Her steely blue eyes were calculating and her tone authoritative as she quizzed Lady Nightingale about the mood for the evening, the number of guests, and desired entertainment.

Her pen was poised over her oversized book as she shared her latest recommendation with Lady Nightingale. "They are magnificent. Nothing like them has been seen in London this season. I have been the first to secure them. For no small price, I may add." Her eyes gleamed triumphantly.

"As this is the only ball I shall host this season, the expense is of no consequence," Lady Nightingale said, waving a dismissive hand.

"Lovely." Mrs. Kensington scribbled another note in her

ledger. "Now, for the unmasking. Guests will remove their masks at the stroke of midnight, then we will have the grand spectacle before the dancing continues for the evening."

"Miss Worthington will assist us with the midnight display," said Lady Nightingale.

Mrs. Kensington glanced up at Rose from her notes, her gaze assessing, calculating.

Rose clasped her hands together in her lap to keep from fidgeting beneath her discerning eye.

"And what sort of display were you thinking, your ladyship?"

"A countdown suspended in mid-air above the guests as the clock strikes midnight. The numbers will be made of fire."

Rose felt the color drain from her face. She knew her success with fire magic had only resulted from her heightened emotional states. To perform such a feat on demand would surely be impossible.

Mrs. Kensington raised her brows skeptically. "Your girls have pulled off some truly remarkable things in the past. Last year's peacocks were divine. But this sounds quite elaborate, even to me."

Lady Nightingale smiled, unbothered by her planner's lack of confidence. "Rose, be a dear and light the fireplace for me? I'm feeling a little chilled."

The room was comfortable. Warm spring air wafted through the open windows and buttery sunlight cast warm rays throughout the room. Rose knew that this was merely another test.

Rose drew a deep breath and closed her eyes. She focused on the patches sun and let the sensation of warmth fill her body. She searched her mind for the tether to her magic, relieved to find it quickly. It rested near the place in her chest that ached with remorse for what she had done to get those papers from Alexander. She grabbed hold of the tether and tugged, directing fire towards the dark hearth.

The sea of power was open to her, endless and sparkling. Rose fought to stem the overwhelming wave of magic as they built and built within her. She released one mental hand from the tether, lessening the flow of power. She didn't want to set the whole house on fire.

As she exhaled a long breath, Rose felt the logs in the hearth kindle and light, the blaze raising the temperature of the room instantly. Her chest, arms, and stomach pulsed. She released her magic, sad to let it go, and opened her eyes.

Mrs. Kensington gave a crisp nod. She jotted another note in her ledger, making distinct marks on the page.

Lady Nightingale waved a hand toward the mantle and extinguished the fire. It was too warm for such a blaze.

Rose smiled to herself as Mrs. Kensington continued to work. She had performed on command, and managed to not only tap into the power, but control it. If she could make it smaller, stem the flow of magic to meet her task, who was to say she could not make it larger if the occasion ever called for it? She would certainly be asked to become a Nightingale now. A proper witch. She had proven her worth, talent, and commitment flawlessly.

She couldn't wait to tell Harriet and Kate.

Her musings were interrupted as Mrs. Kensington swiveled the book to face Lady Nightingale and Rose. She'd drawn a grid of dots amidst the scribbled notes, shorthand Rose could not decipher. The most coveted event planner in London knew how to guard her secrets.

"These marks will represent candles that will be suspended on the wall, high enough so the guests will not detect them before it is time for them to be lit. Miss Worthington, you will light them in the proper formation in accordance with the countdown. Be sure not to leave them burning too long, though, lest they scorch the wallpaper." The thought of scorched wallpaper looked like it might do Mrs. Kensington in.

"Ingenious," Lady Nightingale beamed. "The next dance shall start at five minutes past midnight. This will leave time for the guests to marvel at one another's identities, or at least pretend to, and enjoy the spectacle."

Mrs. Kensington turned the ledger back around and jotting a few more notes in her coded shorthand.

"I believe this is all I need for the moment. I shall be in touch."

Lady Nightingale removed a vial of green liquid from her pocket and handed it to Mrs. Kensington, thanking her for her time.

Mrs. Kensington snapped the ledger closed, slid the vial into her pocket, and bid Rose and Lady Nightingale a good day.

"She's certainly an impressive woman," Rose remarked once Mrs. Kensington had left.

"She is the best at what she does. A pity she had no interest in magic. Though with her talents, she fares well enough without it. And I pay her well to keep our secrets. Year after year, all the other ladies clamor to know how our little spectacles are performed, but she can truthfully say that I buy her silence."

"And what happens when someone else has a better offer, or can pay more to have her divulge your secrets?" Rose asked. It seemed perilous to reveal so much about magic to someone who claimed to have no interest in it.

"The vial I gave her is one of the few tinctures that eases her husband's pain and slows his ailment from taking over the rest of his body. He suffers from a condition which has degenerated the use of his legs. Only I have the herbs in all of London to make it for her. She is intelligent and realizes that should she choose to divulge our secrets, her access to her husband's medicine will cease."

Rose bit her lip. What a terrible thing, to watch the one you care for suffer day after day. It was unsettling, the hold that

Lady Nightingale had over the woman. But Rose herself had just gone to great lengths to prove her loyalty and that she could keep their secrets. Mrs. Kensington willingly entered the agreement for her husband's treatment.

"She must love her husband very much," Rose said, more to herself than to her benefactress.

"Love is a powerful influence, Miss Worthington."

Something pulled at Rose's chest. She thought of Philip, and how he had still not answered her letter. Love. It was a powerful influence. She had been prepared to change her life for love, to run away and start anew with Philip. But then the plan had gone awry, and love had not been enough to save him. Or herself.

She thought of the pleasure of using her magic. The waves of pure power, the sheer vastness of it, made her feel so *alive*. Like she could do anything. She liked the control she felt when she used her magic, calling fire to ignite on her command. It felt warm and comforting, carrying the same weight that her love for Philip did. It made her in control and powerful.

"Magic is also a powerful influence," she said, gazing steadily at Lady Nightingale.

Her love for Philip could not prevent Cornelius from finding her a husband, or forbidding her to see people, or hurting her. Her love could not stop the trajectory of her life. She had tried that, and it had failed. This was her path now, to use magic to achieve her ends. Magic was the answer.

Lady Nightingale's round, smooth face was serious. "I think you begin to understand, Miss Worthington, what magic can do for you. And for us all."

Rose swallowed hard. A solid wall formed around the knife of regret and shame in her chest, blocking the pain.

Lady Nightingale's eyes softened as she studied her pupil. "Come," she said. "Let us practice your candle lighting for the party."

Rose nodded and helped Lady Nightingale fetch enough candles for their lesson.

*   *   *

AFTER TWO HOURS, Rose lit and extinguish all the candles, counting down from twelve to one. She was utterly exhausted. Lady Nightingale gave her much praise for how quickly she had learned to light and extinguish the little tapers. For some reason, it was more taxing to control the stream of power than to let herself open to it completely.

"Keep practicing, and you'll have no trouble dazzling us all at the ball," she said as Rose bade her farewell.

Harriet and Kate waited for her just down the hall. Rose smiled when she saw them, heads close together and whispering conspiratorially. Harriet snapped up at the sound of her approach, and she ran to close the distance between them. Kate followed at an easy pace behind her.

"You said you would tell us *everything*," reminded Harriet as she gripped Rose's hand.

"Of course, I will."

"The whole *ton* is talking about how Alexander Crawford took you to the opera last night." Harriet's eyes glowed with eagerness.

Rose groaned. "*Everyone* knows?"

"It was in the scandal sheets this morning," Kate supplied, bemused.

Icy dread pooled in her stomach. Cornelius would surely know her excursion with Alexander, then. There would be consequences for it.

"Your cousin is a horrible man," said Harriet softly.

Rose dropped her hand quickly, realizing that she had read her thoughts. "It's all right," Rose said dismissively.

Harriet tried to say more, but Kate interrupted her. "So, are you going to tell us how it went or not? I'm assuming you got what you needed since Lady Nightingale let you in."

Rose silently thanked Kate for shifting the conversation back to the drama of her task.

"I was. This masquerade is going to be spectacular," hinted Rose.

Harriet bounced with anticipation. "Tell us, tell us now!" But she paused, and Rose did not like the look that passed over the girl's face.

"Drat, Lady Templeton's coming. This way." She grabbed Rose and Kate's hands and ran down the hall before either of them could protest.

Rose was happy to delay the confrontation, no doubt waiting for at home, and to ignore the twisting pain of regret in her heart.

For now, she would tell Harriet and Kate all about the opera, her visit to the Crawford house, and the plans for the most anticipated party of the season.

CHAPTER 25

Rose could not delay the inevitable scolding from Cornelius forever.

After supper, he summoned her to his study. He sat behind the desk, fingers steepled. Rose stood in front of him. She felt like a child waiting to be reprimanded, and she loathed it. She'd gotten enough of that from Lady Templeton.

A scandal pamphlet lay open on his desk. No doubt there was talk of the wallflower *Miss W* cavorting with the esteemed *Lord C* at the opera. Rose cursed the gossips of this city.

Cornelius peered at her through the midnight black hair that fell into his eyes. His face had once again taken on a sallow look, throwing his cheekbones into stark relief. He had dark circles under his eyes. He looked like he wasn't sleeping or eating properly at all. It was unsettling.

"I thought we had come to an understanding about your dalliance with Lord Crawford," said Cornelius.

"Is that why you've summoned me to be scolded like a child?" A muscle feathered in her jaw. Rose willed it to relax. She did not want Cornelius to see how much he bothered her.

His dark eyes held hers. "You are not a child," he said softly, his voice a cool caress.

A strange tingle crept up her chest to her lips. The feeling felt inexplicably wrong. She crossed her arms and tore her eyes away from his, trying her best to shrug off the peculiar sensation.

"Then do not presume to treat me like one. You may be lord of the estate, but you are not lord over me."

Cornelius sighed heavily. "Can we not have a simple conversation without you biting my head off?"

He sounded defeated and tired. Rose uncrossed her arms and looked at him, really *looked* at him. His shoulder sagged with weariness, his thin fingers trembled, and his hair was flat and dull. He did not look well at all. She wondered what had caused the change in his health. But her anger and loathing for the man seated across from her clouded all else. He had hurt Philip, and he questioned why she couldn't stand him?

Heat bloomed in her cheeks, and she bared her teeth. "You may have everyone in all of London fooled, including my mother, but I know your true character. I know you are a cruel, possessive man who wants nothing more than to be rid of me. You delight in using what little power you have to make my life miserable. So, no. I will not deign to engage in civil conversation with you." The words singed her tongue as if laced with frothing magic.

At her utterance, Cornelius straightened his posture. His dark eyes glittered ominously. He looked like a different man than the one who had been sitting before her moments ago. Gone was the deflated, sickly countenance. A cold, cruel one had taken its place, though he appeared physically unchanged.

"You are forbidden from ever seeing Alexander Crawford again," he hissed. "Should I hear of you keeping any company with him, I will find someone for you to marry *immediately.* There is already one man who has offered to take you."

The bubbling of magic simmered beneath her skin. She knew without question that she could use the magic easily. Rose felt the powerful vibrations within her and slammed a mental door against it. Cornelius could not know about her power. No one could. She needed to leave the study. Now. Before she lost control.

"Fine," she snapped.

Cornelius cocked his head distrustfully, as if he sensed the magic that fluttered in her veins. His nostrils flared. "You agree to these terms?"

Rose swallowed hard. "Yes." She clenched her fists. All her focus was directed on keeping that mental door closed. Her nails bit into her palms. She focused on the pain.

"Very well," he said. He picked up a pen and slid a piece of paper into the center of the desk. "You may go."

She forced herself to close the door softly, despite every instinct telling her to slam it shut and run, run, *run*. She marched down the long corridor towards the main stairs and slowly eased her hold on the mental door of magic.

The candles on the sconces flared as she walked past them, growing bright as she passed before fading to their usual mild glow. Each time a candle flared with sudden light, she felt the demanding pulse of magic lessen. By the time she had reached her bedroom suite, the bubbling magic had faded until it lay silent, asleep for the time being.

* * *

THE NEXT DAY, Rose found a small package waiting for her at tea. A bracelet of black sapphires was nestled in an intricately carved box with a note.

Miss Worthington,

Please accept this bracelet as a prize for your latest demonstration. You are a perceptive student who takes instruction well. I am looking forward to further displays of your progress at the annual Nightingale Masquerade Ball (invitation enclosed). Proper commitment to one's studies opens many doors.

Yours sincerely,

Lady Hana Nightingale

Rose beamed and examined the bracelet more closely. It looked like an ordinary piece of jewelry, but felt oddly warm to her touch, particularly the larger stone at the bracelet's center. She strapped it to her wrist, fiddling with the clasp impatiently.

Her mother marveled at the lavishness of the gift. "I confess, I am eager to witness what demonstrations she is talking about," she said after reading the note.

Rose knew the bracelet was enchanted. She could feel a warm pulse of magic within the stones. They buzzed pleasantly at her touch, calling out to the magic within her own blood. She studied the last line of Lady Nightingale's note. A clue to the bracelet's function was contained within. Her mother would read it as nothing more than praise for her attention to lessons in decorum, but Rose scrutinized the lines for the second meaning.

Opens many doors.

An unlocking bracelet. That had to be it.

"Rose, did you hear me?" asked her mother, interrupting her thoughts.

"Sorry?" she snapped her head up, releasing the bracelet. It lay heavily on her wrist.

"Cornelius was not too harsh? I explained to him it is perfectly within the rules for you to accept an invitation extended by Lord Crawford, but I do not think he felt the same as I did. He does not see the potential for you that I do."

The walls of resolve she had put up around that wound in her chest held firm. "Cornelius was displeased. As a result, I have informed Lord Crawford that our private outings must end."

Her mother dropped her teaspoon. It hit her saucer with a deafening clatter. "You did no such thing."

Rose's eyebrows shot up at the sound, uncharacteristic for her mother, who usually remained so calm and collected. "You actually thought I had a chance of marrying him, didn't you?" She laughed and shook her head.

"It is no laughing matter. I have told you, time is of the essence, and Lord Crawford—"

"—is engaged to Miss Hawthorne," finished Rose. "It wasn't appropriate for us to spend that much time together. Cornelius was right about that."

"I have said it before. Betrothed is not engaged, Rose."

Rose pushed away her small plate of cucumber sandwiches. She wasn't hungry anymore. "Cornelius would have never allowed it. He cares too much for what they all think of him," said Rose in a low voice. She didn't want any of the staff reporting her slander back to her cousin. "And *I* see Lord Crawford as a friend."

Her mother had not picked up her teaspoon. Drops of milky tea dripped onto the pristine white cloth, staining it. "I am going to say something to you, honestly and directly, because you are my daughter, and you need to hear it," she said with calm resolve.

An icy shiver traveled from her head to her toes, as if her mother had dumped a bucket of ice water over her.

"You are letting your *fear* get in the way of your life."

Rose scoffed. "I'm not afraid of anything."

Her mother held up her hand, silencing her. "You are afraid of getting too close to those you care about. *Yes*, you are. I see it. I watch how you refuse to interact with others at balls and parties, how you shut down anyone who shows the slightest interest in forming an attachment with you. You are getting in your own way, and you cannot afford to do so any longer."

Rose was numb. Her mother's criticism was scathing, and

simply untrue. She had no idea what she had been doing during her days at Lady Nightingale's estate. She was making friends. She had Harriet and Kate.

She *hated* large crowds, loud rooms, and feeling like she was on display, but she danced at parties with Alexander, and suffered through forced, meaningless conversations with her mother and other vapid members of the social elite. She should have been enraged at this attack on her person, but she only felt a cold detachment. Her mother knew *nothing* of who she truly was. How could she, when they were so different? When she had *magic* pulsing within her every heartbeat, which now screamed at her to be let free.

Her teacup her shook on its saucer, rattling.

Rose found the mental door and slammed it shut, bracing with two hands. It was becoming more difficult to keep the bubbling power contained within herself. The teacup stilled.

"I'm sorry you're disappointed," said Rose wearily. "But Cornelius made his feelings clear. Speak with him, not me."

She dismissed herself from the table. She half expected her mother to call after her, but she did not.

Rose clutched the arm with the sapphire bracelet to her chest, cradling its heavy warmth. She let her feet carry her where they willed. She felt detached from her own body. Her mind was too focused on keeping the raw power within her from escaping.

After a minute, she blinked, finally able to release her grip on the mental door without feeling like her power would explode from her. She found herself at Cornelius's study door. She still cradled the bracelet, which now pulsed fervently under her fingers.

With her unadorned hand, she reached for the handle and twisted it. The door was locked. Cornelius had taken to his bed today. She didn't expect to see him.

She pulled on the handle again, but it did not budge. Perhaps he had changed the lock. Rose reached for the door again, this time with the hand where dark sapphires sparkled. The stones flared hot for a moment, and the tumblers gave way. The door swung open.

Rose was right. It was an unlocking bracelet.

She entered the study and helped herself to two generous gulps of brandy from the near-full decanter. She sat on the floor, cradled her head in her arms, and closed her eyes as the room swayed.

CHAPTER 26

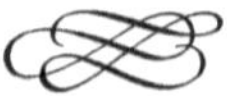

*L*ady Nightingale's masquerade ball was the most highly anticipated events of the season.

In the nights leading up to the masquerade, Rose laid out a grid of candles on her bedroom floor. She practiced lighting them, creating the numbers twelve, eleven, ten, and so on until she could do so with ease. Rose stumbled the first night of practice and had allowed the power to pour through her too strongly. She nearly set her bed linens on fire.

Once she realized it took only a tiny stream of magic to light the candles, she had much more success, even though containing the magic was far more taxing than letting it burn through her.

During the day, Rose and her mother made several flurried trips to the modiste to order adequate clothing. Dress shops took on a festive atmosphere, and shop owners often served tea as ladies waited their turn for fittings. Gossip was rampant. Girls and their mothers snubbed Rose plainly at first, especially in the days after the gossip sheet detailing her outing with Lord Crawford was published. A day later, however, a countess was caught in a pantry with her husband's groomsman. Rose's own scandal was quickly forgotten.

Rose and her mother did not speak of their most recent quarrel. Both were content to pretend that it had never happened. Instead, they directed their energies to the ever-important matter of dresses and accessories. They purchased intricate masks to cover their faces. Rose chose a black mask with silver gems to complement the dark sapphire bracelet Lady Nightingale had given her. In candlelight, the gems on the mask looked like tiny stars that had been plucked from the night sky. Rose had taken to leaving the mask out on her dressing table at night so that she might look at it while she practiced her candle magic.

Until now, Rose had been unconcerned with her wardrobe. Perhaps it was because the ball was Lady Nightingale's, or because she knew she would have a part to play in the night's festivities, but she felt inclined to choose a gown that made her feel special. Which is why the dress she selected for the night's fete differed from anything else she owned. Her mother had, unsurprisingly, found the color of Rose's dress to be too dark, but Rose had insisted on it. As it was the first time Rose had taken any sort of interest in her wardrobe this season, her mother had reluctantly allowed Rose to wear the gown.

As she slipped on the dress the night of the party, Rose felt as if she were draped in the night sky itself. The soft fabric of the gown shifted from the deepest blue to black when she moved. Tiny embroidered silver stars cascaded down the bodice and skirt. Beads and small gems added extra sparkle. The sheer cap sleeves were also embellished with silver gems, matching the ones in her mask. Rose felt beautiful as she studied her reflection in the mirror, fluffing the skirts.

She held her mask in place over her nose as Betsy tied its velvet black ribbon to secure it. A matching ribbon adorned her neck, and she slid black gloves up to her elbows. Her sapphire bracelet was the last addition to her ensemble.

"If every man at that party does not trip over himself to dance with you tonight, then they're all idiots," said Betsy. "You look beautiful, Miss."

Rose could only manage to flash a small, appreciative smile. Her stomach writhed with nerves.

Betsy held the back of her dress for her as she descended the stairs to the foyer. Her mother and cousin waited at the foot of the stairs. Cornelius wore a black evening waistcoat and white gloves. He wore the bronze fox mask Rose had selected for him. She thought it had been the most fitting for his personality.

Tonight, Cornelius offered his arm to Rose instead of her mother to escort her to their carriage. Rose took it reluctantly and kept her gaze fixed in front of her. She could sense that he was in an amiable mood, but knew it was only temporary. He could flip the switch of his personality at any time. She didn't want to be around when he did.

They arrived at the party fashionably late, which is to say they arrived at the time everyone else did. The night was a warm. The Worthingtons stood on the grand steps to Lady Nightingale's house to await admittance. It was odd to see so many people and so much light about the house she had been such a frequent visitor of on quiet afternoons.

As it was a masquerade ball, there was no formal receiving line. Everyone milled about the grand ballroom in their elegant face coverings and costumes, some of which were more elaborate, and scandalous, than others. Most of the mamas wore evening gowns with simple masks decorated sparingly with flowers or jewels. Rose spotted Effie Crawford in a revealing Roman goddess costume. Her circlet of golden laurel leaves looked stunning against her brown skin and ice-blonde hair.

Rose craned her neck to scan the ballroom that was growing more crowded by the second. Alexander was nowhere in sight.

Neither was Harriet, or Kate, who had said they would both be attending the party tonight. All the Nightingales would be here. Rose was also intrigued to see that a flurry of footmen milled about the party, carrying trays of sparkling champagne, taking cloaks, and seeing to the needs of the guests. She wondered where Lady Nightingale had found such a retinue of them, and what would happen once the ball had ended.

Once Rose and her mother were safely deposited on a far wall, Cornelius left to find the gentleman's room, probably for a round of cards or to drink his brandy in peace. Rose wasn't sure when the last time he actually danced was.

As he left, she asked her mother, "Why do you think Cornelius is not dancing, or trying to find a suitable wife at these parties?"

"Who can say? He certainly is of marriageable age, but perhaps he is not quite ready to settle down. He did just arrive in England after all."

Her mother's hand, which had been resting lightly on her own as they surveyed the attendees, stiffed. "Lord Reeves. What a pleasure to see you here tonight." She forced a polite smile.

Rose groaned inwardly. She thanked the powers that Percival Reeves was too old and feeble to dance. He was wearing a hideous Henry the VIII costume, forgoing a mask.

"Miss Worthington. You will take the air with me in the garden tonight?"

It was barely a question. Apparently, he was not taking part in the farce of hidden identities tonight.

"I'm sure you shall grow weary of standing here against the wall all evening. These ballrooms tend to get a bit stuffy after a while," Lord Reeves drawled on.

The insult registered and Rose's face grew hot. She was about to open her mouth and say something she knew she would regret when she heard Alexander's voice over her left shoulder

"There you are, Miss Worthington. I've been looking for you."

He looked handsome in his evening attire. He wore a golden mask decorated with two horses at each temple and a lyre at the center. Dark, strong lines encircled the eyes and brow. Alexander was the Roman soldier to his sister's goddess. The piece enhanced his strong jaw and bright blue eyes. The overall effect was striking.

"A legionnaire emerges to do battle on the dance floor," teased Rose, ignoring Lord Reeve's presence. Her heart fluttered gently against her ribs, soft as a butterfly.

Alexander flashed a genuine smile. "You'll have to excuse me, my lord. I must ask Miss Worthington to dance before her card is filled for the evening."

"Yes, well. I shall take your company later, then." Reeves shuffled off to find another pretty young girl to entice into the gardens.

"Well, Miss Worthington? Would you do me the honor of your first dance?"

"Of course," said Rose, extending her card. She felt the sour tang of regret rise. She hadn't wanted to forsake their friendship. Rose was glad he was acting as if nothing had changed. But she knew that she'd hurt him. It pained her more than she thought it would.

Alexander returned the card after penciling his name. "You look lovely this evening, Lady Worthington."

"You are sweet," said her mother, patting her hair and blushing.

Rose fought to keep the bemusement at her mother's girlish behavior from her expression. A jolt thumped against the walls she had erected around her heart, cracking them. The knife of regret she had plunged into her own chest twisted, but she did not allow herself to feel it.

The musicians halted their soft tune as Lady Nightingale

took center stage on a dais at the front of the room. Her costume was that of an elegant peacock. Large, delicate plumes of feathers arched gracefully from one side of her mask. It complemented the deep shades of emerald and amethyst in her gown. She stood, waiting for the attention of her guests. It did not take long before every eye in the room was drawn to her.

Her warm, inviting voice filled the air once silence had settled over the party. "I would like to thank you all for attending this year's masquerade. Your identities are your own until the strike of twelve. Then, all shall be unmasked." She scanned the room, meeting each guest's eyes.

Something flickered in Rose's peripheral vision as Lady Nightingale continued to survey the room. Two pairs of girls in black form-fitting trousers and shirts entered the room on either side. They each wore matching black masks set upon their faces, and their hair was knotted in slick, tight buns. They looked as if they were exact copies of one another. The overall effect was impressive, if not a little eerie.

"To begin tonight's festivities, I have invited friends from the bohemian quarters of our city to entertain us with a performance." The lights dimmed until only a soft amber glow remained. Candles near the edges of the room were left alight, framing an area of floor space where each pair of performers stood still as statues.

"Looks like no peacocks this year," whispered Alexander as the audience hummed excitedly in the dimming light.

Rose huffed a soft laugh through her nose. She was tempted to jab him in the side, but thought better of it. Party guests pressed close on all sides, and she didn't want anyone getting the wrong impression, especially after her recent appearances in the gossip pamphlets.

The musicians began a slow, sensual melody full of reverberating bass and cello as each girl took up their position, a perfect mirror of each other from across the room. Footmen brought out large iron hoops, each one as tall as the girls. The performers stood inside their hoops, hands gasping the outer rim. Then, they twirled inside their rings, whipping in dizzying circles and traveling across the floor.The music increased in fervor as the performers spun around each other in an intricate, gravity-defying dance.

The crowd gasped in delight as the girls rotated around one another, turning upside down and right-side up again as the metal hoops spun. One girl pressed herself into a tiny ball and let the force of her hoop take her around and around. Just when it looked like she might fall due to the ring's slowing tempo, she unfurled herself to swing right-side up again.

Each stunt was more daring than the last. The hoops traveled around the entire perimeter of the ballroom. The guests clustered closer to the center of the floor to allow the performers more berth for their tricks.

Rose watched with wide eyes. The level of physical skill and coordination it took to swing around like that was remarkable. She briefly tore her eyes away to scan the crowd. They were awed and enraptured. A soft smile danced at the corners of her lips. If they were impressed now, she couldn't wait to see the looks on their faces at midnight.

Rose dared a glance at the ceiling, where the candles attached to the wall, waiting for her to light them. She longed to tap into the sea of magic that she had been dipping into for the past few days. She had grown more confident in stemming the tidal wave of power into a small trickle, only enough to light the wicks of small tapers with. Rose wondered what would happen if instead of stemming the tide, she opened herself up to the lovely expanse of magic she knew lay within and around her.

A warm pulse radiated through her chest, making her fingers tingle. Rose steadied herself, resting the urge to let the magic pour through her. She took a deep breath,, letting her ribcage expand as far as it could within the confines of her dress.

Alexander threaded his fingers through hers, sliding his gloved hand into her satin-clad one with ease. His palm was warm and steadying. Their hands rested in the folds of her billowing skirts, concealed by the fabric and their bodies.

Heat that had nothing to do with the magic bloomed in Rose's cheeks, but she did not let go of Alexander's hand.

As the music reached its final crescendo, each hoop dancer met at the center of the room in front of the dais. Still within their metal rings, they held hands and became one giant spinning wheel. They looked like the petals of a flower, unfurling and shrinking in on each other. With a last flourish, they dismounted and took a bow, hoops clattering to the ground gracefully behind them.

The crowd erupted into enthusiastic applause.

Alexander withdrew his hand from hers, and they joined the crowd's clapping. A small note of disappointment reverberated through Rose, like the fading of a single note plucked on a harp string.

Footmen scurried about the room, relighting candles, though not all of them were rekindled. The lights were dim enough to lend a mysterious air to the room, but it was not so dark to break the rules of propriety.

"Wasn't that splendid?" Rose asked.

"Very impressive," Alexander agreed. "I believe the first dance is about to begin. Shall we?"

Rose nestled her hand in the crook of his elbow as Alexander led the way to the dance floor.

They passed Effie on their way to a more secluded corner. Though she was surrounded by a gaggle of young gentlemen, Rose could feel her icy glare on her back as they retreated to a quieter spot. She felt little remorse for being seen with Alexander. After all, she had said nothing about not associating with

Alexander in public, just that they wouldn't have any more private outings.

"Don't pay any mind to her," Alexander said, noting the stiffness that had settled over Rose as they walked past his sister. "She'll be so preoccupied with entrapping her next batch of potential suitors that she won't have any time for her usual tricks this evening."

"You think so?" Effie's glare had suggested otherwise.

"Oh, yes. We have a wager. I bet she would dance with no one higher in rank than a viscount. There are several earls present, though two of them are already married. I do not believe the Marquess of Devonshire is in attendance this evening, so her choices will be rather limited."

Rose took her place across from Alexander. "And what did she bet you?"

A wry smile crossed Alexander's lips. "Absolutely nothing. I suppose it was more of a challenge than a bet."

"And what do you win should your sister fail to dance with a duke this evening?"

His face flashed serious for a moment. "She will leave me to dance with whomever I wish for the rest of the season, and not be able to say a word about it."

"She must be very confident in her abilities," said Rose. She knew that probably meant a great deal to him, considering he had sought her out again, even after their most recent meeting.

"I daresay she is. But it's a risk I'm willing to take."

The music started before Rose could reply.

* * *

THE FIRST HALF of the evening passed pleasantly. Rose was able to speak with both Harriet and Kate, but only briefly. Harriet complained that she would be forced to return home shortly after midnight, as she wasn't yet formally out in society. Kate had said hello before wandering off to another corner of the ballroom, where a tall, attractive man with rich, umber skin commanded her attention. Rose was still under instructions not to appear too friendly with the other girls who studied under Lady Nightingale, much to her regret.

Rose grew more anxious as time marched towards empty lines on her dance card. The idea of being forced into taking the air with Lord Reeves became a genuine concern. The musicians announced they would return after a brief interlude. Rather than engage in forced conversation with her mother, or make herself available for Lord Reeves, Rose found her way to the balcony.

A cool breeze gusted, refreshing her and billowing her skirts. The tiny gems on her gown glittered like the stars in the night sky above her. Rose tipped up her chin and inhaled deeply. Potted plants and benches had been placed upon the terrace to provide quiet corners where couples could converse in privacy. Or, if they were daring, steal a kiss or two.

Rose pressed herself into one of the quiet corners, hiding from couples who had also taken the air. Soft sparks of gold shimmered in the breeze, settling in her clothes and hair. They smelled of wood shavings and cool water on a hot summer's day. Kate's enchanted plants must be nearby.

As she stated at the twinkling sky, Rose was reminded of Philip and of the night they shared in the glen, watching stars emerge in silence. Back then, her grief had been lessened by his companionship. Now, it was the absence of him that caused her heartache.

The grief in her heart came and went as it pleased, like a monster she could not control. The walls she had built up around her sadness inexplicably weakened in odd moments. Rather than fight it the sudden onset of despair, Rose leaned into the stone railing that still carried warmth from the bright sunshine it had absorbed during the day. She peered down into the gardens and wondered idly, in a speculative sort of way, what would happen if she jumped from the balcony. How long would it take for the revelers inside to notice a sad little wallflower lying broken in the gardens?

She shook her head, clearing the thought. A heavy weight still pressed firmly down upon her. So heavy, she barely had the strength to stand. She leaned into the stone, letting her sadness wash over her.

A loud clock chimed eleven, reaching through the stillness of the moment, and Rose's stomach flipped. The test of her abilities would be in an hour. She thought about running away to hide in the ladies' retiring room until it was time for her display, but knew that solitude would not cure her melancholy. Besides, she needed to focus if she was going to pass her test. She would not disappoint Lady Nightingale.

Rose pushed off from the balcony and forced herself to return to the crowded ballroom. As she stepped through the wide French doors, a stranger in a white mask and hooded cape approached her.

Though he was not quite a stranger. Rose was certain they had met before. She searched for some clue who he might be, but he kept his gaze lowered. He was very shy, or intent on concealing his identity.

"Might I have a dance?" he asked in a low, gruff voice.

"Of course." Rose handed over her dance card, too intrigued to say no. The stranger took it in his white-gloved hands and scribbled a name. Then he vanished into the crowd as quickly as he'd appeared.

Rose examined her card. *Pike* was all he had written. It was a common enough name that Rose didn't know who it could have been. Besides, some gentlemen were using fake names this evening, in keeping with the ruse of the masquerade. Although those names were things like *Julius Caesar* and *a Priest*.

Her next dance of the evening was reserved for Lord Langley, then she would dance with the mysterious Pike. As she scanned the ballroom for her next partner, Rose spied her mother chatting with Lord and Lady Crawford near the refreshments. Lady Clarke had also inserted herself into the conversation. She wondered what on earth they could be talking about. She suspected that it was her. Cornelius, unsurprisingly, had not emerged from the gentleman's card room. She was thankful for that, at least.

The younger, pimply Langley brother finally emerged and escorted Rose to the floor for their dance.

Halfway through the song, Rose's gaze snagged on Alexander. He danced with a beautiful young woman with honey-colored hair and cheeks as pink as strawberries. She wore fairy wings and a circlet of glittering jewels. Her ethereal beauty was only enhanced by her fairy queen costume. From the way she kept her eyes trained on his face, Rose knew that this must be Cecelia Hawthorne.

A surge of bitterness crashed within Rose, the same acrid feeling that had risen in her throat when she saw Caroline flirting with Philip at their dinner party a lifetime ago. She bit her lip, startled by the strength of her jealousy, and did her best to squash it.

Lord Langley spun her around, turning her to face the opposite side of the room. Effie was taking a rare break on the sidelines of the dancing. She gazed toward her brother, her lips gently parted and eyes sparkling.

The dance ended with a flourish of violins. Rose quickly disentangled herself from Lord Langley's arms. She fanned herself as she walked to a table in search of water. Grabbing a goblet full, she pressed herself into a corner and sipped. She relished the feeling of the cold liquid running down her throat. But she did not have long before the stranger in the mask approached.

Rose smiled, but the stranger kept his face stoic. He wordlessly extended his hand, and she placed her palm over his. Another jolt of familiarity swept through her at the touch. They took their places opposite one another and waited for the music to begin. Rose was finally close enough to be able to study the man's face, or what she could see of it given that he was wearing a mask and kept his hood up. He refused to meet her eyes, glancing over her head or towards the musicians.

The first notes filled the room. Rose placed her hand in his once more and noticed that his glove stretched tightly over his fingers. Her breath hitched as her partner placed his hand firmly on the small of her back, guiding her through the dance. The feeling of his hand was so familiar. As they spun around a corner, the man's hood shifted back to reveal the russet brown hair beneath.

Rose's throat grew unbearably tight. Her heart leapt in her chest, and she tripped, losing the beat and steps of the dance. The stranger glanced down to steady her, and Rose could finally look into his forest green eyes.

Her heart froze, and her hearing became fuzzy, as if she'd been plunged underwater. Her lips were numb as she said his name.

"Philip."

CHAPTER 27

*D*isbelief clouded Rose's thoughts as Philip pulled her to the balcony. Her heart pounded in her chest, pulsing all the way to her palms. When they reached in the farthest corner of the veranda, surrounded by greenery and shielded from prying eyes, Philip turned to her.

"I've been looking everywhere for you."

Philip's tawny brown hair and the set of his broad shoulders were unmistakable, even in the moonlight. How could she not have recognized him immediately? Rose felt as if she were watching her own body from somewhere far away as she tried to make sense of the fact that Philip was standing before her. She took a step towards him with her fingers outstretched. She couldn't get enough air in her lungs.

He slid the mask off his face. "Hello, Rose." His voice was tight with emotion.

Tears slid silently down Rose's cheeks. "I thought you were dead," she whispered.

Philip's brow furrowed. "Dead? No, love, I'm not dead."

Something cracked inside Rose's chest. Her body shuddered

with great, gasping sobs. She reached both arms towards him, and Philip stepped into her embrace.

He crushed her to his chest. Rose inhaled deeply, the scent of him overwhelming her. He smelled like home.

They stood, arms wrapped fiercely around each other, for several long moments. Rose savored the feeling of Philip's body pressed tightly to her own. She relished his warmth, the sound of his breath, not caring that they might be spotted.

Finally, Philip stepped back and tilted her face up, delicately gripping her chin. She still wore her mask of midnight stars. She tugged the ribbon at the back of her head, letting it fall from her face.

"You're alive," she breathed.

Philip swept his thumb slowly up and down her jawline.

"Did you get my letter? Is that how you knew to come?" Rose's voice quavered.

Philip shook his head, clearing his throat. "No, I must have missed it. I arrived two weeks ago. I've been trying to find you ever since."

Two weeks. Philip had been in London for two *weeks*. "Where? How?" She couldn't form more complicated questions.

"Charlie's uncle lives on the east side. He's been letting me stay there, helping me track down where you were. He even gave me this," Philip gestured to his evening suit and cape, "in exchange for work, of course."

Rose shook her head. Philip was *here*. "Cornelius told me you were dead. That he killed you."

Philip frowned as he held up one of his right palm, his glove stretched tightly over it. "He shot my hand. It's nearly healed, but it hurt like hell."

Rose took it gently between her own and placed a gentle kiss on his gloved palm. "It's all my fault. I'm so sorry."

"It's not your fault," he said.

"Yes, it is. I never should have agreed to run away with you in the first place. I knew Cornelius was angry, but I never thought he would do anything to harm you."

The hurt in Philip's eyes confused her. "What?" she asked.

"You wish you hadn't agreed to run away with me?"

"Yes," Rose said, voice climbing. "I didn't say I didn't *love* you. I only wish this had never happened."

Philip grabbed Rose's other hand with his uninjured one and pulled her close. "Would you run away with me again? Tonight?"

Rose stared into his warm green eyes, steeling herself for what she had to say. "Not after what happened last time." She wanted to protect Philip from any further harm. If Cornelius had no qualms about shooting his hand, who knows what he might do the next time he had the chance? This time, he might actually kill him.

But it was more than that. A selfish part of her knew she couldn't run away. Rose still had much to learn from Lady Nightingale. She had tasted magic and could never return to a life where she didn't have it. Rose *finally* had the means to shape her own future. She had barely scratched the surface of what she might do. Rose had gone through so much already to prove that she was worthy of it. How could she leave that behind?

If she stayed, she would continue to learn to control her power and use it to her advantage. She knew she could do so much more than clever party tricks. With magic, she could forge a future where she and Philip could be together without fear.

"I can't let anything happen to you because of me," Rose said.

"I came all this way to find you. To be with you," Philip said gruffly.

Rose brushed her fingertips across his face as the fissure in her chest cracked wider. "I still want to be with you."

Philip's mouth was on hers before she could draw breath. He kissed her fiercely, and she kissed him back with all that was in her. She poured herself into the kiss. She tasted relief, regret, and longing in its intensity. Her breath quickened when he parted her lips with his tongue. His lips caressed her jaw and her throat, moving sensuously down her neck. She felt like she had drunk too much. Her head swam with pleasure at the sensation of his lips on her bare skin.

His hands were all over her, everywhere at once. She could feel how much he wanted her, and her legs trembled. A demanding heat bloomed between her thighs, one she had never felt before. She ground her hips into his, the thin fabric of her dress bunching between them. Philip inhaled sharply and trailed more kisses down her neck. He moaned her name over and over like a prayer.

Rose closed her eyes, savoring the sensation of his touch, not fully understanding the strange desires bubbling within her. A small, rational part of her mind knew it was reckless. Anyone could walk by and see them. The *ton* was always watching. She wondered how easily they could escape into the secluded garden.

She lifted her chin, ready to ask him to follow her into the dark, but another voice pierced through the haze of her desire.

"Get your hands off her." Alexander Crawford stood at the edge of the plants, his feet planted shoulder width apart and his jaw set in a hard line.

Rose extricated herself from Philip's touch and smoothed her dress.

"Mind your own business," Philip growled. He stepped in front of Rose to shield her, but she batted him out of the way.

"I'm fine, Alexander." Rose smoothed her hair. She was painfully aware of how swollen her lips were. She had to stop herself from touching them.

"Oh, really? What if someone else saw you? My sister, perhaps? She would love to use this to ruin you." He removed his golden mask. Exasperation etched deep lines into his face.

"Do you know him, Rose?" Philip asked, not bothering to conceal his irritation at the interruption.

Rose sighed. "Lord Crawford, this is Mr. Harlow. Philip, this is Alexander Crawford. He's my friend."

The two glowered at one another.

Rose's patience grew thin. They were behaving like school children, or cats caught in an alleyway brawl. "Oh, for heaven's sake. I'm permitted to have two male friends." She threw her hands up in exasperation.

"Forgive me, Miss Worthington, but it would appear you are much more than *friends* with Mr. Harlow here." A flicker of sadness crossed Alexander's face, barely concealed beneath his agitated countenance.

"If we're *friends*, Rose, I wonder exactly what you have been doing with Lord Crawford," Philip spat.

Rose felt a stinging humiliation, as if Philip had slapped her. The shock of his words pulsed through her.

Tension crackled in the air between the three of them. Philip and Alexander stared daggers at one another, leaving her unmoored. Heartache pulsed through her, rattling the barrier around her magic. What once had been so hard for her to access now wanted to tumble out all at once. A jolt of pain , sharp and jagged as lightning, rocked through her, making her inhale sharply through her nose. She was angry, and hurt, and sad. And she could damn well kiss whomever she liked whenever she liked.

She turned to Philip with tears in her eyes. "You have no *idea* what it has been like for me these past few weeks. *None.*"

She could not believe he thought she'd been *dallying* with another man. And to accuse her of doing so with such contempt in his voice? She couldn't fathom it.

Magic pulsed beneath her skin, vibrating at her fingertips. A harsh gale blew, knocking one of the potted plants over and shattering the vase. Power thrummed in her chest, her palms, her fingertips. It threatened to burst out of her. She couldn't control it.

Rose ran, shoving past the two men.

"Rose, I didn't mean it, I swear," said Philip through gritted teeth as she bumped into his shoulder, the heat of him settling into her skin like a brand.

"Miss Worthington, come back!"

Rose hurtled down the stone steps, skirts billowing behind her as the wind gusted again. She reached the bottom of the stairs and grabbed the flowing skirts of her dress in both hands. She ignored the sound of Philip and Alexander's footsteps on the stone staircase, chasing after her. Magic continued to thrum in her veins.

She ran into the cool dark of the garden, leaving the warm light of the party behind. Rose sprinted around tall hedges and down narrow paths that twisted within each other, that seemed to extend, grow, and change as she ran. She took a left fork and slowed to a jog before nestling into the shadows of a stone statue, catching her breath. In the dark, Rose could just make out the form of the statue, a robed female playing a small harp.

After scanning the path to ensure she was truly alone, Rose opened her palm. She let the burn of magic sear through her until it became fire. An orb of flame hovered above her hand and burned. Slowly, the ache behind her eyes and in her temples faded. Rose closed her hand and extinguished the flame. The magic calmed, shifting from its frenetic boiling to a gentle simmer.

She slumped in relief, glad she'd learned to recognize when her magic was about to cause destruction. Rose took stock of her situation. It was foolish to run off, but she couldn't bring herself to face Philip and Alexander, or risk her magic escaping for them to see. Lady Nightingale had demanded secrecy. She couldn't jeopardize her trust. Rose rested her head against the stone statue and closed her eyes.

They both had acted like complete idiots. How could Philip think that of her? He assumed she would move on so easily with her life after believing her childhood friend, the first man she ever loved, to be dead.

She paced around the statue, irritation making her head pound.

Alexander had no right to interrupt, either. His idea of honor demanded that he do so. He would have done the same for any unmarried woman. But the sadness in his eyes. . .

Yes, they were complete idiots.

She didn't have time for this. Philip was alive, and she should spend every moment she could with him. Besides, it must be close to midnight. She needed to be in the ballroom. Rose tied her mask around her eyes and set off for the manor.

The crunch of gravel on the path a few hedges over made her freeze. She crouched and pressed herself into the shadows.

"Miss Worthington?" hissed Alexander.

"Rose!" Philip shouted.

"Be *quiet*. If anyone finds out that she was out here alone with two men, she is ruined."

Philip snorted. "As if she cared one bit about her reputation with you lot."

"You may not care about it, Mr. Harlow, but I certainly do. If anyone suspected she was dallying with you, no one would want to marry her. Her prospects would dwindle to nothing."

"The thing about Rose, though, is that she isn't ever going to marry. She's told me a thousand times."

"Are you sure she wasn't just talking about you?"

Rose could feel the thick tension in the air from where she listened.

"Give me one good reason why I shouldn't break your jaw right now."

The gravel shifted. She debated making her presence known, just to prevent harm from coming to either of them. She held her breath for a moment longer, ready to step into the moon-light if they should come to blows.

"Because," said Alexander exasperatedly, "you'll need help to get back into the party undetected. Once we find Miss Worthington, we'll come up with a way to get you both back inside with no one being the wiser about your absence. Her honor will remain intact, and you can leave."

"I'm not going anywhere. Rose is leaving with me. Tonight."

"Is that so? And where will you go? What kind of life can you offer her? Her family will hunt you down and have you hanged. London is not as big as you might think. It will not be hard to find you."

"And you think she'll agree to marry you, is that it? You don't even know her."

"I don't recall mentioning that I was planning to propose to her." Alexander sighed. "Look, we could do this all night, but someone else could be wandering the gardens. If they find her before we do, it will not end well."

"Let's split up then," Philip said, irritation tightening his voice. "I'll take this path. You take the other. If we don't find her in ten minutes, meet back here."

"Fine."

They parted ways, their plans set. She waited a full minute before extracting herself and setting off down the path. She did not need them looking after her as if she were a child.

She walked back towards the buzz of the party. The night was clear, and the air warm. The moon was nearly full and glowed with pale, silver light. Rose straightened her dress as she walked. The fabric slid easily between her fingers as she fluffed her skirts back into place.

A strangled cry ripped through the night. Rose jumped, gasping in surprise. She glanced up and down the path, searching for the source. A tight dread wound itself in her chest.

Perhaps she had not been the only one to wander into the garden paths tonight.

She strained her ears, listening for the sound again, hoping she was not about to stumble upon an entangled pair of lovers seeking privacy in the garden. The cry sounded again, but it was not a sound of pleasure. Her heart hammered as she tiptoed toward the sound. Was it Philip or Alexander? Rose held her breath.

"No, please," whimpered a male voice. But it was not Alexander or Philip. The man was on the other side of a tall hedge. Rose pressed her ear to the vegetation, leaves tickling her ear. She reached for the tether to her magic, ready to intervene if necessary, but stopped when the desperate voice spoke again.

"I don't want to do this any longer."

Rose recognized the voice. It was Cornelius.

He sounded hurt and frightened. Rose was about to march around the corner of the hedge when a high, wicked voice sent a chill down her spine and rooted her feet to the earth.

"The deal has already been made," hissed the voice.

Rose didn't dare to take a single breath.

"It is your job to break her and secure what we need. Punish her, if you must."

"No, please. You told me I wouldn't have to hurt anyone again. Please!"

"Silence. Someone is near."

Terror made her blood run cold. She backed slowly away from the hedge, taking great care to not make any sound in the gravel path. It was impossible. She winced at every small sound her footsteps made. Once she was a few paces away, she fled, not daring to look back.

Rose ran, legs pumping and dress blowing wildly out behind her. The sound of gravel crunched loudly under her feet. She ran, the garden twisting in on itself, morphing until she found herself on a wide path that led directly to the house. She made straight for the stone staircase that led back onto the terrace. Her knees grew weak as she entered the comforting glow of the party. Only when she was paces away from the dimly lit stairs did she dare turn over her shoulder to see if she was being pursued.

She was alone.

She took large, gulping breaths of air. Her side burned with the effort of her flight. She walked towards the steps that would lead back to the main ballroom and heard Lady Nightingale's voice clearly over the crowd.

"Ladies and gentlemen! Most esteemed guests! The time has come for us to unmask!"

Rose broke into a jog up the steps, ignoring the stitch in her side. All thoughts of terror vanished.

It was time for the midnight unmasking.

ose scurried through the crowd to take her place. Everything hinged on her ability to perform this trick for Lady Nightingale. Failure was not an option. She reached her appointed spot just to the left of the dais and tried to focus solely on the task ahead.

Before she could truly center herself, someone coughed pointedly. Rose searched for the source and found Harriet. She beamed and mouthed, *"Good luck!"*

Rose smiled, even as nausea made her stomach clench.

Philip and Alexander entered the room, both scanning the crowd for her. Rose turned her back, focusing on the dais. She could not focus on them now. She would deal with both of them after she had fulfilled her part in the spectacle.

Effie Crawford's grating voice sounded over the murmurings of the crowd. "Oh, *there* you are, my legionnaire!"

Rose couldn't stop her lip from curling in disgust.

Lady Nightingale held both hands aloft, gesturing for the guests to quiet. Once again, the lights in the party dimmed dramatically. She glanced down at Rose, ensuring she was in her proper place.

Rose nodded once. Her chest still heaved from her exertions, but she did her best to look calm and ready.

Mrs. Kensington lurked in a dark corner behind the dais, pocket watch in hand. After a moment, she gestured to the musicians to begin the music to accompany the countdown.

On cue, Lady Nightingale began her address. "Please join me in a countdown to the last stroke of midnight. Then, off with the masks, and all will be revealed. Let us not dwell in shadow and secrecy, but step into the light and revel in the company of friends, old and new."

"Hear, hear!" cried a drunken male voice.

Mrs. Kensington looked as if she might strangle whoever it belonged to for ruining the suspense of the moment.

Rose fought to suppress a smile.

Lady Nightingale lowered her hands, unperturbed by the interruption. "Let us countdown to the stroke of midnight."

Rose stared at the spot on the wall where she knew the taper candles waited for her. She could not see the grid of them clearly from here, but she'd practiced so much the past two days that she could visualize their placement clearly in her mind's eye. She reached for the tether to her power and forced the waves of magic to calm into a small trickle. The magic rose easily, as if welcoming her back.

Rose pictured the number twelve within her mind and channeled her power towards the candles., The candles on the wall lit in the same formation. She formed each number in time with the collective chanting of the party guests, winking candles out and lighting them with ease.

The music grew in fervor with each number and the anticipation within the crowd felt alive, as if it were some breathing thing. Rose harnessed the humming feeling and held it, a pulsing orb within her chest. In some small corner of her mind, she realized she was preparing and performing two forms of magic at once, the fire and holding the small orb of vibrant energy within herself. She made a quick mental note to ask Lady Nightingale about simultaneous spell work.

As the crowd shouted, "Two! *One!*" Rose snuffed out every candle in the ballroom, plunging everyone into darkness. The crowd gasped, and some ladies shrieked.

This was not part of the plan. But if she wanted to truly impress Lady Nightingale and show her she was worthy of learning more about her magic, Rose knew she must do something spectacular.

Rose felt such command, such control. The ocean of magic swelled within herself, joyous and sparkling.

Let me out! it said.

She let the trickle widen into a steady stream. Rose knew she could perform the next feat easily.

Rose sent the ball of energy she'd been holding within herself towards the vaulted ceiling, temporarily concealing its light in shadow. In a sudden burst, she created a phoenix made of fire and silver-blue light from the orb, the energy of the excited party goers manifested into power. Rose knew no one could tell that the magic came from her. The light was too sudden and too bright.

The phoenix spread its fiery wings and soared around the ballroom, staying well above the guests gathered below as they shrieked in bafflement and delight. The phoenix heated the room as it swooped and dived, crackling and sparking. It made for the ceiling, wings stretched to their full length. Right as it appeared it would crash and set the entire room on fire, it exploded into a million tiny stars and vanished in a puff of smoke, cloaking the room in darkness once more.

Rose released the tether of magic within herself, sad to let it go. She gently relit the candles around the ballroom, banishing the shadows. A moment of stunned silence suffocated the party.

Then, all at once, the guests clapped and cheered. Lady Nightingale had once again dazzled them all.

Rose lit the hundreds of tapers around the ballroom to create more light as the guests removed their masks. The party-goers squealed in delight and groaned with laughter as they revealed their true identities.

Removing her own mask, Rose spied Lady Nightingale studying her. Her benefactress wore a placid smile, but it did not reach her eyes.

Rose grinned triumphantly and shrugged, acknowledging her deviation from the plan. Her chest swelled with pride as she clapped along with the rest of the guests.

Lady Nightingale curtsied gracefully. "Enjoy the rest of the evening, ladies and gentlemen." She descended the dais, and the musicians readied themselves for the next song.

Guests swarmed Lady Nightingale, praising her for such a spectacular display as she left the dais. Rose stood in her place, waiting for Lady Nightingale to approach her. Happiness buzzed within her. She had pulled off a wonderful bit of magic and knew Lady Nightingale would be proud.

Her happiness dimmed as she remembered that Alexander and Philip had been looking for her. She'd watched them enter the ballroom, but where were they? She craned her neck and spotted the blonde heads of Alexander and his sister easily. They were the center attention, as usual. Alexander was talking to Cecelia Hawthorne. Rose continued to look for Philip. He was nowhere to be found. She did not see Cornelius, either.

She was just about to go back to the terrace to see if Philip might be there when she felt a hand clamp down on her shoulder, squeezing tightly. It was Lady Clarke, dressed as a fairy. Silky wings of transparent fabric glittered when she moved.

"There you are," she said stiffly. "Do come with me, Miss Worthington."

Rose followed Lady Clarke out of the ballroom. The warmth of her self-satisfaction vanished as cool dread took its place. She had been expecting praise for her demonstration of skills, but it seemed like she was about to get a tongue lashing. She fought the urge to crumple in on herself and kept her head held high as they entered the hallway.

Lady Clarke led Rose up a side staircase to the second floor. This area was off limits to guests, as well as students, and Rose felt her heart sink even further. They entered a small dark room, and Rose stood by the door as Lady Clarke lit several lamps, revealing a tidy parlor. One of many private rooms within the manor.

"Sit," commanded Lady Clarke as she removed her wings. "Lady Nightingale will be here shortly." She positioned herself on the opposite side of the room, facing the door like a sentry.

Rose did as she was told. Lady Nightingale strode into the room a moment later.

She looked down at Rose, her hands clasped before her. "Do you care to explain, Miss Worthington?" she asked coolly.

"I don't understand. I did what you asked." Rose's cheeks flushed as her heart beat painfully in her chest. She felt sick.

"You deviated from the plan," said Lady Nightingale. The ever-present warmth in her eyes was gone.

Rose swallowed the bile that pooled in her mouth. "All I wanted was to impress you." It had seemed harmless, creating an illusion from light. She hadn't even really been conscious of what she was doing. She just let the magic tell her what to do.

"She's still only a child," said Lady Clarke softly from her corner of the room.

Lady Nightingale's frosty glare softened, but she shook her head. "You have done a very dangerous thing, Miss Worthington."

"I don't understand." Rose gripped her mask. The sharp gems dug into her fingers.

"We must be *very* careful with how much magic we display in public." Lady Nightingale lowered herself into a chair across from Rose. "We can't risk discovery. There are dangerous people in attendance tonight. We were debating whether to use magic at all this evening. They would do terrible things for a taste of the power we possess. Terrible things."

"Not to mention she posed a terrible danger to herself," Lady Clarke added. She left her post in the corner and took a seat next to Rose. She fixed a stray lock of hair, placing it back within its pin.

The gesture made Rose want to cry.

"You could have seriously injured yourself. Or worse," said Lady Clarke softly.

Lady Nightingale sighed. "I know you were only trying your best. Perhaps it was too much to ask of you, for someone who is so untrained. You must be exhausted. It was an impressive display of power, Miss Worthington. You must have used up all your reserves of magic to accomplish it."

Reserves? Rose's magic was a boundless, endless sea. She didn't know there could be a limit to how much magic one could use, or store. "It was nothing," said Rose as dismissively as she could. She didn't want to share how much magic she had access to. Not when she was being scolded for using a mere fraction of it.

"I think I should take that bracelet back. For the time being." Lady Nightingale extended her hand for the unlocking bracelet Rose wore on her wrist. The jewels had inspired her entire ensemble this evening. She had been proud to wear the symbol of affection from her teacher.

Rose clutched the bracelet with her opposite hand. She tried to swallow the hard lump that rose in her throat. She could not believe she had offended Lady Nightingale so greatly that she would take back her gift.

"It's for the best. The bracelet uses a small store of your magic to perform its spell, and I don't want to tax you. Especially after you burned through much of your own power."

"I'm fine, really. I'm not tired at all." Rose continued to clutch the bracelet. There were other, more important things, than her alleged reserves of magic that they should be discussing. "I need your help. There is something off about my cousin. I heard him tonight, in the garden, and he didn't sound right. Someone was threatening him. They spoke of a bargain."

Lady Nightingale dropped her hand back into her lap. "What did you hear?"

"Cornelius was arguing with someone. He sounded afraid. Whoever was with him said a deal had been made. They are going to use someone to get what they need."

Lady Clarke and Lady Nightingale exchanged a wary glance. "You heard this tonight?"

"Yes. Something is wrong, and I want to find out what it is."

Lady Nightingale shifted forward in her seat. "There may be more to your cousin than we had previously supposed. Did you hear anything else? Anything at all?"

Cornelius hadn't sounded like himself at all. He'd sounded terrified. "I don't think so. Just that he didn't want it anymore, whatever 'it' might be."

After a long pause, Lady Nightingale relented. "I shall let you keep the bracelet for now, but you must promise that you will tell me what you find out about Lord Worthington. It could be very important, Rose."

"I promise. I will." A rush of relief crashed over her, making her dizzy.

Lady Nightingale reached for her hands, her fingers brushing the black sapphire bracelet. The stones grew warm and heavy at the brief touch. A flare of emerald light flitted across the jewels. The bracelet settled firmly onto her wrist.

"Wear the bracelet at all times. I have added a protection spell for you. I do not know what bargain your cousin has made, but it is best to be cautious."

"Why?"

There was a long pause.

"Tell her," said Lady Clarke. She held a fist to her stomach and waited for Lady Nightingale to speak.

"There is a group of men who wish to do us harm. We've encountered them before. We believe some of them are here tonight."

Rose thought of Cornelius and the mysterious voice in the garden. Had the voice belonged to one of them? "What do they want?"

Lady Nightingale's lip curled. "What men always want. Power."

Rose's chest tightened. Anger flared, heating her core. "Don't they have enough of that already?"

"It's never enough for them," whispered Lady Nightingale. Her eyes glazed, as if reliving a painful memory.

The party continued on downstairs, and among the guests were men who wanted to take what wasn't theirs; who wanted to hurt her new friends and her teachers. She wondered if Harriet and Kate knew. They had to be careful. Rose's stomach clenched with dread. What had she done? "Do the others know?"

"No. Only the Council, and now you, are aware. I ask that you keep this information to yourself, Miss Worthington."

Rose flicked her gaze to Lady Clarke, wondering what she thought. It didn't seem right to not tell the others. But Lady Clarke's face did not betray her thoughts.

"We don't want to cause unnecessary panic. Sometimes the best defense is to carry on as normal. We don't wish for any of the girls to live in fear. It's something we try to avoid at all costs," she said.

"Fear is our enemy. Safety is our priority," added Lady Nightingale. "It's why we needed those papers from Lord Crawford. We believe he may be in contact with the men who seek us, even if he does not yet know it himself."

Rose twisted the skirt of her gown. It made her feel a little less guilty, knowing that the theft and betrayal had truly been for a good purpose. She wanted to protect the Nightingales. But her stomach clenched as she wondered if Alexander knew anything about it. She couldn't believe that he would. He was too kind, too genuine to be involved with men like that. She stopped fidgeting and smoothed the soft fabric of her dress.

Lady Nightingale stood. "Don't speak of this to anyone. And do be more careful."

"I will."

"Go back to the party now. We will join you in a moment."

Rose obeyed. As she closed the door, Lady Clarke and Lady Nightingale leaned towards one another in hushed conversation.

With the door separating them, Rose examined the newly spelled bracelet. A tingle of unease crept up her spine, but she ignored it, choosing instead to sink into the relief of escaping her scolding relatively unscathed.

She had used her magic tonight, dazzling all who had witnessed it. For a brief, shining moment, Rose had felt complete and happy. She closed her eyes, remembering the thrill of releasing the magic and creating something beautiful.

Her contentment did not last long. As she descended the stairs to the main level of the house, her pulse quickened. She had to find Philip. He must wonder where she'd gone.

Rose returned to the masquerade and wandered around the ballroom, making sure to avoid Lord Reeves. She searched the hall, and even dared to poke her head into the gentlemen's smoking room, but she could not find him. She ended her search back on the terrace, and waited for him for an hour, then two, until the first rosy streaks of dawn stretched into the sky and her mother called her to return home.

CHAPTER 29

The next morning, Rose ate breakfast alone in the small parlor downstairs. Her mother lay in bed with a headache. She'd been tipsy when they arrived home after the masquerade and would be sleeping off the consequences of her revelry for a good portion of the day.

Rose had woken feeling happy and optimistic. Not even the scolding she had received from Lady Nightingale could completely dampen the pride that swelled in her chest. The magic she had commanded last night had been unlike anything she'd ever felt. Boundless power was just within her reach, and she had performed not one, but two incredible feats of magic almost simultaneously. She wanted *more*. What other unthinkable things could she achieve with that endless, sparkling sea of magic at her fingertips?

As she picked at her plate of fruit, her pride dwindled as her thoughts turned to Philip. She hadn't been able to find him again. Had he been planning to leave before the unmasking all along? He had snuck into the party, after all.

She knew she would have to explain herself to him. She shouldn't have run off, especially when she could have been spending time with him. But his accusations had stung. Did he really think so little of her? That she would fall so quickly for another mere weeks after she believed him dead?

Rose speared a strawberry indelicately with her fork, but did not eat it. She watched the pink juices spread across her plate. He had assumed she would run away with him that very evening. But she couldn't. Not anymore. But she needed to see him again. How on earth was she supposed to find him? The only clue she had was that he was staying in east London.

Footsteps in the hall shook her from her thoughts. She fought to conceal her surprise as Cornelius sat down at the table across from her, looking pale and drawn. He was suffering from another bout of strange pallor, the circles under his eyes bloomed dark.

Rose watched him prepare tea and grip both hands around the cup, as if willing the warmth into his bones. He kept his eyes downcast.

She tried to sense his emotional state but ran up against a solid wall. So much for being gifted at reading emotions. She cleared her throat and Cornelius snapped his head up. The hollowness there was startling. Not that she cared, really, but it was still disquieting.

He smiled weakly. "Good morning, Miss Worthington."

"Morning." She set her fork down on her plate.

Cornelius sipped from his cup. "Your mother is displeased at my insistence that you limit contact with Lord Crawford's son. I hope you know it's for your own good."

Rose crossed her arms and leaned back into her chair. "You claim many things are for my own good, cousin. What is this compared to all the rest?"

He stared into his tea, long fingers still wrapped around the cup. "What would you do if you were me? If our roles were reversed, and you were a man who inherited not only an estate more grand than anything you had ever known but also a mother and her strong-willed daughter of marriageable age?"

"I would *start* by asking the daughter what her thoughts were about her situation, not presume to run her life for her."

Cornelius remained immobile.

"I'm off to make some calls," Rose said. "That is, *if* you'll allow it, Lord Worthington."

Her cousin snapped his eyes to hers once more, taken aback.

She regretted calling him that, even in mockery. The formal title felt like rocks in her mouth. The last person she had called that had been her brother. He was a man who deserved the title. The person who sat across from her now was wholly unworthy. She pushed her chair back to leave.

"Actually, there is another matter I wish to discuss with you."

Rose gritted her teeth, but remained seated. Cold dread pooled in her stomach.

"Lord Reeves has asked for your hand. I have accepted on your behalf."

She thought she might be sick. Revulsion spread through every inch of her being as the blood drained from her face. Her vision blurred as a roaring sound filled her ears. She fought to make sense of the words her cousin had uttered.

She could not, *would not,* marry Percival Reeves. Her throat tightened, and bile crept up her throat. Blood continued to pound in her ears. The walls of the parlor closed in around her.

Rose shot to her feet and clenched her fists, letting her nails bite into her palms. Her chair clattered to the floor behind her. "And I suppose I have no say in the matter? He has not asked *me* to marry."

Cornelius remained infuriatingly calm. "Lord Reeves adheres to a more traditional approach. Your consent is not necessary."

"I won't do it." Tears sprang to her eyes, even though she was furious. The last thing she wanted was to appear weak. She fought to keep her tears from falling. "I will not marry him." It took all her effort to avoid stamping her foot like a small child.

"I'm afraid you must. I can ensure a long engagement, at the very least. Give you until the end of the season until the wedding."

"Why bother? Why not just marry me off tomorrow and be rid of me, since you care for me so little?"

Cornelius finally set down his teacup. "I don't hate you."

"Your actions say otherwise." Rose stifled a sob with the back of her hand, hating herself for it. Her sapphire bracelet grew warm and heavy as her magic pulsed sluggishly beneath her skin.

Cornelius stood and leaned both hands on the back of his chair. "Lord Reeves is a very wealthy man. You will want for nothing. Neither will your mother. He is old, it is true, but that only means you will not remain married for long. You will be a widow. You can choose to remarry, or not. Your title will protect you. He has no heirs. Your children, if you are so blessed, would inherit everything."

Rose looked up at the ceiling. She blinked back her tears, letting her fury wash over her. "I suppose you think you are doing me a kindness."

He stepped around the table and reached for her.

"Don't touch me." She took a step back, widening the distance between them.

"It's the best I can do," he said, spreading his hands helplessly.

"That's not true, and you know it." Rose had enough of this. Enough of him. She turned her back on him and marched to the door.

She thought she heard a muffled sort of cry, but it was drowned by the roaring in her ears and the pounding of fury in her blood. An acrid smell filled her nose. The door slammed shut in her face with a *bang*. She flinched.

Cornelius stood very close to her with one hand on the door, his expression murderous, eyes black and glittering.

Fear crept into her veins, ice cold. The change in his countenance was sudden. He was so calm a moment ago, and now his face was flushed, chest heaving with fury equal to her own. Her throat burned. The bitter tang was coming from him, strong as brandy.

"You're an ungrateful bitch," he hissed.

Rose balked at the slur. Anger continued to pulse through her. Her chest heaved with rage. "If you expect me to grovel at your feet in thanks for arranging a marriage for me, you will be most disappointed."

"You should be thankful I did not marry you off the moment I arrived in England." His hand gripped the doorknob with white knuckles, barring her exit. "You are *never* to see Lord Crawford again. You are to stay in this house unless I give you explicit permission to leave, and you are to cease your visits to that Nightingale harlot. You are *mine*, and you shall do as I say."

Rose's vision went black. She would not be a prisoner here. Her magic pulse dangerously within her, beating against a muddied wall. She grabbed onto the tether that connected her to her power, feeling for it through a thick fog. After a few moments of reaching blindly through the resistance, she connected to her endless ocean of power. It was glittering, expansive, and frenetic. Rage and magic ebbed and flowed beneath her skin in one tumultuous wave. She could not tell where one started and the other began.

Rather than slam the mental door against it, she let it flow through her. One word reverberated through her.

Burn.

Cornelius yelped and jerked his hand away from the metal doorknob. He looked at his hand, mouth agape. His palm was angry and red. "*You*," he whispered.

"You *will not* touch me," Rose commanded again. Her voice

shook with fury. "You will not keep me confined, and you will not prevent me from seeing Lady Nightingale."

"You are mine to command, and to destroy." Cornelius's eyes glittered with wrath and something darker and more sinister than Rose had ever seen.

Rose felt the wave of her power tear through her again. *Burn.*

Cornelius gasped and clutched his hand as angry blisters covered his palm.

She channeled her rage into his hurt. Her vision blurred, and she saw previously invisible threads of power weaving the heat and his hand so clearly. It took no effort at all to cause this pain. Linking the spots of power in her mind was easy.

Breaking them was difficult.

Cornelius fell to his knees. Rose realized she might have gone too far. Panicking, she forced herself to let go of her threads of magic, disconnecting herself from the expanse of power. She breathed hard through her nose. Her face flushed with anger and the strain of what she had done. Perspiration dripped down her back.

She stormed past Cornelius and wrenched open the door, leaving him cradling his burned palm.

* * *

ROSE PACED HER ROOM, her breathing still rapid from her encounter. Her footsteps sank into the garish pink rug as she fought to still her trembling limbs. What had she done?

Her heart beat against her ribcage. Part of her wondered if she had done something wrong, reached too far into that vast expanse. She had inflicted pain upon another person with her magic. It had been so easy. So very easy to let her rage take over, and to direct the bubbling power to do harm. She had *hurt* Cornelius. Not badly, but she had injured him, as he had once hurt her.

She did not feel sorry for it. Rose had stood her ground and had dared to defy his orders. She flexed her fingers and stared at them.

Her breath finally slowed, and the roaring in her ears receded. The demanding pulse of magic settled into a distant hum. She pushed the spot above the bridge of her nose with her thumb, trying to think. Something was not right with her cousin, but it was more than just the decline of his physical wellbeing.

What did she really know about Cornelius? He had spent the last decade in the United States, but she didn't know what manner of business he had conducted. Hell, she couldn't even say what he did each day in London. If she were going to find some way out of this arranged marriage, she would need to persuade Cornelius that she did not need to be married off to the first detestable suitor who made his intentions known. She swallowed, trying to clear the lump in her throat.

Her stomach roiled, and she fought to keep bile from rising to the back of her throat as the hard truth sank in. Marriage was unavoidable.

Lady Clarke and Lady Nightingale had said as much, even insisted that she could use marriage, and the connections that came with it, to get more from life. With the power that she possessed, there was a small possibility marriage *might* be something she could control, or at least manipulate, to her favor.

Fighting waves of nausea, she gripped the back of a chair, willing her body to calm. Rose focused on the glittering black bracelet on her wrist and breathed in and out, in and out, until her queasiness subsided. She was no longer alone, treading water of infinite darkness, only to be shoved back down to its immeasurable depths. She had a lifeline now. She only had to reach out and grab hold of it.

CHAPTER 30

Happy couples in pastel colors walked arm in arm down the wide lanes of Hyde Park. Rose barely acknowledged those who passed her. Her thoughts were a tangled mess. She hadn't been able to stay in the house, and sought the refuge of fresh air, but it did little to lift her spirits. She needed to take her mind off the tumultuous waves of despair and rage that crashed through her. Her magic flickered weakly. Her wrist hung heavily by her side, weighed down by her bracelet.

Betsy followed, keeping a few paces behind. Rose gathered that her maid knew all about the engagement from the pitying glances she had shot her the entire way here.

Rose couldn't muster the energy to visit Lady Nightingale. Not yet. Though she craved Harriet and Kate's company, she didn't think she could form coherent thoughts about everything that had happened since the masquerade. How could she even begin to explain?

It was overcast, but warm, as Rose wandered deeper into the park. The leaves of the trees were broad and full, and the heady scent of lilacs and roses perfumed the air. Everything was vibrant and alive; the complete opposite of her insides, which felt like barren winter.

After an hour of walking, she finally stopped to rest in a white gazebo in a remote corner. The Greco-Roman structure perched on top of a small hill that overlooked a pond laden with pastel pink and purple lilies. Rose sat on a bench and ran her hand over the smooth stone, its surface worn smooth by time. A mournful raven's cry cut through the birds's cheerful twittering.

She was to be *engaged*.

Rose swallowed the bile in the back of her throat at the thought. She wouldn't marry Reeves. But she couldn't see a way out of this mess. She gripped the edge of the stone seat until her knuckles turned white. Her magic lurched nauseatingly.

A lone figure approached the gazebo. Lamenting the loss of her solitude, Rose wrapped her arms around herself and stared into the pond's still waters, refusing to make eye contact with the stranger. But something tugged at her senses, nudging her towards the figure. She couldn't make out his features, but Philip's gait was unmistakable.

She shot to her feet. The world came into sharper focus, tunneling in on him. She placed one hand on a pillar, steadying herself as her pulse quickened.

Philip closed the distance between them swiftly. "I thought you were planning to walk all the way to Ashford," he said, leaping onto the gazebo. "Hello, Rose." He offered her a tentative smile that melted her heart.

Words failed her. She wanted nothing more than to wrap her arms around him and rest her head on his chest. Instead, she took his uninjured hand in hers and squeezed. "I'm sorry," she whispered.

He stroked her cheek softly with the back of his fingers. "Don't be."

She was drawn to him in a way she would never be able to explain. Rose locked eyes with the man who loved her.

A small cough reminded Rose that they were not alone. Betsy pushed herself off her bench, and wandered towards the water, whistling all the while.

Rose pulled Philip around the back of the gazebo where the pillars shielded them from sight. Unless someone was hiding in the trees a short distance away, no one could see them here. Philip, realizing the advantages of such seclusion, bent his head towards Rose's face and kissed her.

The burning need she had felt on the terrace was replaced by an ache that throbbed deep in her chest. Rose let her tears fall as she kissed him back.

He broke the kiss and wiped her cheeks tenderly. "What's all this for?"

"I shouldn't have run off last night. It was stupid."

The fingers of Philip's injured hand felt stiff as they curled against hers. "I said some things I didn't mean. I'm sorry, too." His green eyes were dark and troubled.

The ache in her chest threatened to crush all the air from her lungs. She knew what came next would destroy a fragile part of her. One she safeguarded against the harshness and cruelty of a world that didn't understand her. What she had to say might very well destroy him, too. "There's something I have to tell you. Before I do, I need you to know that I love you."

Philip frowned as he searched her face. "What is it?"

"I'm engaged." She held her breath, waiting for his response, hoping that the fragile love between them could withstand this next storm.

Philip dropped her hands. She would have preferred he stab her in the heart.

"Dammit, Rose."

"It's not like I *want* to be engaged," she said, voice cracking involuntarily.

A muscled twinged in Phillip's jaw. "I bet he didn't have to twist your arm to get you to accept, though. I *knew* there was something going on between you two."

"What?" Rose's brows knit together.

Philip dragged a hand through his hair. "I can't believe this. You'll marry that stuck up prick, but won't even consider getting married to me?"

"Who are you talking about?" she cried, voice climbing an octave.

"That twat, Crawford!"

Rose felt the color drain from her face. "Are you so jealous of Lord Crawford? That you just *assumed* that I would marry him?" She couldn't believe this conversation was happening.

"Well, why wouldn't you? He's rich, right? Unlike me. What happened to never marrying a man just for his money?"

Rose wavered between slapping him and crying. She clenched her fists instead. "My cousin has arranged for me to marry Percival Reeves."

Philip recoiled as if Rose actually *had* slapped him across the face, stunning him into silence. He shoved a hand into his pocket and rubbed his mouth in exasperation. "Damnit."

Rose let him dwell on the truth as frustrated tears spilled from her eyes. He *should* wallow in the mess he had just made. His accusation had cut her deeply. He knew her. He knew she'd never marry for wealth or status. Not if she had a choice.

"I'm sorry. I'm so sorry," he said. He moved to wipe away her tears once more, but she widened the space between them, wrapping her arms around her middle.

Philip looked stricken. "Let me help you. I can help get you out of this." His hand moved in his pocket, clutching something there.

"No. There's nothing you can do about it."

"Perhaps if there was another offer?"

Her heart beat too loudly in her ears. "What are you saying?"

"Rose Worthington," Philip began, but she couldn't let him continue.

"No, Philip." Rose took another step back and shook her head. "I won't play by their rules. I know you understand that."

Philip clenched his jaw. "Then what do you want me to do? What do you want? I am yours. Whatever you ask of me, I will do it. I will run to the farthest corner of the earth with you. You only have to ask."

Rose wiped furiously at her tears. "It's not as simple as that. I have to figure some things out." She couldn't bring herself to say that her fear of Cornelius also played a part in her reluctance. He would do more than wound Philip if they were caught again. He was dangerous, and she would not risk Philip's life. She hated that she couldn't tell him. But if she did, Philip might do something rash and inadvertently put himself in harm's way. She would not lose him again. Even if it meant they could never be together.

Philip stared out at the overcast park, lines of worry etched in his perfect face. He kept his fist in his pocket. "I can't wait forever. Every day that I am not with you is unbearable."

Rose's heart stuttered. "Give me time. Please."

"Why? Aren't I enough? We would be happy together, far away from here." He pressed her hands against his chest. She could feel his heart beating against her palms.

Her shoulders caved inwards as she sagged against him. "I can't run away again. We would be isolated from everyone we care about. And I'm so tired of being lonely," she said, her heart breaking.

Philip stiffened beneath her touch.

"There are people here who make me feel like I belong, like I am a part of something bigger than myself. It's not that I don't love you. I *do*. I just don't want to lose what I've found. My friends. My spirit." She wished she could tell him about her magic. But she'd sworn to secrecy. He could never know. And if he couldn't hold that part of her too, along with her darkness, then could he truly love her?

"It was always you and me before," he pleaded.

Rose's shoulders wracked with sobs. "I know," she choked. "But I am not sure it is enough this time. I don't know if I can see you again. It hurts too much."

They stayed like that, her hands pressed to his heart, for a long while. Her tears finally subsided, and she removed one hand to wipe them away.

"I'm working for Charlie's uncle while I'm staying with him. Mr. Pike. He offered to give me a job. Charlie doesn't want it."

"What sort of job?" Rose sniffed. She had assumed Philip would take over his family's farm. But he had always been a dreamer. It was one of the things she loved about him.

"Mr. Pike runs a spice trading business. He wants me to go on the next voyage as his emissary," he said.

Which meant he would leave England. Rose hated the thought of him going where she could not follow. But perhaps this was the answer. Away from London, he would be safe from Cornelius. "When do you leave?" she asked.

"Could be as soon as three months."

She gripped his shirt. "I'm proud of you."

His eyes softened. He brushed a tendril of hair from her forehead. "I have loved you for so long. I will never stop loving you, no matter the obstacles that keep me from you."

Rose reached up on her toes and poured all her love and regret into a long, searing kiss. She placed her hands on either side of his face. The slight stubble on his cheeks tickled her palms.

He wrapped his hands around her waist and returned her kiss, lips parting.

Rose's knees weakened as the kiss intensified. She trailed her fingers down the column of his throat, feeling his pulse flutter beneath her fingertips.

Philip broke away, placing his forehead against hers. "I'll be staying with Charlie's uncle. If you should change your mind about wanting to see me, I'll be there."

"All right," she said, sorrow threatening to choke her.

Betsy coughed loudly behind them, announcing her presence. Rose disentangled herself from Philip's embrace.

He caught her wrist and shoved a folded piece of paper into her hand. He nodded to Betsy, then took off.

Rose leaned against a column and watched him go as her chest ached with regret. She opened the slip of paper and saw an address written in Philip's neat hand. She shoved the paper into her boot. Raindrops fell, making soft pattering sounds against the gazebo. Rose held her hand out to the rain, focusing on its icy sting. Ignoring Betsy's protests, she left the shelter of the gazebo. The rain fell harder, staining the ground with fat drops. She tilted her chin up to the sky, letting the rain drench her hair, clothes, and face. She let the icy drops cover her until she was numb.

CHAPTER 31

Rose found Harriet and Kate in the greenhouse the next morning. Though the rain had stopped, thin grey clouds still covered the sky. Weak sunlight filtered through the glass walls of Lady Nightingale's conservatory as Rose walked past the vibrant plants within. Her footsteps were slow, made heavy with guilt and sorrow. Her head ached, and eyes throbbed with all the tears she had shed.

Her magic had been pulsing listlessly against her skin and head ever since Cornelius had announced her engagement. It had become a relentless, subtle throb in response to her emotions. The bracelet on her wrist had grown warm to the touch, too, and felt increasingly heavy. It wrenched at her shoulder and neck, but she had promised to keep it on.

Harriet perched on a worktable, legs swinging idly as Kate bent over a delicate seedling with tiny fat leaves. They both perked up when they heard her draw near.

"There you are!" Harriet launched herself from the table. "You were *brilliant* at the masquerade. I thought the phoenix was simply marvelous. Though I heard it made Lady Nightingale and Lady Clarke rather anxious. Oh, but why should they worry? I think it simply added to the whole marvelous atmosphere—" Harriet's excited prattling was cut short by Kate, who placed a hand on the girl's shoulder.

"What's the matter?" Kate asked. Her stoic face was unchanged but for a tiny frown that betrayed her concern.

Harriet's brow pinched as she looked hard at Rose, noting her puffy face and somber expression.

She didn't have the strength to mask her grief. She could not even fake a smile for her friends. Before Rose could protest, Harriet shot out a hand and grabbed her bare forearm. She gasped and abruptly released her grip. Her large, dark eyes filled with tears of empathy. "Oh, Rosie," she said softly.

It undid the tenuous control Rose had over herself. Tears spilled from her already swollen eyes, and she pressed her palms against her face. Kate steered her to a stool and forced her to sit. She handed her a handkerchief, which only made Rose sob harder.

They said nothing as she cried. Rose had thought she'd cried all the tears her body could hold, but her sorrow swelled like an ocean, vast and unending.

After a minute, Rose regained control and stifled her sobs. She dabbed at her face with Kate's handkerchief and took deep, shuddering breaths. Harriet tentatively reached a hand towards her, but only to pat the top of her head. "Do you want to talk about it?"

Rose cleared her throat, making sure no more tears would escape. "I told Philip I cannot see him again."

"Whatever for?" Harriet asked.

Rose stared at the crushed stone on the greenhouse floor, unable to look her friends in the eye. She would start crying again. "I seem to find myself engaged. To Lord Percival Reeves."

"Oh no," Kate said.

"I can't marry him." Rose started twisting the handkerchief in dismay but stopped, remembering it was not her own.

"You can keep it," said Kate. "I've got others."

"What are you going to do?" Harriet asked.

Rose gripped the small cloth, damp with her tears. Her head throbbed painfully. "I don't know."

"Well, what if you married Philip?" Harriet asked tentatively.

Rose shook her head. "I can't marry him, either." Her vision blurred, the edges growing dark.

"But you love him," Kate said.

Rose blinked, trying to clear the black that encroached further on her sight. "It's *because* I love him that I can't marry him. We would be outcasts, forced to flee from my cousin. It would put him in danger, and I will not cause him harm."

The air was thick and hot. She struggled to get enough air into her lungs. And, she thought, there would be no more magic. No more lessons with Lady Nightingale. No more reading books from the magnificent library or spending afternoons with Harriet and Kate. A strange truth clicked into place at the thought. She did not know how, but she was certain that her fire magic would either catastrophically combust or wither and die without continued training. Her magic pulsed strongly against her skull, angry at the thought of being abandoned.

Rose's chest heaved as she tried to get enough air into her lungs. Her vision tunneled and blurred as pain shot behind her eyelids. Everything felt so very heavy.

"Rose," Harriet said, alarm tinging her voice. "What's wrong with her?"

She sounded very far away. Rose felt Kate kneel next to her and place a hand reassuringly on her back. "You're all right. Take a deep breath."

Rose struggled to obey. Roaring filled her ears, and the world tilted dangerously, threatening to tip her into a dark void.

A sharp scent pierced her dizziness. The world righted itself as she regained clarity. Breathing became easier. The dizziness subsided.

Kate held a handful of crushed leaves with a sharp, pine-like scent under her nose. She straightened and deposited the leaves into a bowl on the rough wooden table.

"Thank you," said Rose faintly. "You are a singularly talented green witch."

Kate smiled to herself but kept her focus on her workbench, clinking vials and bowls as she returned them to their rightful places.

"Are you all right?" Harriet asked.

"I think so."

Kate grabbed her hand and placed two fingers over the pulse at her wrist. She frowned. "Have you eaten today?"

Rose's eyebrows knit together. "I can't remember."

"You should eat something," she instructed, dropping her hand.

Rose nodded and began folding the handkerchief she still clutched in her hands. "I'm sorry if I interrupted you both." She felt a little more than embarrassed at her outburst and near-fainting.

"You don't have to apologize for your feelings, Rosie," said Harriet. "That's what friends are for. To listen, and to help if we can."

Rose stood and placed the handkerchief in her pocket. "Thank you. Both of you."

Harriet smiled encouragingly. "Do you want us to come with you to get something to eat? Lady Nightingale left a tray in the parlor."

"No, I can manage," Rose said. "I'll be back in a bit."

She left Harriet and Kate to their work. She did not want to trouble them anymore. The clamminess on her brow was further soothed by a rush of air as she opened the glass conservatory door. Whatever plant Kate had used to steady her had worked to calm her, but the throbbing headache remained. She hoped Kate was right, and that it would easily be cured with food.

The house was quiet as she made her way to the main parlor. Where the manor had been full of light and laughter at the masquerade, it was now cloaked in a quiet gloom, asleep. Curiously, the door to the parlor was closed. Rose hovered her hand on the handle, wondering if she should test the powers of her bracelet, but froze when she heard her name carry through the painted wooden door. Rose bent down, pressing her ear to the keyhole.

"It will be the end of the Nightingales if your little pet Worthington exposes us," Lady Templeton's raspy voice cried.

"I have spoken to Miss Worthington about the need for caution," Lady Nightingale replied, as calm as ever.

"If it were any other pupil, you would have discarded them by now for such blatant disregard for our safety," said Lady Templeton scathingly.

Rose winced. She had never liked her, ever since that first day in the library.

"Are you questioning what Lady Nightingale has seen?" Rose heard Lady Clarke ask, her tone cold.

"Of course not," scoffed the older woman. "If she is who Hana claims, then we have great use for her. I only question her usefulness in this current venture."

"Miss Worthington is a worthy addition to our ranks. She has talent and raw power. She may be the key to finding what we've looked so long for," said Lady Nightingale. "The papers she acquired from Lord Crawford have allowed us to set the stage for the matter at hand."

Rose thought her heart may burst with gratitude at her teacher's defense of her. She pressed her ear firmly to the door, not wanting to miss a word, ignoring the throbbing in her skull. She was intensely curious what was on those papers.

"It's as we suspected," Lady Clarke said. "The King's condition worsens by the day. He is becoming too volatile."

"Yes, Charlotte has been careless." Lady Nightingale sighed remorsefully. "She should never have tried to cure him on her own. Apparently, His Majesty was seen speaking to a tree."

Lady Templeton cackled. "The once mighty King talking to trees. The minds of men are weak."

"We to draw the magic out of him before it gets worse," mused Lady Clarke. "Has the book reappeared yet?"

Book? Surely they didn't mean the book that the library had gifted her. Rose bit her lip, trying to remember the title.

"No," said Lady Nightingale. "And it's rather unfortunate that our most promising lead was banned from the library."

Rose fought to stifle a manic giggle. How sweet it was to hear Lady Templeton berated for punishing her. She could not believe what she was hearing. Lady Nightingale and her council had given magic to the Queen of England. But why?

Lady Templeton squawked in protest, but Lady Nightingale cut her off. "It is no matter now. We will continue to search for an alternative. I pay Charlotte a visit this evening to remind her of our bargain, and what will happen if she does not take better care and discretion."

"Do not be too hard on her," cautioned Lady Clarke.

Sensing that the discussion was drawing to a close, Rose silently backed from the door and tiptoed around the corner. She waited with bated breath until she heard the parlor door creak open. Still giddy with what she had overheard, she sauntered back towards the parlor as if she had just arrived.

"Miss Worthington. How good to see you," Lady Clarke said.

Lady Templeton scuffled past without a word. Rose bit the inside of her lip to hide her satisfied grin.

"Good morning," replied Rose, assuming a picture of politeness.

"Are you all right? You look rather pale," Lady Clarke said, peering at her with keen emerald eyes.

"I missed breakfast," she said. "And supper last night."

"Well, that won't do." Lady Nightingale came to the door. "There are refreshments on the table. Please help yourself. Hunger greatly limits our ability to focus our magic."

"Thank you." Rose stepped to the side to let her mentors pass.

"Your are no longer banned from the library," Lady Nightingale said casually. "I trust you will make use of your time there today."

"I shall." She dipped her chin demurely as they left. She felt the tiniest ripple of suspicion from Lady Nightingale as she passed, but it quickly faded. Rose knew her teacher had more important matters to worry about.

Rose grabbed a cream scone from the table and chewed thoughtfully. Pain still throbbed dully behind her eyes, though it lessened with every bite. The tendrils of a plan wafted through her thoughts like smoke on a wintry day. She examined each thread of smoke slowly, carefully, as they gradually took on more substance. There was an answer here to all her problems, a solution to her arranged marriage and proving her continued worth as Lady Nightingale's pupil.

She brushed crumbs from her fingers and took another scone, taking her time to slather strawberry preserves over it. She savored the sweetness on her tongue.

She flipped through her thoughts as if they were pages in a book, lingering on certain passages longer than others.

You can use what we teach you to forge your own path.

Magic is also a powerful influence.

Your own destiny will become clear to you, Miss Worthington.

We have great use for her.

Lady Nightingale would help her. If she could prove her value, that she *was* a gifted witch with natural talent and great power, then she could ask Lady Nightingale to help her get out of her marriage. She would be of far more use to her unmarried, anyway.

Rose's magic pulsed dully, mirroring the diminished ache in her head. Rose swallowed the rest of her breakfast and made her way to the library. She would find that book again and use it to complete the task Lady Nightingale needed done.

She would draw out the King's magic.

CHAPTER 32

There was no time to go back for Harriet and Kate. Besides, the book had first appeared to *her*. It might only reappear if she were alone. And with how much of a fuss everyone was making about it, Rose didn't want to get her friends into trouble. It was clear the book was contentious, but if it had what she needed to complete her task, what did it matter if its theories were not in line with what the Council wanted its fledgling witches to learn?

Her sorrow and heartache calmed with every step she took towards the library until it faded distantly to the back of her mind. She didn't want to think about the pain of saying goodbye to Philip anymore. She had already wasted days of her life mourning him when she'd thought him dead. This was the best course of action. She would do anything to keep him safe—even if it meant never seeing him again. She let the clacking of her footsteps drown out her self-pitying thoughts.

The library was, thankfully, empty. The great bronze disks suspended in the ceiling began their silent oscillations as she slipped inside. Rose tried not to be intimidated by the vast number of books on the towering shelves. She didn't know if one *could* summon a specific title from the depths of the library. But she had to try.

Rose brought her hand to her neck, fingers finding her necklace. She gripped the carved wooden rose as she approached the freestanding shelves in the middle of the room. She stood in the heart of the room, letting the books close in around her on all sides.

I need a book to help me draw out the King's magic, she thought. Her head throbbed painfully, and she felt her wrist grow hot where the bracelet pressed against her skin. She scanned the shelves for any book that stood out from the others. The spines of the well-worn titles blended together.

I need a book to help me draw out the King's magic. Another throb, yet the library remained unchanged.

Rose fought a wave of irritation, exhaling slowly through her nose. She stopped fiddling with her necklace and closed her eyes, standing in silence for another moment. Then she gingerly reached for her magic. She pushed through a dense wall of fog to the place where it flickered faintly within her. She didn't have time to worry about why her magic seemed so weak. The hairs on the back of her neck stood up as a chill ran down her spine.

She could feel something *other* watching her. She knew the feeling would be gone the second she opened her eyes, so she kept them squeezed tight. Though the awareness of the strange presence chilled her, there was warmth emanating from whatever it was. She felt it circle around her, not daring to get too close, curiously inspecting her.

I need the book you gave me once. Please.

The presence pulsed with approval, and Rose heard a *thunk* as a book hit the shelf on her left. Opening her eyes, she saw the tome she needed was waiting for her.

Thank you.

She felt another hum of satisfaction from the room. Apparently, whatever magic lived in the library appreciated manners.

Rose grabbed the book and opened its thin, dry pages at random. Though the tiny print and flowery language made the passages incredibly dense, this chapter contained helpful diagrams and scribblings of notes in the margins. She rotated the book so she could read the faded ink scrawled down the length of the page. "Summoning and Leeching of Magic. Beneficial in reclaiming gifted magicks or returning magicked items to their original state." It was precisely what she needed.

A diagram on the opposite page detailed symbols and markings that needed to be drawn in a circle on the ground. The enchantress needed to stand in the middle of the circle when performing the spell. Rose had seen other witches making chalk markings on the floor of the library before. Clutching the book to her chest, she marched to the far wall of the library and rifled through the small desks. Her heart thudded when her fingers brushed a few fragmented pieces of chalk. She glanced down at the book, scanning for anything else she might need. Was it really this easy that all she required were some nonsensical markings on the floor?

She gripped the largest stub of chalk in her fingers and copied the diagram from the book, drawing a circle as wide as she was tall and dashing strange runes and lines around its circumference. When she completed that ring, she set to work on the casting ring, a much smaller circle in the center of the first. Taking great care not to smudge any of her lines, Rose stepped out of the circles. She dragged a chair across the floor towards her workspace and climbed atop it so that she might get a better view of her handiwork. Her pulse continued to pound as she checked the diagram twice, making sure she did not miss a single mark. Her embroidery might be dreadful, but at least her sketching was good.

The last thing she needed was a drop of her own blood, placed in the center of the casting circle. She went back to the desks and riffled through them until she found something sharp.The best she could find was the tip of an ink pen. She perfunctorily dug it into her left index finger, hard enough to slice. Blood welled to the surface. Rose stepped back into the rings of chalk, taking care not to let the bead of blood on her fingertip fall. Glancing once more at the book, she drew a crescent moon on the floor. Her blood glistened against the marble.

Gripping the book tightly in two hands, she began the spell. She closed her eyes and reached for her power. The runes on the floor did all the work for her. All she had to do was channel her own magic into the circle where it would do the rest.

A violent throb in her head sent a wave of nausea through her. Again, her magic was difficult to reach. This time, instead of reaching through thick fog, it felt like swimming through mud. It clawed back at her, threatening to drown her as she reached blindly for her power. Fear bloomed in her mind at the sudden feeling of being smothered. If she couldn't reach her magic, she would be in serious trouble. The mud crept over her mind, her lungs, her legs. She was immobile, but she continued to push through, desperate for air.

After a few painfully long moments, she burst through the sludge. Her power waited for her, beckoning her to sink into its lovely shimmering depths. The ache in her head lessened, and she felt air rush back into her lungs.

There you are, the magic said. *There you are.*

The library and the runes felt impossibly far away. Rose gritted her teeth, knowing she would have to pull the magic back through the suffocating mire to channel it to the casting circles.

Distantly, she heard a door open as someone entered the library. She had to hurry. In a gasping, desperate lunge, she plowed through the muck, going breathless again as she yanked her sparkling magic along with her.

She crashed back into herself. Another wave of darkness and nausea threatened to buckle her knees. Every muscle in her body was tense and immobile. She could only move her eyes. Glowing, pulsing waves of magic coursed through her to the circles she stood in. The magic wrapped around her, soft and warm, but her body was seized with the effort of channeling it. Her power was a beautiful and terrible.

"Rose, stop!"

She couldn't see who it was. Everything vibrated. It took all her control to remain standing. The runes on the floor flickered, then shone with such brilliant light Rose thought she'd be blinded.

"Rose! You must stop!"

But she couldn't. She had to complete the spell. She had to prove that she was worthy of this magic; that she could do great things and wield exorbitant power.

"We have to do something!"

Rose focused her determination into her magic and the spell. She couldn't see past the blinding, dazzling light of her magic and the runes on the floor. She felt the bottom drop out of the world.

A deafening silence. Then—

BOOM.

A shock wave of power erupted from the circle. The giant bronze disks swung wildly, caught in the squall of power. Every light flickered, and stray papers gusted through the air, scattering about the library in a torrent.

This did not feel right. Rose was supposed to be leeching power from someone, not sending out waves of her own. She tried to close the book, to cut off the spell, but her arms were stuck, immobile as marble.

"Rose!"

She finally placed the voices. Harriet and Kate.

Her vision darkened. Pain pounded relentlessly in her head. She was frozen, seized by the strength of her power. She couldn't close the book that drained her. Her breath grew shallow, the edges of her sight blackened and threatened to swallow her whole.

There were more voices, shrill and shrieking. The glass ceiling cracked. Spiderweb fissures raced along the dome. More screaming. More pounding in her head.

She couldn't make it stop. Rose tried, with every ounce of strength she had left, to close the book, to move even one inch and disrupt the chalk runes on the floor to break the spell.

Her chest seized, her vision blackened, and a brisk autumnal-scented wind blew over her before she faded into darkest oblivion.

ROSE FLOATED, suspended in a state between waking and dreaming. She felt herself trapped between two places. The library's cold marble floor seeped through her dress. At the same time, her fingers dug into the soft grit of sand and paper-thinness of fallen leaves. Damp and decay, the smell of an autumn forest floor, flooded her nose. She tried to open her eyes. Her lids were so heavy, made of stone. Rose opened them a sliver, letting in a soft golden glow. Wind blew in the trees, sending the fiery orange and ruby red leaves dancing above her. Though her body was too heavy to move, a sense of gentle peace washed over her. Her head didn't ache so much here. She let her eyes fall closed once more, content to lie on the soft bed of leaves.

* * *

THE SHARP STING of a slap on her cheek dragged Rose back to consciousness. She was back in the library. Her stomach heaved. Rolling blindly onto her side, she retched, dimly registering a pair of shiny black shoes hop away from the vomit that pooled on the marble floor. The astringent smell made her eyes water. She struggled to sit up, but she shook so hard she thought her bones might crack. Her head felt like it was splitting in two.

She blinked, trying to focus her blurry vision, and prayed that the spell had worked.

"She'll kill us all!" screeched Lady Templeton. "You vile girl. What have you done?"

"Enough, Margaret." Lady Nightingale said, with steel in every syllable. "Leave us. All of you."

The sounds of shuffling feet, the grunt of Lady Templeton's disapproval, Lady Clarke's whispered plea cut off by a word from Lady Nightingale; everything made her head throb.

Rose shoved herself into a sitting position. She sat, trembling violently as the room emptied.

"See to the wards," Lady Nightingale instructed.

Rose rubbed her eyes. The room gradually came back into focus. The library doors closed, and an oppressive silence weighed heavily on her bones.

Lady Nightingale sighed and waved a hand. The mess of sick and the chalk runes vanished. Stray papers flew back to their rightful piles. The glass ceiling, which had not shattered entirely, became whole. Lady Nightingale crouched next to Rose and grabbed the wrist that bore the sapphire bracelet.

At her touch, Rose's quaking stopped. Her head no longer felt like it would split, but only ached weakly. She felt steadier, but dread kept her rooted to the floor.

Lady Nightingale released her grip and stood. "Miss Worthington." Her voice speared Rose's heart with a shard of ice. "What were you trying to accomplish?"

Rose got unsteadily to her feet, knowing she must face the consequences of what she'd done. Her heart pounded and her lips felt numb, but she forced the words out. "I heard what you were planning to do about the king."

Lady Nightingale inhaled, nostrils flaring. The smallest

frown creased her otherwise smooth face. "You tried to drain the King of England of magic. By yourself."

"I thought—I thought if I could show you how powerful I am that you would keep me, train me." She took a shuddering breath. "I'm engaged."

"And you thought that performing a spell, one I would not attempt with less than three accomplished witches, would convince me to get you out of your engagement."

Rose's stomach clenched. Her plan sounded so foolish now.

Lady Nightingale's frown deepened. "Do you know what you have done?"

Rose shook her head. She didn't dare ask if the spell had worked.

Her teacher clasped her hands in front of herself. "The pulses of magic you released have led the witch hunters right to us. Every being who wishes to do us harm now knows where we are. The witch hunters will come for us all, now."

A chill of dread raced down her spine. "The men you mentioned at the masquerade —" Rose didn't need to finish.

"Yes. Their sole aim is to dominate and destroy us. We have been monitoring their movements, keeping a close eye on them while shielding our abilities. Until today, we were confident that they did not know where to find us. Now they know." Power, strong and ancient, rippled from her teacher. Her lips were bloodless, her eyes flashed with anger.

Rose tried to speak, to apologize or beg for forgiveness, but her mouth had gone dry.

"Thankfully, there are cloaking wards and spells of protection all over this house. The signal you sent will have been distorted. They shall not know our exact location. But we are not safe. You have endangered us all, Rose."

A keening sound erupted from Rose's chest. *What have I done?* Guilt tied knots in her stomach, so violently that Rose thought she might be ill again.

"This is the second time I've had to speak to you about your recklessness with magic. Your thirst to prove yourself has jeopardized our safety. You are a danger to yourself and to others. You are dismissed as my pupil and may never enter this house to study magic again."

Time stood utterly still. Rose's whole body, which moments ago had been wracked with pain, went numb. She had failed.

She didn't care about endangering herself; she would do whatever was necessary to escape her engagement and keep Philip safe. But the spell had not worked, and she had put everyone at risk. Harriet, Kate, Lady Clarke, Lady Nightingale—all were in peril because of her.

"I'm sorry," she choked, her voice barely above a whisper. She wanted to throw herself on the ground and beg for forgiveness. But how could she ever atone for what she had just done? It was a fitting punishment. Her banishment was what she deserved. She would marry Percival Reeves and live out the rest of her wretched life alone. Without magic.

"Go," ordered Lady Nightingale with cold finality.

Rose bowed her head as tears fell down her cheeks. Every step was excruciating.

Traitor. Traitor. Traitor.

The halls were quiet. She saw no one as she left the Nightingale manor. The house held its breath, waiting to be rid of the dangerous thing that wandered within it. Rose opened the front door and stepped out into the street, where the rest of her doomed, solitary life awaited her.

CHAPTER 33

Rose spent the next two days alone in her room, refusing her mother's wheedling pleas to eat, attend parties, or go shopping. She barely had the energy to shake her head, mutely refusing it all. Her mother gave up on trying to cajole her on the third morning. She didn't know if it made her feel better, or worse, to know that her mother had given up on her, content to let her daughter wallow in her grief.

She'd lost everything. Philip, her magic, her lessons with Lady Nightingale, her friends. Guilt twisted inside her at every waking moment. She had placed the other witches in grave danger. If anything should happen to them, it would be all her fault. She cried the whole first day, unable to stop the tears of sorrow, self-pity, and shame. Now she felt like she'd never be able to cry again. A hollowness consumed her. Even more so than when she had first lost Philip. There was a gaping hole within her where her magic had once flickered restlessly, clamoring to be used. Now, there was only suffocating silence and stillness within her.

Rose longed for the dark, dreamless release of laudanum, or the burning sting of alcohol, but the oily, sleep-inducing drops had been disposed of and she couldn't bring herself to wander to Cornelius's study. There was nothing she could do to stop the trajectory of her life now. Everything she had done these last few months to try to maintain her independence had only hastened her journey to an engagement to the last person she would ever want to marry. The thought made every waking hour a torment.

Rose was utterly, undeniably, alone. She sat, watching the shadows lengthen across her bedroom wall with each passing hour before fading into twilight. Time had slipped away. She couldn't recall the last time she had anything to eat or drink.

Betsy opened the door to her room. Rose wasn't sure if it was morning or afternoon. She felt her maid brush her hair and twist it into a simple knot. Betsy pulled her gently to her feet, washed her with a damp cloth and changed her clothes. Her maid tried to take off the sapphire bracelet, but Rose placed a stiff hand upon it, a silent plea to keep it on.

Lady Nightingale had not taken it from her. Knowing her teacher, it was unlikely that it was mere oversight. Perhaps it had been her last gift, letting Rose keep the protection charm in case the witch hunters came looking. A tiny prickle of fear pierced through her gloom. The danger must be grave if Lady Nightingale thought she still needed it.

"Your cousin wants to see you," said Betsy.

The fear faded as quickly as it had come, replaced by a suffocating numbness. Rose nodded once to indicate that she had heard and followed her maid down to the study.

Cornelius sat behind the large desk, a scroll of paper laid before him. It was stiflingly hot. The windows were shut, trapping sticky summer air within the study. Rose stood before him, arms limp at her sides. Cornelius dismissed Betsy and turned his full attention to her. They hadn't been alone together since she had burned his hand. She spied a thin bandage covering his palm, wrapping around his fingers. A mirror to the one Philip wore. Rose wondered what kind of person that made her.

Once, she might have balked at the way he studied her, his dark soulless eyes staring into the very core of her being. Now she stared blankly back at him, waiting for him to speak. There was nothing more he could take from her.

He slid the scroll of paper towards her. "Your marriage contract. I require your signature."

Rose swallowed hard and scanned the shelves behind Cornelius, looking for something, anything, she could use to delay this moment. As soon as she signed this contract, she would be truly lost.

Cornelius let out a high, bitter laugh as he walked around the desk and grabbed her chin between his thumb and forefinger, the linen bandage rough against her skin. *"Look at me,"* he hissed.

She reluctantly slid her eyes to his. His pupils were too large, their black centers taking up most of his eyes. Only a tiny sliver of golden brown remained.

"There is no way to prevent this marriage. None. You made your choice when you refused me, and now you will live with the consequences of your actions. You will also name me as sole inheritor to the Reeves fortune should you fail to produce any heirs."

"You can't be serious," Rose said. Her voice grated against her throat, raspy with disuse. Such a thing was unheard of. Reeves would have a family of his own, no matter how distant, that would be written into the will. It was simply how things were done.

Cornelius released her chin and sneered. "He has already agreed to it. I am the son he never had, after all. All those hours at the club listening to the old man spew his vitriol paid off."

A wave of anger made a crack in the walls of Rose's despair. "Are you that desperate for titles and fortune? Or do you simply find satisfaction in using the people around you to meet your own ends?"

"The estate's considerable wealth go to my business back in New York. Not that it is any of your concern what I do with my money."

Rose had resigned herself to the idea of marrying. After she had betrayed her sisterhood, she knew she deserved a life of isolation and suffering. But Cornelius would not be content to dump her in a country estate far from London. He would use her and her connections for his own personal gain. Her breath grew quick and shallow. Her chest burned. "I won't sign anything. You can't make me."

"Oh, but I can. It wouldn't do for everyone to learn of your little tryst in the garden with not one, but *two* men at the masquerade ball—one of those men being the respectable Lord Crawford." Cornelius smiled wickedly. "What would his family think? Imagine what his sister might do to you if she found out, the possessive bitch."

The walls of self-pity and grief that she had crafted over the last several days shattered entirely. It was one thing for him to manipulate and use her. But she wouldn't stand for the people she cared about to become his targets. Not again. "No one would believe you."

"I think they would when I challenge him to a duel to defend your honor."

Her anger waned as the sound of gunfire reverberated in her head, an echo of the night Cornelius had shot Philip. Heat drained from her face as a dark cloud of foreboding pressed heavily upon her.

Alexander had been nothing but kind. Rose still regretted having to end her friendship with him. He had suffered enough at her hands. She would not allow him to be hurt by Cornelius. Not if she could prevent it. "That won't be necessary," she said through gritted teeth.

"I thought not. You really are a harlot. It's been, what, a few weeks since I shot your last lover?"

Rose wanted nothing more than to slap the smirk from his face. Her rage pounded in her ears as something sinister itched at her fingertips. She had burned him once. She could do it again.

Rose took a deep breath, trying to clear her head of violent thoughts. The breath calmed her just enough to realize that Cornelius didn't know who the second man in the garden had been, or he would use Philip's presence to blackmail her, not Alexander's. She clenched her jaw, not wanting to betray her thoughts. Philip was safe. For now.

Cornelius reached for the marriage contract and slid it towards her.

She could shove past him and bar herself in her room. She could run. But it would only delay the inevitable. Cornelius might shoot Alexander just out of spite for her insolence.

"Sign." He shoved an ink pen across the desk.

Rose picked up the pen. It was cold and heavy in her palm. She stared at the blank space that awaited her signature. Reeves had already signed it.

"I don't have all day."

Rose slowly unscrewed the cap. A bead of sweat trickled down her temple. It was so hot in here, she couldn't think. She needed more time. She had thought she was ready to accept her fate, thought it was the punishment she deserved, but she couldn't condemn everyone she had ever known to be used as pawns in whatever sick game Cornelius was playing. Another bead of sweat dripped down her back. The heat gave her an idea.

Her eyes darted to the hearth as she reached deep within herself. She brought the marriage contract up to her face. "I'm reading," she said as nonchalantly as she could. Her head throbbed and her fingers shook as she burrowed deep, deep,

deep within, fighting to reach her magic. It was even harder to access than it had been in Lady Nightingale's library. Her knees threatened to buckle as she took a pensive, swaying step to her right towards the fireplace.

She was already damned. Why not use her magic to try to save herself?

Cornelius's hand shot out to stop her, just as she finally broke through to the magic that waited for her. *There you are,* it whispered gleefully. She mentally grabbed a fistful of sparkling magic then threw herself to the ground, dodging Cornelius and thrusting her hand into the hearth. She let out a bark of pain as her elbow hit stone. A blaze roared to life, bright and burning as if it has been burning for hours. Rose released the contract into the heart of the fire. Flames shot up, licking the sides of the chimney. The paper burned, its edges turning black. The contract was ruined. Pieces of it floated in the flames before turning to ash. She had forestalled her doom, however temporarily.

Panting and fighting the urge to be sick, Rose rolled onto her back. Cornelius loomed above her, eyes now entirely black and glittering with rage. Something was not right. An acrid smell clogged her throat and burned her eyes, but she could not look away from Cornelius's murderous stare. Sweat trickled from her brow.

"I could no longer sense it on you," he mused, his voice cold and biting. "For days, I have waited and watched. Now, I see." He extended a single forefinger towards the raging flames.

Rose's stomach clenched. The contract lay in the fireplace, untouched by the ravenous fire. A strange, smoky barrier surrounded the paper, protecting it.

Cornelius crooked his finger, and the paper leapt from the grate, untouched. He picked it up before Rose could blink. Magic. Cornelius was using *magic.* She shivered as she lay prone on the floor, mind reeling.

"Intriguing." He peered down at her like she was a specimen to be observed. "The levels of magic you possess appear wholly bound to your emotional state. You have exhausted your meager stores with this little stunt. There's barely any magic left within you."

Rose's hands trembled. She knew what he said was truth. She was utterly exhausted. There was no whisper of magic left within her, only bleak and cold emptiness. After the spell she had attempted in Lady Nightingale's library and this, there was nothing. The endless supply she had tapped into at the masquerade was gone. Dread coiled in her stomach.

"Get up. Your magic may be worthless, but I still have use for you."

She shoved to her feet, limbs quaking.

"Yes." He tapped a long finger on his chin as he observed her shivering. "I knew from the first dinner at the estate that you possessed some magic. It was quite amusing, the way you shattered that glass. So jealous, sweet Rose," he clicked his thong against his teeth. "I thought you might have been the one I am looking for, but I was mistaken. Your stores of magic are practically worthless. Though I wonder..." he trailed off, lost in schemes of malice. His pupils contracted, revealing the golden-brown irises, though they did completely return to normal.

Rose clenched her fists, digging her nails into her palms.

Cornelius set the unblemished contract back on the desk. "Your wish is granted, for now, Rose. There is something I must add to the contract. Return to your room. The next time I call for you, you *will* sign. You will marry Reeves, secure me my fortune, and assist me with another task that I must see to." He turned his back on her, dismissing her.

Rose yanked open the door and walked as fast as she could to her room, her knees trembling and heart pounding. She concentrated on her feet as they carried her down the hall and up the stairs. She blocked out all other thought, all other feeling.

The weight of her failure pressed down so heavily on her it was difficult to breathe. She could not think about it. Instead, she focused on placing one in front of the other.

Her mother was waiting in the garishly pink parlor. Rose stood in the doorway, surprised to see her. Her body was still wracked with tremors.

Her mother took one look at her and wordlessly wrapped her in an embrace.

Silent tears streaked down Rose's face as her mother held her. They stood for a long while, until her tears stopped, her breath steadied, and her limbs finally stilled. Her head still ached, gripped in a relentless vice.

Her mother finally broke their embrace and wiped Rose's cheeks of tears. "I know you do not want to marry Lord Reeves. But it will be for the best."

Rose swallowed. She couldn't possibly tell her mother that marrying Reeves wasn't the sole cause of her misery. Her mother would never understand, and Rose couldn't tell her about her magic, or Cornelius's nefarious plans. She would never believe her. So, she held silent, waiting for her mother to continue.

"All I wanted was for you to find a love match. I would have helped you marry Lord Crawford if you had asked it, or any other gentleman who would have caught your eye. I wish you had let me help you, Rose." She sighed despondently.

Rose had given up being angry at her mother for her narrow ideals for her life. Now, it made her inexplicably sad. Her mother would have done all in her power to see her wed a wealthy man of the gentry. But would she have put forth the same efforts for someone she deemed common?

"And what if the man I love, the only man who I could be happy with, is a farmer's son?" she whispered.

Her mother frowned and shook her head. "What are you talking about?"

"I love Philip Harlow," she explained, chin trembling.

Shock registered on her mother's face as she shuffled backwards. She placed a hand over her heart. "You really were running away with him that night, weren't you?"

Rose stiffened. She knew her mother would disapprove. "I won't condemn myself to a life governed by these ridiculous rules. I can't marry someone just for their money, Mama."

"But you would have abandoned me?" Her mother's face was bloodless, her eyes wide with dismay.

"You are the one who abandoned *me*," Rose cried. "After George died, it was like I wasn't even there. You hardly spoke to me for two *years*. It was only when I came of age that you suddenly took an interest in me again. And it wasn't an interest in me as a person, but in my marital prospects."

There were no more tears to cry. There would never be enough tears to convey the heartache and sorrow Rose felt at her mother's abandonment.

"Rose, I—" she covered her mouth. "I had no idea."

"I don't blame you for your grief," Rose said. "But it hurt so much that the only thing you ever thought I was good for was marriage. That my only value was economic."

"We must marry, Rose." She lowered her hand, face still white. "That is how we survive in this world. You are my daughter. You're shrewd, brave, and kind, not a mere commodity. But for you to have any long-lasting happiness in this world, you must marry. If you had run away with that boy, you would have been disgraced. I would never have been able to see you, and you would have none of the money your father left for your dowry. You would have experienced a few years of passion, but the hardness of your life would have soured any affection you had for him."

"You can't possibly know that," Rose said, crossing her arms.

"You are my daughter." Her mother smiled sadly. "I know you want more than what most can give you."

Rose stared at the floor. She couldn't look her mother in the face. What she wanted was to be loved and accepted for who she was. Her mother might never give her that. Especially when she would never know about the parts of her that mattered.

"I know this is challenging. At this moment, it seems impossible, but I have faith that you will find happiness. In a few years, you will be a wealthy widow. Then maybe you can marry for love."

Her mother pat her on the shoulder as she left, leaving Rose alone with her thoughts.

CHAPTER 34

Rose wrapped her arms tightly around herself. She ignored a summons to supper and remained in front of her suite's windows, watching rain lash against the glass in torrents. She couldn't face her mother, not after what had just passed between them. Lightning cracked the sky, swallowing everything in a moment of blinding, dazzling stillness before plunging the world back into dull shadow.

She had always known her mother upheld traditional ideals about what a woman was meant to do in this world. Rose had hoped she might accept that she could not stand to be suffocated by the rules and customs that governed their lives.

Another crack of lightning broke the sky, and Rose closed off the wound in her heart, sealing it with the cauterizing sizzle of lightning. What she could not so easily ignore was what Cornelius had done in the study mere hours ago. He had used *magic* to restore the contract, and while it did not feel like any magic she had ever experienced, it was the only thing that made sense. The memory of his dark, cold eyes sent a shiver down her spine. Gooseflesh tickled the back of her neck and arms as she recalled the malice in his eyes.

Fragments of thought, pieces of a puzzle, floated just out of reach. She was shocked that Cornelius could wield such power. Everything Lady Nightingale said made it seem like only women had a strong proclivity for magic. But Cornelius was a man, and he had reversed the effects of her spell.

He'd known ever since they met that she had some magic. Even before she knew it herself. But why had he not used that information against her? If he had known for so long, he could have added it to his arsenal of blackmail material. Perhaps he was also afraid that no one would believe him if he said his cousin was a witch. She was sure no one would believe *her* if she revealed the same about Cornelius. No one except Lady Nightingale and the other witches.

Thunder rolled in the distance. Rose unpinned her hair, letting it tumble down her back. She threw the pins onto her vanity as she entered her bedroom.

Even if she wanted to, she couldn't tell the Nightingales about Cornelius's magic. She was banished from the manor and from studying magic. She had ruined all chances at becoming a fell-fledged witch. Rose sat at her vanity and cupped her forehead in her palm. Her throat and stomach twisted into painful knots.

She'd brought this upon herself. Lady Nightingale was right. She had been reckless and selfish, placing her own ambition before the safety of others. She had placed Harriet and Kate in danger after all they had done for her. Witch hunters would stalk them, all because of her. Rose wished Lady Nightingale had said what the witch hunters looked like, at least. Then she would be able to at least keep her head down if she encountered any. Perhaps she did not know the face of their enemy.

Another crack of lightning illuminated the bedroom, and Rose caught her reflection in the mirror. Dark circles bloomed under her eyes, her hair billowed around her in waves. Her face was pale. She blinked as the light faded, unsettled by how much her haggard face looked like Cornelius's own sickly visage.

Rose shot up from her seat, tipping the bench over with a crash that sounded in time with thunder.

Cornelius had thought that she was the one he was looking for. Not looking for a wife, but for a *witch*. Cornelius was a witch hunter. She felt incredibly stupid for not realizing sooner.

Rose bit her lip, ignoring the taste of copper as her mind reeled. Cornelius wasn't through with her yet. She may not be the one he was looking for, but marriage to Reeves, the desire for his fortune, his business in New York, it all had to be related to the witch hunters. But who was he looking for?

She had to warn Harriet and Kate. She had to tell Lady Nightingale and the Council that her cousin was one of the witch hunters. Surely Lady Nightingale would have warned her if she'd known Cornelius was a witch hunter. She wouldn't have let her continue to live in this house when she was so close to danger.

Rose paced frantically, twisting the ends of her hair. There was something that still did not complete the puzzle. Who had been giving Cornelius orders? The night of the masquerade, she had heard him pleading with someone. He was clearly not working alone, but perhaps he could lead them to whoever was heading this pursuit.

She grabbed a cloak from her wardrobe and hastily braided her hair. She couldn't solve the rest of this mystery alone. The last time she'd tried, she put everyone she cared about in danger. She had betrayed Alexander, lost all her friends, disgraced her teacher, and pushed away Philip — all because she thought she could take care of every problem by herself. But this... even if she couldn't aid her friends in eliminating this threat, she had to warn them. There was no hope that Lady Nightingale would take her back as her pupil, but Rose had to tell her what she had discovered. She had to do all she could to prevent any harm from befalling the other witches. Even if it meant placing herself in danger.

Rose threw the midnight blue cloak around her shoulders and crept down the darkened hallway, past the gloomy foyer and silent kitchen to the back door of the house. There was no time to waste. She raced into the night, lightning illuminating her path as she ran. She would warn the Nightingales. But not before she set one last thing to rights.

* * *

BY THE TIME she reached the townhouse on the east side, mist clung to Rose's cloak and eyelashes. She glanced at the paper once more, now smeared from exposure to the damp. Satisfied that she was at the right address, Rose knocked on the door.

Her throat tightened as she waited. Nerves made her stomach twist in knots. She rubbed her arms, trying to dispel the gooseflesh that had erupted across her skin. She knocked again, louder this time. Rose's mouth was dry. The windows were dark. She swallowed, as her hopes began to dim. Maybe it was for the best. Seeing him might only make things worse.

Rose turned to run to her next destination, but halted as the door opened behind her. Philip stood inside, illuminated by a soft, warm glow. His shirt was unbuttoned, his hair disheveled. He stared at her, mouth agape.

The speech she had prepared, the things she yearned to say, vanished at the sight of him. She wanted to beg for his forgiveness, to tell him that she'd been wrong that day in the park. Now, she could only utter one word.

"Philip."

It was all he needed.

He pulled Rose inside, crushing her to him. His mouth found hers, and she wrapped her arms around him. Her heart beat fiercely against her chest as her body melted into his. Philip whirled, kicking the door closed behind him. He trailed kisses down her neck. "Rose." His name was like a prayer on his lips.

She ran his fingers through his hair as he trailed his tongue across the soft spot behind her jaw. Heat pooled in her core and between her legs. She felt as if she was wound too tightly. Ever inch of her burned with need.

Philip pulled away and cupped her chin. "Come to my bed," he growled.

Rose brushed her fingers against his exposed chest. It rose and fell rapidly, pressing into her palm. "That's what I want. Please, Philip. Make me yours."

Before she could draw breath, Philip scooped her into his arms. He carried her up a flight of stairs and into his room, kissing her all the while. She kept her arms locked firmly around him, relishing the feel of his broad shoulders and the warmth of his skin.

He nudged the door shut behind them, and set Rose gently her feet.

Rose felt her cloak slide to the floor, then her dress. She stood before him in only her chemise and stockings. Philip removed his shirt. She swallowed at the sight of him. She ran her hand across the hard ridges of his chest and the planes of his stomach. He grabbed the back of her neck and moaned as he kissed her.

She had thought she'd feel more timid exposing herself to him, but her need smothered all self-consciousness. She was here, with Philip, for what might be the only time. She was about to do something reckless and dangerous.

Rose was not the girl who had asked him to run away with her a few months ago. She was not afraid of chasing what she wanted head-on. Not anymore. Not when danger lurked in the shadows, and witch hunters prowled the streets. Even so, there was no easy way to say what she needed to. But if she were to bare her heart to anyone, it would be Philip.

"I know you are leaving soon, but I love you, Philip. Even if we can't be together as a proper man and wife, I still want you. I want to be with you, always. What that looks like, or means, I don't know. But I can't deny how I feel. I once believed that you were gone, that you were taken from me. It was devastating. I don't want to feel like that ever again."

Philip's eyes glowed fervently as brushed his thumb across her jaw. "Whatever you ask of me, I will do. Whatever you want this to be, want *us* to be, is all right with me."

"I just want you." She pressed up on her toes, and kissed him, pouring all her love and everything else she couldn't say into her kiss.

Philip tugged the straps of her chemise down her shoulders. She stepped away from him, widening the distance even though her body ached for his touch.

He stared at her with fiery eyes.

"Do you want me to take this off?" Rose asked. Her fingers brushed the top of her chemise. Rose could see how badly Philip wanted her. The hard length of him pressed through his thin trousers.

Philip only nodded. His throat bobbed as he swallowed. His lips parted with desire, and his chest heaved.

Warmth rushed through Rose at the sight of him. He was entirely at her command. Philip craved her as much as she desired him. Through heady thoughts of want, Rose realized that this was power. A different sort of power than her magic granted her, but it was power nonetheless.

And she wanted to revel in it.

"Say it."

"Yes." Philip's voice was hoarse with want.

Rose pulled her chemise lower and lower. She shivered as

the smooth fabric slid down her body until it was gathered around her waist. Every inch of her buzzed with tension. Even the soft brush of cloth stirred her desire. Rose slid her chemise down her legs until it pooled on the floor. She was naked, save for the necklace she never took off. The necklace he had given her.

Philip raked hungry eyes over her body, drinking in the sight of her. His eyes stilled on the carved rose. His face softened.

It melted her heart. "Touch me," Rose whispered.

He closed the space between them in an instant. He wrapped his fingers in her hair and brought her mouth to his. The other hand spanned over her body, brushing against her throat, her chest. He cupped her breasts, and she let out a shuddering groan.

It felt so good, but she still needed *more.*

Philip tasted her skin and kneaded her flesh until her knees trembled. When she could hardly stand, he guided her to his bed. He grabbed the top of one of her stockings and slid it with tantalizing slowness down her thigh, her calf, her ankle. Philip let the stocking fall to the floor and he ran his hands up her leg, kneading her flesh as Rose let out a sweet groan of pleasure. He did the same with the other stocking, then joined Rose on the bed. He caged her with his body, propping himself up on his forearms.

"Are you sure, Rose?"

She looked into his eyes. They were filled adoration. For her. Her heart swelled in her chest. She was certain. "Yes. Please, Philip." Her voice wasn't authoritative. It had morphed from commanding to pleading, and she gladly let go of any hope of wrestling control back. She gave it all willingly to Philip.

"Thank God." He kissed her again until their breathing grew ragged. "I can make you feel so good, love." He dipped his hand between her legs.

Rose gasped as pleasure jolted through her. A moan built in the back of her throat as he ran his thumb over the sensitive bundle nerves between her thighs. She'd never imagined being with a man could feel so good. Her body wound tighter and tighter. She needed *something*, she just didn't know what.

"Philip," she moaned. She writhed, her fist gripped the bedcover. "I can't —"

He dipped a finger inside of her, and stars bloomed behind her eyes. She writhed against his hand, needing the friction, reveling in it.

"That's it, love."

The tension built until she shattered. Rose cried out. She arched as every muscle grew taut and pleasure overcame her in waves.

Once her breathing slowed, she opened her eyes. Philip smoothed the hair away from her brow. "How was that?"

"Oh, my god."

His lips quirked. "Good."

"But you —"

He stopped her with a kiss. "That was pleasurable for me, too."

Rose pouted. "But I want you to feel as good as I do." She cupped his face with her hand.

Philip's face pinched. He seemed torn.

Rose ran her hand down his chest and dipped her fingers just inside the waistband of his pants.

He inhaled sharply.

"Take them off," she said. "You don't need to worry about my honor. You said whatever I wanted this to be would be alright with you. This is what I want."

He needed no further encouragement. He slipped off his trousers. The hard, thick length of him sprang free.

Rose swallowed at the sight of him.

Philip shifted his body, pinning her beneath him once again.

"It may hurt a little your first time. I'll be as gentle as I can. I promise."

Rose nodded. She wanted to know what it felt like. All of it.

Philip kissed her, and moved his hips against hers. Pleasure whipped through her whole body at the sensation of him sliding between her wet thighs.

"Ready?" he panted, breaking the kiss.

Again, Rose could only nod. Her head swam with pleasure.

Philip slid into her, easing himself slowly, then withdrawing. He repeated the movement, slowly stretching her.

Rose thought it felt strange. Not unpleasant, but odd. It was such a foreign sensation.

Philip kissed her. "Does it feel alright?"

"Yes," she said, placing her hands on his chest.

"This part may hurt a bit," he warned. But she was ready for him.

Rose felt a quick flash of pain as something stretched within her. She bit her lip, and made a small noise. Philip stoked her hair, and cupped her face in one of his hands. She leaned into the touch.

Philip moved slowly within her, and Rose felt the pleasure of the friction between them as Philip thrust into her again and again, each time a little faster. Desire built within her once more. The sensation of Philip filling her provided a different pleasure than what she had felt moments ago.

Her fists gripped the sheets again as she felt her own hips rocking to meet Philip's. She moaned deep in her throat as they moved together. Philip moved within her faster and faster until she felt him stiffen and quickly withdraw. He moaned and shuddered, gripping himself with one hand and clutching the sheets by her head with the other. His seed spilled from him onto the bed between them.

When he slumped onto the bed next to her, Rose kissed his forehead and wrapped her arms around him, as he had done after her climax. Instead of rousing, as she had, Philip nestled closer to her. His eyes drifted closed.

Rose stared down at his handsome face. He looked so peaceful. She felt her heart clench as watched his chest rising and falling in even breaths.

She allowed herself a few moments before she extracted herself from the bed. Rose dressed as Philip continued to doze. The bliss of their love making faded with every passing moment. She had forgotten, for a little while, about what lay ahead. Now the black cloud of fear settled over her once more.

She heard movement on the bed as she bent down to tug her shoes on.

"Where are you off to, Rose?" asked Philip, voice gravelly with sleep.

"I have to go. I'm sorry."

He sat fully upright, not caring that he was still naked. "What do you mean, go?"

"There's something I have to do." With her shoes on, she straightened to meet Philip's hurt gaze.

"What is it?"

Rose shook her head. "I can't tell you. But other people are depending on me, and I don't have a lot of time left. I needed to see you before I — before I left."

"Did I do something wrong? Did I hurt you?"

She felt her face soften. "It was the best thing I've ever felt. Truly. I would do it again right now if I didn't have to go."

Philip looked like he would very much rather she removed her clothes again, but there was hurt there, too. "I know I've asked you before, but I will ask again, and a hundred times after that. Stay with me. Come with me. Just *be* with me."

"I want to." Rose pressed the heels of her palms into her eyes. "But I *can't,* Philip. I can't. I won't put you in danger. Not again. I won't."

Philip stood abruptly, clutching the bedsheet around his

waist. "What danger? If you mean that damned cousin of yours." He placed a hand on her shoulder.

"You have no idea what he is capable of," she snapped, unable to keep her frustration contained. "You have no idea what *I'm* capable of."

"Of course I do. You're smart, determined, beautiful, and never take no for an answer. But if he's said anything to you, or threatened you, then let me help you."

Rose swallowed an incredulous laugh. Philip couldn't possibly understand.

"He can't follow you across an ocean. Come with me. I'm not asking you to marry me. I know that's not what you want. But there's no reason we can't be together." He dragged a hand through his disheveled hair.

If only she could tell him, but Lady Nightingale had forbid her from ever revealing her power to anyone. Rose had chosen magic over everything else.

Now she was suffering those consequences.

"What are you not telling me, Rose?" he asked irritably.

She sighed. "It's not because I don't trust you. It's because I promised I wouldn't tell."

"If you're in trouble, let me help you. You never let anyone help you with anything. It's not a sign of weakness."

Rose blanched. "I never said it was."

"Well, you certainly act like it is." Philip folded his arms and glowered at her.

The warm glow of contentment vanished. "I'm sorry, Philip."

There was nothing more to say. She'd dallied too long already. Once again, she'd placed her own desires over the safety of others. Cornelius was a witch hunter. The Nightingales had to be warned. What had she been thinking, coming here first? Shame heated her cheeks. She had to go. Now. "Goodbye."

She didn't give Philip a chance to respond. She scooped her

cloak up from the floor and dashed from the room. He didn't follow her.

Rose wrenched the door open and plunged into the night. Rain fell in torrents, pooling in the streets. She ran headlong into the storm and let it swallow her whole.

CHAPTER 35

The back gardens of Nightingale Manor seemed to bend and twist and morph as Rose ran through them. Turns that she was sure hadn't been there before sprang up, leading her further into the maze of blooms and greenery. Leaves shuddered as the wind and rain whipped through the hedges and plants. She thought only of reaching the door, of warning the women inside, as she pumped her legs. Rose could barely see through the sheets of rain that fell, puddling onto the gravel paths. She was soaked to the bone, but would not slowed by mere water.

Suddenly, the garden spit her out. Hair clung her to cheeks and forehead. The windows glowed, a beacon in the dark that beckoned her forward. Rose slammed her fist against the back door, praying that someone inside would hear her over the thunder that continued to reverberate throughout the city. The rain had numbed her feet, which were cut and bleeding. Her soft slippers were not meant for running through cobbled streets and gravel paths at breakneck speed.

She pounded on the door for a third time. *"Please."* The rain continued to fall in torrents. A moment later, the door swung open. She pitched forward, knocked off balance. No one let her inside. Rose let out a little laugh of relief as she stepped into the manor. The house really did respond well to manners. As soon as she stepped over the threshold, the door swung shut behind her.

Dropping her soaked cloak to the floor in a wet heap, she peered into the quiet house. The soft glow of a fire and distant candles flickered down the hall. Rose headed towards the light.

The parlor door was ajar. With a soft nudge, Rose opened the door. Lady Nightingale and her Council sat inside, bent towards one another in hushed discussion. Lady Nightingale sat at the head of the circle, directly across from the entryway. Her eyes locked with Rose's, and a bemused smile flitted across her lips.

The other witches turned to see who had disturbed them. Rose was unnerved by the feeling of thirteen pairs of eyes all fixated on her at once.

"How did you get in here?" choked out Lady Templeton. She stood and pressed her lips into a thin scowl. The other witches, Lady Clarke among them, also got to their feet. Soft, confused chatter filled the room. Rose recognized some of the ten other women, but not all of them.

Lady Nightingale lifted her hand, silencing the chatter. "It appears my house has let her in, despite my instructions never to do so."

Rose's heart thudded against her chest as she stepped fully into the parlor. "I have something I need to tell you. All of you."

Lady Nightingale dipped her chin, wordlessly inviting her to continue.

Rose shifted, painfully aware of the puddle of rainwater she was dripping on the fine emerald rug. She didn't have time to wonder why Lady Nightingale, who had banished her in such quiet fury, was now allowing her to speak. She balled her hands into fists so the others would not see them shake. "First, I must apologize. I have been shamefully reckless and have placed you all in danger. I'm so sorry. No words can take back what I have done, but I am sorry for my actions."

Lady Templeton scoffed. The other witches simply stared at her, their faces blank.

Rose continued, despite the growing lump in her throat. "I must also tell you, I have discovered the identity of one of the witch hunters. I came to warn you."

The Council erupted.

"Were you followed?"

"How do you know?"

"It is too dangerous for her to be here!"

"Who is it?" Lady Nightingale asked, her voice cutting through the commotion. Everyone stilled, waiting for the answer.

"My cousin, Cornelius Worthington."

The silence was suffocating. All eyes turned to Lady Nightingale. Rose clutched her hands together. She had thought that Lady Nightingale might already suspect Cornelius, especially after what she'd shared about him the night of the masquerade.

But if Lady Nightingale was suspicious, she did not show it. "Explain," she commanded. The witches sat, turning their chairs to her, ready to bear witness to her testimony.

Rose told the Council of each fragment of the puzzle she had discovered, and of the magic she had seen Cornelius use that afternoon. She breathlessly explained what she had overheard in the garden the night of the masquerade, and that he was looking for one witch in particular. After she told them all she knew, she waited, observing the expressions of panic, fear, and anger on the faces of the Council. Rose traced her thumb over the scar on her wrist, waiting for someone to speak.

Lady Nightingale remained calm. "It appears as though your

cousin *may* be a witch hunter," she mused. "Please wait outside while we discuss what you have shared, Miss Worthington."

Rose nodded and stepped into the hall, closing the doors behind her. She leaned against the wall, not caring that she left a damp print on the fine paper. The adrenaline that had fueled her journey here was gone. The cold and damp penetrated her bones. Her teeth chattered, and her feet ached horribly, blistered and raw. She closed her eyes. She was so very tired.

Five minutes passed, then ten. She debated curling up on the floor to wait and rest, but Lady Clarke opened the door and beckoned her inside. Rose obeyed, teeth still chattering.

Lady Clarke retook her seat and muttered something to the two witches next to her. They silently waved their hands in Rose's direction, and she felt her hair and clothes dry instantly. Warmth leapt back into her. As one, the three witches extended their hands to where the fireplace flickered and muttered, "For the Mother." Steam rose from the flames as the water that was siphoned from her evaporated.

"Thank you," said Rose.

Lady Nightingale stood while the rest of the Council remained seated. Something about the gesture did not bode well.

"We thank you for conveying this warning, Miss Worthington. We were not aware that Lord Worthington may be a witch hunter."

Rose stiffened. May *be a witch hunter?* The floor seemed to drop from beneath her feet. They didn't believe her.

Lady Nightingale shook her head, as if reading her thoughts. "It' not that we don't believe you. We simply require more proof."

"I'll gather whatever proof you require. If I can." Rose would not give up so easily. They had not seen Cornelius's violent moods, his utter hatred. They didn't know what he was capable of.

Some of the Council shifted uncomfortably in their seats.

"We have reservations about continuing any sort of relationship with you, Miss Worthington. For all we know, your cousin could have sent you here as a spy. You have been reckless with magic and brought danger to our doorstep. What I have Seen for you also calls for caution."

Rose hung her head. She hadn't wanted to admit she held a tiny glimmer of hope that Lady Nightingale would take her back, that she could rejoin the witches and resume her training. She could not deny her curiosity. If she was going to be tossed out one last time, she wanted to know what the Council knew about her future. Lady Nightingale never had told her. She lifted her gaze to the woman in front of her. "What have you Seen?"

"You will be the salvation or destruction of us all."

Her stomach plummeted. Her hands grew cold, a shiver ran down her spine. "And you don't know which it will be? Or how?" Her voice did not sound like her own. It was full of pain and longing.

"I have not been able to tell. Certain signs point to salvation, others to our ruin. You are an enigma. There have only been a few witches whose futures have been so unclear to me."

She was a danger to everyone here. Rose did not begrudge Lady Nightingale, or the other witches, for wanting to remove her from their circle. Why risk her continued presence, especially after the havoc she had wrought? Rose leaned back on her heels, ready to accept the demand for her to leave.

"However," Lady Nightingale continued, "the benefits of your connection, and the strength of your power, potentially outweigh the risks. There are two conditions you must agree to should you wish to aid us."

Rose's mouth went dry. "What are they?"

"The first is that you must bring us concrete evidence of your cousin's treachery within twenty-four hours. The second is that you must live here for the rest of the season, or until you are married, where we may keep a close eye on you."

Rose held her breath, waiting for the catch. "And you will continue to train me as your student?" she dared to ask.

"Correct."

"And should I fail?"

"You will be banished once more. Not even the house will be able to let you in again."

Lady Nightingale offered her what she wanted most: to help eliminate the threat she had created and continue her training. If there was a disadvantage to the arrangement that she could not yet see, Rose would deal with it later. "I agree to the terms," she said, sealing her fate.

"Then give me your hand," Lady Nightingale instructed.

Rose extended her hand to the matron. The pleasant scent of jasmine wafted over her as their hands met.

"Do you, Rosalind Francis Worthington, so enter into this agreement of your own free will?" Their clasped hands glowed with an emerald light.

"I do," she replied, swallowing a kernel of unease. At her acceptance, the light grew as bright as the cracks of lightning from the storm that continued to rage outside. Rose blinked, temporarily blinded as a sharp pain flared on her wrist. She sucked in a breath through her teeth, not wanting to betray her pain. When the light faded, Lady Nightingale unclasped their hands.

"You have twenty-four hours, Miss Worthington."

Rose glanced at the clock on the mantle. It was two minutes past midnight. Her time was already ticking.

"Bring us proof, and you shall rejoin us."

She nodded and exited the room, ignoring the feeling of thirteen piercing stares on her back as she strode away. She had no time to waste. Her hand gripped the handle of the back door, but the patter of footsteps made her freeze. She spun around, bracing for more stipulations or conditions. Lady Clarke hurried towards her.

"Wait," she said in a soft voice. Lady Clarke gestured to Rose's sodden cloak. "I can shield you from the rain."

Rose opened her mouth to protest, but Lady Clarke had already raised her hands and brushed them over her cloak, drying it. "There," she said, giving it a little shake. "It will repel water for you, too. We can't have you arriving home looking like a drowned cat." She threw the cloak around Rose's shoulders, smoothing it into place. As she did so, Lady Clarke leaned down to whisper in her ear. "The bracelet. Take it off at the right moment, but not before. It was only meant to protect you. You must put it on again straightaway. You must not leave it off for long."

She pulled back, finished adjusting the hood of the cloak around her face, and made her way back to the rest of the Council before Rose could utter a word.

She glanced down at the sapphire gems that encircled her wrist. A symbol of affection — and a shackle. Her stomach clenched. New, white scar tissue had appeared on her skin. Sliding the bracelet back, Rose examined the symbol that had been branded upon her wrist. A bird sitting in an open cage, waiting to take flight. Lady Nightingale's house sigil. Proof of the bargain she had made. She did not want to think about the significance of the mark, or what would happen should she fail to uphold her end of the bargain.

She wrenched the door open. Cool night air blasted her face. The thunder and lightning had moved on, and a shroud of darkest night covered the city. Rose moved unseen between alleys and walkways, cloak shielding her from the damp mist. If only it could keep out the chill that had settled in her heart.

CHAPTER 36

Rose rubbed her eyes, fighting exhaustion. She'd stolen a few hours of sleep. She had less than a day to find proof that Cornelius was a witch hunter. Rose paced, alternately biting her thumb and running a finger over the new mark on her wrist as a red sunrise stained the sky. She knew the Council's desire for tangible evidence and their hesitancy to believe her was valid, but it still stung that they had not immediately believed her.

She yawned, drawing attention from a squat little dog that sat on a velvet cushion in the corner of Harriet Sinclair's drawing room. It angled its white and red face at her, tongue lolling. Rose arched her eyebrows at the dog, and he wagged his stubby tail in response. The dog's ears twitched toward the door before Harriet burst into the room. The dog leapt from its place to greet her, running on short legs towards his mistress.

Harriet scooped up the dog without slowing her pace and settled herself next to Rose on the sofa. "How good it is to see you, Rosie," she beamed.

Rose grinned. "It's nice to see you, too."

"I see you've met Quincy." She gave the dog a kiss on the head. It gazed up at her, mouth open in adoration.

"He's very sweet," said Rose, reaching out to pat the dog's head. It eyed her warily, sniffed her hand, then leaned into her touch, having determined that she was worthy to pet him.

"What brings you here? I am surprised you called. Not that I'm not thrilled to see you, but after everything that happened."

Rose bit her lip and glanced back to the parlor doors. Anyone could be listening. At the very least, they'd think her a lunatic, but there was danger lurking everywhere. Cornelius might not be the only witch hunter in London. She didn't know who she could trust. "May I show you?" she asked, mentally selecting the most crucial scenes from the past day to transmit to her friend through touch. She offered her hand, palm up to Harriet.

"Oh, um," said Harriet, focused on massaging Quincy's ears. "I'm not sure. Last night was a bit much for me." She smiled wearily. "Mama brought me to a party with her, and I spent a long time with other ladies my age who are not yet out in society. There were a lot of feelings. You can't imagine the pettiness and jealousy. It's hard to ignore it all sometimes, even if they're not physically touching me."

Rose placed her hands back into her lap, letting Harriet have her space. "I imagine that must be difficult."

"Yes, some days are more taxing than others, to be sure. Sorry."

Rose fought the urge to grip Harriet's hand comfortingly. Instead, she folded her hands in her lap. "You never have to apologize to me. Especially not about that. Actually, I am here to apologize to you."

Harriet's brows knit together. "Whatever for?"

"I've been a terrible friend. No, I have," she continued on, ignoring Harriet's polite denial of her claim. "You have been a true friend to me, Harriet. I was so caught up in my problems that I didn't notice. I'm sorry I have never called on you before. I should have long ago."

"You're here now," Harriet said. Quincy jumped off her lap to resume his vigil in the corner atop his velvet pillow.

"I'm also sorry for putting you in danger," said Rose in a low voice, eyes sliding again to the drawing room door.

Harriet's eyes followed hers. "Oh, just a moment." She closed her eyes and waved a hand towards the white doors inlaid with gold. Rose felt a tingle of magic brush her cheeks, though nothing had visibly changed about the room or doors. "Silencing bubble," she explained. "No one will eavesdrop now."

"You'll definitely have to teach me that one." Rose's eyes creased with mischief. "Even so, I'm sorry. It's my fault the witch hunters are here now, and that they know where we are."

Harriet shook her head. "They were already here. You just gave them more of a general direction to start looking in."

Rose fiddled with her necklace. "Do you know why they've come? What can they do to us, really? Who would even believe that we are witches?"

Harriet went over to a small table where a tea service was laid out, waiting for guests to partake. She fixed two cups. "They would not publicly oust us. That sort of thing wouldn't work today. There's no widespread belief in magic anymore, so there's no fear. You didn't believe it was possible to be a witch until you had the concrete proof, after all. Even though the magic was within you all along."

Rose accepted the delicate china cup and saucer. "So, what would happen, then?"

Harriet dunked a biscuit into her tea. "They would kill us or try to steal our magic for themselves. One or the other," she said around her mouthful.

"Wouldn't people be suspicious if a bunch of women started dying?"

Harriet chewed slowly, then swallowed. "People die all the

time. No one would pay any mind. People only see what they *want* to see. They'll accept any reasonable explanation as long as it is within the realm of possibility."

Rose set her cup down. It made sense, even if it was disconcerting. "And how do they steal our magic?"

Harriet grabbed another biscuit. "They have to kill us for that, too, I think. But I'm not sure. It's been over a hundred years since the last group were successful in their hunt, and it was mass panic from what I have read. A very public affair. I am not too keen on finding out how they would do it today."

Rose's mouth went dry. If Cornelius was a witch hunter, then he must truly think her magic was not worth the effort of killing her for it. He'd made it clear that he had other uses for her. Her union with an ancient and wealthy suitor, for example, would give him access to status and wealth the Worthingtons did not possess. Another chilling thought made her hands tremble. If she proved no longer useful to him, would he kill her? He certainly wouldn't spare a second thought about killing any other witch he encountered. She couldn't bear the thought of him hurting Harriet.

Quincy let out a low, protective whine as if he, too, could not stand the thought of anything happening to his mistress.

"Cornelius is a witch hunter," Rose said.

Harriet stilled. Tea dripped from her biscuit into her cup. She swallowed thickly; her face turning a shade more pale. "Your cousin is a witch hunter?"

"Yes." Rose relayed what she had told the Council last night. She showed her the new mark on her wrist and explained the bargain she had struck with Lady Nightingale.

Harriet retook her seat and sat in stunned silence for a while. "You came to ask me for help?"

"Yes, but I can't ask you now that I know how dangerous it is."

"Don't be silly. I'm coming with you." Harriet got to her feet and set her teacup and half-eaten biscuit down. Quincy also rose from his velvet cushion, ready to escort his mistress.

"But it will be too dangerous." Rose had had every intention of asking Harriet to accompany her, but that was before she knew her friend could be killed for her magic.

Harriet crossed her arms. "You need my help. It's all right to ask for it. Besides," she tossed her hair over her shoulder, "I've always wanted to play detective. I love mystery novels."

Worry twisted Rose's insides. Every instinct in her shouted to protect Harriet. But beneath that, so quietly she could hardly hear it, the voice of her magic whispered for her to trust in her friend.

Harriet, seeing Rose's hesitancy, brought herself to her full height, which was still a head shorter than Rose. "I am the daughter of Viscount Sinclair. I know for a fact that your cousin has been trying to gain an audience with my father for a few weeks now. He would not risk harming me if he wants something from Papa. If he is a witch hunter, I want to find out what he wants with my father."

Rose studied the fierce determination on her face, a reflection of what she felt in her own heart. "All right, then."

Harriet clapped her hands, making Quincy yip, and rushed about, readying herself to accompany Rose back to her house.

Rose watched her friend gather her little jacket, kiss her dog farewell, and buckle her shoes. Her heart felt full, and tears stung her eyes. Though the worry still made her stomach clench, she was very glad that she would not be going alone.

They stepped out into the weak morning sun. "I don't suppose you know where Kate lives, do you? I thought I should ask her as well."

"Good idea," said Harriet. "I know just where to find her."

She set off down the street, dodging puddles left by the storm, leaving Rose to follow behind her.

* * *

KATE IMMEDIATELY AGREED TO HELP. They found her near the outskirts of the city, tending to tiny seedlings in her family's greenhouse. Her father was a gardener for some of the more well-to-do families in the city. The Millers were not members of the gentry, but they belonged to an ambiguous class of people who lived comfortably because of their service of greater households, while holding no land or titles of their own.

After a brief explanation, the tale got shorter each time Rose told it. Kate had wordlessly brushed off her hands and removed her smock. Now, the three ambled through the park, plotting what they should do before returning to the Worthington townhouse.

"I believe he can sense magic," Rose explained. "It will be too dangerous to perform any sort of spell work to track down anything of importance."

"It sounds like we shall require a more tried-and-true approach," replied Harriet.

"And what would that be?" Kate asked dryly.

"Ransacking drawers, looking for hidden panels in the floor, that sort of thing," said Harriet. "You know, traditional detective work." She tilted her head in thought. "I wonder if I should have brought Quincy. His little nose is quite adept at sniffing out little biscuits he's not meant to have."

"Unless he's trained to sniff out a witch hunter, I think he'd rather stay at home," said Rose.

"You may be right," agreed Harriet.

"There is one drawer in his study that I've never been able to open," Rose said. "I've tried more than once, even with an unlocking spell, and I couldn't get it to budge."

"The most obvious choice is usually the correct one," Kate said.

"Let's start there." Harriet bounced with anticipation.

Her unbridled enthusiasm was concerning, but Rose knew Harriet was well aware of the dangers that lay in store. Or at least she hoped she was. There was no room for fear or doubt. Only action. "All right," Rose agreed. "But it would be foolish for all of us to be caught rifling through his private things. We need to set a lookout."

"I'll do it," Kate said, her tone leaving no room for debate. "You live there, and your abilities may be more useful than mine once inside."

"And I am the picture of innocence," added Harriet, schooling her features into sweet naiveté.

A corner of Kate's mouth twitched. "That, too."

As they made their way to the Worthington's house, they smoothed the details of their plan. It was risky, but Rose had no other choice. She ran her finger over her newly raised scar and tried not to worry that she was dragging her friends into more trouble.

CHAPTER 37

*R*ose refused to acknowledge the anxiety that tightened her throat and made her ears perk up at every sound as she and Harriet tiptoed into the foyer of the Worthington townhouse. They passed open parlor doors, their skirts whispering softly against the hall's polished wooden floors. Her mother was, thankfully, out. Formally introducing Harriet to her would take precious time. It would be better if she did never knew she had been here.

Rose pressed an ear to Cornelius's study door and held her breath. The tightness in her throat lessened at the silence within. The room was empty. He was, no doubt, at the club trying to gain audiences with esteemed members of the gentry. To what purpose she could only imagine.

As per usual, the door to the study was locked. Harriet raised her eyebrows and slid Rose an anticipatory glance. Rose felt it was safe to use the unlocking bracelet, even though they had agreed to not use magic. The spell had never alerted Cornelius before now.

She was afraid. Her last use of magic had left her empty and reeling. What if she reached for her power, only to find it gone?

Rose gripped the handle with tingling fingers and pushed past her own fear, reaching for tendrils of magic. The bracelet grew warm and heavy on her wrist.

After a heart-stopping second of emptiness, Rose felt a sparkling heat pulse through her, no bigger than a candle flame. It was weaker than anything she'd felt before, but it was enough. The lock tumblers slid open. A vicious throb of pain made her see stars. She swayed on the spot and gripped the handle, waiting for the blackout to fade. The pain subsided quickly, and Rose and Harriet stole inside.

Harriet examined the room and rubbed her hands together. "Where shall we start?"

"The drawer is here," Rose said, striding to the desk. She knelt before the lowest drawer and pointed to the tiny keyhole. "I can't find the key, though."

Harriet squinted at the lock. "Have you used the unlocking bracelet?"

"No," Rose said slowly. "Do you think we should risk it?" Did she even have enough power left?

"I don't see why not." Harriet brushed her fingers over the polished wood. "There is something here." She rubbed the tips of her fingers together, as if she'd touched something unpleasant.

Rose gripped the tiny handle. "If Cornelius comes back, stick to the plan."

Harriet nodded solemnly. She continued to rub her fingers together.

Rose gritted her teeth and willed the drawer to open, relying on the bracelet once more to unlock the drawer. Her magic was feeble and wobbly as a newborn fawn. She fought to keep it steady as the stones on her wrist grew heavier and heavier.

The drawer resisted. A black, odious cloud poured from the cracks and seams as the bracelet's magic fought to open the lock. Pain shot through Rose's skull, smoke obscured her vision.

She heard a faint, sluggish scrape as the lock slid reluctantly open. She jerked her hand back, coughing and spluttering. Rose and Harriet covered their mouths and tried to blink away the stinging in their eyes. They waved their hands through the air, dispelling the acrid cloud. The sulfurous stench of the smoke lingered in the air.

"Are you all right?" Rose rasped. She reached for her companion, but stopped with her hand halfway through the air, remembering her reluctance to be touched.

Harriet scrunched her nose and continued to waft the smell away. "Yes. Though I shall require a bath."

Seeing that Harriet had escaped the smoke unharmed, Rose watched the study door. Her heart pounded in her chest. If the smoke alerted Cornelius to the break-in, they would have only as long as it took for him to travel from his current location back to the house.

Rose tugged the drawer open. A leather-bound book and some loose sheafs of paper lay haphazardly inside. She carefully lifted the book out first. The leather was soft with wear. She ran her fingers over the emblem stamped into the cover: an upside-down triangle with an eye in the center, three linked ovals curved above it. She had seen him with this ledger before, back at Worthington House.

Rose flipped open the cover, skimming the pages as Harriet peered over her shoulder. The handwriting inside looked like it belonged to two different people. A neat script dominated most of the pages of the journal, while a scrawling, ink blotted scrawl interrupted the entries with odd missives. She turned back to the beginning of the ledger and removed a loose stack of pages. They were written on different stationery and had been tucked inside.

21 May, 1803

Boston

I have finally arrived in Boston to make my own fortune. Father told me it was a foolish enterprise. He refused to give me the capital of my inheritance outright until I revealed what I knew about my mother's extramarital affairs. Colin is not his natural born son. (Though, I would never tell Colin of his misfortune. He is still my brother, after all.) Father was more than happy to deposit funds into my account after I promised I would never speak of it again.

Tomorrow I will join a meeting of merchants to determine the best course of action for investment. Timber may be a lucrative first venture. There are many untapped resources here. So many that I hardly know where to start.

"It's just a journal," Rose said, not bothering to conceal the bitterness of disappointment in her voice.

"That was under a very odious lock," Harriet reminded her. "Keep reading." She scooted closer to Rose so she could see better.

Rose skimmed through the cluster of remaining loose pages. Details of figures and speculations of profitable trade made up the bulk of the writing, with a few notes about travel from Boston to Philadelphia, then New York. She placed the small stack aside. Then they turned to the book, opening to the first page.

20 August, 1806

New York

Here begins my record keeping as a member of the Obsidian Spiritualists.

"What's that?" asked Rose, pointing to the page, tilting it so Harriet could see.

Harriet placed a finger on the book, right under the strange name, and stiffened. Her face went a sickly shade of grey as her eyes grew wide. Not with joy, or curiosity, as they so often did, but terror.

Rose's own heart stuttered. "What is it?" she demanded, trying not to betray her own rising panic.

Before Harriet could speak, they heard footsteps running through the hall, echoing loudly, and approaching fast.

She grabbed the book from Rose's hands, gagging as she did so, and shoved it onto a bookshelf behind them, nestling it in the space between the wall and the edges of the books. "Lock it," she said, voice tight with fear. "Quickly."

Rose closed the desk drawer and frantically passed her bracelet over the tiny keyhole. Nothing happened.

Harriet lunged for the decanter of brandy Cornelius kept in his drinks cabinet and brought it down to where Rose knelt, still trying desperately to lock the desk drawer.

The footsteps grew louder, their pace increasing.

Panicking, Rose waved her wrist in front of the lock again, commanding it to bolt. Harriet took a tiny sip of the amber liquid and swirled it around her mouth. Rose shut her eyes and pleaded with all her might. Another shock of pain raced through her head, this time jolting down her arm, making her jerk. The lock clicked into place.

The decanter smashed against her teeth as Harriet thrust the bottle to her mouth. Rose took a tiny sip, letting the alcohol linger on her tongue. They smeared drops of brandy on their skin, letting the harsh scent waft into the air and mix with the lingering sulfurous odor. They leaned against the bookshelves with the decanter between them right as the study door banged open.

CHAPTER 38

The door bounced off the wall with the force of impact. Cornelius's eyes were thunderous. He sniffed the air, and let out a low, guttural noise. His gaze darted around the room before finally spotting the tops of not one head, but two, visible just behind his desk. He stalked towards them, a predator cornering his prey.

Rose lolled her head against the shelves, corners of book spines digging into her neck and scalp as Cornelius came into view. "Hello, Cousin."

Harriet brought her hand to her mouth, stifling a giggle. "Oh dear," she said breathlessly. "We've been caught."

Rose could hear the note of panic beneath her laughter.

"Rose." His voice was deadly calm. "Explain yourself."

"Oh, don't blame her, Lord Worthington," said Harriet as she struggled to her feet. She braced herself on the desk, swaying slightly. "It was my idea." She covered her mouth again and let out another girlish laugh.

"You did not have to try too hard to convince me, Miss Sinclair," drawled Rose. Her knees trembled. She could not bring herself to stand, even under the pretense of being intoxicated. Her heart thudded so loudly that she was sure Cornelius could hear it from where he stood.

A spark of recognition crossed his face at Harriet's surname. His eyes darted distrustfully to Rose, before sliding back to the dark-haired girl leaning on his desk.

"Miss Sinclair," he said, rolling her name over his tongue like a piece of hard candy. "I have just had the pleasure of making your father's acquaintance. From our brief interview, I gather he would be most concerned to see you in such a state."

Harriet pouted. Her round eyes filled with tears. "Are you going to tell him?"

Cornelius's dark hair fell into his eyes as he shook his head. "No, I shall not." His eyes flicked to Rose again, and a secret smile turned the corners of his mouth. "Perhaps you could join us for supper? You're welcome to the guest suite until then. That should be adequate time to dispel the brandy's effects."

"How very thoughtful." Harriet clapped her hands together. "I should love to dine with you both."

"Very well. I will see to your room straightaway, as Lady Worthington is engaged elsewhere this evening. I should like a word with you, Miss Worthington, when I return."

"Bring me something good to read when you're done, Rosie," said Harriet cheerfully as she made her way to the door, giving Cornelius a wide berth.

The butler must have been listening around a corner, for he was summoned with surprising speed to escort Harriet to the guest rooms. Cornelius followed them, shutting the study door behind him. Rose heard the click of the lock, but remained calm. It was foolish of him to think he could lock her in when he'd never been able to lock her out. She could simply use her bracelet to leave.

Rose made herself count to thirty before reaching for the journal Harriet had stowed on the bookshelf behind them. She prayed that proof lay within its pages. She flipped to the first entry again.

20 August, 1806

New York

Here begins my record keeping as a member of the Obsidian Spiritualists. I have taken the oath of their order to uphold honor, freedom, and truth always. My brothers have been kind to me, showing me how lost I truly was. My lust for profit and wealth were truly a poison upon my soul. What good is wealth and power if the very core of one's self is lost? I've been shown my mortal flaws and will hereafter seek to remedy them.

I knew I wasn't making any substantial contribution to the world — how could I, as the third born son of a lord of England? I had no purpose to guide me, no calling to a higher cause. Now, I have found fellow men whose aims are to elevate every person to a nobler plane of existence. We vow to aid those in need, relieve the darkness of despair, and wage war against infernal vices. We are the moral fabric of New York and aim to influence others to ascend to higher states for the good of all humanity.

Mr. Taylor has been my stalwart mentor since my arrival two months ago. He has given me a great honor by naming me as a delegate to meet with a notable newspaper to discuss how we might share our creed, perhaps write a weekly column instructing others on how to improve themselves. Although I am a humble initiate of the order, I hope to climb the ranks quickly so that I may expand my contributions.

Frowning, Rose turned the page. Cornelius never spoke in such a zealous manner. On the surface, the order he belonged to did not sound so bad. Their purpose was rather vague, dedicated to some sort of higher good. But she knew there must be more.

She flipped impatiently through the next twenty pages. Cornelius continued to detail strange errands for the Obsidian Spiritualists. He traveled to Philadelphia frequently, staying at a tavern called the Seven Stars. Their plans to publish in their newspaper were unsuccessful, though they found several other small papers to print their letters. They were mostly cautionary tales and homilies. Clippings from them were folded and placed within the journal's pages.

The first scrawl of foreign handwriting interrupted this section, jarring against the careful record keeping. Rose felt a sense of foreboding rise within her as she squinted to read the untidy scribble.

Burn them all.

It was the first hint of something more sinister. The journal entries continued monotonously, never acknowledging the threatening directive on the previous page. Then, there was a gap between February 1807 and March 1812. One year before Cornelius returned to England.

13 March, 1812

New York

Mr. Taylor has called upon me once more. I have finished atoning for my mistakes and have repented thoroughly enough to satisfy the other Scarlet members of the order. This next commission will prove my utmost loyalty and secure my promotion to third degree once I have successfully completed it. I am curious to see what their assignment shall be.

The fits of memory loss have grown steadily worse the past several months. Mr. Taylor has mentioned that a return to native soil may improve my health —more reason for this next assignment to send me to London.

I will be a member of the upper rank. I need to find a way to neutralize the damage that has already been done. Let's hope they don't discover me sooner.

Cornelius was unwell. A creeping unease tickled the back of Rose's neck. There was something here, some piece of the puzzle to who Cornelius was, that lay just within reach. There were little to no details about what he did for this order as a second-degree rank. The journal was missing years of entries. Whatever he had been doing in that time, Cornelius hadn't bothered to write about it. From what he did record, she learned that third rank, Scarlet, was the highest you could go. And Cornelius was very close to attaining it.

Rose turned the next few pages, stopping when she saw another mention of Worthington Estate. This entry was in the strange, scratchy penmanship.

19 February, 1813.

Boston

You are Cornelius Worthington, sole heir to the Worthington Estate in Kennington, England. You are traveling to the estate to assume the duties your title requires. The previous lord's widow and daughter are now under your charge. Take care of them.

The next entry reverted to the tidy handwriting that dominated the rest of the book.

20 March, 1813

Kennington

The Worthingtons have given me a warm welcome. It is far more than I could have hoped for. I am a stranger to them, but I hope they know I will care for them. I will protect, serve, and speak truth in all things — especially this. Lady Worthington seems quite set on finding a husband for her daughter. She is exceedingly pretty. I can tell she is wary of my sudden appearance, but perhaps she will warm to me in time.

I am awaiting instructions from the solicitor on how to best begin my management of the estate. The current ledgers are exceedingly well kept. I wonder who has been keeping a tally of the affairs since the late lord's departure? I shall ask the butler. He seems a good sort of fellow. To think he is my butler now. To have lived for so many years with so little—it is strange to suddenly find oneself surrounded by such riches and lavishness.

Rose bit her lip. Worthington House was hardly lavish. She wondered what Cornelius's previous lodgings were like if he thought their house was so grand. If he knew how frugally they lived before his arrival, his opinion might be different. And he thought her pretty. Something strange, a mix of revulsion and curiosity, twisted within her. He had made it apparent that he enjoyed how she looked in the most disgusting way. But the words within the journal seemed almost... sincere.

She was wasting time. Harriet was waiting for her, and she needed *proof.* There were only a few pages left. Her palms dampened as she read on. The next entry was in the untidy scrawl.

28 March, 1813

Kennington

Arrived safely in England. The Worthingtons are manageable. The daughter is a wild thing — marry her off quickly. I will accompany them to their season in London. Potential candidate: Lord Reeves. Amicable to the cause. Send funds to Mr. Taylor as soon as possible.

Well, so much for that. It was like two different people were writing in the same journal. She didn't know what to make of it. A noise in the hall made her jump.

She watched the door, sure that Cornelius would open it at any moment. After a few breaths, nothing happened. There was only one page left.

Heart still pounding, she frantically turned the last page, slicing her finger. Her stomach sank with disappointment as she sucked on her wounded finger, the coppery tang of blood biting her tongue. The last page was blank. There was nothing here, no concrete proof of his treachery. She had failed.

She'd been so sure that the journal would have the proof she needed. She had dragged Harriet and Kate along with her for nothing. Rose let her head fall back into the shelves, biting back tears of frustration.

Liar. Traitor. Thief. Failure. Another name to add to the list of things she was now. Rose gripped the journal, ready to throw it across the room, but something on the last page made her freeze. The smear of blood from her finger dribbled onto the page, sinking in and around shapes of letters.

She did not dare draw breath as she squeezed her cut, forcing beads of blood to well to her fingertip. She smeared all she could across the page. The journal drank greedily, taking her few meager drops of blood, thinning it into ink that spider-webbed across the paper.

Suspected witches
Lady H. Nightingale
Lady L. Clarke
Lady M. Templeton
Miss R. Worthington

* * *

RECRUITMENTS
Lord P. Reeves
Lord J. Harker
Mr. C. Burgin
Lord A. Sinclair

* * *

FINGERS TREMBLING, Rose carefully tore out the page. The scarlet script had already faded by the time she extracted the list from the journal. She folded the list into a tiny square and shoved it down her stays, where it burned wickedly against her flesh. Rose closed the journal and stared at its cover. The strange eye stared right at her, as if it knew what she had done.

She should be angry or scared. Instead, all she felt was revulsion for the leather book she held in her hands. Shuddering, she waved her bracelet over the lock on the desk. No black smoke billowed out, the trap had already sprung. She placed the journal back into the drawer and resealed it with another wave of her wrist.

Her head hurt after the effort, and a sickening wave of vertigo had her slumping against the bookshelves once again. She drew her knees up to her chest and dropped her forehead as she waited for her queasiness to pass. She went over the names she had seen on the list again and again as her stomach settled.

Cornelius already suspected the three leaders of the Nightingales. Why hadn't he made any sort of move against them? The fact that she was the only other name on that list gave her some small comfort. He did not suspect Harriet, Kate, or any other witch in training, and he hadn't identified the rest of the thirteen members of the council.

She knew why Cornelius hadn't killed her outright or ousted her. Besides getting him close to Lord Reeves, the first name on his list of recruits, Cornelius knew that Lady Nightingale was sponsoring her this season. She realized his threats to keep them apart were only meant to drive her closer to his top suspect. He was using her to get close to the people he needed. She was the link between them.

Rose gripped her knees tighter. Maybe it would be better if she stopped her pursuit of magic. Even if it killed some part of her. If she removed herself as the link between everything, the chain would break, leaving Cornelius without a way to get close to the people on his list. But would that keep the Nightingales safe for long?

Either way, she still had to tell Harriet what Cornelius wanted with her father. To recruit him as a witch hunter. If he was successful, Harriet would be in danger. She needed to know. What would Lord Sinclair do when he learned his own daughter was a witch?

She wondered what Harriet was doing now.

The sound of quick, determined footsteps in the hall jolted Rose from her anxious thoughts.

Cornelius had returned for her.

CHAPTER 39

Cornelius closed the door behind him softly, then took two predatory steps towards the center of the room. The precision of his movements scared Rose more than the violence of a blinding rage. His pupils were blown wide, covering his irises in inky pools.

She swallowed and got reluctantly to her feet, keeping her back pressed against the bookshelves.

"You grow more troublesome by the day," he mused, pressing a finger to his mouth. "I don't know whether to curse or thank you, my sweet Rose. You've been prying into my things. But you have brought me a most welcome guest. One I shall take great pleasure in questioning once I am through with you."

He gestured to the reading chair. "Sit."

Rose sidled alongside the shelves and stood with the chair between them.

Cornelius sighed at her obstinance. He walked to his desk and tugged on the bottom drawer, but it remained closed. "How did you open it?"

She held onto the back of the chair, digging her fingers into the plush upholstery. There was no use lying. He smelled the smoke as soon as he entered the room. But she didn't have to tell the whole truth, either. "I tried to force it, but only horrid black smoke came out of the drawer."

If Rose let him think he'd caught her before she saw what lay inside, she might escape the study unharmed. She glanced up at him through her eyelashes. The rage contorting Cornelius's features made her question whether she'd leave the encounter without injury.

Sweat gleamed on his temple, and deep lines etched into his hollow face. His hair was limp, his skin sallow. He looked very ill. She wondered what manner of sickness he had that caused such a haggard appearance and memory loss.

"And what, exactly, were you hoping to find among my personal things?" he asked.

She squared her shoulders. "Anything to get me out of a marriage contract with Percival Reeves." The lie slid smoothly from her lips.

Cornelius threw his head back and laughed, the sound cold and harsh. "Damn me, I should have known."

Rose waited for his laughter to subside. "Let Harriet go. She had nothing to do with it. She wanted to help me get out of the engagement. That's all. We were commiserating."

Cornelius shook his head. "I doubt that." He stepped closer to her, moving from behind the desk.

Rose stiffened, but held her ground.

"You keep such interesting company these days. I am looking forward to hearing how you and Miss Sinclair spend your leisure time. No doubt you met her through your *bene-factress*."

She'd had enough of this. The interrogations, the posturing, the intimidation. She had what she needed from Cornelius. For now. "I'm leaving, along with Harriet."

He moved to block her path. *"Look at me,"* he hissed.

Rose forced herself to stare into his dark eyes, so soulless she felt as if she might fall in drown within them.

He took another step, towering over her and blocking her means of escape. "I told you the next time I summoned you, you would sign your marriage contract. It looks like the summons shall be unnecessary." He withdrew the thick envelope from his breast pocket. He smoothed the papers open, placed them on the side table nearest them, and reached for a pen.

Rose seized the chance to rush past him. He lunged and snatched for her arm. He was much faster than he looked. She felt his long fingers curl around her wrist. As soon as he touched her skin, Rose felt the terrible darkness within him.

But this darkness differed from the one that called to her in her moments of deepest despair. It was not a bottomless well of night, or a crushing ocean of black water threatening to drown her in her own sorrows. The thing inside Cornelius was tar and smoke, a cloying and smothering dark that crushed the air from her body. She gasped for air as he pulled her to face him.

Rose saw, or felt, a calamitous cloud gather and swirl until it took the rough shape of a man. Horrible scarlet eyes peered out of the formless face. Her wrist was so cold it felt like it was burning. Terror gripped her heart as the red-eyed being reached for her throat with its other hand.

It was Cornelius, and yet *not* Cornelius that slowly crept shadowy fingers towards her neck. She saw her cousin and this monster that slept within him simultaneously, each form fighting for dominance in her vision.

She couldn't think, couldn't breathe. The figure and Cornelius were one. A voice from far, far away broke through the suffocating darkness.

Let me out, let me help!

Rose quelled her terror and reached for the expanse of power deep within her. She reached with all her strength as the long fingers closed around her neck.

There was nothing but cold, empty darkness. She clawed desperately at the wall of thick smoke, now solid around the place where she kept her magic deep within her.

Help me! she thought as she scrabbled against the wall of magic and clawed at the hand at her throat. Dark spots flickered in her vision. Rose closed her eyes, lungs burning. She needed air. She couldn't die like this. If Cornelius killed her, what would he do to Harriet, and the others?

With a last push of her fading strength, Rose tunneled further down into herself, searching for her magic.

She shoved through the thick tar of whatever lay inside Cornelius. Every muscle shrieked in protest. She would have retched if she'd had enough air. The most excruciating pain she'd ever felt threatened to tear her skull, her mind, apart. But she kept going. Until, at last, she felt the weak flicker of her magic, like an ember that had almost died out. At her touch, it roared back to life, pulsing through her with agony and elation.

Glittering waves of power pulsed through her, fighting against the smothering darkness. The thing of smoke shrieked and vanished, leaving behind the same sulfurous stink that had spewed from the locked desk drawer.

Cornelius cried out and released her, stumbling backwards as if she had struck him. His eyes rolled into his head, and he collapsed onto the thick rug.

Rose took a gasping breath, her lungs free to draw air again. Tears streamed down her face. Her eyes stung from the malodorous smoke, and her throat burned with each ragged inhale. She glanced around the room, blinking through her tears as she searched for any sign of the smoke creature. It was gone. All that remained of it was the acrid smell.

She dry-heaved, bracing her hands on her knees. It took several long moments for her breath to calm. Every inch of her ached and throbbed with pain. Sheer will gave her enough strength to raise her head enough to look at Cornelius. He lay on his side, deathly still.

Numbly, Rose knelt by him, unable to stand upright a moment longer. Another grunt of willpower, and she turned him so that he lay on his back.

The deep lines and fury were gone. He was pale, his cheeks sallow. His hair clung to his damp brow. He looked as if he'd had a fever for several days. "Cornelius." Her voice grated against her throat, as if she'd been screaming. She wasn't sure what compelled her to rouse him. Did she really want him to wake? She didn't have the strength to run if that smoke creature should return, or if he tried to strangle her again.

She said his name again. "Cornelius."

Nothing. His eyes didn't even move behind their closed lids. The journal had mentioned that he suffered from some affliction. Was this it? The hair on the back of her neck stood up and gooseflesh pricked her arms. Rose glanced around the room. Though the dark smoke had vanished, she had the feeling that something sinister still lingered.

She had to wake him up. "*Cornelius.*"

His eyes fluttered open, and he trembled. He blinked slowly, eyes still unfocused. Rose repeated his name. The sight of her had some effect, as he instantly tried to sit up.

"Miss Worthington, my apologies," he said in a voice she had never heard him use before. It was deeper, the vowels more round. It suited him, somehow.

After a moment, he pushed himself into a sitting position.

"You're all right," said Rose warily, resisting the urge to help him sit up. She wasn't keen to touch him again.

"What happened?" he asked, brows knit together. His voice rumbled through her chest.

"I'm not really sure," she said. "Are you ill?"

Cornelius's mouth twitched wryly, and Rose noticed the smile reached his eyes. Something she had never seen before. "It would seem so." He wiped his sweaty hair from his brow. "I'm so sorry. I must have frightened you terribly."

"Just a bit," she admitted.

He shook his head, trying to clear his thoughts. "The doctor thought being back in England would help me. I have yet to see any improvements."

Rose wasn't sure if she should feel sorry for him or not. He'd done terrible, unforgivable things to her, to the people she cared about. But this person in front of her was wholly different from the one who had harbored the red-eyed shadow moments ago. She extended her hand, against her better judgment. "Here."

Cornelius took her hand.

No bite of blistering cold seared her skin. He only felt clammy, though warmth lingered somewhere beneath. Rose helped him towards the armchair, her own body protesting each step. The movement caused him to go alarmingly pale.

Once she was sure he wasn't going to pass out again, Rose poured two glasses of brandy. She handed one to Cornelius, who took a small, reluctant sip. Rose tossed back her own glass, swallowing the contents in one gulp. The familiar fire coursed down her throat, soothing her and relieving some of the aching. She stared at Cornelius, waiting for him to say something.

His eyes were… warm. Not cold and soulless like before, the pupils blown. "How long have I been in England now, Miss Worthington?"

"You arrived at Worthington House about three months ago."

Cornelius blinked slowly. "Forgive me. This sickness makes me forget myself."

Rose blinked stupidly. *Forgetting himself* was an understatement.

His brow pinched. "Have I fulfilled my duties with honor? Have I taken care of you and your mother?"

She ignored the question, an idea sparking quickly, though

she longed to tell him exactly how he had treated her these past weeks. Rose snatched the thick marriage document from the table and gripped it. "This is a contract for my marriage. You were about to force me to sign it." Her eyes darted to the cold fireplace.

"Forcing you?"

"Yes," Rose snapped. She ignored the look of dismay on Cornelius's face. She needed to get rid of the contract before he took it and made the engagement official.

"And who are you marrying?"

"You really expect me to believe that you don't remember?" She let the contact hang loosely at her side and took several irritated steps closer to the fireplace.

Cornelius shook his head mutely.

Rose sighed. "Lord Percival Reeves. He's a widower, and about a hundred years old. He is crass, rude, and loathes all women. Thinks the only thing they are good for is having children and being pleasing to look at. *That* is who I am marrying."

"I'm sorry," Cornelius stammered. "I would not have chosen someone like that for you to marry. Had I known —"

"You *did* know. You arranged the whole thing." This was getting ridiculous.

"You have to understand," his voice rumbled again through her chest. "I had no knowledge of this. Of any of it."

Rose narrowed her eyes and studied the man slumped in the armchair. He looked wretched. Rose thought that he might have been striking to look at, maybe even handsome, had he been well. He sat with his shoulders hunched forward, his sorrowful eyes fixed upon her. He was not the threatening, fearsome person she had come to know.

"What do you remember?" Rose asked softly, though she did not loosen her grip on the document.

"I remember flashes of things, only bits and pieces. I remember arriving in London, and the first cup of English tea

I'd had in years. How good it was. I remember arriving at Worthington House. I remember you were sick, and we came to London to find you a suitor. That is all."

Cornelius's cheeks flushed a pale pink, and he shifted his gaze to the floor.

Rose raised an eyebrow. "That's truly it?"

"Well, your mother may have mentioned that I should be the one to marry you, but it's highly improper that I share that with you."

"I see."

"Please, Miss Worthington. Whatever I have done, however I may have offended you, I truly have no recollection of my transgressions. However, that does not excuse my actions. I apologize for anything I have done."

"You have caused me more pain than I care to recall," Rose said.

"What can I do? Tell me how to rectify it."

"Undo it," whispered Rose, gesturing to the marriage contract. "If you have any regard for me at all, you will nullify this."

Cornelius studied the document and frowned. "Have you signed it?"

"No."

"Burn it. Quickly." Sweat broke out on Cornelius's forehead. He gripped the arms of the chair, knuckles whitening. "You must do it now, Miss Worthington."

Rose threw the marriage contract into the fireplace and reached for the tinderbox and fire steel. It would take too much time, and strength she did not have, to use magic to light the fire. Her fingers scrabbled with the fire steel. She struck once, twice, three times before a spark hit the tinder. She blew on the flame, coaxing it to life, not daring to glance behind at Cornelius.

Finally, the paper caught fire. Rose sat back on her heels.

They both watched the contract burn. As the final shreds of paper curled into ash, a small drop of relief coursed through Rose's body. She turned to Cornelius, to thank or scold him she did not know, but scrambled backwards as she saw the thick, dark smoke that gathered around him. The insidious cloud slowly embraced him. His eyes glazed, pupils swallowing his irises once more.

"It's all right." Rose tried to keep the fear from her voice as she crawled slowly away from him. "It's done now, Cornelius."

"*No.*" Cornelius hissed, but the voice was not his own. It was the cold, soulless voice from the garden, the one that he had been speaking with all this time. Black clouds rushed into his mouth, and he straightened, possessed once more by the sinister smoke.

Rose pushed herself to her feet, inching closer to the door. She kept her gaze fixed on not-Cornelius, ready to run if necessary.

"*It is not over.*" He rose out of the chair.

She watched in horror as he extended a hand over the fire. The flames turned dark grey and black. Tiny bits of charred paper and ash floated from the grate into the air. Grinning wickedly, Cornelius snapped his fingers, and the marriage contract was remade. Before she could blink, the document was clutched firmly in Cornelius's hand, the paper a shade grayer than it had been before burning. "So clever," the cold voice said.

Rose grabbed a steel poker and held it with two hands in front of her, keeping her back to the door. She should have known better than to try the same trick twice. She had seen him counter fire before.

"Oh, I won't be killing you now," he said. "Now that I know what you are truly capable of." He clicked his tongue. "Such power, sweet Rose, to draw the boy out. Curious. I cannot sense it on you now. You must have used all your magic again. Pity."

He walked around her, ignoring the poker as if it were an annoying gnat.

Rose kept it trained on him anyway as he circled around her, making her pivot until he stood between her and the door. He had blocked her from the exit. She was not a very good tactician.

"You shall stay here while I ask Miss Sinclair a few questions. I know *you* would never tell me the names of the other witches you keep company with. But she might."

Rose's arms shook with the effort of holding the poker. She let it drop. "Let her go." She hated the note of pleading that came from her.

"I will return later to deal with you." He turned his back on her, strode out of the study, clicking the lock once more into place.

Rose stood immobile as she heard Cornelius's steps fade down the hall. Her mind reeled over what had transpired between them. The person she had come to know was no more than a puppet, being manipulated by the dark thing that wore his skin. And now he was on his way to Harriet. The thought made her sick.

Every inch of her still ached, but she made herself pull on the door handle, made herself wave her bracelet, her shackle, in front of the lock. She didn't know what she would do once she got out, but she had to save Harriet.

A blood-curdling shriek made her blood turn to ice.

She tugged on the door again, crying, shouting. It didn't budge. The bracelet wasn't working. And she was utterly spent of magic. She hated herself for being so helpless, for agreeing to this plan where Harriet had insisted that she be the diversion if they were caught. They hadn't known what that meant. Hadn't known that she would be left to face some sort of demon on her own.

Harriet's blood-curdling shrieks continued as Rose pulled

and tugged against the handle. She beat her fists on the door, screaming, pleading. No one came.

With no strength left, her own voice raw, she sank to her knees, pressing her cheek against the cool wood as her friend's screams filled the house.

The ember of hope that had kindled in her chest died. The familiar well of darkness opened before her, and she let herself slide into the abyss.

CHAPTER 40

*N*ight fell. She distantly noted the shifting of light in the room from late afternoon sun to twilight. She only had four hours left to provide proof to Lady Nightingale. Not that it mattered anymore. She deserved to be banished, to be cut off from learning all magic, after she had let Cornelius torture Harriet.

Rose had nothing left. No plan, no backup, no hope. She was empty of magic. She couldn't free herself from the study, and there was no way for her to signal to Kate that they were in trouble, that the plan had gone horribly, horribly wrong.

Harriet had finally stopped screaming some hours ago. The silence was the most terrifying thing she had ever heard.

Rose had sobbed for hours after he had left, chest heaving. Each ragged breath made her throat burn where the monster inside Cornelius had squeezed her.

She screwed her eyes shut and tried again to reach for her magic. The only thing she cared about now was getting Harriet to safety. She clawed desperately for some fraction of power, but there was nothing. Nothing at all.

She had never realized how warm it had felt, like a little

hearth that blazed near her heart. The place where those embers had once smoldered had gone cold. Now that place felt like a freezing, flat lake. Still and lifeless.

Every part of her hurt so much that she hardly noticed her bracelet grow bone-chillingly cold against her skin as she reached the graveyard of her power. She surfaced, leaving the emptiness within her.

Cornelius would break Harriet eventually, if he had not already. He would get the names he wanted and slowly hunt the Nightingales, one by one, until they were eradicated. Or maybe he would publicly oust them, using the prominent gentry he recruited to his cause to give credibility to his claims. Whichever manner he chose, the Nightingales would be destroyed.

Rose hoped that Lady Nightingale and the Council would realize the danger they were in once she and Harriet did not return. Kate swore to warn them if that should happen. Perhaps there would be enough time for them to protect themselves or flee. Could they stand against the hateful entity that controlled Cornelius?

It would only be a matter of time before he came back to deal with her. What else could he possibly want? She scrubbed her face with her palms. He made it clear that she was only good to him for two things: marrying Reeves and getting close to Lady Nightingale.

If she married Lord Reeves, she'd be shipped off to the estate in Hythe. She'd be kept away from London society, and would either be forced to bear and raise his children, if he could still have any, or simply wait for him to die.

A sudden thought made her straighten. There was one piece of herself left that Cornelius had not taken. One that she would sacrifice to save Harriet, to save all the Nightingales if she could. If she married Reeves, she could make sure that Cornelius lost his tie to Lady Nightingale. She would no longer be her sponsor and have no public reason to see her. She'd be sequestered in a seaside town, far away from Lady Nightingale, her friends, Alexander, her mother. And Philip. She would truly never see him again if she made this choice.

Her heart shattered.

She let it break, splintering into a thousand shards that cut her like glass until she was utterly numb. She used the door to help drag herself upwards until she stood with her chin held high and shoulders back. Her decision was made, her voice as steady as her resolve. "Cornelius," she said. "Let's make a bargain."

CHAPTER 41

The door swung open, creaking on its hinges. Rose didn't dare move and inch. She waited, ears straining for any small sound. Whether the door had sensed her intent, or she'd merely spoken the correct words, she wasn't sure.

She took a tentative step into the deathly quiet hall, fighting every urge to run upstairs, to find Harriet, to get her out. She stilled those instincts. They would not serve her in the task she now must complete.

Her ears pricked at the sound of Cornelius's footsteps on the stairs. She was no longer afraid. Nor was she hopeful. She was simply numb. As numb and unfeeling as the frozen lake where her power once burned.

He stopped before her, head cocked to the side, as he held a candle between them. The light cast shadows across his face, and his dark eyes glittered wickedly. "Tell me, Rose Worthington, what deal do you wish to make with me?"

She did not break his stare. "You will free Harriet Sinclair and vow never to touch her again."

Cornelius sneered. "There is nothing you could offer that warrants such a promise."

"I will sign the marriage contract willingly. I will marry Lord Reeves."

Cornelius blinked, the only sign of his surprise. "You would enter freely into marriage? I would have forced you to sign it, anyway. But you are right. This is so much better. I can taste your will, your desire. So potent. So sweet."

His words sent a wave of revulsion through her. She knew he would like what she offered, but his hunger made her stomach churn. Dark smoke curled from him and encircled her wrist, bending her fingers to clasp an invisible pen as the flame of the candle guttered in a phantom wind.

The bitter cold of the smoke brushed against the cold within her. It burned and ached, but she did not tear her eyes away from the soulless gaze of the monster before her.

"You are a witch hunter. I do not know what you plan to do with the witches you find, but I can tell you this." Her voice was hard, steely with resolve.

The smoke drifted back to its master, and Rose let her hand drop back to her side. "I will expose you as a fortune hunter, shaming our family name, until all of London reviles you. You will be unwelcome in every club, every social gathering, every home of the gentry. I will ruin your reputation."

A muscle feathered in his jaw, and Rose felt a tiny flutter of triumph in her chest before the icy waters within her swallowed it. So fragile, the ego of men.

"And who would believe you?" His lip curled with derision.

"Alexander Crawford, to start. Lord Sinclair dotes on his daughter so. I wonder what he will do when Harriet tells him you are nothing but a simpering charlatan."

Cornelius grinned. "Your behavior can easily be explained. I could have you sent to Bedlam for such claims."

Rose crossed her arms. "Then I wouldn't marry Reeves, and you would lose access to whatever power you think I have. You were right the first time. It's not much."

His face fell a fraction. He sensed the truth of her words.

"Let Harriet go," she pressed. "Vow never to harm her again, and I shall sign the contract."

He rubbed his chin thoughtfully, reviewing every angle of the proposition. "Very well," he conceded. He withdrew the thick parchment, stained that sickly shade of gray, from his jacket pocket and extended it to her.

Rose did not take it. "I need to know you haven't killed her already."

Cornelius rolled his eyes. "She's in no state to leave yet, I am afraid."

Fear pushed through the emptiness in her chest. "Let me see her." Fear made her hands tingle. What had he done to her?

Cornelius gestured for Rose to lead the way. "She remains in the guest suite."

She took the steps at an unhurried pace, even though her heart threatened to burst from her ribcage. Cornelius kept within arm's reach of her. At the door to the guest rooms, Rose steeled herself for what she might find within.

Harriet was unconscious in the four-poster bed, so large it nearly swallowed her. Gauzy curtains draped across the bed like a shrine, enclosing the girl within. She looked even more like a doll in sleep than when she was awake. Her limbs were bent akimbo, as if she'd been tossed there by a petulant child. Discarded until she was needed again.

"What did you do to her?" hissed Rose as she grabbed the girl's hand. It was warm, at least.

"I only touched her." Cornelius thrust a hand hands into his pocket and surveyed the girl like she was nothing more than a specimen. "She's very... sensitive."

Rose whirled on the monster behind her. "Release her. Now. Then I'll sign your damn contract."

He barked a humorless laugh. "Oh, no. You'll sign before I let her go." He tapped a long finger against the papers he held. "It was you who invoked the bargain. You don't want to find out what happens when that agreement is broken."

Rose placed her hand against Harriet's forehead. Pale moonlight illuminated her face. Rose watched her eyes slide rapidly back and forth behind closed lids, as if she was merely dreaming. Her hand rested in a loose fist by her face. Tiny leaves sprouted from between her fingers.

Rose shifted her body, blocking Cornelius's view of her friend as she bent closer to examine the patch of silver-green on the downy blanket. A cluster of vines sprouted from seeds hidden in Harriet's palm. Small and fragile, their tiny tendrils curled longingly towards the silver light. Rose followed their trail. They spilled off the bed, onto the floor opposite them, and out the closed second-story window, creeping around the cracks of the frame before spilling into the night.

Her knees threatened to buckle with relief. Harriet had managed to get a signal to Kate. But where was she?

Rose withdrew her hand and faced her cousin, shielding the vines from view with her own shadow. She needed to distract him, to keep him blind him to the signal that crawled out the window.

"You know," she said in a low, sultry voice that was not her own. "I am curious."

Cornelius arched an eyebrow. "About?"

"Why are you so desperate to marry me away to that old lech? You didn't try very hard to make me your own wife." She edged closer to the revolting man before her.

He licked his lips and caressed the edges of the marriage contract. "I have my reasons." His pulse feathered in his throat, just below his jaw.

She inched closer, stopping a hand's breadth away. She shrugged, nonchalant. "It's only that when we first met, you said you were expecting a proposal. I didn't think you'd give up so easily. Surrender to someone like Reeves."

His fingers twitched.

Rose swallowed her disgust as she reached for his face. The demon inside Cornelius had fled at her touch, skin on skin. Would it happen again, with her magic now fully depleted?

Cornelius stiffened as her hand moved closer and closer to his face. Something in his eyes flickered, warm and bright.

Rose's fingertips brushed his high cheekbones. She felt the horrible, dark presence stir beneath his skin. Only this time, it did not recoil or detach from its host. It leapt at Rose, whipping its dark power against her own empty soul. Ice cracked and broke within her. Her fingertips burned where they touched Cornelius.

She wrapped a mental fist around the monster, trapping it. It fought her, lunging like a snake, looking for a soft place to strike.

Through the harsh pain, she glimpsed the man trapped within his own body. His hand gripped around her wrist, pressing her palm to his face.

"Run," Cornelius said in his true voice, the one that reminded Rose of warm honey. The voice where softness rang in every syllable alongside his urgency. His brow furrowed as his eyes met hers. "Now. Take her and *go*."

Something Rose could not describe tugged deep within her frozen heart. "What can I do?" she asked through gritted teeth. The cold was clawing at her, trying to steal her breath. "Tell me how to stop this. Tell me how to free you!"

Cornelius's eyes rolled back into his head until only the whites were visible. He convulsed.

The monster thrashed against Rose's mental grip, stealing past her brittle fingers. Rose's wrist, her hand, her chest burned with icy fire. She could not remove her hand from him, could not break the contact between them. A stony grip held her fast; it was immovable, unbreakable.

Her heart pounded against her frozen ribcage. Her knees

shook. She was still pinned to Cornelius, shackled by his grasp. Rose's pulse changed from a frenetic beat to a listless thump as her heart slowed. She didn't know why she felt compelled to help him. Maybe it was because she knew the feeling of being trapped, of being bound by things she could not control. She wanted so desperately to be free of them. And she had seen warmth smothered beneath the monster that wore Cornelius's skin. The real Cornelius, who spoke softly, and who had tried to free Rose from her marriage contract, was trapped. Just as she was.

Rose's knees finally gave out. Cornelius's iron grip kept her from hitting the floor. She was so cold. She wanted to lie down and close her eyes, if only for a moment. Darkness crept in. Her ears filled with the sound of wind through trees, of water rushing across a bed of rock.

Suddenly, glass shattered behind her, spraying the room with a thousand broken shards. The sound was sudden and terrible. Rose squeezed her eyes shut as pieces of glass cut into her exposed arms, neck, and hands. They shredded through the curtains draped over the bed, leaving it in ribbons.

Vines as thick as her arms and legs whipped into the room and wrapped around Cornelius. They wrenched his hand from Rose's wrist. She fell to the floor. White spots danced in her vision. Her kneecaps felt like they'd been split. She made herself look up, blinking past the haze of pain.

Cornelius's arms were bound stiffly to his sides. Quivering snakelike tendrils of vine wrapped around his legs. The contact between them broke. The creature settled once more into Cornelius's body, overtaking him. He fixed his eyes, soulless and seething, on her.

Her bones still ached with cold, but Rose pushed herself to stand, ignoring the barking pain in her knees. She ran to the window on unsteady feet, dodging lashing tendrils and piles of glass as she crossed the room. She stuck her head out the burst window and saw Kate, hands planted firmly to the earth, commanding the plants that bound Cornelius.

"Take off the bracelet!" Kate shouted as soon as she saw Rose's head emerge from the window. "Bind him! Make him forget us! *Make him forget, Rose!*"

She whirled, stripping the black sapphires away. A gust of wind raised escaped tendrils of her hair, billowed the curtains, and made the vines shudder. The incessant pounding in her head vanished. Her power roared to life within her, fire igniting once more. Rose took a deep breath, the first she'd had in days. Her mind was clear, eyes focused, as she settled into her own power again. An invisible weight had been pressing down on her, crushing her soul and power. Only its absence made her realize how heavy it had been.

She nearly cried out with relief. She felt so *alive.*

It was only meant to protect you.

The bracelet truly was a shackle, dampening her power, stifling it. Rose had no time to be angry, to let herself feel the raw sting of betrayal. She clenched the gems in her fist. Their sharp edges bit into her palm.

She studied Cornelius, bound in vines, eyes wide with shock. He certainly felt her power now.

Rose stalked towards him as the vines on the floor slithered away, clearing a path for her. She had studied no spells for such an occasion as this. But her magic knew what must be done. She let her power guide her, directing her movements. She placed her finger on Cornelius's brow. A single bead of silver power sparkled at her fingertip, brighter than any moonbeam.

He writhed and shrieked, desperate to get away from the single drop of sparkling magic, but the vines held firm, coiling tighter around his thrashing. Rose touched his skin and felt the sulfurous smoke within him recoil.

"Forget," she commanded. Her voice was layered with others that were not her own. Deep and mournful, high and bright.

Voices that belonged to others who had once borne such power as hers.

Cornelius stilled. The monster within glared hatefully at her and hissed through his teeth. "A bargain was struck. The bargain must be honored."

Her power pulsed, reluctantly confirming his words. With her free hand, Rose summoned the contract to her. It opened and hung, suspended in midair, waiting for her signature.

To save her friends, she would do it.

Rose grabbed a thread of her power, a tiny fraction of the vast amount within her, and used it to sign the marriage contract. Her name glowed silver on the page before fading to black.

Cornelius grinned as the paper folded shut. "The bargain has been upheld."

"And now you shall forget." Rose forced her will into the mind of the creature of malice and smoke. She knew she could not wipe away the memories of the past few months entirely. Her magic cautioned her against asking too much, for the creature was cunning and singular in its purpose.

Just enough to keep you safe, the magic cautioned.

Rose obeyed. Her commands reverberated with power and the voices of other witches, rebounding in the room, echoing a hundred-fold. "You shall not recall the power you have witnessed here tonight, the power I possess. You will still think me weak. You will not remember that Harriet Sinclair is a witch. You shall recall only that I signed the marriage contract after you threatened to keep me from Lady Nightingale."

The thing that was not Cornelius stared blankly at her. She hoped it was enough. Rose removed her finger and let the silver bead of magic seep into his brow.

His eyes closed, and he went limp. The vines lowered him to the floor before slithering back out the window.

Rose stared down at him. Her stomach clenched. She opened her hand, and examined the dark sapphire bracelet.

It was only meant to protect you.

Why put it back on? She had accomplished great magic, had negated the threat of a dangerous witch hunter. Surely it would be better if she kept her power unleashed, ready to be called on whenever danger was near…

A small sound from the bed snapped Rose from her deliberation. Harriet sat up, unscathed by the glass that lay all around her. "Now *that* was an impressive bit of magic," she said weakly.

Rose laughed and tripped over to the bed, shoes sliding on glass. She faltered for a half second, fighting the instinct to wrap her friend in a fierce embrace, but Harriet held her arms open. Rose crashed into her, relief making her breathless.

Harriet did not recoil, or stiffen at her touch, but hugged her back with all the strength she had.

Kate's head popped up from the broken window. "If you two are quite finished, we really must be going. Before *he* wakes up again."

Harriet and Rose let go of one another, still laughing with relief.

"How are you doing that?" Rose asked, processing the absurdity of Kate hovering outside a second-story window, moonlight casting a halo around her curls.

"Vine ladder. What are we going to do about this mess?"

Rose glanced at the shattered glass and the ribbons of curtains that blew eerily on a light breeze. A towering oak with leaves as big as her fist grew a short distance away. "How easy would it be to crash one of those branches through this window?" she asked Kate.

Kate glanced at the stately tree and frowned. "I don't like to *damage* the plants. But I will make an exception. Come down first. I don't want to hit you."

Rose helped Harriet rise from the bed. She kept one arm

around her waist as they made their way to the vine ladder. Whatever Cornelius had done to her had made her weak. She swallowed the ache of guilt in her throat as she helped Harriet climb out the window.

The night air seemed to restore Harriet. She climbed down the vine ladder without too much help, though Kate was right behind her. Kate's eyes never left her back, not even to watch her own feet.

Rose breathed a sigh of relief once they were safely on the ground.

"Hurry," Kate called up the ladder.

Rose placed one hand on the window frame, but hesitated. Looking over her shoulder, she studied Cornelius. Moonlight illuminated his face as he lay on the floor. He looked... peaceful. His handsome face did not betray the danger that lurked just beneath his skin. Something twisted within her. Whether it was regret, remorse, or pity, she did not know.

"*Rose.*" Kate called impatiently.

Rose turned her back on Cornelius, shoving the peculiar feeling away. The bracelet, her shackle, was heavy in her palm.

You must put it on again straightaway. You must not leave it off for long.

She gritted her teeth and slid the bracelet back onto her wrist. The world dulled instantly. Her magic shrank deep within herself, and the wall of dense fog clouded her way to it once more. In the darkness, the sapphires flashed with emerald green light before fading to night-black. A dull ache settled in her bones.

It was the hardest thing she'd had to do tonight.

Cold, empty dark now occupied the space where Rose's magic had blazed. She mourned the loss of it. Though her muscles screamed in protest, Rose made herself climb down the vine ladder.

"Get ready to run," Kate said once Rose had joined them on

the ground. The vine ladder slithered back into the soil, leaving no trace of its existence. Kate extended her arms towards the tree. With a loud *crack,* a large branch, as thick as Rose's waist, snapped off the oak. Kate's brow furrowed in concentration, and beads of sweat gathered at her temples. With a grunt, she swung the branch through the window with a thunderous crash.

"*Go,*" she commanded, dropping her arms.

They sprinted from the garden, towards the streets. Rose paused, feeling for the page she had ripped out from Cornelius's journal. The list of witches. She swallowed as a lump formed in her throat. Should she have made Cornelius forget his list of suspects, too? Would it be enough to keep them safe?

"Rosie," Harriet called weakly. She leaned on Kate for support.

Satisfied she had the proof she needed, Rose ran to catch up to her friends.

They raced back to Lady Nightingale's manor as fast as they could, hands clasped together, mere shadows in the moonlight.

CHAPTER 42

*R*ose woke at dawn and dressed, tying the top section of her hair back with a black velvet ribbon. As she had every morning for the past week since moving into Lady Nightingale's manor, she reported to the cellar where Mrs. Carrow, the youngest member of the Council, waited for her. An adept potion maker, she had been tasked with Rose's training in the brewing of various tinctures and salves. Rose packaged different bits of dried plants and herbs into vials, memorizing their properties. She passed them down the smooth wooden workbench to Mrs. Carrow, who sealed and spelled them. Rose ignored pangs of guilt as she worked, shoving away the image of her mother's blank face after Lady Nightingale had bewitched her to believe she was going on a trip to Bath. It was the only way to explain her change of residence.

After breakfast, Rose joined the other novices, Harriet and Kate among them, in private study in the library until teatime. Harriet had taken three days at home to rest before joining them, sending letters each day to assure them of her progress and convey that Quincy was taking excellent care of her. She didn't speak about what Cornelius had done to her.

Rose wondered if she ever would. She spent long hours of the last few nights awake, worrying about her. It wasn't until Harriet had flounced through the library's doors that Rose had accepted that she would be all right. Even if she still had wounds they could not see.

Perhaps they were like the ones that scarred her own heart. When Rose managed to find sleep, her dreams were plagued by the malicious being with scarlet eyes. In her nightmares, she couldn't breathe, unable to access her magic, as the creature of smoke plunged her into an icy lake, drowning her.

She, Harriet, and Kate had poured over every volume the library offered them, trying to learn more about the creature that wore Cornelius's skin. They had been unsuccessful so far. Rose had a feeling that until she knew more about the creature, her nightmares would continue.

Rose shut her book with a loud thud and scrubbed her face. Kate kept reading. Her eyes skimmed the page of her book rapidly.

Harriet shot her an encouraging smile from across their worktable as she gently closed her book. Her cheeks were flushed as she placed a hand over the book's cover. "Ready for tea?" she asked. "I'm starving." She swiftly gathered her notes and slide the book under the loose papers.

Rose narrowed her eyes at Harriet, who continued to shuffle her work materials. "What were you reading?"

Harriet stood, gathering her notes and clutching the book to her chest. "Nothing of importance." Her cheeks flushed an even deeper shade of pink.

Kate looked up from her studies, intrigued.

"Hattie," Rose sang in a teasing melody. "Let me see it."

Harriet huffed. "My, my, you are nosy today. Worse than Quincy when he wants a biscuit. Let's go, I'm hungry."

Rose held her hand out for the book, a roguish grin plastered on her face.

Harriet relented and passed it to her, tossing her dark hair over her shoulder. *"Really, Rosie."*

Rose read the title, *A Lady's Moral Predicaments.* She raised her eyebrows and flipped through the pages until her eye snagged on a particularly descriptive passage of the main character being pleasured in her sitting room. Rose's eyes grew wide. "This is a *romance* book."

Kate leaned over, trying to get a look.

Harriet snatched the book back. "I like romance novels," she pouted.

"That is a very *detailed* romance book," Rose said, eyes wide with delight. "I didn't know you read such things."

"I don't! I asked for something to read and the library gave me this. It is far more enlightening than you realize."

"I'm only teasing," Rose said, rolling her eyes. "I want to borrow it when you've finished."

"That's what I thought," Harriet said with another toss of her head.

The trio packed up their things and left for tea. Rose made a note to ask the library for a romance book of her own to read before she went to bed. It was another silver lining to the bargain she'd struck; access to the library whenever she pleased. She had to keep reminding herself of those silver linings more and more as the days wore on.

The memory of her magic, the unchained and overflowing sea of it, called to her. She longed to remove her sapphire bracelet. She thought about it in every quiet moment. It was like picking at a scab, remembering how powerful she was, how easily she'd commanded her magic.

Her wrist grew warm, and an ache pulsed at her temples. Even the memory of her power made the bracelet fight against her.

Rose turned her thoughts away from her desires and followed behind her friends. She'd need all her strength and focus for her next set of lessons.

Decorum lessons with Lady Clarke took up the time between tea and supper. Rose found these lessons to be the most difficult, even though she enjoyed Lady Clarke's company. Today she was learning a new quadrille. Her dancing skills still needed improvement. She'd only get by for so long on the good graces of society, and the endorsement of Lady Nightingale.

Rose tripped over her feet. Lady Clarke held her hand firm, saving her face from becoming acquainted with the ballroom floor.

"I just don't see the point," Rose said, straightening. "As soon as I marry Reeves, we'll move to Hythe. There won't be any parties or balls for me to attend." Bitterness made her tone harsher than she intended. It was the other source of her nightmares. When she wasn't dreaming of the monster sleeping inside Cornelius, she dreamt of her impending marriage.

"Do not limit your potential with your own thoughts," said Lady Clarke. "If I had done so, I would still be a lady's maid."

Rose bit her lip, fighting the sudden sting of remorseful tears.

Lady Clarke took her hand and marched her to a giant, gilded mirror that stood on the far wall. She stood behind Rose, a hand on each shoulder. "Look."

Rose reluctantly stared at her own reflection. She looked disheveled next to the poised and fashionable woman behind her.

"All women have an inherent power. We can use our looks, charm, and the way we carry ourselves to influence the people around us."

"I don't want to peacock about to get what I want," Rose muttered.

Lady Clarke placed a hand on her hip. "Do I look like a peacock to you?"

"No," she stammered, embarrassed.

"Then watch."

Rose saw the woman in the mirror become smaller, shrinking in on herself. Lady Clarke's eyes grew watery and her shoulders collapsed inwards. She looked like the sort of person who would be afraid of her own shadow. Nothing about her physical appearance had changed, but the way she stood made even the shining locks of her fiery hair dull and lifeless.

"Now do you believe I was a simple house servant?" Lady Clarke asked in a mousy voice.

Rose's mouth fell open. She blinked, and the Lady Clarke she knew reappeared in the mirror, proud and regal. "How did you do that?"

"Practice. I shall teach you, if you'd like. The way I feel about myself influences how I appear to others. If I believe I'm the most beautiful and fashionable woman in all of London, I will become her. It's not magic as you know it, but something different. It doesn't require any sort of power other than your own belief. The way to increase our power and influence is in how you grow your currency, not just your magic. This is your currency as a woman, and can get you almost anything. And anything *that* cannot get you, magic can make up for. You see?"

Rose blinked stupidly again, making her own reflection come into focus. She had never cared much for how she looked.

"Be bold, be daring. Do the unexpected, but only as much as a person's mind can handle, especially a man's. They can't handle much."

Rose laughed, but something in Lady Clarke's advice gave her pause. She ran a thumb over the white scar tissue on her wrist. An idea sparked. The rules were clear, but it couldn't hurt to ask.

"I would like permission to leave the manor. There is someone I must speak to."

The corner of Lady Clarke's mouth quirked upwards. "I grant you permission, so long as you wear your bracelet."

Rose nodded. They couldn't risk Cornelius sensing the vast amount of power within her. But the day would soon come when their paths would cross. He, too, believed that she was away on holiday. Next week she would re-enter society, after her engagement was formally announced. By then, she and the other witches would be prepared.

The thought of her engagement no longer made her physically ill. She had resigned herself to it. Her mother was, regrettably, correct. All women must marry. But Rose would be damned if she let the rules of the ton and a sham of a marriage dictate who she gave her heart to.

* * *

ROSE THREW her shoulders back and knocked loudly on the door of the small townhouse.

A portly man with bushy eyebrows greeted her. "May I help you?" he sniffed.

"Good afternoon. My name is Rose Worthington. I am looking for Mr. Harlow. Is he here?"

The gentleman's demeanor changed in an instant. His eyes twinkled as he threw the door open wide. "Miss Worthington, you say? Do come in, I shall fetch Mr. Harlow for you presently."

"Thank you." The warm scent of cedar and other exotic spices filled her nose. Rose removed her hat and studied the entryway while the portly gentleman shouted up the main stairs. She hadn't paid it much notice the night she'd first seen it.

"Philip! There's a young lady here to see you!"

"Enough, old man! Give it up," rang a jovial voice from a distant corner of the house.

Rose could not stop the soft smile that spread across her face at the sound of his voice. Her heart fluttered in her chest.

"I'm not that old," muttered the man, before shouting up the stairs again. "Really, lad, someone is here to see you!"

Philip obviously didn't believe him. He made no move to come and greet her.

"Philip Harlow!" she shouted. "Are you going to keep me waiting all afternoon?"

A beat of silence. Then a door banged open, and hurried footsteps thundered down the hall. The gentleman chortled. "He's all yours, my lady. Last door on the left."

"Don't bother, Philip, I'm coming up!" With one hand on the banister, she quickly thanked the gentleman who had let her in.

Rose heard him still chuckling to himself as she climbed the stairs, two at a time.

Philip met her on the upper landing. His hair was disheveled, as it always was, though he was wearing finer clothes than she had ever seen him in. They fit him well, accentuating his broad shoulders. Rose felt her stomach tighten as she took in the sight of him. For a moment, neither of them said a word.

Rose cleared her throat. "Sorry to barge in."

"No, I'm—I'm happy to see you," he said. "Do you want to sit down?"

"Sure." She followed him down the hall to his room. He held the door open for her, his face flushed. He stiffened as she passed, so close he could feel the heat radiating from him.

Trying to think of everything but the feeling of his arms around her, and failing miserably, Rose entered his room. In the daylight, she could see it much more clearly. A large writing desk held neatly arranged papers, inkwells, and maps. The sight of his bed, and the memory of what they'd done there, made her toes curl.

"You can sit there, if you like," Philip said, nodding to the armchair.

Rose sat, and Philip perched on the side of the bed, facing her. Awkward silence filled the room. He no longer wore bandages, but she could see the scar that spread like spider webs over the back of his hand and palm, new skin stretching tightly over red welts. Guilt twisted in her chest. Was it selfish to want him so much, even when loving him came with risks?

"I'm sorry. Again. There are things that I want to tell you, but I can't." Rose knew she could not tell him the truth, but she vowed to share as much as she could. "The other night when we… I left because I was trying to get out of my engagement."

Philip's mouth twisted into a deep frown. "By letting me ruin you?"

"No!" Rose ran a hand through her hair. She was making things much worse. "No. It wasn't like that. I asked Lady Nightingale for help. She's the woman who has been helping me this season. My benefactress."

She clenched her hands in her lap. The weight of her bracelet, usually heavy and stifling, now grounded her. "What I said was true. I love you, Philip. I wanted to ask her if there was a way to break my engagement. She's very powerful. But she said no."

Rose swallowed, the truth left a bitter taste in her mouth, even though she'd reluctantly come to accept it. "But it doesn't matter. I want to be with you, engagement or not. If you'll still have me."

Philip gripped the edges of the bed. "I love you, Rose. Nothing will ever change that. But I want you to be honest with me. If I can help you, let me. Please."

She nodded. Her fingers found her necklace. She tugged on

it, fiddling with the charm. "I will. I just want you. I see that now."

Philip fumbled in his pocket. He held a ring between them. It was simple, with a tiny chip of diamond wrapped in burnished gold. "Then you shall have me. I've been carrying this with me for months, desperate for you to change your mind and marry me. I thought that was the only way for us to be together." He gripped the ring in his fist, hiding it. "But if you don't care, then I don't," he growled.

He stood and brought his lips to hers, unable to restrain himself a moment longer, and Rose felt the world tilt under her feet.

There was no timidity to the kiss. It was all-consuming, burning her from within. She met his passion equally with her own desire, running her hands through his hair as he cradled the back of her head. He kissed her deeply, parting her lips with his tongue.

Rose let herself sink into him. She felt lightheaded, dizzy, and drunk.

"I want to take you to my bed again, Rose," Philip said hoarsely. "But I want to wait until I get back. Can you wait for me?"

They would never be husband and wife. They would never be bound by a mere piece of paper. But they would be bound eternally by their love for one another. They would remain free. Free to love one another as only they could. Rose wanted nothing more than to tumble into the bed behind him, to tear off her clothes and let Philip worship her, but she would respect his wish. "You have waited for me all this time," she said, nestling under his chin, kissing his throat. "Of course, I will wait for you."

Philip tipped up her chin and kissed her. "I love you," he whispered.

She smiled against his lips. "I love you, too."

They spent the afternoon kissing, holding one another. Philip showed her his maps, charts, and navigation instruments, eyes bright with excitement. He showed her the path he would take, across the sea and back again. Back to her. He would leave in two weeks.

Sadness made her heart heavy and throat tight as they parted. She hated to go, but she was needed back at the Nightingale manor before nightfall, another condition of her being allowed to leave the house alone.

But it was not goodbye, nothing so final as that. Rose fiddled with her necklace as she walked. The diamond ring sat next to the wooden rose Philip had carved for her months ago. He had pressed it into her hand as they parted. "It was always meant for you."

Twilight stained the sky purple and gold. A soft breeze kissed her cheeks, drying her tears and hurrying her along as she walked back to Mayfair, where Lady Nightingale and the other witches were waiting. She would not rest until she became a full-fledged Nightingale and banished the malevolent thing inside Cornelius for good.

Until then, she would be discreet. She would learn all she could about her own power and follow Lady Nightingale faithfully. She would keep herself and the ones she loved safe.

No matter the cost.

ACKNOWLEDGMENTS

When I first set a goal of writing a book before I turned thirty, I had no idea what I was really getting into. The journey to completing this story was far more rewarding, and challenging, than I ever anticipated. Three years later, here we are! I never would have finished it without the support of my husband, Adam, who cheers me on every day. Thank you for your belief in me, and your unwavering support. I love you so much!

Thank you to my sisters. This book is dedicated to you. I am grateful to Mackenzie, who was a first reader and my stalwart cheerleader, and Riley, whose editorial feedback and encouragement on many projects have made me a better writer.

Thank you also to the parental figures in my life, who offered support in numerous ways.

Love and gratitude to Leanne, who knew it was going to happen someday!

To my Romantasy Book Club. I am so lucky to have such supportive friends. Caitlin, for beta-reading and listening to my crises; Kara, Jadie, Sarah, and Sam for being my ultimate hype-women.

With every book and project, my writing improves. However, this book is readable today thanks to Dr. Misty Krueger, who took the liberty of highlighting all my use of passive voice in my Austen seminar paper. Thank you for the first firm and kind feedback I ever received on my written work.

Much gratitude to Carrie Jones, whose developmental edits

on my first draft helped me realize that this story was a duology. Her feedback helped make *Season of Fire* what it is today.

To Alyssa, who helped me heal.

To my internet writing community, whose friendship made me feel like I was not going it alone, and who educated me in the crazy world of publishing. Thank you to Yi Shun Lai for your coaching on how to write a pitch. To Demri Redmon, Melody Pendlebury, and Michelle Sanchez for your friendship; and Christina Fitz-Gallant and R.H. King for your proofreading and critiques. To my BookTok community. Our shared love of reading, books, and positive vibes make my days brighter.

If you are a person who always reads the acknowledgements (like me) I hope you know that you are included in my thanks. This book would only exist in computer jail if it weren't for you. Thank you.

ABOUT THE AUTHOR

Cidney Mayes is a teacher librarian and writer of speculative fiction from Portland, Maine. She is currently earning her MFA in Creative Writing from Southern New Hampshire University. With over a decade of book review experience, she decided to write the stories she's always wanted to read. Her work explores themes of feminism and power amidst lush, dark, and often magical settings. When not writing, you can find her playing board games and video games, walking in the woods, or watching reality TV with her husband and two cats. You can connect with her at cidneymayes.com.